Legends of Galria: Shadows of War

Book One of the Galrian Saga

Written by: Tyler Zilkie

Cover by: Donna Vu

In loving memory of Joyce Zilkie, who passed away as this book was going to print.

Special thanks goes to the countless people who have helped me along the way. This book exists because of all of you.

Chapter 1 - Tran, The Village of Trades-People

Dane ran full bore through the forest. The wind whipped past him as he sprinted down the rough, uneven dirt road. His feet left the ground as he leaped over a large branch that had fallen on the path. When he landed, he continued onward without missing a step. He imagined that if he'd jumped a little higher and gone a little further, he could've taken flight. Dane had always dreamed of flying as high and freely as a bird could and to not be strapped down by the bonds of gravity. He wanted to soar unladen by responsibility and to explore all that Galria had to offer.

The boy came to a full stop at the crest of a hill at the forest's edge. Dane leaned forward and planted his hands on his knees, gasping as he tried to catch his breath. He stood overlooking the village of Tran, and from his perch he could see as far as the endless seas of wheat, flax, and oats on the other side of town. The buildings were fashioned out of finely crafted stone and clay bricks, and their windows glistened in the sunlight from their daily cleanings. A plume of smoke rose from the smithy on the southern side of the town as its forges were stoked, preparing for the day's work orders.

There's so many people here this year, Dane thought as he tried to count the number of caravans that were headed towards the market like ants marching to an anthill. *The Harvest Festival is even bigger than last year I bet!*

A breeze coasted inland from the west and ruffled his hair as it passed. The wind carried with it the scent of freshly baked bread touched with the slightest hint of cinnamon. A smile spread across Dane's face and his mouth began to water as he thought about all the wonderful food the villagers prepared. It seemed like the bakers of Tran always put in extra effort around the time of the festival, just to make sure that everything tasted that much better.

I can't wait to see what all those traders brought into town this year. Dane's smile grew wider, and he stood for a moment more in silence before his thoughts were interrupted by the creak of a wagon coming from behind him.

"Stop day dreaming, boy! Haven't I told you before that these woods are dangerous?"

Dane's shoulders slumped and his smile faded.

"There's been too many skirmishes up north," his father Jonathan said. His brow was furrowed as he glared at Dane. "We have no idea if the fighting will spread south."

Jon was a short and graying old man wearing worn hunting leathers that fit a little too snugly over his stout frame. He hobbled up beside Dane while pulling a wagon behind him. It was filled over the top with a pile of animal hides, each having been prepared by the man's expert hands with care.

"Dad, the orcs aren't going to come this close to the Tradeway," Dane said with a groan of petulance. "Besides, those savages are Northpine's problem."

Jon's hand lashed out and smacked Dane in the back of the head, and the boy yelped in protest.

"Don't talk back to me like that. If I tell you to be careful, you listen to me and stay close, got it?"

"I don't see what the problem is. . ."

Jon gripped the top of his son's head and forced him to look towards the town. He then pointed at a pair of half-constructed watch towers. The sound of hammering echoed up towards them. "You see those there? Those watch towers the militia are building? That means this conflict with the orc clan is a serious issue. It doesn't matter how far away Northpine is or how close we are to the Tradeway, we still need to be cautious. If Northpine pushes the orcs back, they might come down here to secure new territory. Understand?"

"I guess. . ." Dane said, though he didn't really get it. There were plenty of places for people to settle. "Why are they even fighting, anyways?"

"It doesn't matter why," Jon said pointedly. "All that matters is that they are fighting, and we have to be prepared just in case." He glanced towards the bow and quiver of arrows in the wagon, just within arms reach. "Now let's get going. We don't have time for sight seeing like last year. We have work to do."

Dane let out a sigh. *Guess I won't get to look around the bazaar after all. . .*

Jon pulled the wagon up the road to the top of the hill and paused, groaning as he set it down again. He rubbed at his knee, then stood up and arched his back, eliciting a few pops as he moved. Dane waited with growing impatience for his father to rest up, knowing that the old wound on his leg was bothering him. He'd seen the scar on Jon's leg numerous times around the home, the flesh discolored an ugly pink and wrinkled as though it had been left in water for too long. He claimed it was from a hunting accident, and from time to time, the old wound would bother him.

Must be a storm coming, Dane thought as he recalled the many times in the past the pain in his father's leg had flared up just before a heavy thunderstorm.

"Let's get moving," Jon said before picking the cart up. "We don't have any more time to laze about." He took the lead as he pulled their goods along a dirt track towards the village proper.

Dane and his father strode through the center of Tran to a spot in the bazaar they had reserved months ago. The festival was always busy, and getting a stall to sell goods was both expensive and required a reservation well in advance. The center of town was filled with merchants that gathered around a reflecting pool that was constructed in the town square. All the cobblestone roads in town eventually found their way to the bazaar, and it was the home of numerous shops and the inn.

"Good morning, Jonathan!" a voice shouted over the growing din of the marketplace. Dane followed the sound to see a man about his father's age leaning against the door frame of the inn. Jon waved to him and pulled his cart over to the side of the road before stopping at the front steps.

The man's name was Ted Langsten, the innkeeper of Tran. He was known in the village for his kindheartedness and friendly demeanor. He had a thick beard and salt-and-pepper hair. He easily dwarfed Jon by a foot or more and had a potbelly, one just large enough to suggest the man lived a life of leisure rather than one of sloth. The white sleeves of his tunic were rolled up to his shoulders and he wore a green apron over the front of his clothing.

"Morning, Ted. How's business today?" Jon asked.

"It's been slow so far. A few people checking in and getting their room keys, but beyond that it's been very relaxed. Once I open the tavern later and things settle down out here I'm sure I'll be swamped, though, especially since Lily can't work as much," Ted said. He glanced past Jon to look at the cart, and whistled as he spotted the head of a bear sticking out from the back of the pile of pelts. "Nice catch. Grizzly, I take it?"

"Yes sir. He was a lucky find, too. I caught the big fella sniffing around the home and bagged him without much trouble. A quick shot to the head saved the pelt from any damage. I'm hoping to make a killing from selling him," Jon said, his face beaming with a smile born of pride. "I still have some smoked meat left from him if you'd like me to bring a couple slabs over the next time I'm in town. Perhaps in exchange for a drink or two?"

Ted chuckled, "Of course, how could I turn such an offer down? I look forward to it. I've not had smoked bear in some time."

"I'll make a point to come by after the festival is over."

Ted turned to regard Dane and gave him a warm smile. "It's been awhile since I last saw you, squirt." He ruffled the boy's unkempt brown hair. "You've gotten taller since the spring."

"I guess so," Dane muttered, taking a short step out of Ted's reach. The man treated him like a distant nephew, though they weren't related, and Dane found his demeanor annoying.

"It's been a pain in my ass," Jon said with a frown. "None of his clothes fit anymore since he hit that growth spurt and I keep having to get him new ones."

Ted smiled and shrugged. "Can't be helped, can it?"

"Easy for a man without a kid to say."

The innkeeper's smile never wavered. "That'll be changing soon, if all goes well. Lily's almost due."

Jon's expression soured and he cleared his throat to cover it up. "How's her health?" he asked.

"She's fine, lively as ever," Ted replied. "She just gets sore once in awhile, and she can't lift much. It's fine though, I can manage the inn on my own."

"Sounds like you have a lot to do then, so I won't keep you. I'd best get set up before it gets too late in the morning. Take care, Ted. Tell Lily I said hello."

"Will do."

Jon the cart up off the ground. "Come along, Dane."

They headed around the reflecting pool over to their stall, to a spot that was wedged between a tailor on one side and a farmer selling baskets of fruit on the other. Both individuals greeted Jon with a wave and a few small words as he walked by, and he replied with a small nod of his head. He wheeled the cart around behind the counter and began to unload the pelts to show them off.

Dane watched for a while as his father worked with an intense focus on making the countertop look presentable. Jon laid the pelts out with such care, as though he feared they might fall apart if he was rough with them. He smoothed out folds and wrinkles, and arranged pelts by color, size, and animal, with the bear hide taking front and center of his display.

After a few moments of watching Jon work, Dane grew bored and decided to look around while his father was preoccupied. Several other merchants were still getting ready for the day. There were a number of performers present throughout the bazaar as bards strummed a few notes on their lutes and tuned them to get the sound just right while dancers stretched and talked amongst themselves in preparation for their routines.

A few of the local militiamen were patrolling the market, keeping a vigilant eye out for any trouble. It was rare that there would be anything more than a drunken and heated argument between neighbors, but the town didn't like to take chances during the festival.

There's more imperial soldiers than I remember, Dane thought as he saw the blue and white standards of the empire's military on several heavily armored and armed individuals. *Come to think of it, were there any soldiers here last year? Maybe dad was right about the orc problem.*

On the eastern rim of the bazaar was a section reserved for the Snowhoof clan minotaur. The great bull-like men and women had already begun peddling their wares. There were countless pelts from beasts not found in the southern regions out on display, such as those from snow leopards, polar bears, and rams. Metal ingots crafted from the ore mined out of the rich deposits in the mountains were stacked on another stall. Others still held oddities and trinkets that were handcrafted by their people, giving Dane a glimpse into their shamanic heritage.

Something glimmered off to Dane's right as it reflected the sun in his eyes, and he bee-lined towards it. Whatever it was, he was drawn to it with a sense of curiosity that nagged at him. As he approached the stall, he noticed rows of polished gemstones laid out on a leather mat that shone in the light. They were arranged in a pattern according to color, starting with stones as black as night on the left, and proceeding all the way to bright, white and clear gems on the right, like a crystalline rainbow. Strange etchings marked some of the stones on the table, and they were set into crude looking necklaces.

The minotaur running the stall was a tall female wearing a brown hide tunic and dress adorned with fur lining around the collar and sleeves. She was busy talking to a few of her neighbors in their native tongue, and Dane waited for them to finish before speaking up.

"Um, excuse me?" Dane said, trying to get her attention.

"Yes, what is it child?" the female asked in the Common tongue as she turned. Though her accent was heavy, Dane had little trouble understanding her. He'd been exposed to the minotaur many times in his short life and he was used to the way their voices sounded.

"May I take a look at that one please?" Dane pointed to a small green pendant that had caught his eye.

"Certainly." She picked up the item in question and held it out in her open palm. "It's crafted out of jade, and has been smoothed and polished into a lustrous sheen by one of our shaman."

The small green stone hung from a thin strip of leather. Dane ran a finger along the smooth stone, and noted that it had a design carved into it that looked like a bear's paw.

"What does the symbol mean?" he asked.

"Let me see. . ." she said before examining it closely. "Ah, now I remember. It's a talisman crafted by my cousin. The bear in our culture is a symbol of strength and courage, and the stone bestows its wearer with these qualities. It was given the blessing of the shaman who carved it.

"Oh wow, really? How did he bless it?"

"Well, between you and me," the woman leaned a little closer, "I don't know much about shamanism myself, but I hear that he slew a bear and embedded its spirit within the stone."

"There's no way a bear could fit inside that!" Dane exclaimed. He reached out to touch it, and felt a strange warmth radiating from the stone. He thought it might have been a trick of his mind or the heat of the sun left on the stone, but when he took his hand away, he could still feel a tingling sensation running up his arm.

"Does that mean it's magic?" he asked. When the minotaur nodded her head, Dane's face lit up. "I've never touched something magical before! Can I buy it? How much is it?" He was already shoving his hands into his belt pouch to retrieve his money before he'd finished talking, and was scooping out a handful of silver coins.

"I think I could part with it for a few silver pieces," the minotaur replied after a moment of thought.

One of the other minotaur snorted as he watched the exchange. "Lora that stuff isn't for a calf. Just send him away."

Feeling the tips of his ears heat up, Dane looked up at the male and said, "I'm not a child, I'm almost fourteen!"

The minotaur looked down at him and sneered. "What's your name, kid?"

"Dane! And stop calling me a kid!"

"And what would you prefer?" the minotaur said, his lip curling into a cruel smirk. "Child? Runt? Pipsqueak?"

Dane frowned. "I would prefer to be called by my name."

"Thrak, leave him alone," the female running the stall said. "He can buy it if he wants."

Thrak laughed. "Listen Dane, you've got guts but you won't get far just getting angry. Face it, you're small and you're weak. What are you going to do if I decide to do something about it?"

Dane's face blanched at the threat. He had only seen the Snowhoof clan minotaur as being friendly, but now that he actually considered how much larger the bullmen were compared to him, he realized he was completely outmatched. Why was he picking a fight with him? His eyes wandered upwards and he saw the sharp points of Thrak's horns, deadly and glinting in the sunlight as though they'd been waxed.

"I guess I couldn't do anything," Dane mumbled. His eyes hurt from not blinking as he stared, fixated on the fine tips of Thrak's horns.

"Exactly. So why don't you run along and --"

"Thrak, it's my stall," the female said harshly, cutting him off. "If I want to sell him the pendant, then I will."

Thrak bristled at this, and he swung his steel-eyed gaze over at her. She didn't waver beneath his glare like Dane did, and he gave a disapproving huff through his nostrils.

"Do whatever you want, Lora." He pushed past her and said, "I'm going to get some food."

Dane followed the minotaur with his eyes, worried that perhaps he would go around him and try something, but when he disappeared into the throng of the crowd, the boy relaxed.

"Sorry about that," Lora said. "Males are so temperamental when opposed. You shouldn't try to argue with one." She chuckled. "I suppose that goes for anything bigger than you." Her tone was soft and not scolding, and Dane nodded in agreement. He would keep that in mind next time he spoke to a minotaur.

"Now then, I believe I said I'd sell this pendant for three silver, correct?"

Again, Dane nodded. He picked out three silver coins and slapped them down on the counter. The merchant smiled and plucked the coins up before she dropped the pendant into Dane's open hands.

"Thank you for your business. May the spirits watch over you, child," Lora said.

"Thank you," Dane said and waved goodbye.

Dane scurried off, choosing to melt into the crowd to avoid running into Thrak. He kept his eyes peeled around him as he slipped the pendant over his head. When the stone passed over his skin, it still felt warm to the touch.

Oh wow, it's magic. Real magic! Father never let me learn anything about these sorts of things. I wonder what I can do now. I can't wait to find out if the bear really does make me stronger!

He wandered around the bazaar for a bit longer and looked at some of the goods the local merchants had to sell, but beyond the baked food nothing caught his attention. He was always interested in the exotic weaponry, but he was too young to even be looking at that stuff, let alone being able to buy it. He began to meander over towards the bakery while examining the stone that now hung around his neck.

"Dane? Dane!" Jon's voice rang out across the market, and Dane felt his heart jump into his throat. "Where did you wander off to?"

The boy's face flushed with embarrassment as a few people nearby looked in his direction. He longed to be able to disappear, to avoid their stares and his father's demands, but such a thing wasn't possible. If only he could perform magic, he could simply slip away behind a cloak of invisibility and never be found again.

Not wanting to dawdle any longer and provoke his father further, Dane scurried back across the bazaar. He hid the pendant beneath his tunic and returned to where Jon was waiting for him.

"Where were you? Get back here!" Jon grabbed him by the forearm and dragged him behind the counter.

Dane looked up at his father and opened his mouth to apologize, but he was quickly cut off before he could make a sound.

"Don't do that again! Didn't I tell you it was dangerous to go off on your own?"

"But. . . I was still in town. . ."

"It doesn't matter! You do as you're told, understood? You'll never amount to anything in life if you always act on every impulse."

A young woman in the stall next to them poked her head over to look at the two of them. "Don't you think you're being a little hard on him, Jon? It's a boy's nature to want to explore."

"A boy needs to learn to follow rules and not spend his time entertaining whimsical fantasies," Jon replied. Then, as if it was an afterthought he added, "With all due respect, miss." He turned back to look down at Dane. "Just go and sit by the wagon and stay out of trouble.

"But I was just --"

"Sit! Down!"

Dane lowered his head until his chin touched his chest. He shuffled over to sit on the back of the wagon and watched as Jon tried to sell his pelts, calling over anyone who walked by to take a look at what he had to offer.

A few children were running around the bazaar, and Dane noted that none of them were forced to help their parents.

Probably because they all have mothers to look after them while their fathers work, Dane thought bitterly.

The day progressed slower than a turtle walking uphill. He lost count of the number of times he yawned. The day moved without incident, until sometime in the late afternoon. Two individuals approached Jon's stall and were talking to each other in a language that Dane hadn't heard before. Despite the heat, they wore large cloaks that were draped over their bodies. Dane could see the glint of metal off a chain mail tunic and he spied swords strapped to their belts. He looked at their armor, trying to find a crest or insignia of some sort to signify what military they belonged to.

They must be mercenaries or adventurers, Dane concluded when he couldn't find any sign of their allegiance. He looked at his father, who wore a scowl on his face and stood with his arms crossed. *What's his problem?*

"Can I help you?" Jon said, his voice slightly raised.

"Just looking around, sir," one of the men replied. Eventually they both walked away without buying anything, satisfied with whatever it was they had come over to look at.

"Bunch of blood-sucking leeches," Jon muttered quietly. "Every time some new conflict springs up those thugs show up to bleed the locals dry of their money and stir up more trouble."

Dane was too busy with his own thoughts to care about what Jon was saying. "I wonder if they're travelers or adventurers or something like that. It would be so amazing to be able to travel the world, and to see new sights and help people or --"

Jon slammed a fist on the counter and spun around. "They were mercenaries, Dane! They are worthless scum-suckers that prefer to leech off our nation rather than help it. The only thing they care about is money, not about helping anyone." Spittle flew from his mouth as he yelled. "So long as you're my son and you're living under my roof, you won't so much as think about something like that. Do I make myself clear Dane?"

Dane knew it wasn't a question. He hung his head as his eyes began to water. His voice quivered as he uttered his reply, "Yes." Dane went back to sitting quietly on the back end of the wagon, and didn't speak for the rest of the day, unless he was spoken to first.

The sun was beginning to set when Jon finally sold off the last of his pelts. The coin purse that hung from his belt was nearly full, and it jingled as he walked. It looked ready to burst and shower the ground with coins at the slightest provocation.

"It feels like I got a good haul this year," Jon said. He lifted the bag up and shook it to guess at its weight. "Hopefully it's enough to fix up the home a bit and replace some of my tools."

Dane hopped off the wagon, his bottom sore from sitting all day. "How about a new hatchet?"

"No. The one we have is fine," Jon replied.

"But it's so dull!"

"I said no. I need the money for things that are more important, like fixing the door or replacing the windows before winter comes. Not to mention there's that bow you broke last month that still needs replacing. Have you forgotten about that?"

Dane winced at the mention of the bow. "It wasn't my fault! It snapped as I drew it back." He looked down at his arm where a large cut was still healing when the splintered wood had snapped backwards.

"That's because you were being too rough with it," Jon shot back. "It's going to cost a good chunk of our earnings just to keep paying for your education and to get us through the winter. Replacing the hatchet is the last thing I need to worry about right now." Dane grew sullen once again, and Jon sighed. "I suppose I can spare a few copper for a whetstone if it gets you to stop whining about it. But you're sharpening it and you're going to be chopping the wood from now on."

I always do the chopping anyways, Dane thought.

Jon strode over to the cart and picked it up. "I'm going to return this to Farmer Mathias and then we're heading home. Stay here and wait for me."

Dane didn't have to wait long for Jon to return, and once he did, he fell in stride behind his father as they headed back to their home in the woods. A large pine forest lay to the north of Tran, and a well-worn path cut through it to the Northpine logging camp beyond. Jon walked with his bow in hand and the quiver hanging from his waist. He didn't have an arrow ready though, and seemed confident that they wouldn't encounter any problems on the way home.

Everything was quiet save for the sound of their feet crunching twigs and leaves that had fallen on the path. The trees cast long, dark shadows across the ground, like claws scratching at the dirt. Few birds were around at that hour, and their chirps were broken up by long stretches of silence before they started up again.

Every sound set Dane on edge. Seeing the construction of the watchtowers and the increase in military presence made him question whether his confidence was misplaced. If everyone was taking the orcs being in the area seriously, then maybe he should, too?

That's not right, they'd never come this far south. Would they?

Some bushes to the side rustled violently, causing Dane to stumble in surprise. He lost his footing and fell forward, skinning his knees. He tried to catch himself but he only ended up scraping the palms of his hands.

A deer bounded across the path and back into the woods on the other side. Jon looked back down at Dane and said, "What in the Pantheon's name are you doing?"

"Nothing," Dane stammered, embarrassed that he'd been startled by nothing more than a deer. He brushed the dirt off his legs as he stood back up, and ignored the aching in his hands as he fell in stride beside Jon once more.

Those orcs will never come here. They have no reason to, Dane assured himself.

After a time they came upon a fork in the path. It was less worn down than the main pathway and the underbrush was beginning to grow back over it. At the end of the path was their home. It was a small, one room log cabin nestled within a clearing. To the side of the house was a small stump with a hatchet buried in it, next to a stack of wood piled up against the cabin. On the opposite side was a workbench and a large rack that Jon used to prepare the pelts he gathered.

The two of them headed inside and Dane bolted to the cellar. He pulled the door open and out popped a small gray tabby cat that they had gotten the year before. It seemed like the only time Dane saw his father smile was when the cat was around. Jon had named the kitten Zoey, though Dane never discovered where the name had come from. He scooped the cat up and rubbed a finger against the cat's cheek, and she purred.

As Dane was occupied with the cat, Jon slipped past him and went down into the cellar to bring up a pair of venison steaks to prepare for supper. He set them down on the table, then turned to Dane.

"Go out and chop some wood for the stove."

Dane grumbled and set the cat gently on the floor. He left the house and slammed the door behind him.

"Knock it off, Dane!" Jon yelled as he got to work preparing dinner.

The boy shuffled over to the stump and yanked the hatchet out. The shaft was gnarled, and it was beginning to splinter in a few places. There was a dull sheen on the blade, and it was scratched from many years of use and poor maintenance.

If father would chop the wood once in awhile, he'd know how badly we need a new hatchet.

Dane grabbed a log from a pile beside the house and placed it on the stump before slicing the log in two, then repeated the process to cut it into quarters. He moved onto the next log, but the hatchet's blade became lodged two-thirds of the way through.

"Piece of junk!" Dane yelled, and with a wordless shout, he lifted the hatchet up and slammed it down until it cut the rest of the way through.

Cheap old man can't even get a decent hatchet to chop his own wood. He continued until he had an arm full of cut pieces to use for firewood, and headed back inside. After tossing half of the pile into the stove, the set the rest down beside it. Dane then grabbed a bit of tinder and a pair of flint stones from the waterproof lock box stored nearby. After a few strikes with the stones, the tinder caught fire and he began to stoke it a bit until a bright orange flame started to consume the wood.

"Stove's lit," he announced.

"That was fast. Did you even cut enough wood to keep the fire going?" Jon asked.

"Yeah, of course. I'm getting stronger you know. I'm not a little kid anymore," Dane replied, remembering the pendant he wore beneath his tunic.

His father shrugged and went about finishing supper while Dan went back to playing with Zoey. The cabin was soon filled with the scent of cooked meat and onions, the latter of which irritated Dane's eyes.

The moons were beginning to crest the horizon by the time Jon was done cooking. A lantern hung from the ceiling and provided the pair with ample lighting. Zoey bounded off into the cellar to find her dinner. Dane slumped down in his chair, disappointed that she left.

Jon brought their food over and set it down on the table. They ate in silence. Dane didn't want to rile his father up with whatever he wanted to say, and he imagined that Jon would only think he was whining.

Hopefully if I keep him in a good mood he won't be such a grouch when we go hunting in a couple days, Dane thought. With the winter months nearly upon them, they needed to prepare their cellar with as much food they could get their hands on. It was usually slim pickings for hunting once the snow fell.

After they ate, Dane cleaned their plates in a small wash basin using water pumped from a well Jon had dug next to their house. He then tidied up the table and made it spotless. His father would accept nothing less than absolute perfection. After he was done, Dane decided to go to bed rather than get involved with anything else. It was too dark to go outside, and Zoey was too busy hunting in the cellar to care about much else.

Dane crossed the room to his bed and ignored his father, who sat by the window with an unmarked book in his hand and a pipe in his mouth. Dane never asked what it was that he was reading, but for more nights than he could remember, Jon had the same book every time he smoked his tobacco. The boy wondered how many times the man had read through it in its entirety.

"You're getting up a little earlier tomorrow," Jon said, "You have a lecture with Lynn in the afternoon, and I need fresh firewood before I walk you to town."

Dane didn't respond as he pulled the covers away from his bed.

Whatever old man. The next few days are going to be an absolute nightmare. Dane climbed under his blankets and turned onto his side. He faced the wall with his back to Jon, and fell asleep.

Chapter 2 - Children of the Goddess

1st Day of Manul
124 I.E.

The red-skinned boy held his hands out and his mother took them in her own before she ran her thumbs over his palms. The orc whelp looked up at her with expectant eyes, waiting for her lesson to begin. The woman's body was lithe and frail looking, yet she commanded the entirety of her tribe because of the power she held within her body. The magic of the orcs' Goddess, Sytarel, coursed through her veins. At a distance, one would see only the soft facial features, thin frame, and long black hair that flowed down to her waist. However, her calloused, scarred hands said she had a life full of hardships and labor.

By comparison, her son Xellik looked very much the opposite of her. He was tall with broad shoulders and naturally thick arms. His black hair topped his head loosely and fell disheveled around his face. He had a pair of tusks growing from his bottom jaw that stuck out of his mouth and curled up against his upper lip, even when his mouth was closed. His knuckles were worn from the constant fights he'd gotten into with the other orcling males, but beyond that his skin was still soft and fair.

"Always remember that you are a conduit through which our Goddess works her magic," Fellis told him as she turned his hands over until his palms faced upwards, towards the ceiling of the tent that was their home. "Never forget to be thankful for the pact that Sytarel allowed you to have with Her."

"Yes, mother," Xellik replied.

"Now, focus your thoughts on the Goddess and speak the words of power exactly as I taught you."

Nodding his head and swallowing audibly, Xellik waited for his mother to take a few steps back before he began. "Sytarel, Goddess of War, I ask you to bestow upon me a blade to cut through my enemies."

Nothing happened, and his mother was quick to reproach him. She gripped his hands and twisted them into the proper position, causing him to wince with pain. "You did not align your body properly and you stuttered. I told you before, it needs to be perfect to work!"

Xellik tried again, but with similar results. Nothing seemed to be working and he didn't understand what he was doing wrong. Every attempt he made failed to conjure a sword as his mother had shown him.

What am I doing wrong? Xellik thought as Fellis became more and more frustrated with him. *This is supposed to be Sytarel's easiest boon to command. So why can't I do it? Come on, please work!* The orcling pleaded, hoping that if Sytarel was listening that she would reward his efforts as he strained to succeed in casting his spell. He shifted his feet and tried again, focusing so intently he feared that a blood vessel in his neck would rupture and splatter the underside of the bear hide that made up the walls of their tent.

There was a sudden crackle of energy and a pop that surprised Xellik, and he lost his focus. The whelp gave the spell one more attempt and as he did so, a swirling vortex of blue-white energy began to coalesce into a physical object. A blade of pure mana sized to fit the young orc appeared within his hands. Xellik wriggled his fingers to adjust his grip. It felt real and solid.

It was a scimitar of simple design, with a curved blade and a flat hilt. Its surface was blue and shimmered as white lines streaked across it, ebbing like ripples in a pond. Xellik lifted a finger to the sword's edge, and quickly drew his hand back as the blade bit into his skin.

I can't believe it. It's real!

Not even his mother had believed that Xellik had cast the spell successfully. Fellis closed her gaping mouth, then nodded her approval. "It's about time you pulled it off," she said. "Now put it away."

Xellik did as he was instructed. Dismissing the weapon was as simple as letting go of it or focusing on something else. His thoughts turned to dinner, and he salivated as the thought of a juicy roast boar. With his concentration broken, the sword faded away as it dispersed into a mist of energy as the mana used to conjure it returned to the air.

"Stopping your own spell effects will always be easier than creating them," Fellis told him. "You can easily dismiss a fireball or cease levitating with as much as a thought, but working most spells in the first place requires focus, training, and devotion to the Goddess above all else."

"Can I try another one?" Xellik asked, eager to expand his repertoire of spells as quickly as possible. "I want to try the other spell that you told me about. You know, the one with the black ball?"

"I suppose it couldn't hurt for you learn another spell. However, you're going to need a target."

Stepping back, Fellis spoke a chant in a low, barely audible voice. She knelt down, issuing an audible pop from her knees as she moved, and placed her hand flat on the ground. As she stood back up and lifted her arm, the dirt began to shift and rumble.

From the ground rose a dirt-caked construct that stood as tall as Xellik. It was vaguely humanoid in shape with a pair of glowing green eyes inset into its head. The earth elemental stood facing

Xellik, its eyes unblinking. The orcling found it more than a little unnerving how it stood before him unflinchingly. He reminded himself that it was a mindless construct incapable of independent thought. It only stared at him because that's all it had been instructed to do.

"Do you remember the words to the spell from the last time I showed you?" Fellis asked.

Xellik nodded and shook his arms a little to limber up. There was no need to worry about it moving around or getting away from him. All he had to do was strike a stationary target.

It should be easy, if I can get the spell right. Sytarel, please grant me Your strength!

Clenching his hand, Xellik imagined the energy around him gathering towards his fist as he spoke. "May despair befall my enemies as the encroaching darkness threatens to consume them whole!"

To his surprise, the spell worked on his first attempt. A ball of shadows appeared around his hand. It was pitch black and cold, completely obscuring his hand. His skin began to sting as if frostbitten and he needed to act quickly. Xellik pulled his fist back and then thrust forward as he opened his hand. The ball of shadows flew as if fired from a crossbow and it struck the elemental square in the chest. The creature exploded in a puff of dirt and dust, leaving only frosted rubble where it had stood.

"Don't feel too proud of your accomplishment," Fellis rebuked him when he cheered. "It was weak, so much so that you could've poked a finger into it and it'd give way like water."

The young orcling was too lost in his own thoughts and he didn't hear what his mother had said. It didn't matter to him whether his spell work had been weak or not. He'd done what he'd been waiting for years to do.

Finally, I'm moving towards the destiny that my mother has promised me. One day I will lead our people, with this power at my command.

There was a rustling sound as the tent's flaps were pushed aside and a male orc stepped inside. His head was shaven bald, as was customary for orcs to do at their coming of age ceremony. On his shiny, red head was tattooed a symbol of the Fergoth clan, an open maw with blood dripping from the fangs. He wore a wolf-fur girdle about his waist and fur leggings beneath that. Around his neck was a talisman of sorts, fashioned from teeth plucked from a bear's muzzle.

"High Priestess, a word if you'd please?" the male said. He didn't bother to acknowledge Xellik with anything more than a casual glare in his direction. Though it confused him as to why people looked down on him, he didn't care. One day all the Fergoth orcs would bend their knees to him.

"What is it now, Bytej?" Fellis said impatiently as she moved outside to join the other orc.

Xellik remained inside, reciting in his mind the words of power for the spells he'd just cast. He worked to commit them to memory to make sure he could get it right every time. There was no way of knowing when he might need a weapon, and if the time came where he did need to take up a sword, he didn't want to risk being in a position where he couldn't conjure one up before his enemies were upon him. The males were the defenders of their clan. They did the hunting, they fought off the bandits, and raiders, and opposing tribes. He needed to be prepared for any situation.

From inside the tent, Xellik could hear the voices of Fellis and Bytej as they spoke just outside. Though the orcling wasn't one to listen in on other people's conversations, his ears perked up when he heard his name. Suddenly the discussion they were having drew all his attention, and he stood near the tent's walls to listen in on what they were saying.

"No one is going to accept Xellik as your heir. No one will listen to him when he grows older. Why do you insist on training him?" Bytej asked.

Fellis let out a sigh. "You've told me this a thousand times since he was born but my response is still the same. I'm keeping Xellik and training him to replace me one day."

"Don't you think there's a higher power out there that might disapprove of something like that? Someone more powerful and all-knowing than you are? Than any mortal could ever dream of being?"

"Are you suggesting what I think you're suggesting?" Fellis laughed. "Are you so ignorant that you can't even see what's going on around you? I can still work my magic, and my prayers have still been answered. Sytarel has not abandoned me or the tribe for my choices."

"Even despite the loss of our home to the human scum? You know as well as I do that you should have sacrificed that bastard child as an offering for a daughter. Perhaps losing our home was Sytarel's punishment?"

Xellik blinked when he heard those words. That wasn't right, was it? He had to have misheard something. There's no way his mother would have ever thought of sacrificing him as an offering to Sytarel, would she have? Though outwardly he denied it, deep down a part of him understood that if Sytarel had wished it, Fellis would have slain him as a defenseless whelp ages ago.

I know the females rule the tribes but that's no reason to kill a defenseless orcling. Is it?

"You forget your place, Bytej, and it is not for a shaman such as yourself to question a High Priestess," Fellis scolded him with a raised voice. "Are you seeking to waste my time with this nonsense? Or is it something else? Yes. . . now I see it. You're ashamed, aren't you?"

There was a moment of silence and Xellik could make out the sound of someone grunting a response. What is Bytej ashamed of?

"That's what I thought," she said, finally breaking the tense quiet.

"You know I'm not the only one that's been unhappy with the decision. We've been surviving since the child was born, that much is true, but how much longer do you think we can last before Sytarel gets upset that you have yet to sire a daughter?"

"When and if it becomes and issue, I'll deal with it. Sytarel has not denounced me in response to my prayers, and I'm confident it won't be an issue. I don't care if the tribe has a problem with my decisions. It is not for them to question. If there's nothing else you wanted to say, then be gone. I do not wish to discuss this with you any longer."

"What about your plans for dealing with the Rogarians?"

"Everything is in motion as we speak. The humans have begun fortifying their settlements but there's one nearby that's ripe for picking," Fellis responded. "Ragash and his warriors have everything prepared and Urzule's out scouting. She should be back soon, if all goes well. Is everything prepared on your end?"

"Everything is set for the ritual. All we need are the final ingredients. I can only hope Ragash can procure them," Bytej said. "If this plan of yours fails --"

"It won't. In two days, Sytarel Herself will bless us with enough power to retake our homeland."

"We should have traveled to Zugrul when all this happened," Bytej remarked.

Xellik clenched his fists, irritated that the shaman would want to give up their ancestral land so easily. He was fortunate that his mother expressed their mutual disbelief for him.

"Are you questioning my decisions, Bytej? That isn't a male's place!" Fellis roared, her voice carrying through the woods. She boomed with power, and likely every orc in the settlement heard her. "We will deal with the Rogarians as Sytarel sees fit, and endure just as we always have. The Fergoth clan has survived for centuries on this land without ever needing to rely on Zugrul for aid. We are the descendants of the Last Empire and we will not be shoved off our homeland as easily as those cowards."

"That was generations ago," Bytej reminded her, "Back when the humans were nothing but a collection of small, disorganized farming communities. Now they have a military and a proper leader beneath a single flag. We can't endure against those odds any longer, especially now that our clan has been decimated."

"We will survive, because it is what we must do. Now if there's nothing else to discuss, I have other matters to attend to."

There was a pause, and tensely Bytej warned her, "You will get us all killed because of your pride. I hope you're aware of that."

Footsteps quickly faded into the distance as Xellik assumed that Bytej had begun to walk off. Realizing that his mother would quickly return inside and find him standing awkwardly doing nothing, he assumed his sword summoning stance and began reciting the words he needed to conjure the blade.

Fellis walked into the tent as he finished the spell, creating a sword of mana. She barked his name and asked, "What are you doing? Who gave you permission to do that?"

Xellik dropped the sword, which caused it to disappear before it even touched the ground. "I was just practicing, mother."

"Not without my express permission. You're not to cast a spell unless I say so or until after your coming of age ceremony. I know how hot-headed you can be and I don't want you using your power frivolously. It would be an insult to Sytarel!" Fellis backhanded her son, turning his cheek a deep red as a welt began to form. "Do I make myself clear?"

Xellik nodded his head and swallowed a lump that had formed

in his throat. His mother never threatened him, but he knew that his punishment would be swift if he crossed her. Getting caught trying to use magic was still far more preferable to being caught eavesdropping on her conversation with Bytej, though.

"Go outside and play with Napir or Sorda or something. I have things I need to do."

Xellik did as he was asked, knowing that remaining in the tent would only anger her. He was lost in thought as he bumbled through their makeshift camp, and didn't notice the larger orc that he bumped into on his way to find his friends. Xellik fell backwards with a grunt as he landed on his backside.

"Well well, look what we have here," spoke a gravelly voice.

Xellik looked up into the eye of Ragash, the leader of the Fergoth clan's warriors. Though he was missing an eye and wore a bandana over that side of his head to cover it, the orc still managed to look intimidating. He crossed his overly muscled arms over his thick chest and grinned, showing off a mouth full of yellowed and missing teeth.

"You trying to pick a fight, whelp?" Ragash asked.

"Do you even know who you're talking to?" Xellik spat. "I should have you gutted for talking to me like that!"

"Oh?" Ragash leaned forward to stare Xellik in the eyes. Rancid breath like rotten meat seeped forth from his mouth, washing over the orcling's face. "And who are you to make such threats? There's not a scar on your body and you're just another male."

"I'm the next High Priest!" Xellik said defiantly.

Ragash laughed at him. "You haven't learned a lot if you think anyone will ever answer to you. We're males, whelp, and it's high time you learned that there's no hierarchy between us. We're all beneath the females, got it?" His hand fell upon the handle of his sword. "If you're going to threaten me, then I won't hesitate to put you in your place."

"Fine by me!" Xellik stepped back, assuming his stance to summon his weapon. He managed to utter two syllables before Ragash struck.

The orc's blade flashed out of its sheath and in a single smooth motion, Ragash slammed the pommel into Xellik's gut. The orcling gasped as the air in his lungs exploded outward.

The ground rushed towards Xellik as he slumped forward. He groaned as he tried to breath, and ended up inhaling a mouthful of dirt that caused him to cough even harder. He rolled over and looked up, seeing Ragash poised above him with the tip of his blade pointed at Xellik's right eye.

Despite himself, Xellik managed to glare down the length of the sword and meet Ragash's gaze. He wasn't going to cower even in the face of death. He wouldn't give the orc any such satisfaction.

Ragash sheathed his sword then knelt down. He grabbed Xellik by a tuft of his hair and uttered in a low, cold voice that seeped with anger. "Don't make threats you can't keep, whelp." Afterwards, he shoved the orcling's head back into the dirt and ground him down for good measure before letting go and walking off.

There was no shortage of laughter from the orcs that had gathered to watch the exchange, and Xellik's face burned with a mixture of anger and embarrassment. One day he would lead the clan. Why wouldn't they see that? He would use his power to teach them all not to laugh at him again.

Once Xellik managed to get air back in his lungs, he rushed through the Fergoth's camp to find someone to take his rage out on. Napir had stolen his hiking stick from him last week. Perhaps, he thought, it was time to get him back for that.

He cracked his knuckles as he went off to find the other orcling.

Chapter 3 - Expectations

2nd Day of Manul
124 I.E.

Dane awoke to the sound of metal scraping against wood and the creak of his father's favourite chair. He blinked his eyes open and looked around to find Jon whittling away on something. A stack of half finished arrows was piled neatly on the floor next to the chair.

"You slept in again," Jon remarked, not looking up from his work as he set one shaft of wood down and picked up another less refined one before he began whittling again.

"You didn't wake me." Dane rubbed the sleep out of his eyes and slid out of his bed to get dressed.

"I shouldn't need to wake you," Jon said, slowly dragging the blade across the wood and sending shavings to the floor. "You'd better hurry and get dressed or you'll be late for your lesson. I don't want you squandering a good education."

"You don't want me to get firewood?" Dane asked.

"You can do it when you get back. You're not missing your tutoring for anything."

"Fine, whatever. . ."

"Don't take that tone with me," Jon snapped, pointing the stick of wood in his direction. He motioned towards the door and said, "Get your shoes on and I'll walk you to the edge of the village."

As Dane stepped outside, he grabbed a thick, wool-lined cloak and draped it over his shoulders. He took a few steps out into the forest and waited for his father to gather up his bow and join him. It was a breezy, frigid autumn morning, but the cloudless sky promised that it would warm up later in the day. Every breath of wind rustled dried and dead leaves from the trees and coated the forest floor with crunchy foliage.

Stupid old man, Dane thought as he marched through the woods. The wind whipped past him and his cloak fluttered in the breeze. He drew it closer to his body and tried his best to stay warm. Soon it would be winter, and he'd be stuck sitting in their home until the snow thawed, unable to go anywhere. He wasn't looking forward to it. The winter months were boring and filled with reading and occasionally chopping firewood.

Dane's body was still stiff from waking up and he wanted to walk slower, but Jon insisted on keeping a brisk pace. The boy stalled even as he approached Tran and crested the hill at the end of the forest. It was the second day of the Harvest Festival, and tomorrow all the vendors and farmers would be packing up their goods and returning to their homes. If only Jon weren't around, Dane figured he could have taken one last look at the goods the merchants had for sale before going to Lynn's house.

"Alright, get moving," Jon said. "I'll be back around twelve, so don't keep me waiting."

"Yes dad. . ." Dane mumbled as he stomped off down the side of the hill.

As he crossed through the town square, he peeked at the sundial in the middle of the reflecting pool, noting the time. Professor Lynn was expecting him any moment, and though Dane longed to be able to gawk at the exotic wares in town a little while longer, he knew that if he was late she would inform Jon.

Dane made his way across the market and down the street, past the inn that Ted and his wife Lily owned. No one stood there to greet him, like they did with his father. Dane couldn't understand how a man like Jon could have any friends with the way he always acted so high and mighty.

The bells in the Church of Laren rang out as Dane passed by the chapel, signaling the start of a new hour. Eight dings echoed across the town. The church was small, about the size of Dane and Jon's cabin with a steeple atop the bell tower in back, but that seemed to be big enough for the people of Tran.

Dane wasn't a follower of the God Laren. Or any God or Goddess, for that matter. He was still young, and too naive to consider whether the Gods really existed or not. Jon had tried to get Dane to go to the church's services at least once a week, but he resisted and despite his father's persistence, the older man eventually grew frustrated and relented.

I don't see why I should have to attend the sermons when he doesn't want to go, either, Dane thought as he continued walking past the church. *He probably doesn't believe in Laren with how often he's always praying to that Xenar God of his.*

Dane kicked at a loose pebble that bounced along the cobblestone road as he came up to Professor Lynn's residence. The home was built out of bricks, a luxury that his father had been unable to afford when he'd build their cabin out in the woods. The windows had sky-blue colored drapes on the inside, with lace edges that added a touch of femininity to an otherwise cold building.

He gingerly knocked on the door and waited for Lynn to open it.

"Good morning, Dane," she said and stepped aside to let him in. "I hope you're ready for today's lesson."

"Yeah, I suppose so," Dane said, not feeling the least bit enthusiastic about the prospect of reading more books and being drilled relentlessly by the scholar.

Lynn was a fair-skinned woman, and tall compared to most others. Her long golden hair fell around her shoulders and down to her waist. Some people around town had said she was of elven blood, and that's what contributed to much of her beauty. No one was sure if such rumors held any truth or not. Lynn was very tight-lipped about her heritage when asked, and her hair always covered the tips of her ears. She wore a blue scholar's robe that matched the color of her eyes.

"You should be more excited. There's so much one can learn from history," she said as she closed the door behind him. "Besides, we're going to be going over the Jintaren Incursion today."

"Great, I can read all about a war that happened before I was born and that has nothing to do with me."

"Nonsense!" Lynn said, waving his criticisms aside as though his words were nothing more than pesky flies. "Such history has relevance to everyone in this province. It's shaped much of our policy and, dare I say it, our ability to prosper since we no longer need to defend our northern border."

"Pity I live out in the woods and live off the sweat of my labour."

"Must you always be so jaded?"

"Must history always be so boring?" he shot back.

"I don't find it boring. Regardless of your opinions on the topic, your father has paid me quite handsomely to teach you about these things so that you can one day become a scholar yourself," Lynn told him as they moved towards her study off to the side of the main room. Dane led the way, having been there plenty of times before.

"What if I don't want to be a scholar?" Dane whined, "Why hasn't anyone thought about what I want? I want to travel and see all the places that I read about. What's the point in learning about all these places if I never get to see them first hand?"

Lynn rolled her eyes at his childish complaints. "One day, your wanderlust will fade and you'll want to settle down. Scholars are well paid and you can have a fulfilling life without having to travel. Besides, how would you raise a family on the road?"

Dane shrugged. He never thought about things like getting married or raising children. Those were concerns for adults.

He opened the door to her study and stepped inside. The room was laid out with bookcases lining every single wall except for a spot behind the desk. A recessed alcove gave way to a panoramic view of the rolling farmlands beyond the town. The window was cracked open just enough to allow the fresh air and sounds outside into the room, and the drapes fluttered in the breeze.

The bookshelves were full of thick tomes that varied in subjects and looked to Dane like they were older than even Lynn. He could only reach the third shelf without having to stand on his toes or use a chair, but what books he had seen when he'd stolen a few moments to himself between study sessions were equally as boring as what he'd been stuck reading.

"Let's get this over with then," Dane said as he shrugged helplessly. He took his place at her desk and Lynn set a large tome before him. All Dane could think about was how long the day would drag out as he saw the book being opened before him.

"I'll be back in a short while to question you on what you've read. Study hard, young Trueshot." Lynn left the room and moved into the kitchen. Through the door he could hear porcelain cups and plates clinking together, which told him that she was going to be brewing some tea later on.

With a defeated sigh, Dane looked down at the page covered in lengthy paragraphs and run-on sentences. Whoever wrote these, he thought, hadn't heard of what it meant to be brief.

He spent an hour studying the text before he grew bored. He was fed up with the slow pace of reading through the book and even after skipping several sections, the end was nowhere in sight. Deciding to sate his curiosity, Dane hopped off the chair and began to peruse Lynn's library, searching for something more interesting than the textbook he'd been given.

Dane got up from his chair and paced around the room, making his way over to a spot on the bookshelves where he had last finished snooping during his previous lesson. He ran his index finger over the spines of each book as he read the titles in a hushed whisper.

"Beginnings of Rogarian Culture... Spiritcalling: The Beginnings of Shamanism and the Snowhoof Minotaur..." he kept on going, finding that the books were beginning to be less about culture and history. "Herbs and their Medical Properties... Understanding Runes of the Arcane Age... Basic Spellwork for Sorcerers..."

He took another step to his right, then doubled back to the previous book as it finally clicked in his mind what it was he'd just passed over. Quickly sticking a finger over the top edge, he hastily yanked the book out from its spot and knocked its neighbor off with it. Dane hastened to catch it before it could strike the floor.

With a sigh of relief, Dane replaced the errant book and flipped open the brown-covered tome about magic. Though the first half of the text disappointed all of Dane's expectations with its liberal peppering of large words and theories he could scarcely understand, the second half fulfilled every promise his imagination had made to him about the contents of a mage's book. An entire catalog of various spells, rituals, runes, and the directions necessary to implement them.

His mouth hung open as he gaped at each page, gently turning them over as he read on. There was a spell for everything, from the majestic like summoning a creature of pure energy to act as a servant or evoking fire, to more mundane things like enchanting a broom and mop to clean one's home without having to so much as lift a finger.

Amazing! I didn't know Professor Lynn had a book like this. Boy, would father get upset if he found out the woman tutoring his child studies magic! I should ask her about it sometime, and see if she can really do what's in this book.

Footsteps alerted Dane to Lynn's approach and he quickly shoved the book back in its spot, making an audible slam as he did so. Cursing to himself, he quickly darted back to his chair and acted as if he'd never left it. The door opened and he raised his head to see Lynn enter, carrying a pair of cups full of tea. It was her preferred beverage, and Dane had taken a liking to it, even though the taste of the bitter drink reminded him of dusty tomes and quiet studies.

"Is something wrong?" she asked and set one of the cups down on the desk next to Dane. "I heard something slam."

"Oh, sorry about that, Professor. I had picked up the book but I guess I set it down a little too roughly. I didn't realize it was so heavy," Dane replied. He wasn't sure if it was a good lie or not, but he felt it was believable enough that he might be able to get away with it.

"You should be more careful. Books like this are hard to come by, even if newer editions are easier to find these days."

"Why's that?" Dane asked as he took up his cup and sipped from it. It was still hot and stung his tongue, but it warmed him from the inside out and sent a shiver up his spine.

"Because it was at the beginning of the Industrial Era that sorcerers developed an inscription spell that could copy the contents of one book to a blank one in a fraction of the time it takes someone to hand-write these texts." Lynn set her cup down and took a seat at a chair just in front of the desk. "It's because of that development that you're able to learn to read and write without having to pay a king's ransom for my services." She blew on her tea before taking a sip of it. "We're very lucky to have come this far so that more people can grow up with an education."

"I suppose so," Dane said, shrugging.

"Now then, how far did you read?"

Dane made a show of flipping the pages to the end of the chapter and beamed a smile at her.

"Alright then, first question. . ."

She drilled Dane on numerous aspects about the war, including events that had lead up to it and the reason it had ended. The boy underestimated Lynn's questioning ability and got many answers wrong, such as dates and names. He cursed his laziness.

I should've just read the whole chapter. I bet she's going to tell father I haven't been studying properly.

"I'm a bit disappointed in you, Dane. I'd have thought you would've mastered such a short chapter easily. You've done better on longer subjects," she said, chiding him.

"I know. I guess I couldn't focus with the festival in town today," Dane lied. Lynn was a trusting woman, and he'd hate to betray that trust by lying to her again, but she had believed his first lie. Perhaps she would believe a second one.

Lynn nodded her head. "Yes, I've heard quite a bit of noise from time to time. Perhaps you're right. We can pick up where we left off next time."

"You mean we're done early?" Dane asked. Only a couple hours had passed since he'd arrived, and he'd been expecting to be stuck at the professor's home for a couple more still.

"Sure, why not?" Lynn shrugged. "Go and enjoy the festivities for a while. After all, it's only here once a year. We can continue two days from now, when the festival is gone." She wagged a finger at him before he could jump out of his seat. "Just remember, I won't hold back next time, so make sure you study hard."

"Yes, Professor Lynn!" Dane said, beaming, "Thank you very much!" As he rushed out of the room, he paused and turned back around. "Um, I had a question."

"Go ahead, ask away."

"Who is Xenar?"

"Xenar, the All-Healer? He's the God of health and well-being. Why do you ask?"

"No reason. I heard his name once and I was just curious," Dane said. Suddenly he was wondering why his father would be praying to Xenar instead of Laren, but he didn't think he'd be able to ask him about it. "I'll see you again in a few days, Professor!"

"Take care, Dane."

* * * * *

"What did you learn about at Lynn's today?" Jon asked Dane when they sat down for dinner later that night.

"Nothing that interesting," Dane said, poking at some boiled carrots on his plate. "It was just the Jintaren Incursion." He popped the vegetable in his mouth and mumbled, "Stupid history lessons."

Jon stiffened in his seat, but Dane was too preoccupied with his meal to notice. There was a brief but tense silence before he said, "And what did you learn about?"

"It was some stupid war that happened a year before I was born," Dane explained. "I know you know this already, dad."

"I want to know if you know it though," Jon replied quietly, the corners of his mouth tightening a little in agitation. "I need to make sure my money isn't going to waste."

"It was the first major conflict on Rogarian soil since the Last Empire ruled the continent that began when a mining town called Stratin was invaded in the Tarqaron Valley."

"And who was responsible?" Jon asked.

Dane picked up on the tense tone that his father spoke in. Had he done something to anger the man? He swallowed the lump in his throat and continued before Jon grew impatient.

"The Jintaren clans from the north. They were retaliating against Rogust for spreading into their lands but they were stopped in Ingrad just outside the valley. Professor Lynn says the war ended when the military collapsed a portion of the mountain above Tarqaron Valley. I don't really believe her though. Those mountains are big, and you only hear about stuff like that in stories about wizards."

Jon was quiet as he drank from his cup. "Sometimes truth is stranger than fiction..." he said solemnly.

Dane wondered what he meant, but Jon seemed unwilling to elaborate. A haunted look came over his eyes, and it was then that Dane wondered how much his father had seen of the war.

I thought he grew up in Wersgrauff, Dane thought. *Ingrad is too far away for the war to have spread this far south.*

Unable to piece together why Jon was so unsettled by the mention of the Incursion, Dane quickly finished his dinner and cleaned up the table. He hoped that his father would be in higher spirits tomorrow when they went hunting, in the hopes that he wouldn't take out his aggravation on him.

Chapter 4 - Aspirations

2nd Day of Manul
124 I.E.

It was a quiet day in the orcs' camp. Even despite the grunts of laborers working and warriors sparring, it was almost peaceful. Too peaceful for Xellik's liking. The orcs were the children of Strength and War. They were meant to be beings of action, not passivity.

"Feeling restless, Xellik?" Fellis asked when she saw her son fidgeting with the fabric of his tunic.

"When are we going to have our home back?" He admitted to her. There was no point in trying to lie about anything when he was speaking with his mother. She always discovered the truth one way or another.

Fellis placed a hand on his head and ruffled his ebony hair. "In due time. You'll see tomorrow."

"What's tomorrow?" he asked as he batted her hand away.

"Xellik," Fellis said in a cautioning tone, "You remember what I told you about asking too many questions?"

The orcling let out a sigh and replied, "I know. Leaders don't nag."

"That's right. If you're bored, then go play with the others. I heard they had plans to go to the Dragon's Tears today."

Xellik shrugged, "Sure." He left their tent and looked outside for his friends. He spotted a few others his age sitting around a bonfire pit in the center of the village.

There was a portly orcling named Napir, who despite his size had proven to be a competent fighter even with the little experience he had. His cleft chin jutted out from his face, giving his round head the misshapen appearance of an eggplant.

The second, lankier orcling was Aiph, who'd turned out to be one of the smartest of their little group. When he grinned at them, he showed off several rows of sharp fang-like teeth, the appearance of which unsettled Xellik. Most orcs didn't have teeth that sharp, but Aiph had always said it was a quirk his entire family had. He was more headstrong than the others, which meant he often butted heads with Xellik.

The final individual was a quiet but observant orcling named Cinra. He always seemed to be watching or listening for something, his eyes constantly darting one way or the other, as if out of some paranoid notion that something bad should befall him if he didn't keep an eye out for trouble. They greeted Xellik as he approached, and beckoned him over.

"Afternoon," Xellik nodded back in response. "You going to the watering hole today?"

Cinra looked sullenly at his feet before taking up his ever vigilant watch. Napir shrugged and pointed to the quiet orcling. "Cinra says he heard something that would make us not want to go."

"What's that?"

Cinra looked at him momentarily, "Sorda and some of the other females are going today. She said we weren't allowed to tag along."

"That's nonsense!" Xellik barked. "Who cares what she says?"

The other three orclings looked at each other in confusion. Aiph was the one to answer him. "Well, you know we'd never go against what a female says. They become the leaders, we're just the soldiers and laborers."

"So, why should we care?" Xellik asked. He pointed to Cinra. "Urzule is your mother, and she's our clan's chief scout. . ." He then pointed to Aiph, ". . .And Ragash is your uncle right? And

I'm the son of the High Priestess. We should be allowed to go wherever we want with families like that!" He puffed his chest out slightly and stared down the length of his stubby nose at them. "Did you want to go?"

"Of course!" Napir shot back. "It's too hot here in camp. But we don't want to go up against Sorda and her friends. I don't want to get in trouble."

"We won't get in trouble. What will they do to us anyways? We're practically immune if Sorda tries anything!"

"I'm still not sure about this," Napir said and looked uneasily for support from Aiph and Cinra. Neither orc seemed willing to back him up, though.

Something clicked in Xellik's head, and he had an idea for what he was going to do. "Let me take care of everything."

"Isn't Napir better in a fist-fight than you?" Aiph asked, "I mean, have you ever beaten him in a fair fight? What makes you think you'd be better off fighting Sorda if even he thinks we can't stand up to her?"

"Trust me on this one," Xellik said, "If you orcs still want to go then let's get moving. I'll teach Sorda a thing or two about messing with us."

The orclings looked at each other again, not sure what to do. In the end, they decided to get up from where they sat and followed Xellik towards the Dragon's Tears. The walk was relatively quiet, except for the chatter coming from behind him.

"What do you think Sorda will do if she sees us?" Napir asked. "She'll probably beat us to a pulp and rub sand in our wounds."

"I bet all she'll do is pound Xellik into submission before he can even do anything," Aiph replied.

"If he can do anything," Cinra said quietly.

"Right. She'll probably just toy with him before she breaks one of his arms or something. It's not like Xellik would actually win in a fight against her."

Xellik scoffed, but otherwise kept his thoughts to himself. *They doubt that I can do anything? I'll show them what I'm capable of.*

As the four orclings emerged from the brush, they saw the pond already occupied by several females. On the eastern edge of the pond was a rocky formation that the orclings had said looked like the head of a dragon, and water spilled out from where it's eyes were. A couple orcs were climbing among the rocks to jump down into the pond below, and one of them was Sorda. The sounds of splashing water and laughter echoed out into the surrounding wilderness.

Cinra kept an eye out for trouble as he always did, and quickly took a perch up in a tree to watch events unfold. Xellik nodded to him. If there was going to be trouble, Cinra would be there to back them up. Napir and Aiph took the rear behind him, but they were both silent, waiting for Xelik to act first.

Everything fell silent when one of the females pointed out the orclings' presence on the beach. Sorda looked up towards them from the water and her smile vanished. She was a unique breed of orc, and was one of very few women to have grown white hair instead of black or brown as was more typical of their race. She was muscular for her age, more so than even the boys, and word around the village was that her early maturation was a sign of a great leader.

"What are you whelps doing here?" Sorda shouted at them.

"We came for a swim, what else?" Xellik replied.

"I told you to stay away from here," she said as she began to swim in towards the shore.

"Yeah, don't you know you're supposed to listen to Sorda?" shouted another orc named Pauti. "You should turn around now and go running home to Mommy, little orc. I'd hate to see what Sorda will do to you if you don't leave."

"I don't have to listen to you. I can go wherever I want and do whatever I want," Xellik boasted and crossed his arms. "I'm not going anywhere."

"You think just because you're Fellis' kid you can do whatever you Gods-damned please." Sorda marched onto the beach towards him. "This pond is mine, not yours! Now get out of here, or else!"

As she came closer to him, he shoved her away. "Kneel before me," he said, "I'm the future leader of our tribe and I --"

His sentence was cut short as everyone, including his friends, all started to laugh at his proclamation. With flushed cheeks, he took a few steps back and waited for the giggling to die down.

"Are you stupid, you inbred mongoloid?" Sorda asked. She gripped her sides as the last few laughs shook her body. "You know males can't lead."

"And why not?" Xellik asked, and none of them had any idea what to say in response. "The greatest leader in orcish history was a male. Grashal was his name, wasn't it?" Xellik pointed out.

"And look at what happened," Sorda said, "He died, and the orcs lost Muriaj to the Coalition, thus ending the Last Empire. Men are worthless as leaders, and Grashal is proof of that." She pointed at herself with a thumb. "We lead the tribes, and you fight for us. That's how it'll always be!"

"I will change that tradition, one way or the other." His boasting elicited further taunts from everyone present. He grew more frustrated, and growled through clenched teeth. "Enough of this!"

With a great wind up, Xellik punched Sorda's giggling face, silencing her as a stream of blood began to trickle from her nose. She growled at him as she pounced, leaping across the space that separated them and crashing atop Xellik.

Napir and Aiph quickly jumped in to pull Sorda off him while the girls swimming in the pond rushed to help their leader. As the two boys were busy separating her from Xellik, the orcling threw another series of punches into Sorda's face. He felt his knuckles crack and his skin broke against her teeth, but he didn't stop until he saw one of them fall out of her mouth.

"I'll kill you!" Sorda screamed and kicked out at Xellik, aiming for his crotch but missing him and catching him in the shin. He kicked her in the chin in retaliation. The blow caused her to fall back and land painfully in the sand.

As she lay there, she reached inside of her soaked tunic and produced a knife. It wasn't that large, nor did it look very sharp, but Xellik could tell that her strength alone would be enough to effectively use it. The other boys backed off a little, their eyes wide with fear.

"Hah, what are you going to go now?" Sorda said as she ran at Xellik.

Xellik began to chant the words to a spell as he leapt backwards to avoid her jabs and swipes. "Sytarel, Goddess of War, I ask you to bestow upon me a blade to cut through my enemies!"

A sword began to materialize in his hand and he managed to parry one of Sorda's swings just in time. He punched the girl in the stomach, throwing her off-balance. Xellik wasted little time in catching her with her guard down. He wasn't aiming to kill Sorda, despite how much he wanted to, but he did want to teach her a lesson and put her in her place. His swing fell short, just as he had intended it to, and cut a large gash along the length of her arm.

Blood spilled out onto the ground and Sorda gripped at her wounded arm as she dropped to her knees. Xellik pressed the tip of his sword beneath her chin. It would have been easy for him to end her life right then and there, and Sorda knew it. A fire burned within her eyes that showed him just how much rage bubbled beneath the surface of her skin.

"I see I've got you on your knees where you belong. Pity I can't do more about that defiant look in your eyes." Xellik took several tentative steps away from her. "Get out of my sight."

There was some hesitation, but eventually the girls began to gather their clothes before they returned back to camp. Xellik watched with no shortage of glee as Sorda fled with the others.

"Wow, Xellik," Napir began after he released the breath he'd been holding since the exchange began. "You're going to be in big trouble."

"No, I won't. I'm the High Priestess' son. Like I told Sorda, I can do whatever I want." The sword disappeared from his grip and he began to remove his clothing. "The lake is all ours."

"You know it's just a muddy pool of water, right?" Aiph asked as waded out into the water after Xellik.

"I don't care. It's mine now, and that's all that matters to me."

The four orclings wrestled in the waters for several hours before climbing out as the sun began to set beyond the tree line and the temperature began to drop. Xellik lay on the grass beyond the sandy shores of the pond, waiting for his skin to dry off before he got dressed. He shivered as the sharp autumn wind lashed at his naked body, sending chills all the way up his spine.

Aiph laid on the ground next to him, resting his head on his hands. "I still can't believe you did that to Sorda."

"Of course. I'm going to be the leader after all," Xellik said, and paused as he waited for laughter that never came. Either they believed him or feared him, but he didn't care which it was. After his coming of age ceremony in a few years, he would show the entire tribe that he had what it took to replace Fellis Fergoth one day.

"You're confident that's what will happen when Fellis passes away?" asked Napir. He sat cross legged with his hands in front of him, covering his pudgy body as best he could.

"I have to be. A leader can't show fear in the face of adversity, no matter what it is," Xellik replied, mimicking the words his mother had told him countless times before.

When they had dried off, the four of them slipped into their clothes and headed back for the camp. It was getting harder to see as the sun set, but as the light faded their eyes began to adjust to a colorless, low-light spectrum that helped them find their way back. Once they returned to camp, the group of orclings dispersed and went their separate ways.

On his way home he was caught off guard by Haij, his tutor in the art of swordsmanship. The orc wasn't the oldest or the most experienced, but he'd been the only one willing to teach Xellik anything about how to use a sword. He stood several feet taller than most of the Fergoth, and were it not for the fact Ragash was a better swordsman, Haij would've been in command of the clan's warriors. He wore fur-lined leggings, fashioned from the pelt of a wolf, which was regarded by him and his father Bytej as being their family's spirit guide.

Since Haij was without a tunic, Xellik could see clearly the bare skin along which he had cut himself once for every enemy he'd slain on the field of battle. Such a practice had been ancient, before the time of the Fergoth clan. Haij was the only orc in the entire tribe that Xellik had seen practice such a tradition.

"We need to talk, orcling," Haij said gruffly.

"Why, is Ragash all out of swords to polish?" Xellik said cheekily as he tried to muscle his way past Haij.

The older orc easily grabbed him by the shoulder and threw Xellik down on the ground. The orcling landed on his backside and felt a sharp pain flare up his spine.

"Ow, what was that for!"

"You know exactly what," Haij said coldly. He rested his hand on the pommel of his sword, not unlike how Ragash often did when he was itching to draw it.

"Sorda?" Xellik asked.

48

"Yes, it's about what you did to Sorda." He reached down and grabbed Xellik by the collar of his tunic, pulling him off his feet. "I don't care about any of your reasons for why you did it so don't bother wasting my time trying to justify your actions."

Xellik tried to worm his way out of his tunic to get away from Haij's grasp, but the older orc was unrelenting.

"Know this, Xellik," Haij said as he exhaled, assailing the younger orc's nostrils with the stench of rancid breath, "Should you ever use the skills I am training you in against a female orc again, I will kill you myself and damn the consequences. You should know better than to cross them, and I will not be held accountable for your childish actions. Do you understand me?"

Xellik glared at Haij, but he knew that the experienced warrior would not let him go until he agreed to his terms. "Ragash put you up to this?"

"No. Bytej told me to deal with you."

"Why does he care?"

"Xellik!" Haij snapped, shaking the orc violently. "Don't change the subject!" The linen fabric of Xellik's tunic tore and he fell back to the ground, this time catching himself with his arms.

With a grunt of consternation, Xellik said, "Fine, I won't use your tutoring like that again."

"See that you don't, whelp." Haij left him, returning to the home he shared with his father.

The orcling winced as a sharp pain shot up his body as he landed on his tailbone. *Damn that shaman. What does Bytej care what I do anyways? He was talking about having me sacrificed yesterday anyways!*

When Xellik returned to his tent, he found his mother standing inside waiting for him. Her arms were crossed and she was tapping her foot, a sign that Xellik was about to be in trouble. Instead of cowering, he decided to pretend that he had no idea what was going on, plastering a big grin on his face.

"Is there a problem, mother?"

"You were using magic without my permission again," she said, cutting right to the chase, "And what's this I hear about you getting into a fight with Sorda?"

"I think you have it backwards. She got into a fight with me."

"You know better than to raise a hand against a female orc from your own tribe."

"I'm hungry," Xellik stated, not looking to have the same conversation with his mother that he'd had with Haij only moments before. "Is that roast boar I smell?"

"Xellik. . . " Fellis shook her head and loosed a groan of frustration.

"I don't see what the problem is, I didn't do anything wrong!" Xellik said. He began to explain everything that had happened, right from the beginning when Cinra had told him that Sorda had warned the males to stay away from the Dragon's Tears, right until the end when he'd drawn her blood with his sword. "She started the fight with me, and I'm the future High Priest! I had to put her in her place."

"What makes you think you'll be the next leader?" Fellis asked, cocking a brow.

Xellik's heart skipped a beat. *She's not going to turn leadership of the clan over to someone else is she?* He tried to hide the worried expression on his face by attempting to act confident. "Because I'm your heir, and I have the strength and will to do it."

"Neither strength alone nor will alone is enough to become an effective leader," Fellis said, "There's never been a male High Priest in the Fergoth tribe, and probably not a single one in orcish history since Warlord Grashal."

"I don't care. I'll do it because that's what I'm destined to do," Xellik told her, then stuck a finger at her accusingly. "I know I should've been sacrificed so you could have a daughter, but you kept me. If my purpose is not to be the next leader, then. . ." he conjured a sword and, gingerly holding the bladed end, he offered the grip of the weapon to his mother. ". . .cut me down now and have the female heir you should've had."

There was a tense silence that hung between them. Xellik remained kneeling while he waited for her to take the sword, but his mother continued to stand there with her arms crossed.

She smiled and batted the weapon out of his hand. The blade sliced open the back of his hand as it spiraled away and disappeared into thin air.

"It's that conviction and determination that I knew you'd have when you were born. I know you'll make a great leader one day, Xellik. Tradition be damned."

"I'm not afraid of anything I must do."

"Good. That's all I need to hear from you. Now I have to go inform Sorda's mother that the matter of your little spat has been handled."

Xellik didn't stand up until after his mother left the tent. He smiled to himself, and reaffirmed his determination. Now that he had Fellis' backing, there was nothing that would stop him from being able to ascend to his rightful place as ruler of the Fergoth clan.

Chapter 5 - A Father's Anger

3rd Day of Manul
124 I.E.

"About time you woke up," Jon said to Dane when he noticed the boy stirring in his bed. He busied himself with filling a pack for the day's hunt, then gestured to a plate of bread and cheese on the table. "We're leaving as soon as you're done eating."

Dane rubbed the sleep out of his eyes and swung his legs out of the bed. He mumbled something about not wanting to go hunting before he sat himself down in front of his plate. After he shoveled his food down, he tossed his dish into the wash basin as he moved over to the door. Hanging on the wall was the bow and a quiver that had been restocked with the arrows that Jon made the previous day. He swung the quiver onto his shoulders and clutched the bow in his hands.

"Let's go." Jon grabbed a sturdy, smooth metal quarterstaff that was leaning against the wall and hiked down the steps.

After leaving the house, the pair walked down towards the main roadway, then cut across it to head into the forest underbrush. Dane snatched an arrow from the quiver and placed it against the bowstring as he walked. He needed to be able to act without any hesitation if they spotted something. There was little room for error when he went hunting with Jon. The older man's patience was as thin as a razor's edge, and any delays could easily cost them the many meals that they needed to make it through the winter months.

After an hour of searching with no luck, Dane spotted some tracks in the ground. He knelt down to take a closer look. "Looks like something's headed north-west. Deer?" Dane asked, and pointed the tracks out to his father.

Jon knelt down and ran a hand over the prints. "They're deer tracks, but they aren't fresh enough. They look to be about several days old. Pay closer attention. The edge of the tracks are worn down by the wind."

Dane sighed and continued walking in silence. He was having a hard time paying attention to such details with Jon breathing down his neck.

They saw few signs of wildlife for the next several hours, and stopped only when they started to get hungry enough to eat the rough pieces of dried, salted venison they'd brought with them. It wasn't Dane's food of choice, but there was little else they could do on a day long hike through the woods.

As mid-day began to approach, the sun crawled further up into the sky and its light soaked the forest between the naked branches of the trees. Dane wiped some sweat off his forehead with the back of his hand. He wasn't looking forward to when or if they would manage to bag a kill. They'd have to work to lug the carcass back to their home, which was only getting more distant with time.

He perked up when he heard the trickle of a stream nearby and headed due west towards the sound. Not only was he thirsty, but his instinct told him that if there was water nearby, then there would be animals around, too. His hunch paid off when he spotted a small deer standing next to the stream as it took a drink. Its sleek, light brown fur shimmered in the sunlight that found its way down through the trees. The two hunters stayed down wind of the animal and ensured they were as quiet as possible.

Dane lifted the bow and took aim. He drew the arrow back with an ease granted to him after years of practice, then exhaled as he let the arrow fly.

He missed his mark and the arrow fell short as it struck the ground between him and the deer. The animal let out a startled cry upon hearing the noise and began to run.

"You missed!" Jon yelled. "How did you miss a stationary target?"

"Sorry! Sorry!"

Dane scrambled to get another arrow ready. He fumbled and almost dropped it, which elicited a groan from his father. He recovered quickly, readied the arrow, and loosed it. The deer bounded around a tree and dodged the second arrow before disappearing further into the woods.

"Fantastic job as always," Jon said.

It's going to be all downhill from here. Dane sulked as he retrieved the arrows and checked to make sure they weren't damaged. He tossed them back in the quiver and began walking again.

Jon took the lead now, and Dane fell in line behind him. He didn't have the finely honed precision that his father had when it came to using a bow, and the way the man criticized his every move only made him that much worse.

Why does he always have to be so hard on me? Dane thought as he picked his way carefully over a thick bush. *Can't he ever say something like 'Hey, it was a good try, we'll get the next one'? I'm still young. Can't I be allowed to make mistakes?*

After a time, Jon held up his hand, signaling Dane to stop. Through the bushes, he could see a wild boar sniffing along the ground in search of food. Dane took aim and tried to get a good shot but he was blinded by a beam of sunlight. He didn't want to move and risk creating noise that would undoubtedly frighten the animal, so he took the shot anyways. He launched the arrow at the boar and managed to strike it in the thigh.

The boar squealed and kicked its legs before it came charging at the two hunters. Dane fell backwards out of the way and avoided the enraged beast. Jon was nearly gored by the boar's tusks before it ran off. The man tried to strike it with his quarterstaff but it whiffed as he missed completely.

"What is wrong with you today?" Jon snapped, furiously tossing the staff aside. Spittle landed on Dane's face as his father towered over him. "How did you screw that up?"

"I didn't mean to!" Dane wailed. "The sun was in my eyes."

"I'm sick and tired of you always having an excuse for everything!" Jon grabbed his son by the tunic and hoisted him up to eye level. The glare he cast at him bore into his eye sockets like hot iron pokers. Dane quivered in his grasp and his legs kicked out in a futile struggle to get free. "Pathetic." Jon tossed the boy aside.

Dane hit the ground hard and landed awkwardly on his elbow as he slid across the ground. It felt like a knife was being jammed up his forearm. The pain he experienced from his injuries hurt only slightly more than the pain of being thrown by his own father.

"No dinner for you tonight. You need to learn that your mistakes have consequences."

"But that's not fair!" Dane whined as he lay on the ground. He winced as he stood, cupping his elbow to keep it steady.

"I'll tell you what's not fair: Not getting that boar because of you! Explain how that's fair to me?" Jon's voice continued to rise until he was yelling. "Hmm? Can you? How is it fair to me that I get to starve all winter because of your failure?"

"If you're so good then maybe you should've taken the shot!" Dane yelled back. "Why blame me every time I make a mistake when we both know you could have just as easily taken the bow? Don't lump all your expectations on me!"

"You're not going to get better if I have to do all the work for you. Don't pin this on me, this one's all your fault."

Dane gritted his teeth as his frustration began to build. "You always blame me for everything!"

"That's because you can't do anything right!" Jon shot back.

"I can so! You just treat me like I'm shit stuck to your boot and you never give me a Gods-damned chance to prove myself!" Dane paused and felt his heart rate quicken. He hadn't even realized he'd just yelled back at his father until after the words spilled out of his mouth. Even Jon looked startled and lost some of his bluster. His father's hesitancy to respond only served to spur him on and overcome his own shock. "Maybe if you didn't pile everything on me like I'm your personal slave, things wouldn't go wrong all the time."

Jon recovered from his surprise and his face turned red. He scowled and lashed out at Dane in an attempt to grab the boy again, but he was out-matched by the youth's agility.

"Maybe if mom was still alive you wouldn't treat me like this!" Dane shouted. He regretted saying those words as they escaped his lips. Jon redoubled his efforts and managed to grab Dane by the shoulder. His father's fingers dug into him as he was squeezed tight. A fist slammed into his lower jaw, and he cried out as he stumbled to the side with the force of the blow.

"How dare you mention her!" Jon snarled. He punched Dane again, knocking the boy to the ground, then kicked him in the side before he could recover. "She died because of you, and I won't let you speak as if you actually knew anything about her! You're nothing but a miserable accident that cost my Celia her life! If I had to choose between having a child and having my wife with me again, I would choose her over you without a second thought!"

Dane coughed and wheezed. Tears lined his eyes and blurred his vision. The wind had been knocked out of him, and he could taste blood in his mouth. "T-that's not my fault!" he said, his voice wracked by sobs.

"Nothing ever is, is it?" Jon's fists were still clenched at his sides.

"Poor Dane, always the victim, right?"

Dane stood up on weary legs and breathed heavily. His eyes burned and he felt his face grow hot. "I'll show you who's the victim!" He charged at Jon and tried to strike him, but he found that his fists alone weren't strong enough to overcome his father's bulk. Jon responded by punching him in the stomach, and Dane dropped to the ground in a coughing fit as he tried to catch his breath.

"Consider yourself lucky I don't send you off to Wersgrauff. I'm sure your grandfather would love to have another child to smack around," Jon said with an unnerving calmness in his voice. "If you think I'm bad, just be glad you haven't met him."

Dane hacked and wheezed as his lungs struggled to get a full breath. He slammed a fist into the ground out of frustration. He pushed himself up and clutched at his side with his good arm while staring down at his father. He wanted the power to strike Jon down, and to beat the man until he begged for forgiveness, but there was simply no way Dane could match his father, let alone overpower him. He could feel his frustration building up as he thought about his next move. In the end though, he just let out a wordless scream and threw his arm up in the air in defeat before he walked away. He was angry, in pain, and worst of all, helpless.

"Where do you think you're going?" Jon asked.

"Why do you care?"

Jon stood and watched as his son removed the quiver from his back and tossed it aside with the bow. The arrows clattered to the ground and spilled out across the forest floor. Jon remained there long after Dane had left his view before he uttered a curse and picked up their belongings to begin the long trek home.

* * * * *

After a few hours of walking, Dane popped out from the underbrush somewhere along the main road. He brushed off the nettle that clung to his leggings and was careful to make sure they didn't prick his hand as he touched them. He looked up at the sky, got his bearings, then headed south along the path. He kept cradling his injured arm, holding it up with his good hand and ensuring it remained still. Movement only caused pain to shoot up his body.

Dane didn't turn down the tiny path that went to the cabin. He scowled and hurried on towards Tran. Every snap of a twig and every rustle he heard put him on edge and spurred him onwards. He expected his father to burst from the trees at any moment and pounce him like one of the jungle cats he'd read about.

"Stupid old man," Dane said to no one, then quickly shut up, worried his father would be within hearing range.

Before long, he found himself outside Tran. The town was winding down from the final day of the festival, and all that remained were a few scattered groups of people going about their daily business. The forges were still lit and the smell of sulfur filled Dane's head. He could taste the metal in the air as he descended the hill and got closer to the village.

Some of the minotaur were already heading out on wagons down the Valarian Tradeway to return to Snowhoof territory. Others stayed behind to wait for morning before they began their journey home. The sun was already setting and it would be dark in a couple more hours.

Dane wandered around Tran for a time, unsure of what to do next. He kicked at the dirt on the ground, and clouds of dust plumed around his feet. His arm throbbed and itched, and even as he held it in place it began to hurt. Dane walked over to the fountain in the center of town and scooped up a small handful of water with his good hand. It was cold, and it stung as it rolled over his scraped flesh. The waters in the fountain began to turn red as he washed his wound.

"I didn't know you and your father were in town today." The voice came from behind Dane, and he let out a small yelp, jumping from where he sat. "Oh, I'm sorry. I didn't mean to startle you."

Dane turned and smiled. "It's okay. I wasn't paying attention." His voice shook and his smile was wavering. "It's good to see you again, Professor Lynn".

She looked him over and gasped. "Oh my, your arm! What happened?" She turned Dane's arm over to get a better look at it. Dane groaned as she twisted his arm around.

"Nothing," Dane lied and winced. He wasn't sure why he lied, but he couldn't bring himself to say something bad about his father even after what he did. "I tripped on a rock in the forest on my way here. I guess I was running too fast and not paying attention to where I was going." He couldn't maintain eye-contact and instead looked down at his arm.

"I see. It doesn't look too bad, but I'm not an expert on these sorts of things. Where's your father?" Lynn asked, looking around to try and spoke him.

Dane bit his lip. "He's not here. I'm, uh, I'm running an errand for him. He's back at home."

She raised an eyebrow, and Dane was worried that she would end up calling his bluff. When she didn't, he breathed a sigh of relief. "Well, here, I can at least help you with the pain in your arm."

"How?"

"I did a bit of studying on druidic magic once to help with my plant studies, and had the assistance of an elf for a time when he was passing through the village. It's been awhile since I've practiced it though, so this might not work very well." Lynn lightly cupped Dane's arm and ran a hand over the top of it. Her eyes closed, and

Dane watched as he hands glowed with a faint golden-green aura. He could feel the pain subside, and when Lynn was done, he moved his arm. It still hurt, but not nearly as much as it had before.

"Wow, amazing!" was all Dane could manage to say as he inspected his arm. The skin on his elbow was repaired, and all traces of the wound were gone.

Lynn smiled and brushed a few stray strands of hair out of her eyes. "It's been awhile since I've done that, so it took a bit out of me. I'm glad I could help."

"Thank you, I really appreciate it."

"Dane, I've never shown my magic to you before. You're not surprised?"

The boy's face flushed red with embarrassment. "I don't know what you mean. I just figured that since you were really smart you would know magic."

"You're a terrible liar. I know you were snooping through my library."

Dane's chin touched his chest. "How did you know?"

"The way you blushed gave it away," she replied with a wry smile.

"I'm sorry, Professor."

"Next time just ask me when you're curious about something, okay?"

"Okay. Sorry." Dane looked up at her. "Does father know you can do magic?"

Lynn chuckled at his question. "Of course he does, Dane. Everyone in the village does. Any scholar worth their weight in gold is a capable sorcerer."

"Would you show me more of your magic some time?" Dane asked.

"Well, only if your father approves of it," she told him honestly.

"It's getting late and I still have some business to attend to before the market closes for the night, so I have to take my leave. Oh, and if you could remind your father that if he still wants a book regarding Xenarian religion he needs to let me know so I can make a copy for him."

"Yeah, I'll let him know," Dane replied and gave her a weak smile. "Thank you again."

Lynn excused herself and left Dane on his own. He needed to figure out what to do for the night. He had no intention of going back home where his father was, but he didn't have enough money or knowledge to be able to survive on his own for very long, either.

I won't go crawling back. Not after everything he did to me. Not until he comes here and apologizes for being a thick-skulled ogre!

A chill autumn wind blew across the bazaar and Dane shivered. The temperature was beginning to drop steadily as the sun set. He rubbed his hands over his exposed, goose-bump covered forearms and looked around to find someplace warm. His eyes settled on the inn.

Through the windows he could see that the hearth was already lit, and though the inn was full of patrons, they were mostly centered around the bar. Dane headed inside and strode over to a table nearest to the fire. He ignored the curious glances several people cast his way, and basked in the warmth offered by the fireplace.

"It's a bit dangerous for a child such as yourself to be walking around all alone, isn't it?" Ted asked as he approached. "You know the forest isn't a place to be alone in at night."

Dane shrugged in response. He didn't say anything and continued to watch the fire.

"Is your father in town?"

"Nope," Dane replied, still not turning to look at Ted.

"Hmm, well if you need anything, don't be afraid to ask." Ted left the boy alone and returned to the bar.

A few moments passed before Dane was approached by Lily, the innkeeper's wife. She was a fair skinned woman with a protruding belly that suggested she was well along in her pregnancy. "Can I get you anything to eat, hun?"

"Maybe. I dunno if I'm really that hungry, ma'am," he mumbled.

"Well, let me get you something and we'll see how you feel when I get back, okay?"

"Yeah, okay." Dane slumped down onto the table and rested his head on his arms. He continued to stare at the dancing flames.

* * * * *

Jon stoked the fire in the stove, turning a log over. It roared back to life, crackling as it consumed the wood. A dinner sat on the table that had been prepared not long after he returned, but he hadn't touched it yet. Zoey had come out from the cellar and was standing on a chair on her hind-paws, eyeing the cold meal. Outside, the sky was orange from the setting sun and the air was cooling fast.

"Stupid child," Jon whispered. He reached over to grab another log and added it to the fire.

A knock at the door interrupted Jon from his thoughts. He strode across the room and opened it, expecting to see his son. He was surprised when he found Ted standing there instead.

"Hello, Ted. What brings you all the way out here?" Jon asked. He stood in the doorway and leaned against the frame with his arms crossed.

"Just came by to see if you knew your son was in town all on his own."

Jon frowned. "You made the walk all by yourself just to tell me that? My boy isn't causing trouble, is he?"

Ted shook his head. "No," he replied, "The boy just strolled into my inn a short while ago. I came by to let you know where he was, that's all. Did something happen?"

"No. Boy's just run off, that's all. At least he's somewhere safe. Care to come in for a drink? It's the least I can do for all the trouble my boy is causing you." Jon stepped aside and allowed Ted in. Zoey scampered away from the table as the men approached. The cat hid beneath one of the beds and eyed them warily, her eyes glowing green in the firelight. Jon began to prepare a kettle of tea as Ted sat down.

"He's not causing trouble or making a fuss. He's just sitting by the fireplace. I got Lily to watch him," Ted explained.

"How is Lily doing anyways? I didn't have time to see her when we were in town the other day." Jon said.

Ted removed his cloak and hung it over the back of his chair. "You're changing the subject. I've known you for far too many years, and lived with you for a good number of them, to know when something is wrong."

Jon sighed. "Yeah, I know." He walked over and sat across from Ted. "Let me tell you about it while the tea brews."

* * * * *

From the confines of the forest, Ragash looked down the hill at the human village below. The oil lamps in the street were being lit for the evening as the sun set. The orc eyed the hastily-constructed watch towers, hopeful that the humans there didn't notice him.

"We'll be lucky if the humans don't see us up here," Ragash snarled in a low voice as he glanced in Urzule's direction. "I thought you said they weren't well fortified, yet I see men in military uniforms and archers manning the towers."

Urzule lay in the grass next to him. A wolf scalp covered her head while the rest of the pelt covered her body. from a distance, even a trained eye would mistake her for an animal. "This is the least fortified village in the region. Do you question my ability to scout?"

Ragash snorted, but otherwise said nothing else. With the military present, they were going to suffer more casualties than expected. This was what Fellis had wanted them to do though, and he wouldn't dare question the High Priestess' orders.

The orc pulled a pendant of smoothed stone from beneath his armor. The rock was carved into the likeness of a sword. He kissed the cold surface of the icon and muttered, "May the Goddess' hand guide our blades."

The sentiment was shared by those around him, as each warrior said their own prayers to Sytarel.

"Alright you lot, you know the plan," Ragash said once night fell over the town. "Secure the area. Kill anyone in your way, but spare the children. Urzule's scouts will deal with them. Are we clear on that? Cover Urzule's retreat and secure any provisions that you find."

After hearing the orcs' affirmations, Ragash nodded to Urzule. The female lifted a hand and a score of her archers rose with loaded crossbows. She spoke an incantation in a strange tongue and the tips of their bolts ignited in flames.

"Aim for the watch towers," she said, aiming down the length of an arrow. "Loose!"

Behind the hail of flaming arrows, Ragash's warriors were close behind as they spilled down the side of the hill like a red waterfall.

* * * * *

Lily set down a small plate in front of Dane. There were a few slices of bread and cheese, coupled with an apple that looked like it had just been polished as its skin shone in the flickering light. Next, she set down a mug full of water, drawn freshly from a rain barrel Ted kept. The boy didn't look up when he was approached.

"Here you go." She slid the plate closer to him, and he finally acknowledged her with a nod of his head.

"You didn't have to make me any food."

"It's alright, I didn't mind. Go ahead and eat up," Lily replied with a smile.

Dane picked up a piece of bread and took a sizable bite out of it, watching her as he chewed. He could tell she was nearing the final weeks of her pregnancy. He gulped down some water then said, "You're going to be a mother soon, right?"

"Yes. As early as three weeks. My husband and I are very excited about it."

"Whoever your child will be, at least he's wanted. I wish my father was happy about having a kid. I wonder if he was ever happy with me," Dane whispered. Tears welled up in his eyes. He found it odd that he could feel sad about not being loved by his father, despite how angry he felt towards him. "He doesn't care about me." He wiped his eyes clear with his arm before the tears could roll down his face.

"Now, you know that's not true." Lily placed a hand on his shoulder. The contact felt strange coming from someone he barely knew, but at the same time, it was comforting. He wondered if his own mother would have been the same way if she'd survived his birth. "I don't know your father as well as you do, and I certainly don't know him as well as my husband knows him, but a man who feeds you and clothes you and pays to have you educated clearly cares about you."

Dane scoffed at the idea. "If he cared, he wouldn't push me so hard."

"Maybe it's just because he wants to see you succeed in life? To give you a chance at something he never had?"

"Maybe," he said, then muttered, "but that doesn't excuse what he did."

"What do you mean?" Lily asked, giving him a strange look.

"N-nothing!" Dane stammered. He quickly finished off the rest of his food and water. "Thank you for the meal, ma'am."

"You're welcome. You can sit there as long as you need." She patted him on the shoulder and stood up, taking the dirty dishes away with her.

Shortly after she left, the sounds of screams echoed from outside. A bell began to ring wildly before it fell silent, and an orange glow spilled in through the windows. The tavern patrons rose, chairs screeching across the wooden floor, as they moved to see what was going on outside.

Dane's heart pounded in his chest. That bell meant the town was being attacked. But who could be attacking Tran? He knew that he had to run and find a place to hide, but his body was frozen in place. He eyed the door as something crashed into it, sending splintered wood across the room. The remaining patrons leaped to their feet and reached for weapons hidden in their clothing as a towering, red-skinned humanoid stepped into the room.

The being's head was shaved clean, and a white tattoo that resembled a set of fangs dripping with blood was painted on his scalp. He carried a large sword with a blade nearly as long as his body was tall. Corded muscles flexed and rippled as he lifted the weapon and struck down the nearest person. Blood splattered across the being's face, and he grinned a sinister yellow grin before shouting something in another language.

"Orcs!" one man shouted. He was cut down before he could strike back with his knife. Another patron was kicked away before the sword was driven into his chest.

Dane stood up and looked out the window just long enough to see the streets in complete chaos. Orcs were dragging people out of their homes by their limbs and carrying children off out of view. He scrambled under the table and tried to crawl to the back room unnoticed. He breathed heavily, gulping down great breaths of air in his panic. He turned to look at the door and saw that the orc was gone. Momentarily relieved, he swung his head back around and caught a glimpse of a great leather-booted foot planted right in front of him.

"Well well, what've we got here?" the orc grabbed Dane's tunic with his free hand and lifted him up to eye level. A smirk spread across his face. "You look young enough. You're coming with me."

The orc's mouth was filled with yellowed teeth and several of them were missing. Dane was overcome by a putrid, noxious odor reminiscent of rotten meat when the monster holding him opened his mouth. The boy kicked out with his legs and hit his captor in the stomach several times in rapid succession, but all his flailing accomplished nothing.

"Let go of me! Please!" Dane shrieked. He twisted and turned inside his tunic.

The orc laughed. "It's futile kid. All you're doing is pissing me off!" He dropped his sword and it clattered to the ground with a loud clang before he lifted his hand up. He backhanded Dane across the face. The boy coughed and a trail of blood dripped from his mouth. The room spun, and he couldn't catch his breath as he lost consciousness and slipped into darkness.

Chapter 6 - The Attack

3rd Day of Manul
124 I.E.

Ted sat at the table with his hands clasped together as he listened to Jon's story. The glass in front of him had long ago been emptied and the shriveled tea bag sat at the bottom of the cup, reeking of stale herbs and dried leaves. When Jon finished speaking, Ted remained silent and thought about his next few words.

"I've known you to have a temper, Jon," Ted began.

"I know," Jon said, hanging his head.

"But to strike your own child --"

Jon interrupted him. "Yeah, I know." He rubbed his tired eyes with a thumb and forefinger and sighed. "I broke my promise to Celia. Didn't think I'd end up being the same kind of person as my own father."

"No one knows how we'll turn out when we get older." Ted wringed his fingers nervously. "I can only hope to give my child a more loving home than how my family treated me."

"I only wanted a better life for Dane than I had," Jon said, running a hand through his thinning hair. "I don't regret my choices but that's no life for a person to live. And now he's run off and probably won't listen to me anymore."

Ted surged to his feet, causing the chair to screech across the wooden floor. "Sitting here moping isn't going to change a thing, now will it? Be a man! Go over there and get your son. Stop being afraid to face him. You've fought jintaren and bandits and orcs and

Gods only know what else, but you can't go apologize to your kid? Do you think Celia approves of the way you're acting? You're just sniveling here in your cabin while your son is out there on his own!"

Jon stared and blinked at his friend. He would've snapped at anyone else for talking to him like that, but not Ted, not someone who had known Celia and traveled with him in the past. "When did you become the mature voice of reason?"

"I've had plenty of time to grow up since we were in the Blackguard," Ted said, staring down at him.

"Alright, I'll go get him," Jon huffed as he stood up. "I suppose I wouldn't have much of a choice at this point, huh? Wouldn't be much of a man if I left him there to rot, would I?"

"Nope." Ted crossed his arms and gazed at him, waiting for him to start moving.

Jon grabbed his leather coat off the rack near the door and put it on before stepping outside with Ted in tow. "Well then, let's go and I'll take him off your hands."

The pair walked back to Tran at a brisk pace, not wanting to dawdle. Jon managed to steer the conversation away from him and asked again about Ted's wife.

"She's doing fine, and we'll be having a kid any day now. I'm hoping that we end up having a boy," Ted replied, his face beaming with pride. "I want to be able to share stories with someone who might find them interesting, and perhaps teach them how to be a brewer like me, to continue the family craft."

"You mean the 'family craft' that only just started with you?" Jon said with a smile. He remembered years ago when he saw Ted with a book that introduced the basic concepts behind brewing ale."My stomach still turns just thinking about the stuff you brewed in the beginning."

Ted chuckled. "Traditions have to start somewhere though,

right? Besides I could help him avoid the mistakes I made when I started out."

"What will you do if you end up having a girl?" Jon asked. He realized that he'd never considered the question himself. How would things have turned out if Dane had been a girl instead of a boy? Would he have treated her the same way?

"I could just raise her as a boy and teach her the finer art of making a good drink. Though I guess if Lily does have a girl, I'd have to fend off would be suitors to keep her safe."

"Figured out any names yet?"

"Lily insisted on picking a girl's name and she let me pick a boy's name. She wants to go with Bella, and I want to name him Maxwell."

Once he got Ted talking, Jon was relieved to have gotten the focus off of him for a while and to discuss something more mundane. He had spent enough time thinking about his own problems today.

It wasn't long before they began to near the edge of the forest and the smell of sulfur began to fill their noses.

"Smells like a pretty big fire," Ted said in a calm voice, the look on his face showing indifference. It had been a dry season and forest fires weren't uncommon in the drier years. Jon had fallen behind though, and when Ted noticed, he stopped to regard his friend curiously. Jon's eyes swept from side to side. "Is something wrong?"

Jon didn't respond, and merely lifted a hand to silence the innkeeper. He closed his eyes and focused, listening to the sounds of the wilderness around them, getting a feel for the direction of the wind, and a sense of the intensity of the fire's odor. He'd done this routine many times in the past, when he hunted things other than just wildlife. He was happy to see that age had not dulled his senses yet. He trusted his instincts as he got a feel for the area around them, even though he could barely see a thing with the sun having set a short while ago. He stood there for several moments, thinking, focusing, before his eyes shot open.

"Gods, it's coming from the village!" Jon took off running, sprinting past Ted. The sudden declaration sent a chill down the man's spine. He spun around and bolted after Jon.

The forest was nothing more than a blur as the pair sprinted down the path. They crested the last hill and were greeted by a sight that stopped them cold in their tracks.

A great, black pillar of smoke rose up above the village as the buildings burned. Screams could be heard coming from the streets below. Bodies littered the gutters and roads, painting the cobble red with blood. Jon darted down the hill to investigate the situation with Ted close behind. The smoke was so acrid that Jon nearly choked as he walked through the streets, searching for the cause of such destruction and the source of the screams.

"This is impossible!" Ted yelled. "How could this happen? I left a couple hours ago and everything was fine!"

"Hello? Is anybody here?" Jon called out, ignoring his panicked friend.

He crept along the street and watched every nook and cranny for signs of life. Jon's long buried instincts were slowly resurfacing as he plunged deeper into the village. It was still too dangerous, and he knew that such feelings weren't caused by the fires raging around them. Years of experience had taught him to know better than that.

Some movement in the distance caught his eye as a bulky creature shambled along the end of the street. A large red figure moved towards the east, pulling something behind it. Jon ran ahead, and as he passed through some of the smoke the figure became clearer. An orc was dragging a small girl behind him, holding her by her arm. The girl struggled against the orc's grip, kicking and screaming and pounding on her captor's arm with her little fists. She shouted for him to let go. The orc grunted and lifted his free hand to strike the girl.

Jon clenched his fists and charged at the invader. He tackled the orc, knocking the beast down. The girl shrieked as she was pulled along for a short distance before the grip on her wrist was loosened and she could get free. Not wasting even a second, Jon began to pummel the other being's face with his fists before it could recover from the ambush. His hands stung from smashing into the orc's skull, and he could feel the male's tusks slice through his skin. He gripped the beast's head in his hands and began to slam it into the stone street until his skull cracked open. Blood and other fluids leaked out the back of the orc's head and he ceased to move beneath the hunter.

A battle cry echoed down the streets and Jon looked up to see another orc charging from behind Ted.

"Ted, behind you!"

Without missing a beat, Ted spun around while reaching into his cloak. He produced a knife and chucked it as hard as he could. The blade spun and hit the orc in the head, causing it to lose its stride and fall to the ground dead.

"Looks like you haven't lost your touch," Jon said as he joined his friend.

"Neither have you," Ted replied and grabbed his knife from the orc's corpse.

The girl Jon saved looked up and scrambled towards Ted to get away from the orc's body. She clutched at the man's cloak and pressed her face against his leg, soaking the cloth with her tears. Ted reached down and picked her up. She curled into his arms and continued to grip the cloak in her hands.

"Are you okay, little one?" Ted asked, and the girl nodded. "Do you know where everyone else is?" The girl hung her head, then shook it from side to side. "What's your name?"

"Francine," she replied meekly.

Jon knelt down to inspect the orc's body and turned the corpse's head to the side. His attention was drawn to a tattoo on the scalp that looked like a fanged maw.

"I've seen this tattoo before," Jon declared as he stood back up. "They're Fergoth clan orcs. Damn military didn't fortify Tran well enough for the Festival." He reached down to grab the orc's weapon, and slid the heavy sword into his belt.

"Everything all right?" Ted asked as he strolled over to Jon's side. Fran clutched harder at his clothes as he drew closer to the orc's corpse, and he stopped his advance.

Jon shrugged. "I'm just trying to think why these orcs attacked the village. I know Northpine was having problems with the Fergoth a couple months back but why would they attack Tran when we're so far south? And during the festival when the town is reinforced by the military."

"Does the why really matter right now?" Ted asked.

"Maybe, maybe not," Jon said, shrugging a second time. It felt natural falling back into his old habits. Even back in his mercenary days with the Blackguard guild, he'd always been a strong thinker, which stood in contrast to Ted's impulsiveness. Though the other man had matured and eased up in his old age, Jon was still as pensive as he'd always been.

Jon unsheathed the sword and inspected the blade's edge. It was not the best crafted weapon in the world, nor was it very well maintained. It was clearly of Rogarian make and looked several years old, which meant they must have stolen it from some soldiers at some point.

It would have to do. His own equipment was still locked up in the cellar and there wasn't time to spare to run back to the cabin to retrieve it. Jon turned to Ted. "Let's go check your inn. I hope that

Lily and Dane found someplace safe to hide."

Taking the lead, Jon was on full alert as he stalked through the burning town. Ted was close behind him as he carried the girl in his arms, though he kept one hand near his knife.

When they reached the inn, they found that the wooden door had been shattered. Large pieces of wood littered the floor. The tavern had been spared from the fire, but everything that wasn't tied down had been smashed and left in shambles. The bar was cleaned out and the hearth had been extinguished. Bodies covered the floor, but none of them were of people either man recognized. Ted noted that they were all customers that planned to stay the night before they left town.

Ted sat Francine down and began calling out to his wife. "Lily?"

Jon slipped around to the back room, his sword in front of him and at the ready. There was nothing there other than more overturned tables and scattered dishes. Jon waved Ted over. "It's clear. No one's alive in here." He paused when he heard a faint thump from beneath the floor. "Wait, do you hear that?" The faint sound of muffled voices echoed from somewhere close by, but he couldn't pinpoint their location. "Is the cellar door locked? Could anyone be in there?"

Ted knelt down and tugged on the handle of the door, but it just thumped as the bolt held it in place. "No good, it locks from the inside, so we'll have to-" The man stopped as he realized what he was about to say. He began to beat on the door, shouting his wife's name.

The lock clicked and Ted stepped back as the door swung open. Lily rushed up the steps and embraced her husband. A scant few survivors crawled up out of the cellar, many of them tavern patrons from earlier in the evening.

"Gods, Ted! It was horrible! I was so worried," Lily cried, tears staining her cheeks. "Oh thank Laren. I'm so glad you're okay."

She leaned on Ted as he wrapped his arms around her.

"Is Dane down there with you?" Jon asked.

"Jon, I'm sorry." Lily lowered her head and avoided his eyes. "I hid as soon as they broke the door down. They took him away somewhere. I'm so very sorry, Jon."

Jon turned his back to them and began to walk away. "I'm going to check the rest of the village for more survivors to help. Take the girl and hide down in the cellar. All of you. I'll come back and check on you once I'm done. I shouldn't be long."

"What about Dane?" Lily asked. "Aren't you worried about him?"

"I am, but if I don't find his corpse somewhere in town, then it's likely he's still alive somewhere. And I'll need clues to figure out what the orcs wanted him for if he isn't dead."

"How can you be certain he's even still alive?" Ted asked.

"Because, the orcs killed everyone else," Jon said flatly. "Would you kidnap a child just to kill it when you got home?"

"I suppose not. Will you be okay? That sword looks like it's seen better days," Ted asked, indicating the dull, nicked edges. "Let me come with you at least. I'll go grab my knives."

"No, stay here with your wife, where you're needed. If you come with me, who will be left to defend her and the others if the orcs come back? Just get down there. I'll be okay. I've been in worse scrapes, remember?"

Ted mulled over his friend's words. "Okay, but you better come back in one piece. We don't have a healer like we had in Ingrad, like with Celia."

"Yeah." Jon cut him off, his voice wavering as memories of his time living in Ingrad with his wife came flooding back to him.

Jon left the inn behind after ensuring the cellar door was secured. He crept along the streets towards the next intact building. His footfalls were more quiet than those of a cat's. He was slowly getting back into a rhythm as his muscle memory worked to help him remember everything he had trained for when he was younger. He pushed the splintered door open a crack, peeked in, and when he found no hostiles in his line of sight, he shoved the door open.

All he found were more bodies and the destroyed belongings of the deceased owners. He discovered some small children's toys lying amongst the wreckage.

I'm not liking the looks of this. Where's the children's bodies? Jon thought. As he worked to double check and make sure Tran was clear of orcs, he made sure to look out for any bodies of children. His heartbeat quickened as he discovered more and more heaps of corpses. They were all only the aged.

What do they want with children? Jon thought. *They'd be too weak for labour, and too small to be used as food. What is going on here? Celia, I'm sorry. I should have never driven Dane off.*

Jon continued his search, but his mind was elsewhere, constantly thinking about the fate of his son.

* * * * *

Where am I?

Dane could feel the cold ground beneath him and a throbbing pain on the top of his head. He wriggled his hands and feet as he woke from his slumber. After a time, he became aware of the sounds around him as he returned to the waking world. He could hear deep, gruff voices talking a short distance away. Closer to him was the sound of crying. Further off he could make out the faint crackle of a fire combined with the sounds of livestock from all around. Dane opened his eyes, but found that he could not focus.

What happened?

His eyes adjusted to the low light cast by a nearby fire. Dane groaned as he lifted his head, the throbbing sensation becoming more intense. He looked around and found himself surrounded by children he recognized from Tran. A great deal of them looked to be from outside of the village, and there was a small number of minotaur children huddled together in their own little gathering. The faces of the humans were white as chalk and their cheeks were stained with tears.

A figure moved off to the side, just out of Dane's field of vision. He turned and caught sight of a number of orcs milling about just beyond a small wooden fence. Patched, leather hide tents were erected in a circle with their flaps facing towards a large bonfire in the center. Orcs sat around the camp on polished stone benches that looked like they were carved from rocks gathered from the nearby mountain side. They partook of drinks from large kegs marked with a regal R that Dane recognized as the empire's seal.

Seeing the orcs filled Dane's mind with the memories of what had happened prior to losing consciousness. His features sunk as he took in his surroundings, realizing that he and the other children were being kept inside a large holding pen.

Two guards watched the pen's gate. They stepped aside as a female orc approached while carrying a large jug. She opened the gate and stepped inside, but before she could close it again one of the human children took off screaming and darted past her.

The orc woman shouted something in orcish and one of the guards drew his sword. In a single smooth motion, he sliced the girl's head clear off her shoulders. The head rolled away in the direction of the guard's swing, landing on a soft patch of grass near the pen's gates. Screams rose up from the remaining children, and Dane thought he heard someone shout above it, crying for their sister. The sound sent shivers down his spine and churned his stomach.

Dane had never known the girl, but he felt like screaming all the same. All he could do was stare dumbfounded as fear rooted him in place.

Gods, this isn't happening! Dane could feel his last meal threatening to come up his throat, and he struggled to suppress the urge to fall back down on the ground and throw up.

"Shut your mouths! All of you! Otherwise we'll just kill everyone right here and now," the female orc hollered in the Common tongue. "Let that be a lesson to all of you. Your lives are ours now, and if you wish to live even a moment longer, you'd best just keep quiet and don't try anything stupid." No one made a sound after that. The orc set the jug down in the center of the pen. "Drink," was all she said before she left the holding pen and began conversing with the guards in their language full of grunts and hoarse sounds. When they were done speaking, one of the guards picked up the body of the slain girl and carried it off as he followed the woman.

"Why did I leave home?" Dane said out loud, wishing he could wake up again and find himself in his own bed.

* * * * *

Jon rushed down the street with his sword in both hands. His sword sliced one orc open from the shoulder down to the waist as he met the invaders head on. He spun on his heels, narrowly avoiding an axe blade as he cut another orc's stomach open, her entrails spilling out onto the cobblestone road. She clutched at her wound with weak, feeble hands as she fell to her knees. A third orc screamed at him and raised a club above his head. He took a swing at Jon, missing as the more agile human doubled back. The second swing clipped his arm and threw him off balance. With a grunt of effort, Jon brought his sword to bear and barely managed to parry the third strike.

He was out-matched in straight up hand-to-hand combat against the orc, as he was smaller and weaker than his club-wielding opponent. Jon had been getting by on surprise attacks alone, and none of the orcs so far had been capable of recovering from his ambushes.

He strained to repel the orc's repeated attacks, and each swing of the club missed him by only fractions of an inch. Mustering all the strength that he could, Jon roared as he deflected the club before delivering a swift kick to the orc's stomach. The orc stumbled backwards a few steps and took a second to recover, but Jon didn't give it the chance as he brought his sword back around and thrust it into the orc's midsection.

"Give my regards to your maker, filth!" Jon twisted the blade, then pulled back and knocked the orc away. The body fell to the ground with a dull thud.

Panting, Jon surveyed his progress once he was certain his attackers were dead. He had made it to the other side of the village and the three orcs that now lay dead at his feet brought the total number of hostiles slain up to eight. He took a moment to examine the bodies as he had done with the others he'd encountered, searching for some clue to explain the situation or where they were headed or why they had remained in the village. However, he discovered nothing he didn't already know.

The adrenaline from the battle was beginning to wear off, and he could finally feel the pain in his arm from where the club had nicked him. A large gash cut across his forearm and was bleeding out slowly. Ripping off a strip of cloth from his tunic, Jon tied it around the wound as a makeshift bandage. He yanked the cloth tight with his teeth and knotted it. There would be time to properly tend to the injury later. Right now he had more pressing matters to take care of. Jon rushed back through Tran, glancing about to make sure he didn't miss any orcs on his first time through.

He returned to the inn and proceeded to the back room. He knocked a few times on the cellar door and called out to Ted. A moment later, the lock clicked open.

"Is it all clear? Is it safe?" Ted asked, leaving the others alone in the cellar as he clambered out.

Jon nodded. "Far as I can tell, it is. The fires are starting to die down too. There weren't very many survivors though. Most of those who are left were already holed up in their dwellings by the time I got there." He motioned for Ted to go back into the cellar. "They may be gone for now, but we don't know when or if they'll be back. Stay here for the time being."

"Why? Where are you going?"

"To Wersgrauff to summon the military," Jon said.

"You're going without a horse? And alone?" Ted asked, and Jon nodded. "But at that distance, it'll take you at least a day to make it, and that would be assuming you were well rested. In your condition it'll take even longer. At least stay the night and rest up!"

A new voice spoke up, cutting off Jon's response. "Yes, stay here and wait. We'll take care of things from here on out."

Jon turned to regard the new comer, a tall man wearing the blue and white colors of the empire. He wore a suit of full plate armor with a tabard draped over his chest. The regal R of the empire was embossed in white thread on the center of the cloth. Even though he wore wide pauldrons, Jon could tell the man naturally had a broad build. He had olive skin and a pointed nose, with a face framed by neatly trimmed black hair. The man carried his helm underneath his arm and he stood up straight with his chest puffed out.

"And you are?"

"Colonel Nicoli of the 32nd Armored Infantry Division. We came as soon as word reached us of the attack."

"How did you know about it so soon?" Jon asked, confused.

"A scholar living here teleported into our barracks, taking us by surprise, and alerted us of the attack." Nicoli shrugged. Jon figured it must have been Lynn, being that she was the only mage in the village. He was grateful to at least know she was safe.

"Are there any other survivors?"

Jon filled Nicoli in on the situation, about the locations of the other survivors, about the orcs found in the town, and about the fact there were no children among the bodies of the slain. Nicoli listened intently to the entire report before he excused himself to go issue his orders.

"I'm going ahead of them to find Dane," Jon declared after the Colonel had left. "The Fergoth no doubt left a trail behind. An attack of this size would be impossible to conceal."

Ted was about to talk his friend out of it, but the fiery look in the old hunter's eyes showed him that there would be no sense in trying to get him to wait in Tran. He sighed, and gave Jon his best before returning to the cellar where his wife waited.

Jon sprinted out of Tran and through the forest back to his cabin. The military paid him no heed as they took up the search and rescue efforts within the town. Regardless of what the military was going to do, Jon decided that he was going to get Dane back from the orcs, even if he had to do it alone. He was determined to find out what was going on and to keep his son's life out of the hands of both the military and the Fergoth.

I don't trust those bastards anymore than I would trust the orcs, Jon thought, ignoring the pain flaring up in his leg as he ran.

He only hoped that he would be able to get to Dane in time, before the orcs did whatever they were planning to do to their young captives.

Chapter 7 - The Hunt

4th Day of Manul
124 I.E.

Xellik yawned and stretched his arms as he woke up to the strong, smoky scent of fire. After a moment, he realized that the stench was coming off his tunic. He rubbed his eyes and strolled over to the tent's flap as he was scratching his head.

"I'm gonna go find Napir!" Xellik shouted to his mother, who was stooped over a stone covered in a number of materials the orcling couldn't recognize. Whatever it was she was working on, it made the tent smell of wax and iron.

Bytej stood next to her and spoke in hushed whispers. The only words Xellik could pick out were something about some orcs not coming back from the raid.

"Alright," his mother said, turning to look over her shoulders at him, "but make sure to stay away from the holding pens."

Xellik rolled his eyes. "Yes, mother."

He left the tent and ran around the center of the camp where the smoldering embers of last night's bonfire remained. Orcs were scattered about on the ground, snoring loudly as they slept. Many of them had drank more than their fair share of the stolen Rogarian ale in celebration of their attack on Tran. Xellik stepped carefully over them as he plodded his way across the camp. He looked up as someone shouted his name and he spied his friends a short distance away. They waved to him, and he waved back.

"Just one second," Xellik shouted to them. There was something he wanted to do first.

Xellik moved towards the pens where the Fergoth were keeping the human children imprisoned. He walked over to the fence and looked at the captive humans inside. A few of them turned to regard Xellik with fear, while others glared at him.

"Move along, whelp."

Xellik looked up at the guard that stood before the pen's gate and scowled at him.

"Oh, you're Fellis' kid," the orc said, "Uh, never mind."

At least some orcs understand their place.

There was one boy that caught Xellik's eyes. He wasn't skinny, but he wasn't very muscular looking either. The human had a large bruise on his face that looked vaguely hand-shaped, and he wore an indifferent expression on his face, as if he'd already resigned to his fate.

The orcling pointed to the human boy and said to the guard, "Bring him here."

The older orc hesitated. He looked to his fellow guard, but he just shrugged. Not knowing what to do, they opened the gate as ordered and stepped into the pen. One of the guards grabbed the boy harshly by his arm and dragged him out as he began to protest. Or that's what Xellik thought he was doing. He couldn't be certain, since he could barely understand a word of Common.

The human was plopped down before Xellik and the two of them stared at each other. The boy made no move to try to escape.

"What did you want him for?" the guard asked.

"I've never seen a human up close before. I want to see what kind of people we lost our home to."

The guard made a short, huffing noise. "Good luck trying to understand it."

Jabbing himself in the chest with an index finger, the orcling said, "Xellik."

The human raised an eyebrow and looked between Xellik and the guard.

Does he not understand what a name is?

Xellik repeated the action, saying "Me Xellik" using one of the few Common words he knew. He then poked the human harshly in the chest. There was no change in the boy's expression, but he did say two words.

"Dane Trueshot."

"Tell me something, human: Do you know why you're here? Do you know what you've done to my people?" The orcling cracked his knuckles. "You can't answer me, of course. That's fine. I've been wanting to do this for a long time."

The orcling's fist flashed out and caught Dane in the stomach, causing him to cough as the air exploded from his lungs. The human caught the next fist with his hand and launched his own attack, his foot coming out but only barely grazing Xellik's shin.

"So you do have some fight in you!" Xellik taunted.

The guard made a motion for his sword but Xellik bade him not to interfere. The orc wanted to take his frustrations out on someone who so rightfully deserved it. Dane and Xellik grappled for a time, but slowly the orcling was beginning to win the engagement. He started to push him down to the ground.

Are all humans this weak? How could we have lost our homeland to this race of pathetic beings?

In his over-confidence, Xellik hadn't seen the foot coming up between his legs. He yelped like a pup and rolled off Dane, clutching at his loins. The guard next to him was laughing, along with a few of the children in the pen. There was some cheering coming from the prisoners, and that only further angered Xellik.

"Enough of this farce!" Xellik said through gritted teeth as he tried to roll away before Dane could slam a foot into his side. He clenched a fist and focused, "May despair befall my enemies as the encroaching darkness threatens to consume them whole!"

Dane's eye twitched as Xellik worked his spell, and he paused his attack before catching a blast of freezing shadows in the chest. The boy was flung backwards by the force of the spell and he landed hard on the ground with a groan. Xellik got up on weak legs and stood over Dane before he clasped his hands together and struck him in the temples, knocking the boy out cold.

All the captives fell silent after seeing the orcling's spell work. The guard threw Dane back into the pen before Xellik spat blood on the ground and limped off to catch up with Napir. He hoped that he would get a chance to get this human back for this embarrassment. He didn't care what his mother or the rest of the clan had planned for their captives. Dane Trueshot would be his to do as he pleased.

* * * * *

Dawn was but a faint glimmer of a promise on the horizon by the time Jon returned to his cabin. As soon as he burst into the clearing he bolted straight for the door and headed into the cellar. In the back corner underneath a hidden hatch in the ground was an iron foot locker. He hauled it up out of the ground while brushing Zoey aside with his foot. His hand ran over the top of the chest, feeling the rough texture of the rusted surface beneath his skin. Jon paused for a moment, his hand falling upon the latch on the front of the box.

I had hoped I'd put this part of my life to rest for good the day Dane was born.

Shaking the thoughts out of his mind, Jon opened the chest. Inside lay a chain mail vest. A pair of glimmering mithril bracers rested on top of it. Rows of magical runes skittered across the surfaces of the bracers as they came back to life, energized once more by the mana in the air. Lying at the bottom of the foot locker was a sheathed short sword.

"Never thought I'd be putting these things on again." Jon sighed as he put the armor on and slipped his arms through the bracers. The metal rings of the chain mail clinked together like a sack of coins, and the cold steel sent shivers up his spine. He secured the sword's scabbard to his belt before he stood up and retrieved his bow and quiver.

By the time Jon returned to Tran, the fires had been put out and clean up operations had already begun. It seemed like no one had set out to go find the missing children. He frowned and wondered why they were still fooling around moving corpses when actual lives were at stake.

Typical imperial dogs, only concerned with material wealth instead of the lives of the civilians.

Jon headed towards the center of the village, and on his way he looked around for Colonel Nicoli, but he had no such luck finding the man. Deciding it would be futile waiting to speak to a military officer, he headed to the inn to speak to Ted.

Jon called out as he knocked on the cellar door. "Ted, are you awake?" The lock clicked and his friend pushed it open.

"Lily and most of the others are sleeping," Ted whispered, pressing a finger to his lips. He looked his friend up and down. "What are you wearing? You're not planning to head out there alone are you?"

"Yeah, I'm going."

"But you can't! The odds are against you! At least wait for the military to head out first," Ted pleaded, but Jon was having none of it.

"The military doesn't give a damn about those kids. If they did, they wouldn't be piling up bodies in the center of town," he shouted, frustrated that his friend continued to insist relying on the army for help. Remembering that people were still sleeping in the cellar below, he lowered his voice and said, "The only useful thing they've done since they got here was put out the fires."

"Jon, please!" Ted pleaded.

"I'm going. I have to make it up to Celia," Jon said. He corrected himself and added, "And to Dane, too."

Ted gripped Jon's shoulders. "Please, listen! They can handle things just fine. You don't need to endanger yourself. We went through a lot in the Blackguard, but even these odds are too much for one man."

"If you're so concerned, then come with me and help." Jon shrugged his shoulder, brushing Ted off. "I don't intend to sit idly by while a bunch of savages do Gods only know what to my son and countless other children. Those redskins could be picking their rotted teeth with his bones for all we know. I'm going, and your words will not stop me."

"And if I decide to stop you by force?" Ted asked, balling up his fists.

Letting out a boisterous laugh, Jon replied, "I've seen you fight. I'd take you down before you could even lay a hand on me. Either help me, or stay out of my way!"

Jon turned to leave when Ted spoke up one final time. "Do you have a death wish?"

"No," he said, peering over his shoulder. "But I have nothing left to lose. Isn't that the same reason we joined the Blackguard when we were younger?"

Ted opened his mouth to reply, but no words escaped his lips. Jon continued to walk away, and didn't stop until he reached the eastern edge of the city.

There's only a few places the orcs could have gone, Jon thought. *They couldn't have traveled north, otherwise Ted and I would've crossed paths with them on the road to town. And with the forest so thick, it's unlikely they'd take off with so many stolen goods and captives if they had to avoid taking the roads.*

He scratched at the stubble on his chin, feeling a persistent itch that wouldn't go away. *Wersgrauff is to the west and it has tight patrols in the region, so they couldn't have gone there. The south just opens up to plains and more fortified regions the closer one gets to the capital.*

Jon looked towards the horizon, where the sun was just peaking over the tips of the mountain tops.

The only direction they could have headed is east, and there's a good chance they avoided the Tradeway entirely, he thought as he moved to the edge of the village and began to search the ground for clues. He needed to find some kind of tracks or footprints or blood. There had to be something out of the ordinary that he would be able to use to hunt down the orcs who had attacked Tran. He was certain his tracking skills hadn't decayed any over the years, but he knew it had been a while since he'd last tracked something other than wildlife.

Jon knelt down and ran a hand along the ground. There was a loose patch of dirt and he brushed it aside to reveal a narrow rut in the ground. Within arms reach as a second patch of dirt that hid a second, parallel line cutting through the earth and towards the east.

"Wagon tracks," Jon muttered to himself. "That would explain how they took off with so many prisoners. They must have concealed the path as they fled."

Jon stood up and looked to the east. "How far could they have gone? There doesn't seem to be any hoof prints, so it's unlikely they came on horseback. Can I still find the orcs in time while on foot?" It was still too dim to be able to make out the tracks more clearly. Waiting until the sun had fully risen would take too much time. Time that Jon didn't have.

His thoughts were interrupted by a steady rumbling noise

coming from the town. Jun turned to see a squadron of mounted soldiers following Nicoli. A woman rode alongside him, wearing tanned leather armor. She came to a stop next to Jon, gave him a passing glance, then inspected the ground before her.

"What is it Lieutenant?" Nicoli said to the woman.

"Wagon tracks, headed due east," she replied.

Nicoli thanked her then looked to Jon. "So you're planning to go after them, huh?" he asked. Jon grunted in response. Sighing, the commander shrugged. "If there's no stopping you, then just follow my orders and stay out of the way."

"I've participated in military operations before. I know how these things work," Jon said.

"Fine. Take a seat with one of the privates in back then. There should be enough room for you to double up on one of the horses." Nicoli pointed behind him with a thumb over his shoulder.

Riding with someone wasn't a dignified position to be in, but Jon didn't let the snickering of the soldiers get to him. If it was the only option to get to Dane quicker, he'd take it and he wouldn't complain. He got on to a horse and sat in front of one of the lower ranking soldiers, a tall yet imposing man that made Jon look like a dwarf.

"Alright men, let's move out. Lieutenant Rojen, take the lead," Nicoli ordered, and his men gave their acknowledgements before falling in line.

Jon remained quiet and spoke only when addressed directly by Nicoli. He ignored the glances cast by the other soldiers and didn't bother to engage in conversation with the man he sat in front of. His mind was elsewhere, filling with thoughts of the battle that he was expecting to come, and how it would play out. He couldn't help but worry about Dane's safety.

As the sun rose, Rojen had no trouble picking up the trail left behind by the Fergoth. Despite the orcs' care in trying to hide their tracks outside Tran, they didn't seem to care once they left the town's limits. Eventually, the party came to a point where the tracks split off into two separate directions.

Rojen indicated the fork with a wave of her hand. "A set of tracks continue to the east, while another one snakes off to the south."

"Trying to throw us off the trail, huh?" Nicoli thought out loud.

Jon took his opportunity to speak up. "May I offer my opinion?" he asked. Rojen turned to Nicoli, and the commander eventually nodded his head. "I doubt they would've headed south." He hopped off the horse and moved up to where Rojen was looking. "The tracks here are less dense, and even if they were smart enough to walk in each others' boot prints, their trail should be more prominent, and deeper, too," Jon explained. "Not only that, but the Valarian Tradeway is to the south, patrolled by Rogarian and Snowhoof soldiers alike. It's unlikely they would go near it and risk being spotted. They headed east, I'm sure of it."

"Lieutenant, what do you think?" Nicoli asked as Rojen considered Jon's words.

The woman seemed to be thinking for a second, as if she doubted his reasoning. After a moment of muttering quietly to herself and looking at the tracks again, Rojen said, "Surely you must have been quite the ranger in your day." Jon grunted and turned away, returning to the horse he was riding. "I agree with him. We should continue east."

Something doesn't feel right, Jon thought as he climbed back onto the horse, sitting uncomfortably against the large man behind him. There was something about the whole situation that didn't sit well with him, especially where the children were concerned. The reason for the kidnapping still escaped Jon, and that bothered him. He hoped that they would find the answers they were seeking to the east, before it was too late.

* * * * *

Day turned to night and the orc camp grew cold and dark as the sun had almost set. The prisoners were hauled out of the holding pens and dragged to the center of the camp. The orcs pulled harder than they needed to and spat insults, laughing as the children cried. The bonfire pit had been cleared, and all that remained was a charred, black circle upon the ground. Dane moved to the center of the huddled prisoners, trying to get as far away from their captors as possible.

Armored guards surrounded the pit, and each of them was armed with a loaded crossbow. A female orc stood atop a stone on the western side of the ring, wearing a black and red robe that had runic patterns embossed in a blue thread. Her shoulders were adorned with a pair of wolf-scalps, each of them with their toothy maws open in a snarling expression.

"Listen up, you sniveling wretches," the orc woman barked at them in Common. "If any one of you thinks to move outside of that circle, you'll have about a dozen holes in your torso in less than a second."

While she was issuing her threat to the captives, a number of priests in robes placed lit red candles at regular intervals around the pit. The flames atop the candles flickered and bent towards the center, seeming alive with sinister thoughts and desires of their own. Dane shifted uneasily on his feet. He didn't like how things were playing out. If they were going to kill or eat or enslave anyone, why go to such elaborate lengths to do it? There was a feeling in the pit of stomach building up that told him that what the Fergoth were doing was far worse than any of those things, and he swallowed the growing lump in his throat.

Whatever the orcs were doing, it had to involve sorcery, he thought. He wasn't sure what his intuition was based on, but there was some part of him in the distant corners of his mind that told him magic was about to take place, a dark kind of magic that made him feel more nauseous than he'd ever felt before. The kind of horrible ritual that existed only in fairy tales about evil wizards and spiteful deities.

After the priests had finished placing the candles around the bonfire, a much larger onyx candle placed atop an ornate metal stand was brought forward. It was set in front of the woman that stood before the prisoners. Each of the robed orcs moved and stood before a candle of their own, and every one of them drew a dagger from a sheath on their belt in perfect unison. The orc woman pressed her dagger against the palm of her hand, and all the priests around the ring followed suit.

The priestess slowly drew the dagger across the inside of her hand, and Dane winced as he watched. "This is the blood of our ancestors, the essence of our very beings, the gift given to us by our Creator at the dawn of creation," she began, her voice taking on an unnerving dual-tone quality. She spoke as if she were two people, with one voice using Common while the other used orcish.

The woman paused momentarily as she waited for each priest to each slice the palms of their hands open. "We shed our blood willingly in reverence to our Goddess, to show that we have the strength and will to do Her bidding."

The orc held her hand out over the candle until a single drop of blood kissed the fire. The flame was doused for but an instant before it reignited, fiercer than before and with a deep red color. The priests around the pit did the same thing, and soon the circle was surrounded by a red glow.

"As the sun sets to the west, Manul, the Eternal Watcher of the Night Sky, rises to the east. He shall bear witness to the sacrifice we are about to give to our Lady Sytarel, Matron of the Orcish race!"

Sacrifice!? All the blood in Dane's face drained when he heard that word and he began to pant heavily as his heart leaped into his throat. The children around him renewed their cries and he was deafened by the noise. The sun was but a glimmering, orange line upon the horizon. His eyes darted around the pit, searching for a way out. He wanted to escape, to run away, but he was unable to will his legs to move. They were held in place not by physical bonds, but by the cold stares from the crossbow wielding orcs that surrounded him.

The priests standing around the circle began to chant a mantra in Orcish, and a sharp, throbbing pain filled Dane's head. It felt like a knife had been jammed into the back of his skull and some being was continuing to push down on it. He dropped to his knees and clutched at his head.

An ear-piercing scream escaped his lips and he shouted, "It hurts! Someone, please! Make it stop!" Dane was only scarcely aware of the other children following suit as they, too, were wracked by pain.

The high priestess threw up her arms and shouted over the cries of the children. "Sytarel, my Mistress! Heed the prayers of your loyal followers! I ask of You to accept these lesser beings as our gift. We sacrifice the innocence of our enemy's children in exchange for the power to crush the humans who have pushed Your sons and daughters off their ancestral lands!"

"I-it hurts! It hurts!!" There was no other thought filling Dane's mind other than the pain that coursed through him. He no longer cared what the orcs were planning, or that he would be dead in mere moments. He only cared about ending the pain.

"Our Mistress comes!" the high priestess shouted in a frenzy. Lightning crackled around the circle as the moon crested the mountains. The energy arced between the candles, slowly turning from white, to blue, and then into a blood red like the candles' flames. "Yes! Just a bit longer and --"

The high priestess was cut off as an arrow punched through her skull and exited through her forehead. Her face maintained its manic expression as her lifeless body toppled forward from the force of the blow. She knocked her candle over as she fell, an act which broke the circle and disrupted the ritual. The energy fizzled out and began to dissipate.

A second arrow struck one of the guards and he too fell to the ground.

As the ritual came to an abrupt close, the stabbing pain in Dane's head began to subside until it was nothing more than a sharp memory. His relief was short lived as he saw the orcs mobilize their warriors to defend against whoever was attacking.

An alarm rang throughout the camp and the guards quickly tried to defend against the ambush, but they were being picked off left and right by an unending barrage of arrows, with no decent cover to hide behind. Any cover they could find was quickly stolen from them as arrows encased in flames struck the dwellings, setting everything ablaze. Above the panicked shouts of the orcs, Dane could hear a cry rise up from the forest.

"For Tran, and for the Empire! Charge!"

The camp was bathed in light as the tents were consumed by fire, and Dane could see more clearly what was going on around him. The other children had decided that they'd had enough and fled, scattering into the woods as fast as their little legs would carry them. They ducked and weaved beneath the much larger orcs, who were too distracted with defending themselves to notice them.

* * * * *

A streak of red lightning filled the sky, and sank beneath the foliage in the forest above Xellik. He and his friends were finally returning to camp from the Dragon's Tears after a long day of hunting game. They weren't tracking anything big, just smaller animals like rabbits. They'd had no luck catching anything, but it was good practice nonetheless. It was an exhausting experience for all four of them, and they had spent a few hours simply relaxing by the watering hole and trying to avoid Sorda.

Haij had been asked to go with them. Xellik wasn't sure why they needed someone to watch over them, but the older male was more adept at hunting and made for a good tutor. He'd been insistent on not returning to camp until much later at night, and his increasing desire to keep them away only infuriated Xellik.

"I go where I please," Xellik informed him as he marched off to the Fergoth's camp.

"Wait, Xellik! Get back here!" Haij cursed under his breath, and after telling the other orclings to wait where they were, he chased after him.

Before even reaching the orc's village, Xellik could hear the screams coming from the camp. The lightning had faded and all that he heard was the clang of metal against metal and the shouting of many people. He couldn't even make it to the camp before he was intercepted by Bytej and several other shaman.

"Haij! What are you doing here?" Bytej demanded when he saw his son.

"Sorry, he got away from me," Haij replied, smacking Xellik in the back of the head. "What's going on?"

"We're leaving this place behind. Our plans failed. Fellis is dead and Ragash has called for a retreat. There's no hope of us reclaiming our land now." The shaman urged the other two orcs back into the woods. "We must flee!"

"What happened to my mother?" Xellik demanded. "Who killed her!?"

"But father, we can't leave our homes behind. This is our land!" Haij pleaded.

"Who killed my mother!?" Xellik repeated, his voice rising.

"The Rogarian scum, who else?" The shaman shot him a cold look. "If you want to end up just like her, then by all means, stay. But the rest of the clan are leaving. Without Fellis, we are powerless. We've lost Sytarel's blessings and without that, our warriors are no match for their numbers."

"We're not leaving! We'll stay and defend our home!" Xellik insisted. Orcs weren't supposed to run from a battle. It was shameful to turn tail and run. He was going to be a proud warrior one day, and he didn't want to make a mockery of himself by retreating.

"No!" Bytej snapped. "It's suicidal to go back there, you idiot! If there's one thing your mother should've taught you, it's that a good leader knows when a situation is hopeless! Why else do you think we ran from our home on the lake when the humans came? Because she knew better than you did!" The sounds of fighting drew closer, and the shaman growled. "We don't have time to discuss this right now. We'll head for Zugrul. It's the only safe haven for us now."

Haij nodded his head. "Lead the way."

"No, we're staying!" Xellik screamed back at him. "I'm the leader now, so you listen to me!"

Ignoring Xellik's ravings, Bytej said to Haij, "Shut that whelp up and let's go!" before running on ahead.

Haij stepped up behind Xellik and clubbed him in the back of the head with a fist, knocking the orcling out cold. Quickly picking him up, he began sprinting after his father. On their retreat eastward, they gathered up Napir, Cinra, and Aiph as quickly as they could and headed further into the mountains.

Behind them, the death wails of their kin faded into the

distance.

* * * * *

"Show them no quarter! I want every last one of them brought to justice for the lives they've stolen!" Colonel Nicoli drew his sword and leg the Rogarian soldiers into battle.

Jon came up behind the line of soldiers with his bow at the ready. He moved at a slower pace and let arrow after arrow fly, thinning the orc's numbers one by one.

The soldiers engaged the orcs in combat, their swords flashing out with trained precision. Though the average orc was stronger than the average human, the orcs' natural advantage was lost as they were caught unarmed and unprepared. They scrambled for their discarded weapons. Hatchets, clubs, and anything that wasn't tied down and could serve as a weapon was picked up in a hurry.

Jon drew another arrow and loosed it, striking an orc in the head before he could fire his crossbow at him. He heard a shout over the din of the battle, one in the orcish tongue. Jon wasn't that fluent, but he managed to understand what was being said.

"Don't let the human offspring get away! Kill them all!" a voice cried out, and the orcs scrambled to strike at anything that moved, including their former captives.

"They're trying to kill the children!" Jon shouted to the soldiers around him. He looked about frantically, and spotted Dane across a clearing. He took aim, but found he couldn't get a clear shot with the Rogarian soldiers in his way.

"Dane, get down, now!" Jon bolted around the edge of the camp to get a better shot, keeping the arrow firmly against the bow string.

Dane jumped at the sound of Jon's voice, and on command he dropped low just as an axe swung a hair above his head. He quickly shrank away from the orc before it could pull his axe back for a second attack. The beast was never given the chance as it fell to the ground with a thud, an arrow sticking out of his throat.

Jon fought his way into the camp to help his son. His bow was back over his shoulder, and he drew his sword. The blade was already coated in blood as it sliced through one orc after another. An orc charged at his side and swung at him. Jon deflected the blade of a sword with his bracers, and the runes on their surface glimmered briefly as magic reinforced his strength to aid him in shoving his attacker away. Jon thrust his blade between the orc's ribs and cut through his organs. He pulled the sword out and knocked the body away.

He spotted Dane scampering behind a rock to hide. Jon came around and appeared to Dane's left, startling the boy.

"Come on, let's get out of here." Jon held his hand out to Dane. He was hesitating to take it, and he regarded him with an apprehensive look.

Jon read the expression on his son's face and took a guess at what he was thinking. "We can talk about it later. Right now we need to move!"

There was no hesitation this time as Dane reached for Jon's outstretched hand. As his son's smaller hand grabbed his own, the boy's face turned pale and he opened his mouth to shout a warning.

"Father!"

Jon tried to turn around, but an orc caught him by surprise as a spear was thrust deep into the man's back. He coughed, spattering Dane's face with blood. Jon fell to the ground as his legs gave out beneath him. The world felt like it was slipping away, and he knew only darkness as his vision faded and the sounds of battle disappeared along with it.

Chapter 8 - Respite

13 years ago. . .
23rd Day of Xenar
111 I.E.

The muggy summer air hung in the room, and Jon tugged at his sweat-soaked tunic to pull the sticky fabric away from his skin. Even though the sun had set hours ago, its heat could still be felt as if it were high in the sky.

A door creaked open to Jon's left, and a small woman poked her head out. She wore simple white robes, and her golden, silk spun hair fell around her shoulders. She swung her gaze towards Jon and beckoned him over with a wave of her hand.

He spied the blood covering the lower half of the nurse's robes, and he knew at once it was Celia's blood. He choked on his words as he spoke.

"Is Celia okay? What about the baby?" Jon asked as he got up and rushed over to the door. The nurse blocked his path and wouldn't let him look in.

"The delivery went well, but. . ." the woman bit her lower lip, seeming unable to continue. She exhaled, looked down at her robes, then said, "You need to understand that she's lost a lot of blood. She might not make it. The birth was hard on her."

Jon's features drooped and his face blanched. Tears brimmed at the bottom edge of his eyes.

"I'm sorry. We tried to stop it but --"

"Take me to her."

The woman bowed her head and stepped aside, motioning for Jon to go in first. Celia was laying on a bed in the center of the room, with a thick white blanket over her. Her auburn hair was splayed around her on the pillow and matted with sweat. She looked tired and ragged and had deep, dark bags beneath her eyes, as if she had aged several decades over the course of the last few hours. Two other women were in the room, dressed in the same white robes as the first, and also covered in streaks of blood.

In Celia's arms was a baby wrapped in a blue blanket. The child's cries were nothing more than mere whimpers. Jon hurried over to the side of the bed, brushing past the nurses tending to his wife, then knelt down and kissed her on the cheek.

"Hi," she said with a wavering, weak smile. She slowly turned the baby in her arms, so that Jon could see him. "Say hello to Dane Trueshot."

"He's beautiful. He's got your eyes." Jon fought back the tears that wanted desperately to come.

Dane kicked his feet and opened his mouth wide as he started to wail.

"And look, he's got your loud mouth," Celia giggled, then began to cough. Jon panicked, but she dismissed his concern with a wave of her hand. "I'm alright, really."

Jon placed an arm around Celia and pulled her into a hug, kissing her again.

"Jon?"

"Yes?"

"Promise me that you'll take care of Dane for me. Always," she spoke between ragged breaths.

Jon took one of her hands in his own and held them tight. "Don't talk like that! You'll be fine. I'm sure of it."

Celia smiled. "I'm not a foolish woman, dear. I know I won't make it. I've already made peace with that fact, and with Xenar.

Just please, before I go, promise me. . ."

"Yes, of course. I'll watch over him and take care of him." Jon sobbed, unable to hold the tears back. "This is all my fault. If only I hadn't pushed to fight in the war, you wouldn't have been in Ingrad and you wouldn't have been hurt."

"Don't blame yourself. I chose to stay by your side." Celia said, putting a clammy hand atop his own to offer him some comfort. "It's a dangerous world now, Jon. There's always war around the corner. Please make sure you give him everything he needs to survive. When he's old enough, give him the bracers I made for you, to keep him safe. Please raise him right."

"Of course." Tears flowed freely from Jon's eyes and he squeezed Celia's hand. "Please don't go. I don't want you to."

She seemed not to hear him. "It seems fitting to pass during my deity's month." Celia let out a sigh of relief. "Thank you, Jon, for the years we spent together. I'll always be watching over you." She turned her head to the side towards her husband, and her eyelids sagged until they closed completely. "I love you." She exhaled once more, then ceased to continue drawing breath.

"Celia? Come on, stay with me!" Jon shook her as he shouted, but there was no response. Her body was still, she had stopped breathing, and he couldn't feel her pulse through his fingers anymore. "Celia!" As he cried her name, Dane joined in and let out a screeching cry of his own.

* * * * *

Present Day
4th Day of Manul
124 I.E.

Jon reached out into the darkness, like a drowning man reaching for the surface of the water. A burning pain shot out from a point in his back and spread all throughout his body. He couldn't seem to catch his breath and he realized that something had punctured one of his lungs. He opened his eyes, and found that his vision was blurred. He could see shapes moving around him, and could hear voices, but they sounded as if they were many miles away. His mouth was full of something that tasted like iron, and he spat it out, feeling a line of it dribble of his lips.

I'm dying, aren't I? He felt dizzy and he couldn't focus.

"Father!" Dane shouted over the sounds of the fighting. He backed away from the orc who now stood over him, a bloodied spear at the ready. "Help me!"

Jon feebly felt around his armor. The weapon had pierced through his chain mail, and he could feel shattered bits of metal stuck in his wound. The orc had stabbed him with such strength that the spear had penetrated his armor. He could faintly hear his son screaming for him.

Dane. . . ? I can't die here. I need to help my son.

He pushed himself up onto his hands and knees, reaching for his fallen sword as he stood upon his shaking feet. The pain from Jon's wound flared up as he moved, but he ignored it. He had to if he was going to protect Dane. He brought his sword to bear, and the blade wavered as he held it before him. Reaching up with a second hand, Jon steadied his grip before tilting the weapon forward to point it at the orc that stood over his son.

With all the strength that Jon could muster, he rushed forward and thrust his sword through his killer's unprotected back. The orc came to a sudden halt as he choked on his own blood and fell forward, nearly crashing atop Dane.

"Father!" Dane scurried over to Jon's side as the man fell back down onto his stomach. "Hang in there, please!"

Jon rolled over onto his back, regretting it the moment he

started moving. His eyes met Dane's, and they reminded him of Celia. He brought his hands up to his chest and rested for but a second to fight back the overwhelming urge to fall into unconsciousness. With fingers that wouldn't steady, he managed to unlatch his bracers and hand them off to Dane. Bloody hand prints stained the metal as he touched them.

"Your mother made them. Said to give them to you when you grew up." Jon coughed and wheezed, splatting himself with his own blood. "I know I've not been the best father to you. . . that I've made many of the same mistakes my own father made. . . and I know my apologies might not make up for it. But I'm sorry, Dane."

"Please, don't talk like that!" Dane pleaded. He looked up and shouted, "Help! Somebody, I need help!" However, his cries were unanswered.

"Grow up strong, Dane. Do something great with your life. Be a better man than I was." Jon looked up towards the sky and fixed his eyes on the moon. "You know, there's so much. . . that I wish I could say, and do, and take back. I never even told you about your mother, or who I was before you were born. I'm sorry." It was getting harder to think, as if a thick fog was rolling in on his mind, preventing him from hearing his own thoughts. He struggled to stay conscious, but he knew it was a losing battle. "Celia, I'm coming. . . to join you. . . ." Jon's eyes closed and he went silent.

* * * * *

Tears burned Dane's face as they rolled down his cheeks. He remained kneeling by his father's body as the flames around him consumed the orc's camp. The sounds of battle began to die down as the orcs were being routed by the Rogarian military. He choked on his words, opening his mouth but hearing no sound escape his lips. There was a feeling of desperation as he tried to cry out his father's name in frustration and despair. But the side of him that grieved over his death warred with the side of him that still resented the man. Dane had no idea what to feel.

As the battle came to a close, he cried. He held the bracers close to his chest and lowered his head. Tears rolled off his face and dripped onto the metal, and arcane runes shimmered briefly with each tiny impact.

I'm alone. They were the only words running through his mind. He was all alone in the world, without any family to take him in. *This was not what I wanted! I just wanted to get away from, to get away from his rules. I didn't ask for him to die! I just wanted him to leave me alone!*

"Aw, damn it. The old man didn't make it," a voice said, coming from behind Dane. The boy turned slowly to regard the soldier standing there with his sword sheathed and blood stained on his armor.

"Who are you?" Dane said, sniffling.

"I am Colonel Nicoli, from Wersgrauff," the main responded. "You're that man's son?" When Dane nodded, Nicoli added, "For what it's worth, I'm sorry." The boy said nothing and turned back to stare at his father's corpse.

A woman ran up to Nicoli and saluted. "Sir!"

"Status report, Lieutenant."

"We've routed the orcs and recovered most of the children. We also located a number of stolen goods that would aid Tran in its recovery efforts. We took a number of casualties, and many more injuries. A handful of children also fell during the skirmish."

As the two soldiers were busy talking, a third one approached as he inspected the battlefield. When he got near Dane, he eyed the bracers held by the boy. The soldier knelt down and said, "What'chya got there, kid?"

Dane looked warily at the man, and clutched the bracers tighter.

"Kids shouldn't be playing with those kinds of things, you know." The man reached out for him.

"No! Stay away!" Dane shouted.

Nicoli turned and realized what was happening. "Stand down, Private! The old man there was wearing those. Lay a hand on the boy or those possessions and I'll have you court-martialed."

"But sir!"

"You know the rules. Now hands off!" Nicoli barked, and that appeared to be the end of it.

"Sir, yes sir!" the soldier stood up and saluted his commander before he scurried off.

"Thank you. . ." Dane whispered, sniffling a little.

"Best hide those kid, before someone else sees them." Nicoli walked off and continued to talk with his lieutenant.

Dane rolled up his pants and latched the bracers onto his legs. They were too large for his own arms, but they fit well enough around his calves. He'd also be able to hide them using his leggings. He noticed the runes, and realized that those were probably what the soldier saw, too. Dane didn't intend to have the bracers taken away from him. It was all he had left of his mother and father.

"Wait!" Dane shouted. A thought occurred to him that the soldiers might be preparing to leave, and he didn't want to get left behind. Nicoli turned to face him. "What happens to me now? Are you taking us with you?"

"We'll be taking you and the other children back to Tran." Nicoli helped Dane to his feet. The boy wiped his face clean with the back of his arm.

The body of the orc was still lying face down in the ground right next to them. Dane looked at it, then looked to his father's body. He could feel the tears in his eyes welling up again. When he looked around at the camp and all the slain children, his eyes began to burn as he scowled. Dane clenched his fists and he kicked the side of the orc's corpse.

"It's all their fault!" Dane howled as he kicked the body a second time, then a third, unrelenting in battering the dead orc. He reached forward and grabbed his father's short sword, pulling it out with a grunt, and raised it in the air to strike at the beast. A hand gripped his wrist and pulled him back while another took the sword from him.

"Easy kid." Nicoli let the sword fall to the ground and led the boy away. "I know you're angry and hurt, but right now we need to head back."

"Fine," Dane said flatly, and followed the Colonel to where the horses were waiting.

It was nearly dawn by the time the soldiers from Wersgrauff had rounded up the remaining children, counted their losses, and returned to Tran. During the ride back, many of the survivors slept in the arms of a soldier upon the horses they shared. Dane seemed unable to sleep, as there was too much on his mind. He couldn't simply fall asleep after seeing everything he saw.

I've killed animals before but those were people! Dane thought, *They had lives, and dreams, and thoughts of their own. And they died just like that, like they were nothing at all.* His stomach twisted as images of bloodied corpses that had been hacked to bits flashed in his mind. *Those red skinned bastards took their lives. It's all their fault!*

By the time they returned, people were already beginning to emerge from their shattered homes to pick up the pieces of their broken lives. Bodies that had once littered the streets were being piled up in the town center to be cremated, where the rubble from the destroyed fountain now lay.

The soldiers split off and took the children to their homes, if any remained. Those that didn't have a place to go to were taken to the inn, teary-eyed and wailing about the loss of their families. The few families that remained were unable to take in any children other than their own. Worst of all, the people refused to take in any of the minotaur that had been orphaned. Despite everything, they had enough energy in them to angrily turn the young minotaur away, telling the soldiers that they need to "take care of their own kind."

Why are they acting like that towards their allies? That isn't fair to them! The minotaur suffered as much as us. Taking long strides, Dane rushed over to where the minotaur were huddled together near a group of soldiers arguing with some Tran locals. *This isn't right!*

"Is this any way to treat someone's friends!?" Dane shouted, feeling a rush of adrenaline as everyone fell silent. "You people welcomed the minotaur into Tran with open arms, but now you shun their orphaned children like lepers!? What in the Pantheon's name is wrong with you lot?"

"Stay out of this, kid," one of the soldiers said and pushed him away before turning to start talking to the locals again.

Determined to not allow the soldiers to push him around, he continued. "How is this fair to them, huh!?"

"Like we care what happens to them," a local tailor said. "We're ruined. We got better things to deal with than to look after some cows." A few of the other locals expressed their agreements with this sentiment.

"Who will help them get back to Valar then if you won't take them in?" A perpetual scowl found its way onto Dane's face. Something about how the villagers were treating the minotaur orphans got under his skin.

"Who cares."

"It's not our problem, it's theirs."

The soldier grabbed Dane by the shoulder and shoved him away. With a grunt of pain, the boy landed on his backside on the uneven cobblestone road. "I told you to get lost!"

Dane could feel the anger building up inside him, and deep down he knew if this kept on, he'd do something stupid like try to attack them like he did to his father. His hands felt abnormally warm as he wished to be able to do something to help the minotaur.

A soft hand touched his back and snapped him out of his fit of rage. Dane looked up to see a minotaur girl looking sadly at him. "I appreciate what you're trying to do," she said, "but we're a strong people. We can take care of ourselves. If we have to."

"But they --"

"Please, don't trouble yourself on our behalf. You have lost enough, haven't you? I appreciate your concern, but worry about yourself for now." A sad smile spread across the girl's muzzle. "We live long lives, and I for one will remember that there's at least one human out there who cares for someone other than himself."

Dane bowed his head, and all the anger left him. He was beginning to feel numb, as though all emotion was slowly evaporating from his body, leaving him as an empty husk. "If you're sure." Taking the girl's hand in his own, he then said, "Take care on your journey home."

"We're two days out from a Valar outpost. We'll get home just fine."

With that said, the girl began to speak to her kin in their own language, and they shuffled off, bringing an end to the entire argument. Dane watched them for a moment before he meandered back to the inn and sat down on the porch as people began to work on cleaning up the town.

Nicoli was talking to Ted as they stood in the doorway. More and more children were slowly beginning to congregate outside the inn, each one of them now homeless and without a place to stay.

"He died fighting," Nicoli said when the innkeeper asked of Jon's whereabouts.

Ted sighed and looked down at the ground, rubbing the back of his head. "Jon, I told you not to go. Well, I've known him for a long time. I'm sure he gave them hell."

"He did," Dane said simply without turning around. "I saw the eagle feathers on the arrow that killed their leader. I know he got them good." His voice was filled with a strange sense of pride that he couldn't explain. It came out of nowhere, and the statement had escaped his lips before he'd even realized what he was about to say.

"That sounds like the old Jon I used to know," Ted remarked. "Never content to sit idly by when he could take the lead."

"I'm sorry we couldn't bring his body back," Nicoli stated, though it sounded halfhearted. "We weren't able to bring our fallen soldiers with us either."

"Understandable." Ted looked at the growing number of orphans outside his inn, and to the gathering of bodies in the center of the town. "It's a sad sight to see so many being left homeless. It wasn't this bad up at Ingrad, but at least then we knew when the attack was coming. What happens to them now though? The town is ruined, and we don't have the ability to take care of so many. I've already taken in one little girl who lost her family. I can't afford any more with a child of my own on its way, either." There was a pause, almost as if he hesitated to say the next words. "Sorry, Dane."

The boy shrugged in response. *I don't care. I don't want to be a burden on the Langstens anymore than I already have been.*

Nicoli leaned against the door frame and crossed his arms. "We'll be escorting them to Rogust. The orphanage there will take care of them."

"That's a long journey, at least several days pace even by

horseback. Why not just take them to Wersgrauff?"

Nicoli snorted and spat. "Wersgrauff has a terrible reputation. I'm sure you know how bad that place is. We don't have the capacity there to take on this many children, either. They'll be given out to whomever is willing to take them in, and all too often they'll be given to some sailor who needs a new cabin boy."

"I do remember what it was like but that was almost twenty years ago," Ted said. "I'd heard things had gotten worse but I didn't really think the rumors were true." He sighed and gave a heave of his big shoulders. "Well, you're all welcome to rest here for the night. I don't have many rooms left undamaged, but we can clear the bar of debris and set you all up there. I'm not about to let anyone sleep outside after everything you've all endured, and it's the least I can do to offer you a night of comfort before you head off."

"Thank you. It'll be better than a tent."

Ted nodded his agreement. "I could use a few extra hands getting the inn cleaned for tonight, if you have any men to spare." With a nod of his head, Nicoli agreed and went to recruit a few soldiers to help while Ted went inside.

After a few moments of thinking, Dane slipped into the inn. He wanted to talk with Ted and Lily privately so that he could thank them, and to be near someone who would talk to and understand him. He was alone and he didn't know what to do. He could hear the sound of wood scraping across the floor as he spotted the tail end of a broken table being dragged into the back room.

Following the sound, he found Ted, his wife, and a little girl working to clean the inn together. Dane couldn't help but feel a pang of envy at seeing them all work with each other to achieve a common goal, without any complaints or animosity between them. He had never gotten a chance to know anything close to that. Dane dismissed the thoughts as quickly as they had come, and cleared his throat to get their attention.

"Dane, I'm glad to see you're okay!" Lily hurried over to the boy's side and gave him a hug. "I'm so sorry to hear about Jon." Dane stood there, stunned that she was hugging him. He kept his hands at his sides, feeling uneasy as she embraced him.

"It's fine," Dane said, but he wasn't sure why he said it. "I wanted to thank you for taking me in the other night, and for talking to me."

"You're welcome," Ted said. "I wish we could do more for you though. But, we've already promised to take care of little Fran here, and with another child on the way we can't possibly afford to take care of you on top of that." There was a hint of sadness in his voice as he spoke. "Please, forgive me for not being able to do more for the son of an old friend."

"It's okay. I don't want to be a burden on you any more than I already have been."

Lily was still kneeling in front of Dane and she placed a hand on his shoulder. "You're very strong for someone so young."

"Strong?" Dane remembered that he still had the talisman around his neck, the one he bought from the minotaur on the first day of the festival. "Maybe."

He'd forgotten that he was wearing the trinket, and was momentarily amazed that the orcs hadn't noticed it either. Was he truly strong, or was it the magic of the stone? He placed a hand over the stone and it felt warm even through his tunic.

"Is there anything we can do?" Ted asked.

Dane thought for a moment. Ted was already putting them up for the night before the trip to the capital city. Then, he remembered his home, and who still remained there. "Yeah, there's one thing you could do, if you don't mind."

"Anything."

"There's a kitten in my father's cellar named Zoey. Can you take

care of her for me, please? I don't think I can take her with me."
Dane didn't want his kitten to be all alone. "There's a lot of food
and other supplies in there as well that will go bad if someone
doesn't use them. Father and I were saving them for the winter, so
please take them. I think you'll need them."

Fran smiled and cheered. "Yay, a kitty!"

"Of course, Dane. We could certainly use a cat right now to
keep the pests away while we rebuild." Ted scratched at his chin as
he spoke.

"Thank you."

A few moments after their exchange, a number of soldiers came
inside and said they were ordered to aid in whatever repairs they
could. Dane offered his help as well, seeking a distraction from his
thoughts. He was relegated to performing simple jobs, such as
removing small pieces of debris and putting them outside,
salvaging bedrolls from the unusable bedrooms and from ruined
houses, and aiding in keeping the hearth lit to prepare a meal for
everyone.

Ted left sometime in the early evening and returned a while later
with a wagon full of goods from Jon's cellar. He handed Zoey to
Dane and left to make sure everyone was comfortable. The boy
stayed up for a short time and tried to amuse himself by playing
with Zoey, but his mind was elsewhere and he had trouble
enjoying the encounter. When he finally clambered into his bedroll
on the tavern floor, amidst the sleeping bodies of the soldiers and
survivors, Zoey crawled over his body and curled up on his
stomach, purring contentedly. Dane let the tears flow freely as he
cried himself to sleep.

The next day, everyone in the inn awoke as the sun began to
rise. Dane was slow to wake, spending his last few moments with
Zoey and watching as Nicoli got his men together and asked for
volunteers for the escort trip to Rogust. There would be no need to

bring the entire platoon with him. Those who chose not to go were ordered to return to Wersgrauff and to send any supplies and labor to help with Tran's recovery effort.

The horses' packs were loaded with supplies to make the trip south. They were filled to the point of bursting with dried meats and bread and water to feed the entire convey.

Dane said his last goodbye to Zoey, hugging the cat and kissing her atop the head one final time before handing her off to Lily. She took the feline in her arms and held her like a mother would hold a baby. Zoey curled up in her arms and purred, closing her eyes when the woman reached up and scratched behind her ears.

"We'll take good care of her, Dane."

"Thank you." Dane turned when he heard the last call for the wagons to be loaded. "I hope you'll all be okay."

Ted nodded. "We'll be fine, son. Take care of yourself."

"I will," he replied. "Thanks again." Dane hurried off to board the wagon that the other children were loaded onto.

Once everyone had been accounted for, Nicoli motioned with his hand and snapped the reins of his horse. "Alright men, we're moving out!"

As they left Tran behind, Dane looked behind at the ruined buildings and at the surviving villagers milling about as they began to rebuild their shattered lives. He was leaving his home behind, and deep down Dane realized that he'd never be able to go back to the way things were. He spun around and faced south as he began to wonder what the future would hold for him.

Chapter 9 - Rogust, Capital of the Human Empire

2nd Day of Shinixuroc
124 I.E.

"Damn these accursed headaches!"

Talia Frostfire set the parchment she'd been reading down and rubbed her temples with her forefingers. The throbbing headache felt like her mind was filled with many tiny demons stabbing at different parts of her skull. She leaned forward and laid her head in her arms, trying to blot out the light from her window. She focused a portion of her magical energies and flicked the alchemical lamps off around her, darkening her room.

The door to her study slowly opened and creaked noisily as someone stepped in. The sound lasted for what felt like forever, and the screeching was only adding to her suffering. With a low snarl, the half-dwarf sorceress reached out with her magic and pulled the door wide open until it slammed into the wall. Her headache reached its crescendo when she saw the grinning elf standing in the doorway.

With a dismissive wave of a hand, the parchment on Talia's desk floated into the air, rolled itself up, and disappeared with a pop. It reappeared somewhere on the overflowing bookshelves that lined the walls.

"I'm sorry about that, dear Talia," the elf said as he stepped into the room, closing the door at an excruciatingly slow speed behind him. "I hadn't realized you were experiencing such a strong headache." His silver eyes shimmered as he examined her. "Perhaps you should see a healer about it."

Talia jabbed a stubby finger at the elf. "Don't patronize me, Sylenthros! You know full well the cause of my ailment."

Sylenthros looked down at the half-dwarf with a thin smile as he approached her desk. "Well, perhaps you are wrong. Usually when your headaches start, you can find the adept rather quickly. But this time around you haven't found anyone to blame for your suffering."

"There's something preventing me from scrying their location," Talia rubbed her eyes. Her frustration with the elf wasn't helping anything.

"Maybe you're wrong. Maybe there is no new adept out there. You have been incorrect before." Sylenthros wore a pensive look on his face and tapped his lips with the tip of a forefinger. "Or maybe you have no real skill as a wizard after all? Perhaps I should alert Ancherad that we need a new mage to fill in for your position."

Shooting Sylenthros a hard look, Talia hopped off her chair and moved past him to grab her staff from beside the door. "If I have no skill as a sorceress, what does that say about you?" She cinched the sash around her red and blue robes tight and left the room. Sylenthros was quick to fall in line behind her as they stepped into the hallway.

The hall was lit with the dim, orange glow of lamps that lined the wall, set within stone sconces. Magically enchanted mops and brooms scrubbed the floors, keeping everything neat and tidy. As the two sorcerers came close, the household tools rushed to the sides of the hall to get out of the furious half-dwarf's way.

"Do you intend to follow me?" Talia said in a grating voice. She waved her hand and the great double doors at the end of the hall swung open, allowing the sunlight from outside to pour in.

"I'm concerned as to whether or not you plan to attend our meetings. Have you so quickly forgotten your duties as one of the

Five?" Sylenthros asked.

"Five? When was the last time there were five of us?" she snapped.

"My apologies, it's a force of habit."

With a scoff, Talia continued, "I've not forgotten my job!" She stepped out into the sunlight and turned to look up at the elf. "If the Council had anything worth discussing, I might have left my study despite my condition. But there is nothing urgent to talk about, and I am therefore not needed. Or are you all so incapable of handling administrative concerns like what color robes the graduates get this year?"

Sylenthros shrugged. "Perhaps we merely need the opinions of a woman on matters such as style," he said with a cheeky grin. Talia loosed a disgusted snort and stomped off. "I only jest. We all know you have the style and grace of a newborn cow."

"Damn it, elf! Don't you have some trees to tend to?" Talia shouted over her shoulder. She muttered a short cantrip and winked out from sight with the pop and crackle of electricity.

Smiling, Sylenthros cast a spell of his own, reappearing behind the fuming half-dwarf on the other side of the Academy near the gates. The guards turned their heads towards the pair of sorcerers briefly before returning to their watch.

Continuing from where they'd left off, Sylenthros said, "That depends, don't you have a keg of ale you should be drowning yourself in?" Talia could hear the grin in his voice as he spoke.

She stopped when she realized that the elf was still following her even after she teleported away. She sighed and spun to face him. "I assume it's of the utmost importance if you're still following me. Come on, let's have it. What's so urgent that you must pester me?"

Sylenthros flicked his wrist and a scroll appeared from out of his sleeve. He handed it off to Talia. "I assume you've seen this report?"

Talia quickly glanced over it's contents. "Is this about the orcs that were east of Tran? I was already aware of what happened. That tribe had been there for some time and they weren't a major threat. They certainly aren't anymore, that's for sure." She handed the scroll back to Sylenthros, who slid it back into his sleeve and it disappeared again, all within one smooth motion.

"There was more regarding the incident though. It's not in the official report we were given, but it seems that sorcery was involved."

"Of what kind?"

"Elder Summoning."

Talia's breath caught in her throat. "The Gods are in play?"

"It seems that way. An educated guess would suggest it was Sytarel."

"This could be a problem." Talia sat down on the grass. She suddenly felt like her headache had become ten times worse. Holding her head in her hands, she took a moment to let the pain subside before speaking again. "Do we know why Sytarel is becoming involved in mortal affairs?"

"No, and that's what's most troubling," Sylenthros said. "Perhaps the Fergoth meant to obtain power to prepare for an attack on the human settlements to the north. I hear there was some friction between them and Northpine prior to this incident."

"That's possible, but the threat was neutralized wasn't it? I don't see why we should worry for the time being."

"It would seem that way. We'll have to wait and see if this was a one time occurrence or not. I'm going to return to my study. I hope your walk helps relieve your headache." Sylenthros bowed, then disappeared through another portal.

Talia remained on the cold ground for a moment, lost in thought. Knowing that the Fergoth clan had been so close to summoning one of Sytarel's avatars left a sickening feeling in

Talia's stomach. She stood up once the pain went away and resumed her walk out the front gate.

The orcs were dealt with. It won't happen again, she thought.

Winter was fast approaching and the ground already had a thin layer of snow covering it in a soft blanket of powder. Though it was cold out, Talia's magics kept her warm and warded off the winds. While others were bundled up in furs and heavy cloaks, she walked as calmly and comfortably in her silken robes as if it were spring.

Talia proceeded through the intricately shaped steel gates as they swung open on her approach. The guards, clad in the blue and white colors of the empire's militia, saluted her as she passed. Before her stretched a small park filled with enough trees to blot out the sun. In the summer-time it created a refreshing shade for all who walked through it. Beyond the park lay the Eastgate Market, a street filled with stores, stands, and kiosks selling all manner of goods from both local merchants and those from beyond the empire's borders.

After leaving the park, Talia veered away from the Market, as she didn't want to be in the middle of a street full of screeching merchants. She took a sharp turn and headed in a roundabout way past the market towards the Temple of Tranquility. It was an ursar temple known for its quiet and peaceful surroundings that seemed to block out the sound of the bustling city around it.

The temple courtyard was filled with a lush garden during the summer months, but now all the plants were leafless and lacked the life they normally held. Thick bushes lined the pathway and streams ran through the entire yard, snaking around trees and going underground into the temple proper. Even in the winter, the water flowed, staying unfrozen due to the magics granted to them by Talia herself.

The bear-like ursar looked at home in the cold environment

with their thick pelts of fur. They wore flowing, elegant robes and moved with a grace that belied their great size. They were all either priests, monks, or servants. The temple had no guards looking over it. There was no need for such things, as the ursar kept nothing of value within the temple's walls and no one ever had an issue with them since they kept to themselves.

The half-dwarf strolled through the gate and was greeted by an attendant. "Greetings, Mistress Frostfire. Here on business or for a more personal matter?" When he smiled, the corners of his mouth lifted slightly, showing the promise of pristine white teeth.

"I'm just here to relax, Othur. Bit of a nasty headache I'm afraid," she said.

"Would you like to see a healer? Or perhaps you'd like to try a herbal remedy? Or we could even arrange a massage for you."

"No thanks, not today. A quiet place to meditate would suit me just fine."

"Certainly. Please, follow me." Othur turned and walked through the temple's halls, his foot paws making not a sound upon the tiled floor.

Talia was led into the temple's cloisters, towards a room on the side. The small room was bare, save for a plush pillow for someone to sit on. The side walls had holes near the floor that allowed a stream to flow through, bringing with it the fresh, clean scent of the outdoors and the quiet trickle of water. The room was lit with a light that shone with a faint green glow, like sunlight pouring through dense forest foliage. The inside was warm and welcoming, and it reminded Talia of the spring season.

"Thank you, this will do just fine," Talia said as she propped her staff up near the door and removed her shoes.

Othur bowed. "If there is anything you need, please let me know," he said, before turning and leaving the half-dwarf to her thoughts.

She moved to the pillow, turned to face the door, and sat down cross-legged. The plush fabric sank beneath her weight as she settled in, cushioning her body and enveloping her in its soft embrace. She closed her eyes and took a deep breath, then focused her thoughts on the sound of the stream, on the rise and fall of her chest as she breathed, on the sigh of her muscles as she relaxed.

All conscious thought was pushed out of Talia's mind, swept away like dust by a broom. The thoughts of faraway conflicts and of the problems at the Academy were erased. Her breathing began to slow, and to any bystander, it would appear that she had fallen asleep while sitting upright.

She spent the better part of the afternoon in meditation, but much to her dismay the headache returned. It worsened as the day progressed and her focus began to slip, causing her to grimace and bringing her out of her trance.

By Laren's beard, will this infernal torture ever cease?

Her thoughts trailed away, becoming increasingly discordant. She was no longer able to focus on her meditation. She was drawn elsewhere, away from the temple. Something pulled at her consciousness like a kitten tugging at a string. Her pain peaked, and she lost all sense of where her thoughts were taking her.

Talia fall backwards as she opened her eyes. "I was so close!" she exclaimed. "Where is that damned adept?"

She remained in the room until dusk, looking up only when Othur had returned to check in on her and make sure she was okay.

"Perhaps I'll take you up on that offer for something to take care of this headache," Talia said as she stood up and smoothed the wrinkles in her robe.

"Certainly. Right this way, Mistress Frostfire," Othur said with a bow.

*****

When Dane had first arrived at the orphanage, he wished he could return to Tran. The walls were crumbling and in desperate need of repairs. The hedges around the property were slowly turning to dust. Many of the windows were cracked, and some were completely shattered, requiring them to be boarded up. The doors looked as if they were about to fall off their hinges at any moment. It was hardly fit for anyone to be living within within its walls.

Things only managed to get worse over the months. Ever since the children from Tran had been dropped on the doorstep of the orphanage, there was simply no way for the Matron to take care of everyone and maintain the property anymore. Daily lessons had become a matter triage, of who the Matron could keep on task and which individuals she could afford to ignore.

Dane hated being forced to live in such a place. The cracked windows allowed drafts to seep into their sleeping quarters and he was left wanting thicker covers. The food was slimy with the consistency of slop. It was made from what Dane could only guess to be the cheapest ingredients imaginable. The orphanage was surrounded by a stone wall and the gate was kept closed, preventing him from being able to go outside. The Matron had been cold and unloving, and Dane wondered if that was because she just didn't care for any of the orphans or if she could scarcely manage the increased number of children. It was a worse existence than being under the tyrannical rule of his father.

Dane tried to suppress the thought. Despite the history between his father and himself, he felt a pang of guilt for thinking ill of the dead, let alone someone who had died for his sake. His guilt had increased threefold when the first day of Shinixuroc had come, known as the Day of Mourning. It was a day when the humans of

Rogust remembered the lives of the loved ones that they lost in years past. Dane prayed for his mother and father, but he didn't know why. He had explained away his unease as being part of never having known his mother and hating his father.

Several of the children from Tran had killed themselves on the Day of Mourning, and that only added to the pain of surviving. The number of survivors was being reduced day by day, as more of them decided to take their lives into their own hands.

To make matters worse, the Tran children were alienated by the native Rogarian orphans, and most had suffered beatings from the older children. Dane had failed to escape being on the receiving end of someone's wrath, and was nursing a black eye. For the most part, Dane tried to keep to himself so he could avoid any confrontations with other people. He'd barely spoken to anyone since leaving Tran.

In another year, it was likely that Dane would be kicked out of the orphanage and deemed an adult. Whether he was fit enough to survive on his own or not didn't matter. The Matron would soon be rid of him and the other children, and he'd have to find some way to make a living when he knew nothing about the city he'd been thrust into and without any money in his name.

This wasn't the change that I was hoping for, he thought. He began to miss the days of studying in Lynn's library and going out hunting with his father. At least then he was somewhere safe, even though he hated doing either of those things.

Dane was sitting near the edge of the grounds within the shadows cast by the orphanage. Even on a cool day at the beginning of winter and sitting in the shade, he wasn't the least bit cold. In fact, he'd already shed his cloak earlier because he'd been sweating in it. He was content enough to sit around in the shadows with nothing more on his back than a set of linen clothes. The other orphans thought he was weird, and the Matron had warned him that he'd catch ill if he kept doing such foolish things. But weeks went by and nothing bad happened to him, and since he was comfortable, he didn't change a thing about his attire.

A few children were playing some sort of game in the field just around the corner, but Dane wasn't interested in it. He sat with his knees pressed up against his chest. Most of his time was spent thinking about the events of the previous month and whether he could have done anything different, about whether he could run off and live on the street, to get away from this squalor, and about whether he'd be prepared for the inevitability of living on his own in just a short year.

But most of all, he thought about how he wanted his revenge, to get back at the orcs that had stolen his family from him.

He scowled at the thought. *Filthy red skins.*

A rock flew by and struck Dane in the side of the head. He recoiled and nearly fell over. He could feel blood trickle down his cheek, and the freshly opened cut throbbed with the hastened beating of his heart. He could hear laughing coming from the yard, and he swiveled his head around to see a group of three native Rogarians, the same ones that had given him the black eye earlier that week.

"Sulking out here again, Dane?" the eldest of the three grinned. The boy had an upturned nose that reminded Dane of a swine, and a scar cut across his fat, bottom lip.

"Leave me alone, Chris. I don't want any trouble today," Dane said. He stood up and attempted to leave, holding a hand to his bleeding wound. The trio maneuvered themselves to block his path.

"Who said you could talk to us like that?" Chris asked. He wound up and swung at Dane with a fist.

Dane ducked to the side, but was quickly flanked and shoved to the right by the smallest one. He fell full force into the ground, landing on his shoulder.

Chris looked down at Dane as he stood over him. "You think you're so important that you lot can come here and do whatever you want? This is our home, not yours!"

Dane rolled to the side and sprang up to his feet to avoid a kick that would've struck him in the side. He tried to attack Chris with a punch of his own, but his swing was dodged and he was struck in the back. Dane's teeth slammed together as his chin struck the dirt.

"Gods damn you," Dane cursed under his breath. He slammed his fist down and the ground cracked from the impact. He swept his leg out and tripped one of his attackers, the quiet one of the three named Corey, but the action only caused the bullies to redouble their efforts. Booted feet slammed into his side and Dane groaned with each hit. He shot a hand out and grabbed an ankle as it swung at him, stopping it before it could strike him in the chest.

"Don't touch me!" The short one named Theodor shouted before he spat in his face.

I can't do anything like this. It's three against one. I should just let them win quickly so that way they'll go bother someone else. If only I had the power to put up a real fight. His pride would not allow him to back down without a fight though, and he pulled on the leg in his hand, dragging the other boy down to the ground with a hard thump.

Dane's resistance only infuriated them more, like a bunch of aggravated wasps. He was left on the ground bruised and bloodied, coughing as he tried to catch a breath. The three older boys laughed at him as he writhed beneath him. They left Dane alone after that, patting each other on the back for a job well done before they moved on to go cause trouble for their next victim.

Why am I so weak!? Dane pounded the ground again. *Why does nothing bad ever happen to them when all they do is make life hell for the rest of us?*

Dane struck the dirt again in a fit of rage, and suddenly, all three of the bullies tripped on the same raised piece of earth. They landed flat on their faces, much to the laughter of everyone who saw their fall.

Blinking, Dane stood up on legs that strained to hold him upright. *Was that rut in the ground always there? That's so strange that they would all fall at the same time.*

"See? I told you this place was haunted!" one girl said when the bullies picked themselves up and were out of earshot. "The ghost struck again!"

"There's no such thing as ghosts, stupid," a boy responded, but then his voice dropped low and he added, "They were just being clumsy. They always are."

"Yeah but what about what happened with the latrine?" the girl asked.

"We don't talk about that, remember?" the boy replied with a shudder.

Dane listened to the gossip for a while longer. It was impossible to say whether the orphanage was haunted or not, but there had been a lot of strange things going on lately.

It doesn't matter, he told himself. *It's just another incident on a big pile of oddities here.*

Dane decided to head back inside. The cuts on his face and chin weren't clotting fast enough and he needed something to clean them with. Dane hobbled back into the orphanage to look for the Matron. With any luck, she would have something to treat his open wounds.

Chapter 10 - Gengistahn, Last Orcish Bastion on Muriaj

16th Day of Sethyr
125 I.E.

"I'm tired of following you around, shaman!" shouted a female priestess named Tamril. It had been several days since the Fergoth fled into the mountains, and she had constantly been at odds with Bytej and those who wanted to head to Zugrul. "We should be turning back to retake our homeland instead of running from our enemies and headlong into the problems that we'll face in Zugrul. Nothing awaits us there but squalor."

"Zugrul is safe. We know this continent is no longer hospitable for us," Bytej reminded her.

"Safe? For who?" she shouted, "We're without a High Priestess. That makes us caste-less! Have you so quickly forgotten what your forefathers taught you about that place and its customs?"

"This would imply that I cared. I'm thinking about the safety of our people. Do you think that returning to the human's lands is any better? We'll be driven away like the last two times, only this time we won't have Fellis' magic to protect us."

"We don't need that weak orc's excuse for magic to fend for ourselves," Tamril shot back. "We have enough strength between the lot of us. More than enough to make up for her loss if we tried."

Ragash stepped forward and shoved Tamril away. The orcs around them reached for their weapons, glancing nervously between each other and they tried to determine who to fight alongside. Tradition demanded they side with Tamril, but they knew that fighting with Ragash and his warriors would be disastrous for them.

"It's suicide to go back there," Ragash said. "We barely have any warriors or capable mages left after that last attack. What do you hope you'll accomplish by going back there? Bytej has the right idea: we should flee to Zugrul until we can recover our strength."

"And you would wait to take back our land when it's right here within our grasp?" Tamril asked coldly. A few other Fergoth nodded their agreement with her, voicing concerns that now would be the time when the humans would least expect a counter-attack.

"I would rather wait generations to ensure the children of my children can once again lay eyes upon these mountains than rush headlong into our clan's doom."

"Ragash has the right idea, Tamril," Bytej piped in, stepping forward to stand beside the seasoned warrior. "We can always return later, whether it's us or our descendants doesn't matter."

Tamril sneered at them, pacing slowly from side to side as she pointed accusingly at them. "And why should we listen to a male? You have no authority here!"

The argument between the orcs was threatening to reach its violent inevitability. Xellik watched as they shouted back and forth at each other. After days of thinking and watching silently from the sides, he was beginning to see the validity of Bytej's plan. Even if they were unified as a single clan, they did not have the numbers to stand up to the Rogarians.

"Then who should lead?" Ragash said with a huff. "You?"

"You're an idiot if you think you can compare to Fellis' powers," Bytej added, advancing on Tamril and getting in her face as he yelled.

"And you're both more stubborn than braying asses!" Tamril

shouted and jabbed Bytej in the chest with a forefinger. "Returning to Rogust may not be the safest thing for our tribe, but at least there we'll have control. We'll be able to handle the situation in any way we see fit. If we go to Zugrul, then we'll just end up cast out from the city's walls and forced to live in something even more pathetic than our little shanty town back in the foothills."

Xellik was growing tired of listening to them fight and shouted above them all. "Enough!"

Both orcs turned to regard Xellik. The orcling clenched his fists and scowled at both of them. Their behaviour was unbecoming of true, honorable warriors. They shouldn't have been arguing about it, Xellik reasoned, because they should both be following his orders.

"I'm tired of the fighting," he said before the others could say anything else. "I'm Fellis' son. I don't care what your rules or traditions say. All that matters is that what I say is law for our tribe."

Tamril loosed a hearty laugh from deep within her chest. "You've got guts, whelp, but you're forgetting your place." She kicked Xellik over and then stepped on him, digging the heel of her boot painfully into the orcling's back. "The males listen to the females. That's how it's always been and that's how it'll continue to be. As a priest of Sytarel, I'll take the place of your failure of a mother and lead this tribe." She held out a hand and a ball of golden fire appeared in her palm. "This tribe has no place for an accident like you."

Sytarel, I require aid! Xellik prayed, matching Tamril's cold gaze with a fierce determination of his own.

His arms moved of their own accord as his body sprang into action. Without calling upon his pact, a blade of mana materialized in his hand mid-swing. Tamril barely had time to pull her hand away as the weapon sliced the tips of her fingers off. She screamed as she doubled back, giving Xellik enough time to stand up again and bring his sword up. He was about to finish Tamril off when another sword crossed in front of his swing, knocking his weapon out of his hands and causing it to disappear.

"Do not bring shame on yourself by killing one of your kin," Ragash told him.

"You. . . wretched worm!" Tamril screeched, raising her other hand as she worked another spell. "I shall see you burned to a crisp for this offense!"

Bytej stepped forward and clubbed her outstretched hand with his staff, breaking her wrist with a resounding crack. Her spell fizzled out before she could release it against the orcling.

"Enough of this foolishness. Regardless of what you think, there is a higher power that would take exception to killing the heir of a High Priestess, regardless of whether it's a male or female."

Tamril clutched both hands against her chest as she dropped to her knees in pain. She seethed at them, hissing through clenched teeth. "Sytarel doesn't care for the male sex. You're for working, breeding, and fighting. You're not fit to be leaders, not since Grashal cost us our empire."

"That's not for you to decide."

Urzule stepped out from the tree line, her hands on her bow as she stalked forward. Her son, Cinra, was close behind, watching the others around them. Her wolf fur scalp was pulled down over her face to ward off the harsh winds atop the mountain, granting her a fearsome visage.

"I agree with Ragash and Bytej," Urzule said. "This land is inhospitable to us. You would know this if you ever lifted a finger to help us, Tamril." Her fingers played upon the nock of the arrow that sat against her bowstring. "Our odds of survival are greater if we go to Zugrul, regardless of whether they consider us casteless or not.

The two orcs stared each other down until Tamril finally relented and stood back up.

"Fine, do as you please, blasphemers," she told them, then turned to the rest of the tribe and shouted, "If anyone else wants to join me in retaking our land, then come with me. We'll deal with the human scum on our terms. If you'd rather turn tail and run like a mongrel, then you know who to look to."

Tamril stomped off, back in the direction they had come from. Nearly half the tribe turned and left, muttering amongst themselves and casting disapproving looks towards those who remained.

Bytej offered a hand to Xellik and helped the orcling to his feet. "I'm surprised you would side with me. Until a few days ago I was sure you would've turned back around the first chance you got."

"It's not for lack of wanting to return, but rather because I realize we won't succeed in our current state. We need more power."

"And where do you intend to get that from?"

"Sytarel Herself, if necessary."

Ragash walked over to Xellik and crossed his arms, sizing the orcling up. "For a whelp, you have some stones. I suppose there is hope for you after all, son of Fellis." He walked off, taking the lead as they picked through the mountain trail. Before Xellik could even register the compliment in his mind, he heard Ragash shout back, "Just don't let it go to your head."

Over the next three months, the Fergoth that followed Bytej journeyed across Muriaj. They scaled over the treacherous Rogarian mountain range and through the massive Kelial Plains as they skirted human and dwarven territories. Winter settled in with a blanket of heavy snowfall towards the latter weeks of their journey when they finally arrived at the orcish town of Gengistahn along the south-eastern coastline. The town was nestled against a cusp of trees, hidden well away from the dwarven and elven kingdoms that surrounded them.

Compared to the Fergoth's old village, Gengistahn was significantly fortified with a mishmash of stone and wooden walls around the entire settlement. Its stone houses were like pimples poking out of the snow-covered fields. Despite the cold weather, the town was always alive with activity, as it was a fully self-sustaining home for its inhabitants that actively engaged in trade with Zugrul across the sea.

Xellik sat on the beach after finishing a sparring session with Haij. It was a mild evening, and a light wind blew loose snow across the ice floes that had coated the coast. He looked up when he heard the sound of approaching footsteps crunching on loosely packed snow. From over his shoulder he could see Cinra walking towards him in a slow, meandering manner.

"Was there something you wanted?" Xellik asked finally as the other orcling came to a stop behind him.

"Haij and the others are going to take us hunting tomorrow morning."

"Where did you hear that?"

The orcling shrugged.

"Good. I need the experience, what with my coming of age coming up in a few years," Xellik said. "I can't wait to go hunting with them and leave this place for a while. I'm tired of the way these Gengistahni look at us like we're diseased."

"Perhaps to them, we are," Cinra said cryptically. "Casteless are bad luck to have around. They just tolerate us because killing us would be an affront to Sytarel."

"Still, I'd have half a mind to wipe the smirks off their faces with my own two hands if I could." He looked out across the frozen sea. "If only we weren't stuck here. . . ."

"If only," Cinra said. Xellik wasn't sure whether the other

orcling was patronizing him or not. "We should head back. I think Bytej was looking for you."

"Another rumor you heard on the wind?" Xellik asked skeptically.

Cinra didn't respond.

The two orclings left the frozen beaches and took a short walk up between the tree line and Gengistahn. Cinra led Xellik around the town to the area that was being used by the Fergoth. Hastily erected tents were put up and acted as a temporary home for the displaced tribe. Cinra took this moment to depart and left Xellik on his own to go find Bytej. The elderly shaman was always in his tent, preparing for dinner or for some ritual he had cooked up for his magic.

He was greeted outside the tent by Haij, who waved him over. "It's about time you showed up. Bytej is waiting for you."

"So I heard. What does he want?"

"I don't know. He didn't say. Just go and ask him yourself." Haij motioned for Xellik to enter the tent. "I have a lot to do before tomorrow and that's not counting all the crap Ragash is dumping on me. Don't do anything stupid, Xellik."

"Same to you," Xellik responded before he entered the tent. Bytej was sitting in the center of it, preparing a number of herbs and powders that were laid out on a cloth on the ground.

"What are you doing?" Xellik asked, curiosity getting the better of him.

Bytej ignored the question and asked, "Off daydreaming again, whelp?" The orcling didn't give a response.

The old shaman had aged considerably on their journey, and it was little wonder why. He'd been forced to take the reins in place of Fellis, and Xellik knew that was a tall order to fill for someone who had never had any real authority before. The wolf fur garments he wore were tattered at the edges and stained with his sweat. His hands were calloused and covered in scars from all the extra labor he was forced to endure. Wrinkles ran along his face and down into a thick gray beard. Dark bags hung under his eyes, which only served to highlight his drooping features.

"Well, at least make yourself useful. I need a test subject." Bytej produced a knife from a hidden sheath in his clothes.

"What for?" Xellik asked warily. Bytej grabbed his wrist without a word and cut a thin line across the palm of his hand. Xellik clenched his teeth as the blade sliced through his skin. He fought back the urge to yank his hand away, refusing to make a noise or show that the pain bothered him.

Strong orcs didn't whine or cry.

Next the shaman grabbed a number of blue leaves and rubbed their oily surface against the wound. It only caused the pain to intensify, and it showed on Xellik's face as he winced and pulled his hand away.

"Hurts?"

"You think?" Xellik snapped, "What in Sytarel's name is that?"

"I was hoping some sort of pain reliever. I guess I was wrong." Bytej grabbed a skin of water sitting next to him and spritzed a small amount onto Xelik's hands. The water did little to ease the stinging sensation that he felt on his open wound, but the coolness of the liquid was a little soothing. He jotted a few notes in a leather-bound tome and muttered something about using the blue plant as a toxin before setting it aside.

"Let's try another one." The shaman held up a three-pronged, red leaf.

The orcling glanced at him and said, "Red means it's bad."

"This isn't poison ivy if that's what you're thinking." Bytej told him and began mashing it in a mortar and pestle until it was a fine dark red paste. He slid a finger along the bowl's surface and scooped up a liberal amount of the substance before he smeared it across Xellik's wound.

The orcling had expected it to hurt, but nothing happened. In fact, the pain was subsiding.

"Is the dragonspine working better?"

"Yeah, it is actually," Xellik said, surprised.

Bytej began to clean up his mess and made some more notes. "I have a job for you, Xellik."

"What kind of job?"

"I want you to grow strong. I'm sure you've seen how things are with these orcs here. It's not going to get any better once we cross the sea."

"I already understand our situation," Xellik said, confused. "I thought you wanted me to do some work? That wasn't much of a request."

"Being strong is work. Understand this, Xellik: You're the son of our High Priestess, and that means you are capable of more at your young age than the rest of us." He turned to face Xellik. "Those born under a High Priestess of Sytarel have great potential. The blood of the First Orcs flows through your veins, passed down to you by your mother's family for generations past."

"I still don't understand what you want me to do."

Bytej placed a hand on Xellik's shoulder. "Very soon you'll come to understand the nature of our society, and you'll understand why I said you need to be strong. We have no power in this world, but that will change because you are here." He took his hand back and stood up straight. "I'll be training you to ensure you live up to your potential."

"What is this potential you keep mentioning?" Xellik asked, but the older orc dismissed his question with a wave of a thick, calloused hand.

"I'll tell you in due time. For now, rest up and get ready for tomorrow's hunt. Take this time in Gengistahn to relax, because as soon as we board the first boat out of this place, I won't be going easy on you." With that said, Bytej shooed the orcling out of the tent while he went about some of his alchemical experiments.

Xellik would be lying to himself if he said he wasn't a little scared. The uncertainty of what was to come made him feel uneasy, and his stomach churned. He decided that there was no use fretting over it. If whatever Bytej had in mind was going to happen, there was no point in being worried about it. He would face these trials head on, as he was taught to do in the face of uncertainty.

As the orcling lay in his bedroll, his hand snaked out from under the covers and he examined it. He could remember faintly the way his mother had held his hand and touched his palm when she was giving him lessons on magic.

I am a conduit through which Sytarel works her magic, he thought, repeating Fellis' words in his mind. *How am I to harness this power without mother's teachings?*

Xellik let his arm fall back down to his chest and heaved a big sigh before rolling over and closing his eyes. He had months to think these things over before Bytej would feel like sharing with him. There was no point in wasting precious time worrying about it when he should be asleep. After all, he had to be up at the crack of dawn with the rest of the hunters.

Chapter 11 - Awakening

30th Day of Xenar
125 I.E.

Dane heard the boy's screams before he saw where they were coming from. It was followed by a loud thump and a crack as one of the Tran children flung himself off the roof and struck the cobblestone walkway. Dane didn't recognize who it was, but he doubted he would have known the boy's name even if he had. All he could do was stare blankly at the broken, bloodied corpse that lay on the ground.

In the beginning, when he had first arrived in Rogust, he'd been strong and hopeful. Though the beatings he received left him bloodied, he always told himself that he'd be free in a year's time. However, he quickly began to feel as if there was no opportunities outside of the orphanage, and after witnessing the eleventh suicide since he arrived, he was beginning to think there was no way out. He was far from the forests of his home, and though he knew enough about hunting that he imagined he could get by, he lacked the equipment to be able to do it.

It felt like there was no way out. No matter what he could potentially do, there was always more problems to deal with that would make it impossible for him to make a better life for himself.

I need to get out of here, Dane thought as people clamored past him to investigate what had happened. He found the orphanage suffocating, it's brick walls containing a musty stench that he felt might never leave his lungs.

The gate to the orphanage was left slightly ajar, and Dane took the opportunity to slip out and wander the city streets. The rumble of thunder off in the distance promised that a storm was coming, and when he looked up, he could see the darkening clouds rolling in from the west.

He meandered around without any purpose and no destination in mind. Dane sought to dissolve and become one with the crowd of people and merchants, so that no one would notice him while he took in the sights. This was the first time he had left the orphanage, and being invisible to the crowds allowed him to see more than he had expected, or even wanted. He saw happy children with their parents and he both envied and hated them. Their existence only reminded him of something he couldn't have, that he'd never get the chance to know.

As the hours passed by, Dane eventually found himself in front of a church dedicated to the God Laren. Neither he nor Jon had been overly religious individuals, and looking past the priest standing outside shouting for donations, he didn't see why that should change now. He walked past the man as he rang a small hand bell, annoyed by the sound as it echoed in his skull.

The sky was beginning to grow dark as the clouds blotted out the moons. A gentle breeze carried the scent of wet grass along with it, an odor that Dane found comforting. Rogust stunk compared to his home back in Tran; it reeked of filth and refuse. Being able to once again fill his lungs with the smells of nature reminded him of a time not too long ago, one that he wished desperately to go back to.

With nothing else to do, Dane decided he'd take a walk towards the piers and look out at the sea for the first time since he had arrived. He always wanted to swim in the ocean, but he didn't picture that the waters would be all that warm until summer arrived.

As Dane headed towards the docks, he passed a set of buildings that stood out from the rest of the city. They were constructed out of stone and red clay bricks, with strange, triangular roofing. The largest building in the center was tiered, as though a series of smaller structures were built one on top of the other, each with a slanted, red rooftop.

It looked foreign to Dane, and he wondered whether they were of human construction or not. He'd never seen or read about anything of the like in all his time studying with Lynn, since she focused entirely on Rogarian history in all his lessons. He followed the outer walls until he came to an opening. Inside the courtyard he could see strange, bear-like people walking around in robes.

Dane dared to creep into the courtyard of what looked like a temple. He held onto the wall, fearing to let go of it as he walked around and into the garden. He saw a network of streams running through the center of the compound, with pink flowers and green lily pads floating along with the water's current. It was quiet in the courtyard, and upon entering the temple's walls, the sounds of the bustling market a short distance away seemed to dim until he could no longer hear any of it.

"Greetings, young man. May I help you?" A black bear that stood as tall as a mountain casually moved towards Dane, spreading his arms wide in a welcoming gesture. The boy couldn't help but notice the shining tips of the beast's sharp claws. The bear's voice had a thick accent, one that Dane had never heard before. He was still able to understand him fairly well as he enunciated each of his words and spoke slowly.

Gods, a talking bear! Dane stared wide-eyed at the creature, unable to move. *I mean, I know minotaur are just talking cows but talking bears!? I never even knew they existed.*

"Is something the matter?"

"You can talk." Dane felt stupid the moment he said it, and he could feel his face heat up.

"Never seen an ursar before?" The bear seemed mildly amused by Dane's confusion. "I take it you're not from around here are you?"

Dane shook his head, and felt unable to voice a reply. *How much of the outside world have I missed being stuck in the Professor's study?*

"Then allow me to introduce myself. My name is Othur of the Xenarian Order," the ursar bowed low, his robe flowing along with the movements his bulky body was making. "We come from Xenaria, a country situated on Yasuragi to the south."

Dane tried to recall a map of Galria, but he couldn't place where this land was located. There was little that he understood about the world outside of Rogust's territory, and he felt ashamed of his ignorance. He was left wondering why his father was paying for his education if Lynn never gave him a broader view of the world.

"Is Yasuragi full of bear people?" Dane said. The island's name sounded awkward as he stumbled over each syllable.

"Bear is considered an offensive term to my people. Would you call a minotaur a cow?" Othur smiled, speaking simply and without any anger or annoyance in his voice.

"I didn't mean to be rude."

"It's alright. You didn't know and fortunately we are an understanding people. Now then, what brings you here today?"

"I was walking towards the pier when I saw this place and it looked so different from everything else around it. I wanted to see what it was. I've never left the orphanage before so I don't know anything about what's in this city."

"You're an orphan?" Othur asked. Before Dane could reply, he added, "I'm deeply saddened for your loss."

"I suppose someone should be," he replied flatly.

The ursar motioned for Dane to follow him. "You seem

139

troubled. Perhaps you would like to come with me. We can talk and I'm sure I can help you relax."

"I don't have any money," Dane said, hesitating. He was a bit nervous about following the ursar. What if they planned to eat him? He shuddered to think what they could do. Othur was so much larger and stronger looking than him, and he wouldn't be able to put up a fight if something bad happened. He wasn't sure why he distrusted the ursar so much, but perhaps his recent experiences played a part in that.

"We don't charge for our services. We have a wealthy sponsor here in the city that keeps our temple running," Othur said and smiled.

"Well, as long as it isn't any trouble," Dane said, allowing himself to trail off. He was still feeling nervous, but he began to follow after Othur anyways.

"Come along, there's no need to feel scared," Othur assured him.

The ursar escorted Dane through the courtyard and into a cloistered room beyond the temple's inner walls. The entire room was lined with countless doors spaced equally apart. In the center of the cloister was a fountain, in the design of a group of four fish all springing up out of a river. Dane realized that they were facing the four cardinal directions.

"Everything here looks so clean. And strangely symmetrical. Is there a reason for that?" Dane asked as his curiosity surfaced and drowned out all other thoughts. He couldn't help but feel enamored by the uniqueness of the Xenarian Temple.

"We subscribe to a belief that everything has a place and alters the flow of ki that permeates all living things. By keeping things neat and orderly, we reduce the harmful impact on ki and help promote health and well-being."

"What's ki?"

"It is the body's natural energy that affects our well-being. Someone with lots of good ki tends to be healthier and happier than others." Othur opened a door and stepped aside to allow Dane in. "I can tell just by looking at you that your ki is in disarray. It's a maelstrom, like a hurricane, when it should be calm, like a stream."

"How can you see it?"

"It's a gift the ursar possess, but it's kind of hard to explain to someone who can't sense it," Othur admitted and shrugged. He urged Dane to head inside. "After all, we would both have difficulty explaining what the color red looks like to someone who is blind, would we not?"

"I suppose."

Dane stepped into the simple, yet elegant room. There were a pair of pillows that looked incredibly plush and appeared big enough that he could curl himself up in them and sleep comfortably. A set of wind chimes hung in front of a window and jingled lightly as a gentle breeze blew into the room. A small stream of water came out of a hole in the south wall and ran up to the north side of the room. There was a tasseled rope hanging over one of the pillows, and it ascended up into the ceiling above.

"However, you're not here to learn about our beliefs." The ursar took a seat on a pillow and gestured for Dane to sit down on the one across from him. "Something else brought you here."

"What makes you say that?"

"Because someone who is merely inquisitive would not have followed me into the temple, and I'm sure you're aching to talk about something if you took me up on my offer." Othur crossed his legs and interlaced his fingers before dropping his hands into his lap. "No one else cares to listen?"

"No," Dane admitted, though he didn't mention the part where he never tried to talk to other people. "Why do you?"

"We believe in helping other beings no matter what the personal cost is. Do you like tea?"

"I used to drink it, but not since I arrived here in Rogust."

Othur reached up and pulled on the rope. A tiny bell jingled somewhere above them, and after a moment, two saucers with cups resting on them began to float into the room atop the water. The ursar stood up and retrieved them, offering one to Dane.

"Thank you." Dane took a cautious sip of the steaming drink. It tasted like the tea Lynn used to brew for him, but it was considerably sweeter. "What's in here?" he asked without thinking.

"Honey." The ursar smiled at him. "It's a personal favorite of mine."

Dane lifted his cup up and took another sip to hide his smirk. Something about the ursar enjoying honey filled his mind with comical images of Othur ravaging a bee's hive to get at it.

Setting his cup down on the floor, the ursar cut right to the chase. "Would you like to tell me about why you look so distraught?"

"I can, but you'll probably regret it. I'm sure I could go on for hours."

Othur smiled. "It is a good thing my race is long lived then. I'm all ears."

Dane spilled his entire story to the ursar, baring his soul to the being that he had known for only a few short minutes. Othur was kind enough not to interrupt him, but he made sure to let him know that he was still listening with a periodic nod of his head.

Though Dane found the chance to open up to be somewhat cathartic, he was surprised to feel upset over what had happened in Tran and lost his calm demeanor several times while telling his tale to the monk. Tears stained his cheeks and he sniffled, wiping his runny nose on the back of his arm. Even after all this time, he couldn't believe he was still crying over losing his father. He reached up and gripped the bear-paw talisman around his neck and clutched it, wondering why it wasn't making him stronger.

"Do you still feel upset with your father?" Othur asked when the boy was finished.

"For a lot of things, yes."

"Do you feel guilty too?"

"Yeah, of course. Who wouldn't feel like that after he died trying to protect me?" Dane said, and he found his voice rising. "Sorry."

"It's alright to feel the emotions you are experiencing, or to even lash out at others. They're all natural feelings, but that's no reason to give up on the world."

"Maybe it isn't, but I simply don't see anything after this orphanage that's worth struggling through," Dane admitted. "I'll probably end up on the streets with barely any food in my stomach."

"*Nanakorobi yaoki,*" Othur said in a language that Dane could not understand. "It's an old Ursese proverb. It means that if you fall seven times, stand up eight. You should never give up on what you hope to accomplish in life, and you shouldn't let anything hold you down. Didn't you used to have dreams about what you wanted out of life?"

It was a topic Dane scarcely thought about anymore, and he wondered why he stopped looking at the world with the same wonder as he had before. He had lost his family and his home, but he was still alive.

"When I was studying to be a scholar, I hated it. I always wanted to be something more, to be an adventurer who travels around the world and meets new people."

"If that is what you truly want to do, then you shouldn't let anything hold you back. If you see an opportunity, take it and don't look back."

"It can't be that easy."

"It can be, if you want it to be."

It's easy for an adult who has money, and a big temple to live in, Dane thought bitterly, but he quickly dismissed it. The ursar was only trying to help him and there was no reason to turn away his advice or get angry with him.

"You don't believe me," Othur stated.

"How can you tell?" Dane asked. He was sure he'd kept his sour expression hidden well enough.

"Ursar are empathic." The monk tapped the side of his head. "That's why we're so good at what we do. I can feel the doubt you exude. It's just an extra sense, one that detects emotions like your nose picks up smells."

"Sorry, I suppose it's a little hard to believe."

"It's always hardest to have faith in something new when you're down on your luck and nothing else has worked."

"Yeah. . ." Dane glanced out the window, and began to wonder what time it was. It had rained during his talk with Othur, but now the sky was clear and he could see at least one of the moons overhead. He was feeling hungry too, and figured it would be a good time to head back to the orphanage. "I should be getting back. I appreciate you taking the time to talk to me." He stood and offered his hand to shake. Othur instead pressed his palms together and bowed. Hesitantly, Dane mimicked the action and could feel his face heat up. The action felt awkward to him, and it was only made worse as Othur let our a great bellow of a laugh.

"You are very accommodating. You don't have to bow if you don't feel comfortable, but it is appreciated." The ursar flashed him a grin, revealing the rows of sharp white teeth to the boy. "Come, I'll see you to the gate."

Othur escorted Dane back out of the temple and to the gates before bidding him farewell.

"Thank you for talking to me today."

"It was my pleasure. I hope we'll see you again."

"Yeah, maybe," Dane said, and smiled genuinely for the first time in months. He still felt like his situation was inescapable and dismal, but at the same time, the talk with Othur had given him a faint glimmer of hope that perhaps one day he would be able to go out and do something exciting with his life.

As he walked back through the market, he plodded along slowly, taking his time to return to the orphanage. He wasn't sure if he'd live up to the half-hearted promise of returning to the Xenarian temple, but their beliefs and way of life that he'd witnessed intrigued him.

"Where were you?" said a voice that snapped him out of his thoughts.

Dane hadn't bothered to sneak back into the orphanage like how he'd originally snuck out, but he didn't expect to run into the three bullies standing right inside the gate.

"Hello, Chris," Dane said dryly. The bully and his goons were the last bunch of people he wanted to deal with. His stomach was rumbling and his legs felt weak from hunger. Even the gruel that they were served was more enticing than another fight with the older kids.

"I asked you a question," Chris crossed his arms and tapped his foot in an exaggerated gesture.

"Yeah, answer the boss when he asks you something!" Theo replied, and reached out to shove Dane in the shoulder. he let the other boy have his way and just glared at him as he righted himself.

"It's none of your business where I went or what I did," Dane replied. Even without trying to be antagonistic, he found his tone of voice was giving off how irate he was. "But if you need to know, I decided to go for a walk to clear my head. Is that illegal?"

"Did we say you could go?" Chris asked.

"I didn't realize I had to ask you for permission to use a public road."

Corey spat on the ground near Dane's feet. "I don't like his tone."

"Neither do I," Theo said.

"Let's fix it for him." Chris reached out and tried to grab hold of Dane, but the other boy had been waiting for them to make the first move.

With the swiftness of a cornered house cat, Dane dodged Chris' attempts to grab a hold of him, then stepped forward and landed an easy punch in the other boy's face. He could feel the crack of crumpling cartilage against his knuckles, and he found it oddly satisfying to finally land a blow against Chris, yet absolutely terrifying at what the consequences could mean.

"Why you little shi --" Theo tried to tackle him but he missed and toppled forward when Dane stepped aside and kicked his leg out to trip him.

"I don't even care what you do to me anymore. I'm tired of being pushed around!" Dane yelled. Before Chris was able to recover, he delivered a swift right-hook to his jaw line, then reversed direction to slam his elbow into the boy's already broken nose.

"Gods damn you!" Chris shouted as he staggered backwards, holding his nose as blood dripped from between his fingers.

Corey kicked Dane in the side while he was dealing with Chris. The second kick failed to land as it was caught in his hand.

"Ow! What did you just do?" Corey screamed. He pulled back out of Dane's reach. The bottom of his leggings had turned to cinders and the skin beneath it was a bright red. The boy looked back up and saw smoke rising off Dane's hands. The other two began to slowly back away from him.

Dane hadn't noticed what he'd done, and was puzzled by their behaviour. They outnumbered him three to one, so he couldn't understand what they were afraid of. His hand flashed out, grabbing the collar of Theo's tunic and pulling him forward. He punched the boy several times in quick succession before he hurled him to the ground. The other two boys turned and ran.

"Oh no you don't! I thought you wanted a fight?" Dane hollered. His hand came up seemingly of its own will. "You're not going anywhere."

As if to answer some unspoken request, the ground beneath the fleeing boys turned to mush. Their feet sank down past their knees before the earth solidified again. They were locked in place and unable to move as an orange glow filled the courtyard. An explosion of fire scorched the spot where they were standing.

Dane paused in horror upon hearing the boy's screams as they were flung out of the ground and against a wall. He didn't have time to process what was happening as Theo leaped onto Dane's back and knocked him to the ground. They struggled, and Dane managed to roll onto his back. He ignored the pummeling coming from the boy on top of him and placed both his hands flat on the other boy's chest. A blast of heat exploded from Dane, knocking the boy up and off of him. Theo landed several feet away, and the front of his tunic had turned to cinders.

Dane eased himself back onto his knees and lifted his hands up to inspect them. Both of them felt uncomfortably warm to the touch, and they continued to get hotter. He felt a dull ache in the back of his head that was swiftly increasing in intensity. His hands shook and his eyes were wide with fear.

"What's happening to me?" Dane's voice quivered. A sharp pain cut through his thoughts and he doubled over. He covered his head with his hands and began to scream as the pain reached unbearable levels.

Lightning began to form around Dane and it crackled as it exploded upon the ground, sundering the earth with their power.

Cracks in the ground crept outwards like snakes as they slithered away from him. The few children left in the yard ran inside, screaming and crying for the matron's help. The windows shattered as an explosion of lightning erupted near the building, scattering glass shards all over the inside of the orphanage.

Dane rolled onto his back and arched his body upwards. He fell back down and squirmed around as the pain only increased. The heat in his hands had begun to spread downwards and was threatening to engulf his entire body.

Just as it peaked and he feared his body would be consumed by flames, it disappeared in an instant, and he felt overcome by a sudden drowsiness. A cool wind caressed his exposed skin, stealing the heat from him as he slipped into a quiet, peaceful sleep.

Before he lost consciousness, he could hear a tearing sound as if someone was ripping a great piece of canvas in half, followed by the sound of a woman's voice. "Ah, so that's where you are, adept." There was a small pause, and then she added with a sigh, "Finally, the headache is gone."

Chapter 12 - Journey to Zugrul

1st Day of Nova
125 I.E.

A ship arrived early in the morning at the Gengistahni port, anchoring at the long dock that extended out into the ocean. It was a great galleon named the *Berserker*, and it towered over Xellik as he stood near the shore to watch it pull up. It had a sleek wooden hull painted black, with spikes made of blackened steel mounted on the front. Above that was an idol carved in the likeness of a female orc with her arms crossed over her chest, holding a pair of swords. The mast towered above the ship, with great canvas sails hanging from it. The ship looked like it could easily hold a large number of people, probably the entire town if they tried.

Merchants came off the ship and began to unload their goods. Once they spoke to the locals, they began to ignore the Fergoth and they would occasionally shoot them dirty looks or rude gestures.

As soon as the ship was emptied, they began to load some new crates back into the hold. There weren't as many going in as what had come out. Xellik saw that some of what they were loading up were things belonging to the Fergoth clan. He strolled over to where Bytej was standing and watching the sailors work.

"When will we be boarding the ship?" Xellik asked.

"Later tonight," the shaman replied. "We'll be staying below decks and tomorrow morning they'll be casting off to head back. Just stay out of the crew's way."

He won't need to tell me twice, Xellik thought. The crew looked like they were itching for a fight. Their bodies were covered in huge scars and many of the senior shipmates had large weapons strapped to their belts. It was enough to deter Xellik from going near the ship until it was time to board.

When the crew of the *Berserker* were finished loading the ship, it was nearly dark out. The Fergoth tribe was ushered on board and stuffed below decks, almost as if the orcs of the Zugrul-bound ship were trying to hide them from any prying eyes. The oarsmen and much of the rest of the ship's crew were asleep already, so the refugees were ordered to stay quiet.

Once everyone was settled, Bytej beckoned Xellik to follow him above decks.

"What is it that you want? I'm tired of these cryptic little games you and Haij have been playing on me since we left Rogust," Xellik said, not caring that he was speaking informally to his elder. He was Fellis' heir, and he should have been the one calling the shots, not the shaman.

"Understandable," was all Bytej said. He waited a moment, taking time to collect his thoughts, before he spoke again. "You're aware of the importance of the High Priestess in a tribe, right?"

Xellik rolled his eyes, irritated. "Yeah, we went over this already. Do you think I have the memory span of a common ogre?"

"Fair enough," Bytej said, then was silent once more.

The sound of the gentle waves lapping at the shore and of the flag above the mast served as ambiance for their meeting. It was too quiet and peaceful. Xellik much preferred to have the sounds of laborers working and of warriors sparring, like back home.

"Ours is a matriarchal society, Xellik," Bytej began. He leaned on the ship's railing as he spoke. "While the males have their roles, we are still only second class citizens to the females. For our tribe in particular, we're worse off because Fellis died without an heir who is old enough to take her place."

Bytej looked over the edge of the railing to watch the water caress the ship's hull. "The High Priestess is supposed to give birth to a female. A first born male of a Priestess is traditionally sacrificed in offering to Sytarel in the hopes of giving birth to a female child. However, your mother chose your life instead of trying again."

"Yeah, I already knew that. I heard you talking to mother."

"You heard?" Bytej shrugged, unfazed by this revelation. "In any case, I've come to learn that no matter how strong our race is, mothers like Fellis have foolish and emotional attachments to their children. Your mother was weak." He heard Xellik growl behind him, and he shrugged again. "Learn to accept the truth, whelp. It'll make life easier if you don't try to resist facts. Your mother had trouble bearing a child, and when she finally gave birth to you, she refused to sacrifice you for a daughter. Its as simple as that."

"So then why should I care?"

"Use your brain for once in your life instead of having other people think for you!" Bytej said, exasperated. "When the High Priestess passes away, her daughter is supposed to take up that title and all duties that come along with it. There's supposed to be a ritual involved whereby a transference of power occurs between the High Priestess and the heir, whereby she grants her gifts and knowledge to her child."

"However, with you as her heir, even without performing the ritual, you already have a huge fount of power to tap into because of your bloodline."

"You've already made me aware of this fact. But neither you nor any other members of our tribe are allowing me to exert any authority, nor have I been taught how to use this power you speak of," Xellik said, jabbing Bytej in the chest with a finger.

"You think we'd allow a whelp like you to run our tribe?" Bytej laughed, an act that only infuriated the frustrated orcling further.

"Don't delude yourself, Xellik. Until you come of age, you will never have any authority here. But until that time comes, I'm going to help you become stronger. I've grown sick of this matriarchal society of ours. Tired of people like Fellis and Tamril who do as they please without consulting the needs of their whole tribe. I want to change things, and you are the vessel through which I will enact that change. This journey across the sea will take at least a couple weeks to complete, and during that time, I am going to make sure you know everything there is to know to fulfill your duties as our new leader."

"And what exactly does that involve?" Xellik asked. The new responsibilities and power had been everything he'd ever wanted, and he was finally going to get it. Xellik expected it to be a grueling experience, though. Bytej was harsh on his pupils from what he'd seen of him trying to train younger shaman, and he wondered what the orc would have in store for him.

"Haij will continue training you once we're ashore. While we're on the ship, I'll be making sure you know the teachings of our Creator, and I'll also instruct you in some more advanced magic. Something stronger than your weak mother was willing to share with you. But do not think I will be going easy on you!" Bytej made sure to emphasize the last part of what he said by raising his voice, and Xellik knew he wasn't lying. "We'll begin in the morning. Make sure you're well rested."

When Xellik awoke the next day, they stayed below decks where they wouldn't bother the ship's crew. Haij was with the two orcs as well, standing off to the side and leaning against the wall with his arms crossed.

"Alright, first off, let's start with learning everything there is to know about Sytarel," Bytej said as he opened a book he'd dug out from one of his packs earlier. Xellik couldn't remember when the shaman had time to obtain a book, or where he had gotten it from.

There was no way he could have returned to the Fergoth camp for his tiny library earlier, and he didn't recall seeing Bytej with a pack of books when they fled the camp. The shaman seemed to be full of surprises.

"She is the Goddess of Strength and War, and seeded Galria with the orcish race early on. It's said that at the time, the other races living on Muriaj were nothing more than scattered villages with no real military structure. This lent to the orcs' ability to conquer the continent under Warlord Grashal."

"But Grashal eventually lost --" Xellik began, and was interrupted as Haij backhanded him hard enough that it split his lower lip open.

"Don't interrupt," the orc said, and went back to leaning against the wall. "Just shut up and pay attention."

Bytej continued as if nothing had happened. "Sytarel wasn't the first God to look at Galria and seek to deposit Her children here. Nova had been the first, bringing with Her the dragons and Her disgusting elves, followed by Laren who, in his jealousy of the other God's works, gave birth to a few races, among them being the humans and dwarves. Despite that, we as a race have proven to be stronger and more organized than the lesser races."

Reaching for a cup of water, Bytej took a sip from it then set it back down on the floor next to him. "However, over the years, the races of the other Gods formed an alliance and worked to drive the orcs from Muriaj. We were all but exterminated, save for the few scattered groups, like our tribe and the Gengistahni, that managed to hide on the continent. The rest of our race fled to Rhavik to create Zugrul, far away from the Freedom Coalition's influence.

Bytej ensured that Xellik was learning by asking him questions about what they had discussed, and drilling him relentlessly. When he got something wrong, Haij would administer physical pain as his punishment. Only when the orcling recovered did they ask him again, only to beat him until he got it right.

During the several week long journey across the sea, Xellik spent all his waking hours studying with Bytej, breaking only when it was necessary to eat and sleep. The older orc constantly grilled Xellik about the things he learned, and made sure to reinforce wrong answers liberally through Haij's brutality. It motivated Xellik to pay closer attention and to make sure he remembered everything.

Even with his increased efforts, he still failed to please Bytej and was reminded of how much of a disappointment he was. Over time, the orcling found the pain and abuse strengthened him and he faced his punishments with a grim determination. There was no longer an urge to flinch when Haij made a motion to strike him, and he no longer cried out in pain. He wore the blisters and bruises with pride.

The weeks passed as Xellik trained with Bytej. The voyage across the sea to Rhavik took less time than the orcling had anticipated, and soon they could hear the calls from above decks that they had spotted land. The crew was busy preparing to dock, and Xellik shuffled his way past them to get up top to see Zugrul as they approached.

Xellik stood by the boat's railing, watching as the port pulled into view. The harbor was filled with more ships than he'd seen in his life, though most of them had hulls covered in barnacles and rust, suggesting they were not taken out often. The few ships that did look sea-worthy were being heavily worked on as laborers moved to unload their hauls. Xellik wondered if that meant there were other orc settlements somewhere that ships would be necessary to visit.

He looked closer at the beings working on the docks, and noticed that the workers weren't orcs, but rather boars that walked upright. These boarmen wore tattered rags, well worn and dirtied

154

with sweat as they moved about.

Bytej joined Xellik at the railing and saw where the orcling's curious eyes had wandered. "Those are korcyn," he explained. "They're slaves that serve the orcs that live here."

"If they're so weak that they can only serve, they should be killed off," Xellik said, frowning.

"The Zugruli orcs created them expressly for that purpose," Bytej told him, "Or so I've heard. They would be a good asset for our clan to have if we can get a hold of one."

"We've always done things ourselves. Why would we need some smelly slaves?"

"We don't know anything about this land. They would be helpful to have. Don't discount their use just because they're slaves. Korcyn are supposed to be strong, and we could use all the help we can get to establish ourselves here."

Xellik nose wrinkled at the idea. "They look like they stink." Why did the Zugruli keep slaves in their city if the casteless were thrown aside as soon as they arrived? Even if the Fergoth were without Fellis, their lives mattered more than these korcyn.

The ship pulled into the harbour and the Fergoth orcs were the first things unloaded. The crew was glad to be rid of them as they all but pushed the orcs down the ramp and onto the boardwalk. The humidity had been intense on the boat, but the further inland Xellik traveled, he found it almost stifling how thick the air was with moisture. This jungle was nothing like the forests of home, and he almost wished he had sided with Tamril when the clan split.

"Ugh, more casteless filth," muttered a dock worker as he wiped off his brow. "They're worse than korcyn."

Another orc nodded his head. "Shame it's a crime to kill them off. They're nothing but rodents anyways."

Growling deep in his chest, Xellik whirled around as he pulled on his connection with Sytarel, materializing a blade in his hand. He was going to teach these orcs a lesson. He didn't care if they were of the ruling class or not. No one spoke that way around a High Priestess and he deserved the same respect now.

Before he could take more than a couple steps, Bytej was able to intercept him and tug the enraged orcling away.

"What are you doing?" Bytej whispered harshly through clenched teeth. "If they see a male with Sytarel's power, do you know how much trouble we'll all be in? Tamril was an idiot about most things but she's right in calling us blasphemers." He dug his fingers into Xellik's arm until the orcling released his weapon. "The Zugruli will not take kindly to knowing you exist, so don't go causing a scene! Got it?"

Xellik yanked his arm away from Bytej. "Fine, I'll try not to do anything too flashy." He frowned in the direction of the dock workers, and then trudged off with the rest of the clan.

The Fergoth orcs moved off to the slums that hugged the towering walls between the city and the jungle. Everything was built tight together, and it was almost claustrophobic to be in. Wooden shacks slanted to their sides as they sunk into the damp dirt they were built upon. Rubble littered the land, and it looked like all the earth moved out from the city proper ended up here as great hills of dirt rose above them.

"Our first order of business should be to find shelter," Bytej said as he walked with Ragash. "The weather here is unpredictable and the last thing we want is to be caught in a monsoon."

Ragash grunted. "I'll see what I can do about that."

"My scouts will find some shelters for us to use," Urzule said, and moved to go relay her orders.

Xellik watched as the older orcs moved about to get their clan set up in the slums. He was irritated that they weren't including him in their plans. Didn't his opinion matter?

"This is absurd!" Xellik ranted as he stomped about. "I'm the High Priest! Can't they understand that my word is law?"

Haij cuffed him on the back of the head.

"What was that for?"

"For whining. You can't change anything about whether Ragash and the others will listen to you, so you might as well observe and learn something from them. No one is going to let you lead if you continue to act like a petulant child."

"Whatever you say," Xellik scoffed before he walked off, not wanting to listen to Haij any longer.

The slums could hardly be called part of the city. It was like a stinking wart stuck on the outer edges of Zugrul. The buildings were ruined and crumbling, and they only vaguely resembled the domed structures they had seen in Gengistahn. Though most of the huts were falling apart, there looked to be enough spare rubble that with time the Fergoth could carve out a small home off to the side of the slums for themselves.

The insects on Rhavik were ravenous, and the mosquitoes were far worse than they were back in Rogarian territory. They were bigger than Xellik remembered, too. One landed on his arm, but a concentrated gaze on it spared a small bolt of flame that incinerated the pest.

Napir and Aiph joined up with Xellik a short while later as he was exploring his surroundings. Aiph had grown skinny over time, but his muscles were more well defined from the work he'd been forced to endure during their travels. Napir hadn't slimmed down at all and seemed to always be carrying around more weight than any of the others in the tribe. It made Xellik wonder if Napir was finding a way to eat more food than the rest of them.

"We were wondering where you were headed," Aiph said as he fell in line beside his friend. "It's not like you to be so solitary."

"Since when?" Xellik asked.

"Around the time we were chased off."

The orcling made a grunting noise. "I'd like to see you feel sociable after what happened."

"You're not the only one who lost something," Napir pointed out. "Keep in mind we lost a lot of our tribe that day, too. There's not a single one of us who didn't lose someone important."

"I don't wish to hear anymore of this," Xellik said. He didn't want to be lectured by his friends anymore than he wanted to stab himself in the stomach. They weren't in any position to question his desires anymore. "Where's Cinra?"

Napir pointed in the direction they had come from. "Out scouting over there, or so he said."

"What for? There's nothing here but homeless orcs and ruins. The most threatening things here are the insects."

"I'm only telling you where he is," Napir snapped. "No need to get so pissed off about it."

Xellik clenched a fist at his side and growled, but before he could make a move Aiph stepped between them.

"Enough. You two are so childish."

"What did you say?" Xellik snarled at him.

"You heard me. Enough. You want to lead? Then it's high time you grew up and started acting like a leader instead of being a brat all the time." Aiph raised a hand and pointed his palm at Xellik as magical energies formed a flaming sphere. "You're not the only one who studied magic under Bytej during our journey, and I'm not afraid of you, Xellik."

"You're threatening the leader of your tribe?"

"You're not the leader yet, Xellik. This is exactly what I mean. You're just picking fights and lashing out. Grow up."

"I'm four months older than you!"

"Says a lot about you then, doesn't it?"

Napir jumped in, grabbing Aiph's wrist and pulling it down.

"Can we stop? Please? We're here now and we need to make do with what we have. There's so few of us left, why are we burning bridges between us?"

Xellik was aware that his friend was right, but he didn't want to openly admit it. He was supposed to have all the answers to their problems, regardless of his age.

"Fine, fine," he finally relented and relaxed. "I'm going to look around a bit more. I want some time to think." As he started to walk away, the other two orclings decided to follow him. "Alone," he added.

"Aye, chief," Aiph said, and took off. Napir lingered a moment longer, looking between his friends, before he too left.

So this is where we're stuck, huh? Xellik took note of everything that he came across as he moved through the slums. There were a few scattered orcs praying to Sytarel, asking for forgiveness and a second chance, but judging by their frantic tone, likely none of their prayers had been answered in a very long time.

As he kept walking, Xellik came across a sight that made his blood boil. Near a fire pit, it looked as if a group of orcs had constructed an effigy of Sytarel, complete with scrawny twigs fastened together to form all six of her arms. As they took a torch to the wooden construct, they began to cheer and curse the Goddess' name. The plume of smoke coming off the burning effigy rose high into the sky and over the jungle as it was carried away by the wind.

Words to a spell were on Xellik's tongue as a sword of mana appeared in his hands. He stomped towards the celebrating orcs with a single purpose in mind.

Who in Sytarel's name do they think they are, doing something like that!? I'll kill every last one of them for this offense!

Before he could make his intentions known however, a hand fell upon his shoulder and he could hear a ghostly voice calling his name. The sword fell from his hand as he turned, and the magical blade vanished into thin air. When Xellik looked around him, there was no one there. All he could see was the jungle further beyond the slums. There was nothing there, yet something compelled him to follow the voice. He gazed at the tree line, but saw only the dark green wall of foliage.

The whisper caressed his ears once more before it fell silent. Xellik waited to see if it spoke again, but nothing happened.

I must have imagined it.

When Xellik turned to regard the effigy burners again, the wind kicked up momentarily and shifted direction. The flames were stoked and lashed out at the nearest orcs, igniting their clothes. They screamed and ran away from the pit while the stench of smoldering flesh filled the air.

Xellik smiled, inhaling the scent. *Guess I won't have to do anything after all.*

With nothing left to see but the ocean, Xellik headed back towards where he left his tribe and decided he'd help them get settled in.

Chapter 13 - The Rogarian Academy of Arcane Sciences

1st Day of Nova
125 I.E.

As Dane regained consciousness, he could feel his body being engulfed by a soft, plush bed. He wasn't sure how long he had been sleeping, but since he still felt exhausted he figured it couldn't have been for very long. He stretched his arms and yawned. It felt like he was floating on a cloud. His eyes peeked open and he looked across the room. At a table near the window sat the matron of the orphanage, who was having a cup of tea with a squat little woman dressed in blue and red robes. Dust motes floated in the sunlight coming in through the window as the sun was starting to set.

The small woman lifted a cup to her lips and drank from it before she spoke. "The R.A.A.S. will contract some masons to repair the damaged walk in the yard. We'll also have them tidy up the building and fix the cracks in the foundation. New windows will be purchased to replace the old ones, and a druid will come by to tend to the yard itself." She set the cup down and crossed one leg over the other. "We'll also be offering a small sum to compensate for the inconvenience."

"That's fine. This dump needs repairs, so I'd say this event was a God-send," the matron said simply. "Even if a few children were hurt, they'll be fine."

"You're cold, Matron," the shorter woman said with a wry grin.

Neither individual had noticed that Dane was awake. As his senses started to come back to him, he felt as if something was missing, that despite the fact he was clothed, he still felt naked. He looked around the room and quickly discovered what it was. His bracers sat on the ground next to a small walking staff, with his pendant draped over them. He sprang up and scampered over to the wall to retrieve his possessions, not caring to move quietly. Dane returned to the bed and put them back on, clasping the bracers around his legs once again and slipping the pendant over his head.

"I see that you're awake."

Dane sat up straight with a start, and turned to see both women regarding him. "They're mine," he said, and suddenly felt stupid for saying it.

"Children don't usually own magical items, let alone three of them," the shorter woman in robes said.

The matron spoke before Dane could respond. "He came to Rogust with them, Mistress Frostfire. I've no idea where he got them. He never speaks."

"My mother made the bracers. She gave them to my father and he gave them to me when he passed away." He'd never spoken the words before except in his talk with Othur, and hearing them sent new waves of sadness through his body. He took a deep breath and tried his best to recompose himself.

Talia pointed at Dane's chest. "It wasn't just the bracers I was talking about. That talisman, does it have any runes on it? Etchings, markings, whatever."

Fishing the pendant out from his tunic, Dane ran his thumb over the bear paw that had been carved into the stone. "The only thing on it is this bear's paw. But that's always been there. I bought it at the harvest festival from a minotaur." How could she tell that it was magical? It didn't seem to do anything when Dane wore it.

"I'm surprised that merchant sold it to you, unless they were ignorant enough to not know anything about their own people's magic." Talia rolled her eyes. "I don't know much about Snowhoof shamanism since their secrets are well kept, but I know enough about the minotaur culture to know the bear is a symbol of strength and courage. I'd imagine that even though the magic in that talisman is weak, it's probably helping you somehow. I can sense that there's a faint bit of power inside of it."

Dane looked down at the pendant. "The merchant said it would give me power and courage. I doubt her words, even now after everything I've been through. I had no power when I needed it and no courage when those orcs fell upon Tran."

"You're from Tran?" Talia looked to the matron with surprise.

"I didn't think it was important," she said in her defense and shrugged.

The half-dwarf seemed deep in thought for a moment before she spoke again. Dane observed her, and wondered what it was that she was thinking. He didn't like when people kept secrets from him like that.

"Is that a problem?" Dane asked upfront. "Do you not like Tran?"

"No, there's no problem with Tran." Talia looked hard at Dane for a moment. He felt uneasy under her gaze as she stared at him with hawk-like focus. Reading other people's expressions wasn't something he was skilled at, but he knew that something was going on in that head of hers. "Tell me boy, do you know what happened last night?"

"I hurt others and nearly killed myself?"

"I was speaking more specifically. Those bracers you're wearing suppress magic and have enhanced protection because of the runes on them, which explains why your power erupted all at once instead of gradually over time like most adepts."

"Adepts?" Dane asked. "What are those?"

"Adepts are young individuals with the gift of magic. People like you," Talia told him as she indicated him with a finger. "There's a lot of reasons for why you could have become an adept, but I would rather not speculate on it as it would be a waste of time. I'm not interested in the how or why, only the what. And what I know is that your bracers were protecting you by suppressing your magic without you even knowing it. Even though you had the Gift, your own subconscious was willing those enchanted bracers to suppress your power."

Dane knew the bracers were magical in some way but he didn't know the first thing about using them. The runes engraved on them were a mystery to him, and he could scarcely recall a time where he felt as if they were helping him in some way.

"So what changed?" he asked.

"Your childish temper tantrum and your desire to hurt others overrode what your mind wanted the bracers to do, allowing you to bypass their magical protection. That allowed you to tap into your natural power."

Talia paused to take a sip of her tea, tipping the cup back to finish it off. "Not only that, but the magic contained in those bracers blocked my scrying spells, and they made it a lot harder to find you."

"Find me? Why would anyone want to find me?"

"The empire has rules and regulations regarding adepts. I know you've lived in the boonies all your life kid, but by the Gods you are ignorant."

"Hey, that's not fair! I only know what my father let me learn from Professor Lynn!"

Rubbing her eyes with a thumb and forefinger, Talia sighed in frustration. "Persons with magical ability are required to attend the Rogarian Academy of Arcane Sciences and pledge their service to the empire. Individuals who do not wish to hone their skills and work for the empire are forced to wear dampeners so that they cannot use any of their powers."

"So that means you're here for me?"

"Yes, isn't that obvious? I wouldn't be wasting my time here talking to you if that wasn't the case." She quickly turned to the Matron. "No offense to you, of course." The other woman said nothing, and continued to sip gingerly at her tea. "I've placed a temporary warding spell over you to prevent further use of any magic until we can safely train you on how to properly wield it."

Talia eyed Dane, and he could feel himself wilting beneath her gaze like a malnourished plant. She clearly had a great deal of power at her fingertips, not to mention the knowledge and authority to use it. Her cold stares did nothing but make him more anxious.

"The road towards the mastery of our trade is a winding and difficult one to traverse. No one is going to hold your hand."

"No one held my hand for anything before," Dane said, annoyed that she was treating him like a child. "If I don't go with you, I'm stuck here and can never learn magic, am I correct?"

"If you want to say it that simply, then yes, those are your options."

"And how would I pay for my education?"

"We'll manage something," Talia replied casually. "Yours is not the first case where we've had an orphan turn out to be an adept. The value of magic users is greater than the material cost of training them, so the Empire is willing to do what it must to accommodate individuals in positions such as yours."

Dane began chewing on the inside of his cheek a bit. He didn't know what to do. Though while he was growing up he'd always had a fascination with magic and with stories involving wizards and sorcerers, he never once imagined that he would be one of those gifted few himself. Learning more about his innate powers would give him the excitement he had always sought to experience, to learn more about the world, and to experience all sorts of new things.

Never before had a choice so important been laid before him, and he was always being led around by others. It was a big decision to make, and he doubted there would be any turning back once he decided.

If you see an opportunity, take it and don't look back, Othur's words echoed.

The two women sitting at the table watched him with growing impatience. The sound of Talia's fingers rapping on the wood filled the room. "I don't have all day, boy! What will it be?"

"If I go, will I have to keep living here? Or somewhere else?"

"We have dormitories within the academy to provide for students who are studying from afar or may be in situations like yours," Talia answered with less annoyance than she had spoken with thus far. Perhaps, Dane thought, she merely wanted to get down to business instead of dealing with his ignorance. "Since you have no money in your possession, you'll likely be put to work to earn your keep. I won't lie or sugar-coat anything for you though. The man responsible for assigning tasks to adepts is a jintaren, and he won't be going easy on you."

Dane swallowed hard. He didn't want to be stuck in the orphanage, and even if his time at the academy was short, it would give him a route to being able to have a better life than living on the streets.

"I'll go with you."

Talia stood up and her chair screeched along the wooden floor. "Then it's settled." She turned and addressed the matron. "Thank you for the tea. It was nice catching up with you. Hopefully it will be awhile before we do this again."

166

"I'm sure you'll be back soon enough," the woman said. "There's always one or two of those brats coming through here."

Talia urged Dane towards the door where her staff was propped up. "Let's get going. I have plenty of work to catch up on now that my headaches are gone."

Dane wanted to ask her what she meant regarding her headaches, but he figured she'd already had enough of his questions.

Staff in hand, Talia recited a few words and waved her hand in the air. The air ripped open around them as if cut by some great sword. Dane stared, transfixed as the borders of this window into another realm opened wider, revealing a swirling pool of something that looked like frothing water. The blue-white light enveloped them as Dane gave a yelp of surprise. He held his breath as the liquid-like portal washed over him.

Dane could feel his stomach churning as they were taken through the portal. It was a winding tunnel of blinding blue and white lights that swirled all around him. His body felt drenched by torrents of water and he could hear thousands of waves crashing upon unseen shores around him.

Then, everything vanished and the two travelers were dropped in the middle of a garden. Dane couldn't hold back the bile rising in his throat and fell to his knees as the portal closed behind him. He clutched at his chest with one hand and held himself up with the other as he emptied the contents of his stomach upon the elegant stone walkway. A mop appeared before him and began to clean up the mess.

"Sorry," Dane muttered and looked up. He screamed and fell backwards onto his rear when he found the mop was not being held by anyone. It glided above the ground of its own accord, back and forth, wiping the ground clean. A faint trail of golden sparkles emanated from the metal band that tied the mop brush to the handle.

"I forgot most people aren't prepared for teleportation," Talia mused out loud. "Oh well."

Dane hadn't heard her speak, as he was transfixed on the mop working in front of him. "How is that thing moving on its own?"

"That's just an enchantment. It's something our more skilled sorcerers learn to do." She stared at him in disbelief. "You really have no idea about any of this stuff, do you?"

"No. Father forbade learning about magic," Dane admitted. Though it was the truth, it felt to him like he was making an excuse.

"You'll learn quick enough." The sorceress' silken robe fluttered as she whirled around. "Come, let's get you settled for the night and we can discuss things in the morning. I have a meeting to keep, and you're likely still tired."

"Yeah, a little," Dane said, surprised. He hadn't been awake for very long, and it was clear that he'd slept most of the day away. "I don't understand why though."

"Most sorcerers feel that way after their awakening. You'll be fine in a day or so."

Talia led Dane across the academy's grounds, and he found himself in awe of the sights he was seeing. The sun was obscured by tall, ivory towers and they seemed to come alive with an intense glow. Their long shadows were like fingers as they stretched across the ground. Ivy spiraled along the walls of the buildings, wrapping them in thin green tendrils. Guards kept a watchful eye on the grounds and stood at attention throughout the campus. He wondered why a school would need guards at all.

Dane was taken to a large, rectangular building that stood several stories high. Guards saluted Talia and opened the doors for her as she proceeded through. A mild pain coursed through Dane's body, like a tightness that constricted him as if he were wearing clothes several sizes too small. The sensation faded after a moment, much to his relief. "What was that?"

"Children are irrational creatures and are prone to acting up without reason. Due to space limitations, we're forced to keep all of our students together in this dormitory," Talia explained. "Did you not notice the sigil above the door? The building itself as a dampener and prevents most magic from working in here, to keep unfortunate accidents from occurring."

After Dane's experiences with the bullies in the orphanage, he didn't want to think what someone like Chris could do with magic at their disposal.

"Is that why there's soldiers here?"

"No, they're there to protect the grounds from thieves," Talia replied bruskly.

The inside of the dorms opened up into a large atrium, with trees that ran in a row down the center. The walls were lined with several floors accessed by stairs on the sides of the building. Each floor had countless doors lining the walls, each of them labeled with a number.

Talia led Dane past a stairway that wound its way up a pillar and then towards a plain wooden door on the bottom floor. A piece of silver metal was cut in the shape of a seven and hammered to the door. Talia opened the door, then moved to the side to allow the boy entry.

Dane stepped into the room and looked around. It was small, but clearly luxurious. It had a window facing the southern garden, with a bed in the corner and a small dresser on the opposite side of the room. Above the dresser hung two small, empty shelves. The center of the room had a simple blue rug over top of a hardwood floor. A lamp hung over the bed and gave the room a soft orange glow.

"You'll be staying here during your training. I'm sure you're hungry too, so I'll have a servant bring you some food. I'll also have her bring along a tome containing some basic knowledge about magic and how we do things around here," Talia explained, leaning against the dresser. "I'd recommend reading some of it, given how little you actually know, especially since it's the entry level text we give to all our first year students. You'll be starting your studies a few months late in the semester, so you have lots to catch up on."

"I'm used to reading long texts," Dane told her, recalling all the work he had to do in learning about history from Professor Lynn.

"Frankly, I'm surprised you can even read. Most who come here need to spend at least a year in just learning their ABCs, never mind the nuances of the language."

Dane was beginning to get the impression that she wasn't too fond of children, and while he was annoyed with her constant disparaging remarks about his lack of knowledge, he didn't dare say anything out loud. She was giving him a chance at a better life and he wasn't going to spit in her face for it, no matter how many times she insulted him. "So what will I be doing at this academy then?"

"Get some rest and we can talk more about that in the morning." Talia headed out of the room and grasped the doorknob behind her. She stopped to gaze at him. "One more thing: Don't wear those trinkets of yours around campus. Magic you don't know how to control is a problem we'd rather not have to deal with." She then shut the door behind her and left Dane to himself.

He removed his bracers and pendant as Talia said to do, then stowed them away inside one of the drawers in the dresser. He then strode over and opened the window, letting a breeze into the room. It brought with it the scent of roses and lilacs, cherries and apples. A light trickle of water could be heard above the chirping of birds and the smell of clean water also reached his nose. It looked so perfect and pristine. Magic had to be involved in this little paradise's maintenance.

Dane smiled, thinking on how much better this place was than the drab, crumbling orphanage he'd spent the last few months in. The garden reminded him a lot of home, away from the sooty skies of the capital. His face felt wet, and he realized he'd been crying. He wiped the tears away with the back of his hand.

A light knock came from the door. Dane paused for a moment, expecting whoever it was to just stroll in. After a few seconds, Dane said shyly, "Um, come in?"

A white-robed woman carrying a silver tray stepped into the room. "Here is your meal, sir," she said, setting it down on the dresser. There was a large tome on one side of the tray, and on the other side was plated a meal of fish with a piece of buttered bread, cheese, and a few slices of an apple. A glass of iced milk was also on the tray. "Everything a young sorcerer needs to stay healthy."

"Thank you, Miss, uh. . ."

"My name is Isabella, sir. I'm here only to serve. Leave your empty dishes outside the door. I will be by to pick them up later." She bowed, and excused herself from the room.

She was gone before Dane could say anything or even introduce herself. Was she busy? For that matter, he wondered if the woman was a slave of some sort. What did she mean by being there only to serve? It seemed like an odd choice of words. Either way, it didn't appear that Isabella minded, judging by the way she spoke.

Unless she's a good faker, Dane noted as he pondered over her brief entrance into his new room.

Dane quickly shoveled the food into his mouth, unaware that he had been so hungry, and downed the meal with the milk in one quick gulp. He sighed with a smile. For the first time in a long time, he'd felt something he scarcely felt before: happy.

"I could get used to this," Dane said aloud to the empty room.

Even if he was indentured to the Empire after his training, it would be worth it. At least, he hoped so anyways.

He set the plate down on the tray and, as he had been instructed, placed d it just outside his door. He felt exhausted and was contemplating going to sleep, but his curiosity overtook him and he decided to read the tome as Talia had recommended. He grabbed the book as he moved to sit back down on the bed. The title, *Introduction to Magic and the Rogarian Academy of Arcane Sciences*, was inscribed in gilded letters on the front cover. He flipped past the table of contents and skimmed through the section detailing the rules and regulations of the Academy. He came to a stop at the page that detailed the fundamentals of magic, and began reading.

Dane's eyes glossed over topics like how to maintain a mental hold on spells to make them persist longer, words of power that were required to cast spells, and the tools a mage needed to be proficient with, from basics like chalk and ink to more specialized utensils like a hammer and chisel for etching runes.

A section titled *The Test of Magehood* resided at the end of the book, and it captivated his attention. The Test was described as the final test all mages under the banner of Rogust had to take to be accepted into the Empire's ranks.

Each Test is tailored specifically to the individual and their chosen occupation. While no specifics may be detailed here, there are a few general rules that all Tests have in common. They are conducted before the heads of the academy's faculties, to most accurately assess the adept's prowess. Prospective students will also be evaluated on their repertoire and use of a variety of magics.

Dane shut the book and leaned back against the wall. He felt positive that he'd do well in his studies and master this Test, even without knowing anything about what he'd face at the academy. It was both refreshing and odd at the same time, and he wondered where such confidence came from.

It was dark outside by the time he decided to set the book back on the dresser. It was an interesting read, on par with the book he'd snuck a glance at back in Lynn's library, but he was becoming too exhausted to keep reading it any further beyond the little bits that had caught his eye.

Dane flicked off the lamp and it dimmed until all light faded from within. The room was now only lit by the moonlight pouring in from the window. He smiled as he lay himself down on the bed, and allowed sleep to overtake him. No dreams plagued him that night, and he was grateful for the reprieve.

Chapter 14 - The Council

2nd Day of Nova
125 I.E.

Dane was woken the next day by a loud knocking at the door. The room was still dark, and the smell of the morning dew filled the room. He opened his eyes slowly, giving his vision time to focus as a red and blue blur stepped into the room. He rubbed the sleep out of his eyes with his hands and looked again to find Talia standing over the bed.

"Did you get enough sleep?" she asked.

"I think so," Dane replied, sitting up. Seeing that Talia had barged in his room almost unannounced made him glad that he'd passed out with his clothes still on. Though he stunk and felt sticky from sweating in his sleep, it was far preferable to the embarrassment of being seen in only his underwear.

Dane looked outside the window, at the indigo sky and at the fading stars. "It's a bit early, isn't it?" He couldn't remember the last time he was woken up before dawn.

"This isn't early, not by any stretch of the imagination." She shook her head. "You're training begins tomorrow, but the Council of Five has requested to meet you before classes start this morning. Once we're outside I'll be teleporting us again, so be ready for it."

"Who are the Council of Five?" Dane asked as he hopped off the bed. His hands moved up to his head and smoothed out his hair as he tried to make himself look presentable. The Council sounded

174

important if they ran things at the school, and he was always taught by Jon to look clean when speaking to someone with more authority than himself. He only wished he could have a bath before meeting them.

"They are the heads of the faculties at this school, and include myself, the headmaster, a druid, and a warmage. They're all in the top of their fields," Talia answered.

"Where's the fifth?"

The sorceress remained silent for a moment with a downcast look on her face. She quickly regained her composure and replied, "Some things are better left unsaid. Let's go, you don't want to keep the most powerful people in the Empire waiting, do you?"

Dane didn't question her any further. He may have been young, but he still knew when someone was upset about something. He wanted to know what happened, but he also acknowledged that it was none of his business.

Dane moved out of the room behind Talia, but stopped for a moment to glance back at the drawer where he stowed his bracers. He didn't want to leave his only and most valuable possessions behind.

As if reading his mind, Talia said, "No one has access to the room except for high ranking individuals such as myself, and you. The door itself is registered to your own unique biological signature, and cannot be overridden except by one of the Five. Like I said yesterday, nearly all magic is prohibited here, but this is one of several exceptions. Your toys will be fine."

Dane shut the door behind him and followed the half-dwarf outside.

"Are you ready?" she asked, holding her hands out once again.

The boy shook his head. "No, but let's go anyways. No sense in wasting time."

"Wise lad," Talia muttered. She cast her spell and the blue-white light enveloped them once again, drowning them in a sea of energy. The world reappeared around them as quickly as it had faded, and Dane fell to his knees. Ragged breaths filled his lungs as he fought to maintain his composure and to keep from throwing up.

"Good, you're here."

Dane looked up and saw an elf standing before him. He was clad in deep-emerald robes. On his right shoulder, there was a tome with an 'R' on the cover embossed in a blue thread. It was the same insignia that Dane had seen on the tabards of the academy's guards.

The elf smiled to him and offered his hand to Dane. "I am called Sylenthros. And you must be the adept that's been causing our dear Talia so much pain these past few months."

Talia scoffed at Sylenthros' remark.

"I was causing her pain? I'm sorry, I didn't know." Dane took the elf's hand and shook it. For someone who looked very frail and lithe, he noted that Sylenthros had a firm grip. "My name is Dane Trueshot."

"Trueshot huh? Are your parents Jonathan and Celia Trueshot?" Sylenthros asked.

"They were," Dane corrected with a hint of bitterness in his voice. "Wait a moment, how did you know my parents' names?"

Sylenthros bowled slightly. "They passed? My apologies then, I didn't mean to touch on a sore spot. Master Trueshot was the son of a renowned fletcher from Wersgrauff and a former ranger employed in the Blackguard. I knew Celia had been pregnant but I never heard anything from either one of them about the child's birth."

"She died when I was born, so I'm told." Dane didn't know much about his father or mother's pasts, as the old man had kept quiet about such matters while he was growing up.

This bit of information regarding his parents piqued his interest, and contradicted some of what he thought he understood about his father. The Blackguard was a mercenary guild, and he knew how his father felt about those types of people, which left Dane feeling confused about this revelation. He didn't know why his father always spoke poorly of adventurers and mercenaries, and yet if what Sylenthros said was true, then Jon had once been a mercenary. He wanted to learn more about the man who had died to save him, yet a part of Dane still fought tooth and nail to tell him that he shouldn't care because of how Jon had treated him for most of his life.

His curiosity eventually won over. "My father was in the Blackguard?" Dane asked.

Another individual cut in before Sylenthros could respond. "Can we get on with this? I didn't get up early just to listen to you prattle on like this, elf."

Dane looked over to the table at the front of the room, towards a tall, scarred and imposing man that was glowering at them. He wasn't wearing a shirt, and he had his arms crossed over his chest. A steady thumping could be heard from where the man sat as he tapped his foot impatiently. The man was very tall, Dane noted, and concluded that he was from the jintaren tribe of people. Was that the man that Talia was referring to yesterday?

"Of course, Heshun. We can speak another time, Dane." Sylenthros strode over to a table and seated himself behind it. Talia and Heshun were already seated there, as well as a much older individual that had yet to be named.

"Now then," the eldest looking man said, idly stroking his long, white beard. He sat in the middle of the table, with Heshun to his right, and Sylenthros and Talia to his left. The second chair on the far right was empty, and Dane's thoughts were drawn back to the sad look on Talia's face from just a few minutes ago. He wondered why no one was seated there.

The old man spoke, oblivious to where Dane's eyes had been diverted. "Welcome to the Rogarian Academy of Arcane Sciences, Dane Trueshot. I am Archmage Ancherad, the head of this school. You have already met Talia Frostfire, our resident master of elemental magics. Sylenthros, who you just met, is the head of our faculty of druidic magic. And this man here," Ancherad gestured to the man who sat on his right, "is Heshun Halgrind, head of our battle-mage corps."

"Pleased to meet you all," Dane said, standing rigid and hardly moving from where he'd teleported in. He resisted the urge to fidget.

Ancherad addressed Talia next. "Mistress Frostfire, your report if you please. Let us all know what you have learned thus far about our young adept here."

"Certainly." Talia rose from her seat and produced a scroll from the sleeves of her robe. She unfurled the parchment and began to read its contents out loud. She told of how Dane had come to Rogust, based on the testimony of the matron from the orphanage, and of the events that led to Talia finding him. Dane hung his head, sullen as she went over the events from the other day. He was embarrassed that he allowed his temper to peak like that, and that he'd nearly killed someone with a power he couldn't understand, much less control.

"Of interest, the adept seems to exhibit proficiency over all the elements, most notably his control of lightning and fire. During his escalation of power, the adept was fully capable of evoking lightning with little effort and minimal expense of energy, a feat not even possible for the most gifted of our students. It is therefore my recommendation that the adept be placed under my own tutelage, and not of any of the others in my faculty, to better hone his capabilities."

Dane was surprised to hear this information. Without any thought or effort, he had done something that someone else couldn't do. He smiled. It was the first time he had ever been recognized as being better than someone else, and he liked it.

"Do you doubt the rest of the faculties' abilities to teach a new adept, Talia?" Heshun asked sardonically.

"I doubt your ability to teach anyone, Halgrind," Talia hissed as she dismissed the scroll she'd been reading from. "It's amazing that such a sub-par sorcerer could make it onto the Council of Five merely because of combat prowess, when he's nothing more than a jintaren warlock."

Dane watched as the two bickered back and forth, then noticed that Sylenthros had a mixed expression on his face, one of both boredom and amusement. This behaviour was not something new to any of them.

"What did you say, short-round!?" Heshun roared as he surged to his feet.

"Enough! Both of you!" the headmaster shouted. "I'm tired of these petty squabbles. Must I treat a pair of such prestigious mages like mere children?" Neither sorcerer responded to Ancherad. Talia sat back down, and neither she nor Heshun spoke again.

"Thank you." Ancherad leaned forward on his elbows and tented his fingers. "Now then, the question becomes what do you wish to learn while you're here, Dane."

"What do I want?" Dane repeated. "I want to learn magic, of course, but is there more to it than that?"

Sylenthros took this opportunity to cut in. "Well, we could get you started in earning a generalized education here for your first year, and then go from there. It would cover everything a fledgling sorcerer needs to know, like scribing and teleportation." Dane paled and he stuck his tongue out at the mention of using portals. "You get used to it eventually."

Ancherad nodded his agreement. "I think that would be the best course of action. So Dane, what will it be? Will you work with Mistress Frostfire to hone your skills, or will you cast your gifts to the wind and forever be forced to live the life of a normal human being?"

"I'll join your school," Dane said without hesitating. "How long do I have to wait to begin learning?"

"Almost immediately," Ancherad smiled, "Though it may be some time before you are placed in a proper classroom since it's so late in the year. Until then, you'll be working on remedial instruction until the beginning of the next semester."

Dane would have hated to be put into a new environment in the middle of the term, with no knowledge of what was taught before he arrived, so this arrangement worked well for him.. After a short orientation on the rules and regulations he would be expected to follow while he was at the academy, he was to be dismissed. He thanked them and moved towards the door, not expecting that anyone would offer him a portal back to the dorm.

"Just one moment, Dane," Ancherad called. "There was something I forgot to discuss with you."

"What's that?" Dane asked, moving back to his spot in front of the Council.

"What do you remember of Tran?"

The question ran through him like a knife through butter. His blood felt cold, and he could feel a sweat break out on his brow. The question brought back the horrors that he'd seen in that place, the deaths of his many countrymen, the sounds of their screams, and most of all, the sinister, faceless expressions of the orcs in his dreams.

"You're breathing quite heavily," Sylenthros said, snapping him out of his memories.

"Why do you want to know about Tran?" Dane stammered,

trying to keep the panic out of his voice. He didn't want to remember that night he ran away. He wanted to flee from his memories, to sprint until he was so exhausted that he couldn't think anymore.

"The orcs tried to use an ancient form of magic, one we're not altogether familiar with," Ancherad explained. "We've been trying to determine what happened up there, but no one has come forward with anything more concrete than what the military reported to us. As a survivor of that attack, I must begrudgingly ask you what happened so we might learn the truth of the incident."

"How much do you need to know?" Dane sat down on a chair. He didn't even realize there was one behind him. He didn't recall seeing one there before, either. He rubbed his arms with his hands, feeling cold all of a sudden in the meeting room.

"Everything you can remember."

Dane closed his eyes and took a deep breath. He looked first to Talia, then Heshun, and finally Sylenthros. The elf seemed to be the only one who looked concerned, despite the jovial attitude he had displayed earlier.

This was not something that Dane wanted to think about first thing in the morning.

Taking another moment to compose his thoughts, Dane explained everything about the night the orcs attacked. He remembered the fires that consumed the new watch towers, the explosions that had shook the foundations of the inn, and the orc that had captured him. He could remember everything in such startling detail it was like a painting had been created in his mind, freezing that terrible moment in eternity.

"When we were gathered together on the last night, I think their leader was there. She spoke like two people, one voice in Common, and the other in Orcish," Dane said, his voice feeling hollow and monotone. "She said something about sacrificing innocence for power. I... can't remember exactly what she said. Afterwards, a terrible pain ripped through my head. It felt like someone was driving a spear past my eyes. Everyone was screaming then, and I could see flashes of red lightning through my closed eyes.

"Then it stopped, and when I looked up, there was an arrow sticking out of the orcwoman's head. That's when everything turned to chaos."

There was a moment of silence as the Council considered his words between themselves. There was some whispering, but Dane couldn't make it out from where he sat. He saw that Heshun was glaring at him, though for what reason he didn't know. He didn't have the heart to stand up to someone that big. His encounter with the minotaur at the festival had taught him that much about people larger and more powerful than himself.

"We'll have to look into this some more. Do you know what happened to the Fergoth after the attack?" Ancherad asked.

"They ran east. After that, I don't know. The military took us back to Tran after the fighting stopped."

Ancherad nodded, and seemed about to ask another question when Sylenthros cut him off.

"I think we've pestered young Trueshot enough about what has obviously been a traumatic incident," the elf insisted. Heshun scoffed at his remark, but offered no comment. "It would be best if he was given the day to rest and to tour the grounds so that he can better familiarize himself with our school before he starts classes tomorrow." He looked to Ancherad for approval. "Wouldn't you agree?"

The headmaster nodded. "So be it. Thank you for sharing your side of the story with us, Dane. You're dismissed."

Chapter 15 - The Slums of Zugrul

3rd Day of Lumine
125 I.E.

It was a hot, humid summer day in Zugrul, and Xellik sought shelter within the shadows of the city's gigantic walls. The temperature had been much milder in the Rogarian Foothills, and the change from a temperate climate to a tropical one was difficult for him to bear. He frequently wondered why anyone would chose to settle in such an awful place. Save for the Gengistahni orcs, no orcs called any other continent home. The jungles on Rhavik were all any of them had, and he thought it was pathetic.

If you tried to take an animal's territory, they would fight tooth and nail to defend it, especially if their young were present. Nothing was more fearsome than a mother bear protecting her young, as several of the Fergoth hunters had said in their stories over the evening bonfire. So what did that make the orcs that fled Muriaj to settle in Zugrul? They were worse than stinking beasts for fleeing their homelands, for not banding together and fighting to the death to keep their ancestral lands.

Xellik tried to shake the thoughts out of his mind. Those thoughts eventually turned to anger, keeping him from thinking clearly. The weakness he felt from hunger wasn't helping any, either. The clan hunters had been having difficulty finding food in the jungles. The Fergoth didn't know these lands, and they didn't know the creatures that lurked in the shadows, flitting from one tree to another as they stalked the orcs in their daily hunts.

Perhaps Bytej is right about getting one of those pig-spawn as a slave, Xellik thought when he mind cleared enough to think more calmly. He didn't like the idea of having a korcyn among their tribe, but the bastard spawn of Zugrul magics would know the jungle better than them.

"Hey runt."

Xellik looked up to see Sorda standing nearby with her hands on her hips. She stared at him with her lip curled into a sneer. He'd seen little of her after the tribe had settled in, and the orcling had hoped that meant she'd learned her place. He wasn't fond of dealing with her, but the way she walked with a swagger in her step told him that she was just as stubborn and ill-mannered as before. It didn't matter that she was a female, she was beneath him as he had the blood of the First Orcs in his veins.

"What do you want, Sorda?" Xellik asked with a snarl. He wasn't in the mood to deal with her.

"Is that any way to talk to a female?" she replied.

"You forget who your leader is." He indicated himself with a jab of his thumb. "If you have nothing important to say, then get out of here and leave me be."

Sorda staggered towards him on wobbly feet. Something about her was off, but Xellik couldn't place it. She leaned forward and exhaled. The stench of alcohol wafted from her mouth and he leaned away from her.

"Yes, you're right, I did forget." Her speech was slurred. She drew a line down the center of Xellik's chest with a finger. "Perhaps you could remind me."

Xellik batted her hand to the side and scurried away to bridge a gap between them. "What in Sytarel's name is wrong with you?" She advanced on him. "Get away from me!"

"Why? You're in your fifteenth year aren't you? You're turning into quite the attractive orc."

"Get lost!" Xellik shouted. Though the advances of a female would be welcoming to the young orcling, who had yet to know the pleasures of an orcwoman, he was disgusted that it was Sorda of all orcs. There wasn't a force on Galria that could convince him to mate with someone like her.

The words to a spell left Xellik's lips and he blasted Sorda in the chest with a wave of arcane force. It wasn't strong enough to wound her, but it did manage to push her back onto her behind and distance the two of them.

"You're no fun," she pouted as she picked herself up and walked away.

Breathing a sigh of relief, Xellik relaxed his tense shoulders and slumped back down against the city's walls.

After a moment, footsteps sounded off the walls and Xellik wondered if Sorda was coming back to try again. Instead, Cinra stepped out from behind a rock and joined his leader over by the wall.

"She's a strange one, isn't she?" Cinra asked.

Xellik was slightly surprised to find the young scout skulking about. "How long have you been there?"

"I was following her. I didn't expect her to be seeking you out."

"Why were you following her?" Xellik asked with a raised eyebrow.

Cinra shrugged. "It's something to do."

"Yeah, but Sorda of all orcs?"

"She's a troublemaker. Someone has to keep an eye on her, sir."

"But you can't take her on in a fight."

"I won't fight her. I'm only observing things."

Xellik's stomach began to rumble as he grew frustrated with his friend, reminding him that he needed some food. "Whatever. Have you heard when Haij and the others are going hunting again? I haven't eaten since yesterday."

"Tomorrow morning, but the tribe is getting hungry, so I wouldn't be surprised if the hunters do something desperate like head into the jungle tonight," Cinra explained. "Mother says they should not be rash but no one seems willing to listen to her right now. They're thinking with their stomachs, not their heads."

"So then we need to figure out something for ourselves while the adults bicker, huh?" A plan began to form in Xellik's head. If the only person he could depend on was himself, then he wasn't going to wait for the hunters to get him his next meal. "I don't feel like waiting for them to make a decision, so I'll just take matters into my own hands. Think you can track down a few things for me?"

"Anything, chief."

"I need a few sturdy sticks. At least four, and they need to be flexible, but not brittle," Xellik began, and Cinra nodded as he listed each item off. "We'll also need four lengths of twine or rope, about five meters long, maybe more if you can manage it. And finally, I'll need some thin strips of metal to make into hooks. Grab as many as you can find."

"I take it we're going fishing?"

"Right. Find Napir and Aiph while you're out, and meet me back by the shore as soon as you're ready."

The other orcling pounded a fist on his chest in salute then took off to go scavenge for what Xellik had asked for. Though Cinra was frail looking and a bit thin compared to the average orc, he made up for it with his speed and remarkable grace as he hurried through the crumbling ruins of the slums. Xellik had to commend the other orcling for being able to turn his weakness into a strength that suited him.

Xellik began to meander through the slums on his own, heading east towards the shoreline. As long as he and his friends avoided the piers, the Zugruli orcs should leave them alone. Though they had yet to run into any trouble with the locals, no doubt they wouldn't want caste-less orcs wandering around unchecked. It wasn't something Xellik did by choice though. He had been warned by Bytej numerous times to avoid causing trouble with the Zugruli orcs. Their time would come when he could strike back, but for now the Fergoth needed to get back on their feet and get settled, even if it took years or decades for that to happen.

Xellik spotted a rocky outcropping that extended like a long claw out into the water. The water split upon it as waves crashed into the rocks, and the air was peppered with sea spray.

Thinking that such a spot would be perfect for fishing, Xellik stepped tentatively out onto the wet rocks. It was easy going, until he slipped and smashed his shin into a jagged edge, cutting a deep cut along his skin. The sea spray splashed his wound and he winced.

It was bleeding heavily, and Xellik didn't have any knowledge of healing magics. He didn't want to go back to camp just to have the wound looked after by one of the tribe's shaman like a spoiled orcling crying to mother. He began tearing strips of fabric off his tunic to make a bandage. He tied it tight and watched as blood soaked the cloth.

"Xellik!"

The orcling looked up and saw Napir huffing his way towards him with Aiph and Cinra in tow, each of them carrying a stick while Cinra carried the rest of the materials that Xellik had requested.

"You don't waste any time," Xellik remarked when they had joined him upon the rocks.

"If my leader commands it, I shall go," Cinra said.

Aiph took a strand of twine and began to secure it to his rod. "I don't know why the hunting party doesn't try fishing for our meals. Zugrul seems to do well enough with all the fish they catch. Besides, our hunters aren't having much luck with those tigers prowling the jungle."

"We've never had to fish for food before. We've always hunted or grown our own," Napir said. His stubby fingers fumbled with the twine and it fell, only for Aiph to catch it and tie the knot for him.

Even though the Fergoth had lived on the shores of a lake back near their ancestral homeland, they only used it for drinking water or for ritual cleansing. The thought of fishing for their food was considered beneath them, and they preferred to have red meat, something that was always in abundance in the forests that had bordered their land.

"We're no longer in the foothills, so we'll have to take what food we can get," Xellik told them. "We should also face the fact that we need to learn to take care of ourselves or we'll starve."

"I think he could use a bit of starving, eh?" Aiph grinned as he poked Napir in the side with the butt end of his pole. The fatter orc rubbed the spot where he was jabbed and grumbled.

They finished fashioning their crude fishing poles and walked to the edge of the rocks. Xellik took a seat at the front and let the cool water spray him in the face and against his bare chest. He cast the line off from the rocks, but after that he realized he had no idea what he was doing.

"This would be a better idea if any of us knew how to fish," Xellik thought out loud. "Or if we had some bait."

"Only way we're going to learn is by doing. We don't need other orcs to hold our hands through it, am I right?" Aiph asked, and looked between the other three for confirmation.

"I won't argue with you there," Xellik said. "I'm tired of being told what to do by everyone."

The four orclings continued to sit and talk as they waited for a fish to bite their lines. Xellik placed his rod firmly between a set of rocks so it stood upright. He then leaned back and closed his eyes to rest for a moment. Napir and Aiph seemed content to yammer on without him participating. Cinra was always quiet, neither giving nor being asked for his opinion on any topic the other two were talking about.

Xellik.

The voice rang out in his mind and he tried to open his eyes, but found he couldn't. The sound of waves crashing upon the shore faded away until it was replaced by the quiet whistle of air passing through a tunnel, accompanied by the faint drip-drop of water on stone from somewhere nearby.

Xellik, come to me.

The voice sounded closer this time. Finally able to open his eyes, Xellik found himself in a blurry, dark room lit by the faint glow coming from roots hanging on the walls. The plants shimmered and almost seemed alive as something slick seeped off them. Everything was faded, like a charcoal drawing smudged by an infant's hands. Even as he rubbed his eyes to try and clear his vision, nothing changed.

Xellik tried to call out, but he discovered he couldn't make any sound.

Where am I? Who's calling me?

A large, blurry form seemed to melt off the shadows and moved towards him. The creature towered over him, its head rearing up towards the ceiling. Xellik gaped in horror as the mostly formless shape clomped towards him. Horns protruded from the sides of its head, and a thick tail moved back and forth as what looked like spikes thrashed menacingly behind the monster. But what really terrified Xellik was the look in the creature's eyes. They were a pair of red orbs set within a featureless face, glowing with the brilliance of a fire. If he had believed demons walked Galria, then this was certainly one of them.

Xellik looked down, away from those eyes. He felt that if he stared any longer he would scream and lose his mind to sheer terror. The hollow echo of the beast's footsteps filled the room as it stalked towards him, and he quivered in his boots. Why couldn't he move his body? Why couldn't he run? Not even his magic would come to him.

Xellik tilted his head up and met the beast's eyes again. It reached out for him with a hand that glowed green, and he tried to back away from the thing's touch.

No, get back!

The orclings attempts to call for aid failed. He continued trying to utilize some of his magic to escape the beast's clutches, but all his efforts were for naught as every one of his spells fizzled out with a pop.

The glow around the creature's hands turned from green to a deep sky blue as it opened its mouth and spoke, but the only sound Xellik heard was a swarm of insects buzzing with every flap of the thing's mouth.

Darkness closed all around him as the hand clutched at his face and he could feel something burning him. Finally able to make his voice work, Xellik screamed as he felt his flesh being flayed from his bones.

"Xellik, wake up!"

In a flash, the orcling's eyes opened and he saw a hand coming towards him. He sprang to his feet and summoned a sword as he stood there, breathing heavily. It took him a moment to calm down and realize that the apparition had not followed him. It had all been a dream.

"Xellik, calm down, it's just us," Aiph said. Xellik could sense the shift in mana as the other orcling began to prepare a spell of some sort.

He dismissed his blade then said, "You shouldn't have startled me. I could've killed you." His face felt strangely taut, and when he ran a hand over his brow to wipe the sweat away, it stung him. He'd gotten too much sun, and his skin had turned a deeper shade of red where the light had burned him.

His head pulsed with a terrible headache as he tried to make sense of what he'd just experienced. How long had he been asleep? The sun didn't look like it had moved much since he passed out.

What was that place? And that. . . thing? Xellik shivered when he thought of the beast again, the burning red eyes staring back at him when he closed his eyes, as though the creature resided within his own mind. He was not one to be afraid of simple nightmares, but something about that creature made him feel uneasy because he didn't know what it was. Everything in his life had made sense, and it was logical. That's why he could never be afraid of something, even if that something was a person like Ragash who could cave his skull in with a single blow. But this creature was unknown, and it had details unlike anything he'd ever seen before.

"Your fish is getting away," Aiph said, calling Xellik's attention to his fishing rod.

The orcling spun around and grabbed hold of the rod as it began to bend towards the sea. He gave it a firm tug and felt it fight back.

"I think it's a big one," Xellik proclaimed.

"I hope so. I'm starving," Napir said, rubbing his paunch belly.

"You're always starving," Aiph told him.

"Shut up," Napir said and began to sulk.

The fishing line went rigid and the pole bent towards the sea, but it didn't snap. Xellik pulled his arms back, tugging harshly on the line and he felt it resist. Bracing his foot against a flat, angled piece of rock, he yanked harder on the pole until he saw a splash a short distance away in the water as his catch nearly flopped out onto the shore.

"I saw it!" Aiph shouted.

With one last hard tug, the fish cleared the water and landed a few feet behind Xellik, still attached to the line with the hook protruding from the side of its mouth. It flopped around a little, trying to get back to the water, before its movements slowed as it suffocated.

Xellik wasn't familiar with what kind of fish it was. It was as long as his forearm and nearly half as tall. He was certain it would be enough to last them the rest of the day, at least until they could get a chance to go fishing again.

"One question," Cinra spoke up, drawing the attention of the other three. "How do we cook it?"

* * * * *

It was nearing dusk by the time Xellik began to head back to their encampment. He picked between his teeth using the pointed end of one of the fish's rib bones, scraping the last bit of meat off. It hadn't been the best tasting meal that he'd ever had, but it was good, and he wasn't as hungry any more. Xellik had sent Cinra to skulk about the docks and see how the Zugruli fishers prepared their catches, and had returned about an hour later with a stolen knife. They'd nearly butchered all the meat on the fish trying to scale it and remove the bones, but the effort had been worth it.

Next time they went fishing, they would know how to do a better job of cooking it.

Xellk strolled confidently into the section of the slum's that his tribe had built for themselves. It wasn't anything glorious to speak of, but the crumbling ruins filled him with a sense of home and community. Even if they were treated like scum, at least here they were safe, where they could recuperate after all their losses.

A ramshackle, two room building made up a home for Xellik, which he shared with Bytej and Haij. He popped the door open and headed inside.

Somewhere within the home, Bytej shouted to him, "You're late!"

"For what?" Xellik shouted back.

Bytej came from the other room and stood in the doorway, barring Xellik from going to his bed. "Training, what else whelp? You should've been back hours ago."

"I was hungry."

"So our tribe is to be ruled by a brat who thinks that his stomach is more important than his own training and worship of Sytarel?"

"I'd rather be able to focus on my tasks than to be wondering when I'd next get a chance to eat," Xellik shot back. "Why haven't our hunters caught us anything yet?"

"Because we're not prepared for dealing with the threats lurking in the jungles. Do you have any clue what's out there?" Bytej asked.

"Yeah, so what? Tigers and flesh-eating plants should be no danger to our warriors. If you're getting slaughtered by grass then perhaps the problem lies with the skills of our hunters."

"You don't even know the half of it until you've seen it for yourself. If you were of age I'd have half a mind to send you out with the next party to learn first hand the new challenges our tribe is facing," Bytej said with a shake of his head. "There's still the Korcyn rebels that rove the jungle, howling for orcish blood. We've been finding villages of sentient gorillas that like us even less than the Korcyn, if that were possible, and to make matters worse, there's even some less than friendly ogres lurking in there."

"I've never heard of these gorilla men. You're making that up."

"I'm not. They're only a minor nuisance, but they've hindered our hunting parties efforts nonetheless. You'd know this if you actually paid attention to the thoughts and needs of your own tribe."

"And weren't you supposed to be my counsel on such matters!?" Xeliik snapped.

"Yes, if you actually attended your training I could tell you these things."

Xellik didn't have a response for that one. The older orc had him cornered. "Whatever you old codger. Let's get on with it then."

"That dismissive attitude will get you in trouble one day," Bytej remarked as he led Xellik into the other room to begin their lessons for the evening.

Chapter 16 - Heshun of the Jintaren

15th Day of Gaia
125 I.E.

The noise in the Academy was almost deafening to Dane as young adepts moved through the halls towards their next lecture or back to the dorms. He could scarcely recall a time in his life when he'd been surrounded by so many people all at once. Not even the Harvest Festival brought in as many people as there were crammed into the tight hallways. He kept his tome close to him and tried to shuffle past the writhing bodies that talked and laughed amongst themselves in the middle of the walkways. He almost felt sad to be excluded from it all, but aside from the occasional glance in his direction, no one talked to him. He couldn't seem to bring himself to approach anyone either.

The only people that Dane ever talked to back when he lived in Tran were all adults. He never had any childhood friends. It wasn't for lack of a desire to have any close friends, but because he simply didn't know how to talk to others his age. The few times that he had attempted it back at the orphanage, he'd been teased about his manner of speaking. That shut Dane up quickly, and now he feared the same rejection from the adepts at the academy. Instead of regarding them as people, Dane thought of them as nothing more than nameless, faceless obstacles on his way to and from his various destinations in the academy.

Dane had finished a class with Talia. It had been a history lesson about the origins of the human's magic. He hated the subject, and it made him feel like he was back in Lynn's study and learning about all the boring wars that had occurred across Muriaj. He still had yet to learn how to cast a spell, but he'd been told it was because he was in a remedial class and needed to catch up first.

Normally on an odd numbered day, Dane would be headed back to his dorm to study and prepare for his next lesson. However, on this day he was headed to Professor Heshun's dojo, where he was going to begin his lessons in swordsmanship. He'd been waiting months for the jintaren's class to start over so he could begin the semester with a new group of students.

The dojo was attached to the building that housed the main lecture halls, at the edge of the Academy's grounds. Dane had only seen it in passing, and had never been inside of it. On some days when he walked by, he could hear the grunts of exertion and the clatter of metal against metal through the thick wooden door. He wondered what kind of magical apparatus or conjuration the jintaren professor used to train his students, and he felt excited at the prospect of finally finding out.

Dane snaked his way through the halls and made his way towards Heshun's dojo. When he arrived, he stood outside it, suddenly feeling nervous. He recalled how the jintaren had spoken when he first met the man, and he feared the worst when he walked in.

The door had a metal emblem nailed to it. The design was a stylized mammoth head, similar to a belt buckle that Dane had once seen Heshun wearing. It was painted red where the fur would've been, and the tusks had a pristine white color. It shone as if it was polished daily.

With his eyes closed, Dane took a deep breath and pushed the door open slowly. The hinges creaked as it moved and he suddenly felt self-conscious. He could hear someone talking, then they stopped as the door continued to move.

When Dane opened his eyes, he nearly jumped out of his skin as a sword spiraled towards him, narrowly missing him and becoming stuck in the hardwood flooring.

"Sweet merciful Xenar!" Dane shrieked as he fell backwards. The classroom erupted in a chorus of laughter, but they were quickly silenced by a sharp reprimand from Heshun.

"You're late, runt!" the jintaren shouted. He was shirtless again, wearing nothing more than a green, plaid kilt that was cinched tightly with his mammoth-buckled belt.

"What's the matter with you?" Dane yelled as he stood up, feeling his face hot with embarrassment. Just like that, his hopes of perhaps trying his hand at making some friends were dashed by Heshun's actions. "You could've taken my head off, you crazy son of a --"

"If I had intended to hit you, you'd already be dead," Heshun said, cutting him off. "Pick it up and get in here."

Dane hesitated and looked at the weapon embedded in the ground next to him. He'd never seen a sword up close, except at the orc's camp. The surface gave off a distorted reflection of himself, and he could see the uneasy expression on his face.

"Are you just going to stare at it all day? Hurry up! I have better things to do," Heshun said, exasperated. "Pick it up."

The boy reached out and let his hand grab the smooth leather grip. He swallowed hard and pulled the blade from the floor, tugging harder than was necessary and losing his balance because of it. He held it out to get a feel for the weight of the weapon. Even though the sword was fairly long, he was impressed by the fact that the tip didn't wobble around nearly as much as he expected it to when he swung the weapon.

"Don't just play with it!" Heshun snapped. "Get over here!"

Dane's face flushed again and he dropped his arms, holding the sword at his side. He walked towards Heshun and tried to ignore the snickering coming from the other students. His eyes scanned the room as he tried to avoid their gaze, and he realized that the room was lined with weapons. There were only a few spots where he could see the russet colored brick walls. The rest was covered in hooks and racks that held all manner of armaments, including swords, crossbows, longbows, halberds, spears, axes, and even hammers. They were sized for all kinds of people, from the small to the large. Dane could only gawk in amazement at the sheer selection of weapons that Heshun had at his disposal. A part of him hoped he wouldn't have to learn how to fight with all of them, and that he could stick to lighter weapons like the sword he currently held in his hand.

"Stop right there. That's close enough," Heshun commanded, snapping Dane from his thoughts.

The boy obeyed and came to a halt. He was still some distance away from the jintaren. I thought he wanted me to bring the sword to him? Why am I stopping here? He looked to the other students to figure out what was going on, but their faces were unreadable beneath their chuckling exteriors. He frowned at their behaviour. What kind of teacher allows people to act like that?

"Prepare yourself," Heshun said before he unsheathed his own sword and rushed towards Dane.

The boy only had a moment to realize what was going on before he moved out of the way of the jintaren's swing. He felt a breeze as the blade sliced vertically in front of him, and his heart began to race.

"What are you doing? You're going to kill me!" Dane exclaimed as he moved around the dojo, desperately trying to avoid Heshun. "I don't even know how to use a sword!"

"Then you'll have to learn quickly, won't you?" Heshun slashed horizontally and Dane moved back to get out of range. He wasn't nearly agile enough, and he could feel the blade bite into the skin of his arm, tearing through his robes. Dane couldn't help but scream in pain and pull his arm away, causing him to drop his sword.

He cut me! He actually cut me! Dane thought frantically as he clutched at the wound with a hand, trying to cover it and stem the flow of blood. He could feel the crimson fluid running between his fingers. *I didn't sign up for this!*

"What are you doing? You can't just drop your weapon!" Heshun told him as he hacked at Dane's undefended chest with a series of shallow cuts that assaulted him from several different directions.

Each time the sword raked his flesh, Dane let out a howl of pain and tried to stay one step ahead of the jintaren, but he was quickly finding it impossible to keep up with a veteran warrior like Heshun. He lacked the experience to be able to stand up to him, and once again, he found his powerlessness only infuriated him.

"Why are you doing this?" Dane asked.

"I wish to see what Sylenthros' favorite is capable of." A heavy booted foot swung out and struck the boy in the stomach, causing him to crumple and tumble backwards. Dane's breath was knocked out of him, and he struggled to stand again. Streaks of blood marred the ground from where Dane had hit. "Apparently, not much."

As he coughed, Dane managed to say, "Of course I'm not capable of anything, I don't even know how to fight! Why would you think otherwise?" He sat up on his knees, and realized that Heshun had ceased trying to attack him. Dane remained sitting there and tried to catch his breath. He wiped blood away from the corners of his mouth. His body screamed at him to stop moving and he could feel his heart thumping away in his throat. "Do you do this to everyone in the class?"

Heshun wouldn't respond to his question. Instead, the jintaren moved to where Dane had dropped the sword. The professor put his foot on the hilt and then gave it a firm kick. The blade slid across the ground and came to a halt just in front of Dane.

"You're not getting off that easy boy. Pick it up and let's go."

"Why should I?"

"If you want to complete your training as a mage, then you'll need to complete my course," Heshun replied simply. "And I only train those I deem worthy of my time. So far, you've done little to prove yourself to me."

Dane grabbed his sword, but didn't stand up. "Why should I let you hurt me? If I wasn't jumping around to get away from you, I'd probably be missing an arm!" He looked to the other students in the class. "Did he do this to you, too?"

One boy, a round child that wore a robe several sizes too large, tried to say something, but Heshun put a hand out to silence him. The jintaren moved into position and brought his sword to bear once again.

"I think you have more important things to worry about than them!" He shouted and charged at Dane once again.

Dane let out a squeal as he rose to his feet and jumped to the side. When he landed, he stumbled as his feet threatened to give out under him. Heshun was quick to follow up and attacked his unprotected flank, an act that sent Dane back to the ground.

He's much too quick for someone that size, Dane thought, trying to figure out some way to avoid Heshun's blade.

"Do you think you can win a battle by dancing around?" Heshun spat. When he tried to attack again, Dane tried to bring his sword up to deflect the blow like he'd seen soldiers do, but the force of the jintaren's attack caught him off guard and he dropped the sword again. This time, however, he scrambled to pick it back up and tried again. "Looks like you can learn."

Now Dane was trying frantically to parry Heshun's attacks. He was succeeding most of the time, but with each attempt the jintaren's attacks became more aggressive as he tried to poke holes in his defenses. He began to combine his maneuverability with his new found ability to parry attacks, which succeeded for a time. He was quickly tiring himself out while Heshun was still going at him full force.

How am I supposed to attack him? He's not giving me a chance to do anything! Dane looked over his shoulder and realized he was getting close to the wall. He'd be cornered if he didn't try anything. When he tried to step to the left or right, Heshun pressed that side and prevented him from moving. He was forcing him to move back towards the wall, where Dane would likely be unable to get away from his attacks.

Just before reaching the wall of weapons, Dane made an attempt to cut Heshun's sword arm. However, his weapon was slapped aside by a fierce parry and he received another gash across his chest for his efforts. A thrust was met with the same results, and he nearly dropped his sword for a third time.

Still the wall was getting closer, and Dane began to panic. *Why should my fate be decided by some unfair match up against a more experienced fighter? This is absurd!*

As they distanced themselves from the students, Heshun got in close to Dane and whispered, "If this is how you fought in Tran, it's no surprise those orcs overpowered you so easily."

"What?" Dane gawked in disbelief, and he could feel a sharp pain in his side as the blade bit his skin, just above his robe's sash. "You have no right to talk to me about Tran! You weren't there."

"I don't need to have been there to see that you're just a weakling," the swordsman sneered.

Dane could feel a hot flash surging through his body. What right did Heshun have to judge him because of what happened?

Keep a clear head, Dane told himself. He remembered how his frustration got in the way of doing things when he was back home. He couldn't aim a bow when he was angry, and it would be the same thing with the sword if he gave in to his emotions.

Dane parried a swing to the side, then faked left. Heshun tried to bring his blade around but the boy was too quick, ducking under his arm and darting to the right. Finally free of the threat that the wall presented, Dane was able to maneuver around and attack the jintaren's unprotected side. Heshun proved quick enough to turn around, but Dane had anticipated it. He stepped towards Heshun, trying to get closer so his larger opponent couldn't use his sword as effectively. His own blade came up and he managed to get a small, shallow cut across the jintaren's exposed stomach.

Dane tried to follow through and strike again as confidence washed over him. He would win whatever game Heshun was playing at. As he swung, a thick hand harshly grabbed his wrist and twisted until he let go of the sword.

"Don't be so proud of yourself. That was just beginner's luck." Heshun reached down with his other hand and grabbed Dane under his arms. "But since you seem so happy, here's a reward for your efforts." The jintaren hoisted him into the air. The boy kicked as he was lifted above the man's head before he was hurled across the room, back towards the door. Dane hollered as he soared through the air, and he tried to catch himself on the floor. He fell with a loud thump and felt his chin split as he hit the ground. All Dane could manage was a weak groan as he tried to stand back up.

"Go get yourself cleaned up, and come back after class has adjourned!" Heshun yelled at him, then began to go back to instructing the rest of the students.

* * * * *

There were no healers at the Academy to Dane's knowledge. The only person who could treat his wounds was a doctor that worked on campus who was in charge of looking after the students. He was an elderly man and his hands felt ice cold as he applied bandages all too tightly to Dane's wounds while he muttered complaints about Heshun's harsh teaching methods. Every time the old doctor's frozen skin touched Dane's, he shivered and fought the urge to pull away as he was being patched up. It was like being touched by the hand of Shinixuroc, and he wondered how much time the doctor had left in this world.

Once his wounds were taken care of, Dane walked back through the Academy to get to the dojo. The door creaked open as he pushed on it, and he found no one inside except for Heshun, who was busy cleaning up some of the armaments.

When the professor heard the door open, he turned to Dane and said, "Hurry up and close the door. I don't have all day." He took the sword he'd been cleaning and placed it back on its rack before moving to meet the boy in the middle of the room.

Dane walked cautiously and kept a close eye on Heshun's movements. He didn't know what to expect, but he surmised that nothing good would come out of meeting the jintaren one-on-one like he was. His wounds still stung and he felt light headed, even after having some magical poultice derived from elfin herb applied to his cuts to soothe the pain.

At least he's unarmed, but he still looks like he could rip me in half with his bare hands. No wonder the jintaren thought they could conquer Rogust.

"Sit." Heshun took a seat on his knees at the center of the room, and gestured for Dane to follow suit. When he didn't make a move to sit on the floor, the jintaren's face scrunched up in a scowl. "I told you to sit. I expect you to listen, especially if you want me to train you."

Dane eased himself to the ground and tried to kneel the same way Heshun was, but he found it hard on his knees and he ended up adjusting so he was sitting down on his backside, propping himself up with one arm. There was a short silence between the two of them before he asked, "Do you intend to tell me what that whole ambush was about?"

"What is there to discuss?" Heshun asked, "I wanted to see why Sylenthros has so much hope for you. Nothing more, and nothing less."

"I've barely spoken to Professor Leafsblade, let alone been instructed by him," Dane replied. "I have no idea what kind of 'hopes' you're talking about."

"Human children are too ignorant. They are unaware of their surroundings."

"And I suppose the jintaren are so much better?" Dane shot back.

"The jintaren are raised to be aware of what's occurring around them," Heshun said. "We're not left in the dark because of petty ideas about whether children can handle reality or not. Only a fool thinks a child can be brought up properly by sheltering them from everything."

"I wasn't brought up ignorantly!" Dane said as he began to feel hot in the face. "How can I be blind to something that doesn't exist?"

"You can't see it because you've closed yourself off to the possibility. One day, perhaps you'll realize it."

Dane tried to think back on the few times he'd spoken to Sylenthros, but nothing stood out to him that would suggest the elf was playing favorites with him.

"You don't like Professor Leafsblade, do you?"

"That's none of your concern," Heshun said with a grunt.

So that's probably a 'no', then, Dane thought, unsurprised by

Heshun's response. The jintaren was all business. He didn't have time for fooling around, and more importantly, he was impatient. He wanted things done his way, and he wanted them done yesterday. On the other hand, Sylenthros came off as jolly, almost a bit fey in his behaviour. He liked to joke and grind on people's nerves on purpose as he gauged their reactions. Sylenthros and Heshun were like water and oil. Those two would never get along.

"At any rate, you've passed your first test, and you can begin training with the rest of your classmates starting tomorrow."

"What, that's it?" Dane asked, snapping his head up to look at Heshun. "That spar was the first test?"

"I won't train anyone who can't learn to hold a sword, and I'll push them until they can." Heshun gestured to the cut across his stomach. It looked like nothing more than a cat scratch that had dragged its way across his torso. "You were sloppy and your technique needs work if you're going to succeed in my class, but that's why I'm here."

"Will I only be learning how to use a sword?"

"Hardly. I have weapons from all over Galria, in different lengths and sizes. The greatest warrior is a well-rounded one who can improvise and use any weapon in any given situation. Just because you can hold a blade doesn't mean you can handle a poleaxe or a staff."

"And what about magic? I haven't even learned any yet," Dane told him. So far all he'd been taught was the basic theory behind magic and how to inscribe and understand simple runes.

"That can come later," Heshun said. "There's no point in working magic into your swordplay if you can't wield a weapon yet."

"Did you do that same test with all your students?"

"Yes," Heshun replied simply. There was a short pause, then he added, "Is there anything else?"

After thinking about it, Dane couldn't come up with anything. "I suppose not. I'll learn more as I go along."

"Good, because I'm not answering anything else," Heshun said as he rose to his feet. "Be here promptly tomorrow afternoon after your final lecture of the day. If you're late, you'll have to spar against me again to stay in the class."

"Yes sir," Dane said. He hoped that Heshun would go easier on him in the future, now that he'd passed the man's test.

Just keep a cool head, he reminded himself, *and you'll do fine.*

Chapter 17 - Acquisition

3rd Day of Aegis
125 I.E.

Xellik was awoken by the crash of the door. He sprang out of bed, half expecting that perhaps one of the other casteless in the slums were trying to steal something. He stomped down the hall to see what the noise was as the handle of a sword began to materialize in his hand.

He stayed his blade when he saw Ragash silhouetted by the sunlight pouring in the doorway. He was holding someone by a length of chain that rattled in his hands.

"Get in there!" Ragash shoved a manacled korcyn into the hall as the beastman fell to the ground. The chains linked to his collar made a ruckus as they clattered on the floor.

The korcyn squealed as he smacked his snout on the ground. He curled into a tight ball and held his now bleeding nose, trying in vain to keep the blood from dripping all over the place. Xellik looked down at the thing before him with hate in his eyes. What were on of the Zugrul's pets doing in his home? It stunk of sweat and grime, and he wondered whether the filthy thing even knew how to bathe.

Bristled grey fur covered the korcyn's body. A mane of disheveled black hair ran from the top of his head all the way to the base of his short tail. The only clothing on his back was a sleeveless cotton vest and baggy cotton pants that were cinched closed with a piece of frayed rope. His clothes were stained yellow with sweat.

It was probably all that this slave owned. Xellik didn't imagine many of them were allowed fresh clothes or even a place to keep them. Giving them clothes was likely an industry in itself, and he wondered why the Zugrul bothered to waste resources clothing their slaves, even if they were only giving them third rate goods.

"Why did you bring this disgusting thing into my home?" Xellik demanded, looking up at Ragash with a frown.

"Bytej asked that I obtain a slave," he replied with a huff. "Damn thing put up a fight as I dragged it through the slums. It's little wonder why the Zugrul dockworkers wanted to be rid of it."

"We can barely feed ourselves as it is. How are we supposed to feed this thing?" Xellik asked. He poked the korcyn with the tip of his boot and watched it wilt away from him. "Pathetic. Why should we have one of these things around anyways?"

Ragash shrugged, rolling his thick shoulders as he moved. He turned his nose up at Xellik and his lip curled. "Just following the leader's orders."

"I'm the leader of our clan."

"A whelp like you can barely lead your little troop of orclings," Ragash rebuked. "I've heard how you and my nephew fight. Almost completely one-upped you, hasn't he? He's stronger and thinks things through better than you do. It's amazing you're Fellis' child. You should be stronger than Aiph, yet somehow you manage to screw even that up."

Xellik's face contorted with rage, yet he did his best to control himself. Nothing good would come out of trying to raise his hand against Ragash, and it was clear that the seasoned warrior was trying to rile him up. Maybe he wanted to be rid of him just as much as Tamril did back in the mountains, and he was looking for an excuse to draw his blade. Xellik watched Ragash's movements carefully, seeing how he thumbed the sword sheathed at his hip. He was itching to have an excuse to draw it.

Despite how physically outmatched Xellik was, he wanted desperately to try to put the other orc in his place. He should have been bending his knees in service of him, not opposing him at every turn. What was the point of being the future leader of the clan if no one listened to him? Perhaps things would change in a couple years after his coming of age ceremony. Until then, he supposed he would have to bide his time and wait to show Ragash that he was beneath him, even if it pained him to do so.

Bytej came out of his room as he toweled off his hands. He seemed more than a little overjoyed to see that Ragash had acquired a korcyn slave, and grinned widely from ear to ear.

"Excellent work my friend. How much did you have to pay for him?" Bytej asked, tossing the cloth aside on a nearby table.

"Had to trade a pair of swords," Ragash said, and frowned. "I feel like we were ripped off. They were going to kill it anyways, I don't see why they wanted anything for us taking it off their hands."

Bytej knelt down to inspect their new slave. "It's a shame to lose those weapons, but at least now we have someone to help us get more acquainted with our surroundings. Looks a little on the young side, from what I can tell." He prodded the korcyn when he had stopped writhing on the ground, and looked up at him with black, beady eyes. "Name and age, slave."

"Garro. 13." The korcyn's voice was harsh and scratchy. Xellik wondered if it had made it's throat hoarse from screaming every time its masters beat it, or if it always sounded like that. In either case, the sound of the thing annoyed him.

"A bit stringy, too. . ." Bytej murmured as he held up the korcyn's arm and examined it.

"We tend to have a growth spurt near our twenties," Garro replied. The shape of his mouth and positioning of his tusks made him difficult to understand as he stumbled over the orcish language.

"Did we say you could talk, slave?" Xellik shouted. The thing deigned to speak out of turn. He raised a hand to smack it, but Bytej grabbed his wrist.

"That's not necessary," he said, admonishing the young orcling. "That's knowledge that I didn't have before. It would be a pity if we taught him not to speak about something important when the opportunity arises."

"Why are you being nice to it? It's a slave. It's supposed to be beneath us!"

"I'm not being 'nice', I'm merely trying to learn more about him," Bytej said. "How is a slave to perform if it's always beaten by others?"

Xellik found he couldn't come up with an answer. He still didn't understand how they planned to keep the korcyn in check and to prevent it from rebelling if they didn't reign it in with physical threats. He begrudgingly acknowledged that Bytej had a point. An injured slave was a useless one. If they were harmed, they wouldn't be able to work.

Damn it all, I hate when he's right.

"You may go," Bytej said dismissively to Ragash. The warrior nodded, cast a disapproving glance in Xellik's direction, then walked out into the morning sunlight. Bytej stood up and close the door behind him, muttering his aggravation at Ragash's lack of civility.

"Why did you want one of these things so desperately?" Xellik asked.

"For a lot of reasons, whelp," Bytej said, helping Garro to his feet. "What kind of work did you do before?"

Garro looked thoughtful for a moment, "I've had lots of masters in the past --"

"Must have been useless at your job, slave," Xellik said. Bytej smacked him in the back of the head. "Fine! I'll let it finish."

Garro looked uneasily between Bytej and Xellik, and continued after the older orc gave him the go ahead to speak. "I worked the docks for the last year, but before that I was a carpenter, a scribe, and a gardener."

Bytej nodded his head. "Good. I could use some help getting a garden started for food." He met Garro's black eyes. "That will be your first task. Understood?"

The korcyn nodded. He looked relieved to be given such a simple task, and it disgusted Xellik. If the dock workers were going to have him gutted, he couldn't have been good at anything. It was bad enough this slave had likely seen the splendor of the city itself, and supped on better food than what the Fergoth had been eating, but to now know they were relying on someone like this infuriated him. The korcyn were slaves, created by magic to serve the orcs. It should have been relying on them to survive by the orcs' sheer will to allow them to live, not the other way around.

"Haij! Get out here!" Bytej called, his voice so loud it shook the already fragile foundations of their home.

The other orc stumbled down the hall, exhausted and rubbing his eyes. "What did you need? I was having a good dream. . ."

"This is Garro, our clan's new slave," Bytej said, gesturing to the korcyn. "He'll be assisting us in getting a garden started for our clan. You're going to look after him for the time being."

"What?" Haij asked, surprised. "Why me?"

"Because Xellik is more likely to kill him than use him."

"Hey!" Xellik snapped, whirling on Bytej. "What do you mean by that?"

"Exactly what I said." Bytej handed Garro's chain off to Haij. "Don't be too rough with him. We need him to work, not to beat. Got it?"

Haij grumbled a response and left with Garro to obtain the

supplies they needed to start growing some food. Xellik glared as he watched the korcyn leave. Just as it was about to leave the door, he could have sworn he saw Garro glaring back at him with an equal intensity.

"I don't trust that thing," Xellik grumbled.

"Noted. Now if you'll excuse me, I have things to do," Bytej said, leaving Xellik to fume on his own.

Xellik didn't understand. Garro acted cowed by the orcs' actions, but that final look he gave him suggested something else underlying the korcyn's mind. Possibly even something sinister. Xellik decided that it would probably be best to sleep with his door barricaded at night.

Chapter 18 - Sylenthros

27th Day of Manul
125 I.E.

The largest building on campus was Mauro Hall. It sat planted in front of the Ivory Tower, and housed all of the school's lecture halls and training rooms. It was given the name of the Academy's founder, Doctor Van Mauro. In addition to Heshun's dojo, there were several research and development rooms for spell work, one of the largest libraries that Dane had ever seen, the infirmary, and more lecture halls than he cared to count. He couldn't fathom how everything fit into Mauro Hall, and yet somehow, it did.

The Hall's unusual shape encompassed the majority of the academy's land, and it was clear from how brick met plaster in places that the building had been expanded to allow for newer facilities in more recent times. The latest addition that Dane had had the pleasure of seeing was the observatory constructed and run by a gnomish scholar. The gnome had a peculiar notion that the Gods were somewhere in the sky and that one need only see far enough to be able to prove they existed. He had wide-ranging theories on why this was, but unfortunately he had little ability to communicate them with others. As the gnome grew more excited explaining his research, he would begin to talk faster until his words were a high-pitched, jumbled mess of sounds.

While Dane wasn't sure whether to believe his theories or not, he did enjoy seeing through the telescope at night to view the stars while listening to the scatterbrained professor's stories. The sky was beautiful up close, and on rare occasions it was even possible to see other planets that shared the sky with Galria or even the pock-marked surfaces of the moons.

That's where Dane wished he could be. Instead, he was in Mauro Hall's northern wing, listening to a lesson being given my Talia Frostfire. He shifted uncomfortably in his seat. The chair was cheaply made and poorly cushioned, and he wondered if it was made that way to keep people from falling asleep during lectures.

The class was still discussing the most basic rules of magic and had only touched upon theoretical topics. There had been countless written tests that put Lynn's questions to shame, and despite all his best efforts to avoid having to become a scholar, it seemed as though he had no other choice if he wanted to become a sorcerer.

Despite what his imagination told him, reality had proven that magic was more about being cautious and discussing the hypothetical rather than actually doing anything practical.

Dane leaned forward and rested his chin on the palm of his hand. The only thing he was grateful for was that he was ahead of most of the class. He'd memorized the earliest chapters of his texts and was performing better than he'd expected during proficiency tests. He supposed that Lynn's lessons had been good for something, afterall. They'd certainly done their job of preparing him for a scholarly life.

The class of students was made up of a palty group of individuals who had come into the academy mid-semester, and were therefore required to play catch up with the rest of the students. Dane quickly learned from his time attending Talia's lectures that, while she was thorough in explaining topics and the why behind them, she had a lot of problems making said topics interesting. Her manner of speaking was dry, devoid of humor, and lacked any real world application.

"Magic is not fun and games. It has its limits, and you need to be aware of them," Talia said. She stood at the front of the classroom, reading periodically from a large tome. "The mana that fuels our magic is in the air and in everything around us. Even inside us. We practitioners of the arcane are able to manipulate that energy to fuel our spells. We focus on channeling mana from our surroundings to keep us from burning out own body's natural mana."

She looked up from her book and sighed. A few students had their heads down in their desks, clearly half-asleep. She slammed her thick book shut, causing a noise akin to a thunderclap to echo through the room. The individuals not paying attention were quick to jump upright in their seats and face forward.

"Adepts are people born with the physical ability to manipulate mana," Talia continued when she saw that no one else was napping during her lecture. "That's what makes us different from other mortals, who are incapable of learning how to perform magic. It's important to keep in mind that channeling mana results in our bodies storing excess energy, resulting in a condition called Mage Poisoning. This is because of the body's physiological inability to handle excess mana without burning up. Skilled sorcerers are able to channel mana to such a degree that they store less and less energy within their bodies to keep from burning out as quickly."

"Using your own body's mana would be equally as foolish, as you'll rapidly cause yourself to wither away and die. This means learning to channel is necessary, but it has drawbacks. If you channel too much mana without resting and letting the energy dissipate from your body, you will suffer for it. You can cause yourself to bleed out from spontaneously erupting wounds, cause internal hemorrhaging, or any number of other things."

It can't possibly be that bad, Dane thought. The books he read touched on the consequences of abusing magic, but it didn't worry Dane. There were healers at the ursar temple down the way. If he was injured in any way, it wouldn't be hard to get outside help.

"Always keep in mind how much energy you require for each spell you are casting. Careless, rapid abuse of magic will get you killed, even from simple scribings spells if they are taken to the extreme," Talia explained. She licked a finger and flipped the page. "Though such foolishness is rare, there are still morons out there who think they can handle more than their body is capable of. Please refer to case study #367B: The Fiend of a Thousand Quills in your texts for more information."

It was a simple enough lesson, but that's what made it so boring for Dane. He thought magic would be more about learning how to control the elements or work wonders. He never expected to have to learn such boring topics as conservation of mana and scroll work.

"It is important that you remember this, as it will be a key element in your final proficiency test at the end of your studies."

Dane perked up when she mentioned the Test of Magehood. The professors at the academy often mentioned it whenever they discussed something important, but the students had no idea what the test entailed. Their texts offered no help either, and gave only vague and cryptic clues. He was certain that it wasn't a good thing that so much of the Test was shrouded in mystery, and the professors mentioned that the test was a dangerous one undertaken only when a wizard was truly ready for it, in both mind and body. Dane could only imagine what kind of work it would involve, and how dangerous it could be.

"That's it for today," Talia said as she slammed her tome shut again. Dane slumped back in his chair. He was hoping she would reveal more about the final Test, but as always she remained quiet about it, never giving more than a tiny hint throughout her lectures. "Go to your rooms and study chapter eleven from your textbooks. We'll be beginning basic elemental magic starting with fire evocation next class, so be prepared. Class dismissed."

Finally, Dane thought, *I've been waiting forever to get into magic. I'm so tired of theory!*

Everyone stood up at once and their chairs screeched across the floor as they scraped the wooden floor boards. People rushed out of the room to get to their next lecture, colliding in the doorway and squeezing their way through one at a time like a pile of debris through a small stream. Dane remained seated for a few moments until the stampede was nothing more than a trickle. He didn't like shoving his way past a crowd of bratty children, and he didn't want to get trampled on the way out. He snatched up his book and left the lecture hall once he was one of the only few students remaining. As Dane walked out of the door, he was greeted by a voice coming from behind and to the right.

"Greetings, young Master Trueshot."

Dane looked over his shoulder to see Sylenthros standing at ease against the brick wall next to the open door. He wore the same forest green robes that he always wore, and that never seemed to get dirty. His hair framed his face perfectly, as if he had maintained its luster and health through the use of his druidic magic.

"Good morning, sir," Dane said.

"Do you have a moment? I was hoping I'd have a chance to speak with you today." Sylenthros stepped towards the boy, keeping his hands behind his back and smiling. The elf's silver eyes shimmered in the light cast by a luminescent globe that hung on the wall behind Dane.

"Master Heshun said there was no class today. I have nothing else to do until tomorrow."

"Ah, splendid." Sylenthros stepped forward and placed a hand on Dane's back, between his shoulder blades. "Come, walk with me. Let's talk in the garden where it's quiet. It's a fairly warm day out, too, so I'm sure you could use the fresh air."

"Can we talk as we go?" Dane asked, and the elf nodded in response. "What did you want to talk to me about?"

"I wanted to know if you were still curious about your father."

"Why would I want to know about him? He was nothing but a tyrant all my life."

"Well, you had expressed such an interest when we first met that I'd only assumed you'd become more curious with time, Master Trueshot," Sylenthros pointed out. "But, if you've changed your mind, that's fine, too. I understand that it's been awhile since we last spoke, so you'll have to forgive me if things are different now. I often forget that humans have a shorter life span and are prone to seemingly random changes in mood and disposition." The elf grinned at him and Dane could swear he saw a gleam in his eyes as he looked down on him.

"Stop calling me 'Master Trueshot', I hate that name! And human beings aren't as flighty as you make us seem!" Dane shot back, then mentally slapped himself for the remark. He realized that was exactly the response that Sylenthros had wanted.

"Oh, so I take it then that you're still interested?"

"No! I mean, I thought I was before --"

"Well good! Good," Sylenthros cut him off, insuring that Dane could not continue his line of thinking. "I can tell you about him, and maybe even a bit about your mother. I'm sure you've been dying to know what they were like." Sylenthros began to walk out of the building, and Dane found himself reluctantly following the druid.

"I met your father in a little village north of Tran called Ingrad. I doubt you've heard of it, since it's a rather small agricultural town," Sylenthros began. Dane didn't have the heart to correct him. He was well aware of the town that had played a vital role in the defense of Rogust during the Jintaren Incursion so many years ago. "It was an unimportant plot of land as far as the Rogarian

Empire was concerned, though." The elf shrugged as he walked. "It was a time of peace, and the Empire's military was --"

"I'm not really interested in a history lesson, sir," Dane interrupted. He didn't care if it was rude, he didn't want to listen to someone ramble on about some war from so long ago that it was barely relevant to him in the first place. "I've already learned plenty about the Jintaren Incursion from my teacher in Tran."

Sylenthros smiled, but Dane could tell it annoyed the elf as he cocked a single eyebrow and looked at him out of the corner of his eyes. "Very well. Long story short then, the military had few resources and the jintaren from the Northlands were pushing down into Rogarian territory. That's where the Blackguard and your father came in."

"Why was he in Ingrad?"

"He'd been living there for a number of years with a friend while they were employed in the Blackguard, and he was present when the jintaren began their march into our territory. The military forced the mercenaries stationed there into helping with the defense effort."

Stepping through the gate into the garden, Sylenthros pulled his robes to the side as he ascended a short staircase, ensuring the bottoms did not get marred by dust and dirt. "I was up there doing some research. This garden here is the fruit of my labor." He noted the bored expression on Dane's face, then rolled his eyes. "Your father had been living in Ingrad and I'd met him several times before hand. I'd even employed him myself at one point. I'll leave the details about that out, since I seem to be boring you."

"Did he ever say why he was in the Blackguard?" Dane asked, "Growing up, he taught me that mercenaries are the bottom feeders of society."

"Pity. He never said why."

"So what did he do with the jintaren came?"

"Humans. Always so impatient. . ." Sylenthros sighed before continuing. "The military abandoned the village after their general was killed in the opening battle. Master Trueshot managed to rally the villagers together and we bottlenecked the jintaren forces in the valley north of town until we could collapse the mountain pass right on top of their armies. He saved that village, and countless lives from the surrounding area."

"Wait, that man was responsible for the collapse of the Tarqaron Valley?" Dane asked. "The books I'd read and Professor Lynn both said that the collapse was engineered by the military and its mages."

"Is that so? Hah. That's a good one," Sylenthros said with a hearty chuckle. "As if a human mage would be capable of creating a landslide. They're about as skilled at the Craft as a newborn is at walking. To set the record straight, the book and your teacher are both wrong. I should know, since I was the one responsible for causing the earthquake that collapsed Tarqaron."

Dane was confused, and he scratched at an annoying itch on the top of his head. "That's impossible. How could one person do that? You're pulling my leg."

"Am I?" Sylenthros asked.

Dane was going to respond, but then he began to feel a tremor in the ground beneath him. It grew in intensity until he heard the crash of some clay shingles from off a nearby roof.

"What's happening?" he asked, looking around him.

"It would appear we're experiencing an earthquake," Sylenthros said, standing casually before him.

The shaking started to become more intense by the second. Dane gaped at Sylenthros in surprise. Was he playing a game on him?

"You created an earthquake just to prove a point?"

"I'm hurt you would ever accuse me of such an awful thing."

Sylenthros mockingly swooned as if his pride had been wounded. The tremors eased off and ceased all at once, and everything was strangely quiet. "But yes, I did cause the earth to shake just now."

"But. . . that can't be true! The books I read said that it took a score of the military's mages to collapse the mountain side."

"Well, it seems the military likes to bend the truth to protect its image. I can assure you that I was the one responsible. I wouldn't lie. Besides, I'm many centuries older than the longest lived human. I've had plenty of time to hone my Craft and become a master of druidic magic."

"Okay fine, I'll just say I believe you." Dane tried not to sound too annoyed by the elf's antics, and decided to change the subject. "What was my mother doing in Ingrad? Father never spoke of her."

Sylenthros stroked his chin. "I can't tell you much. I only knew her as a healer working for the military in that village. Frankly, I didn't even know her name until after the opening battle when she was wounded by a jintaren sorcerer. While she was pregnant with you, in fact."

"So. . . it was the jintaren who killed my mother?" Dane asked.

"Perhaps indirectly. Their magics may have affected both you and her. There's a reason we tell mages not to cast spells on pregnant women, and why mages who are themselves pregnant should wear dampeners to prevent harming the child. I imagine it would've been rough on your mother, who had expended all of her energy fending off the jintaren while simultaneously being struck by a spell of their own."

"I didn't know my mother was a mage."

"She wasn't. She was a cleric of Xenar, the All-Healer."

Dane nodded his head. "So, that's why father prayed to Xenar every night." He fell silent again. It was a lot to take in at once for the young boy. His mother knew how to use magic while working with the military, and his father was a mercenary in an adventurer's guild. He clenched his fists and gritted his teeth, wishing he could ask his old man why all this information had been hidden from him.

"Are you happy to know more about your family?" Sylenthros smiled.

Dane scoffed. "What family? I never had any family. I only ever lived with a tyrant, and he died last year. He forced me to become a scholar against my will. I never wanted to study history or to be stuck in a library all day!"

"Isn't that what you're doing right now?" Sylenthros asked. "By my recollection, you're still studying theory."

"We're starting magic tomorrow. And I'm working towards becoming a sorcerer, not a scholar!"

Sylenthros shook his head in dismay as he clicked his tongue. "There isn't a single scholar in Rogust that isn't also a mage."

Dane paused. "That's what Lynn said, too." He was silent for a long moment, and Sylenthros afforded him this as he thought. "But, that means I was always fated to become a sorcerer, wasn't I?"

"I can't speak of your father's plans," Sylenthros said, "But he was aware of your mother's condition. He knew you would likely end up with the Gift for magic. You would have ended up in the capital to train at some point. That's probably why he pushed you so hard in your studies."

Dane almost dropped to his knees, but the elf proved himself more deft than he initially appeared as he caught him and held him up. He couldn't believe what he was hearing. "Does this mean he died for nothing? I ran away and fought with him for no reason?"

The elf turned his head away from Dane to inspect a large-leafed plant. He reached out with a hand and ran his fingers along the veined surface of the leaf, leaving behind a trail of shimmering green lights that slowly faded away. "That's possible, but that's also part of life. We don't know what the future is like, so we can only make decisions in the present. You may think ill of your father, but to myself and many others, he was a hero. He earned the respect of his peers and many more."

Dane frowned, seeking solace in his anger. Whatever guilt he may have felt was quickly buried beneath his animosity towards his father. "You respect a hero who struck his own son? That's pathetic."

"Perhaps." He looked back over his shoulder at Dane. "Or perhaps I think highly of the hero who saved his son, and countless others when they needed him."

"You are aware that it's aggravating when you undermine me like that, right?"

"Perhaps." The elf repeated, smiling knowingly.

Dane hesitated before speaking again. He was trying to keep his frustration in check, and to avoid talking himself into a corner. "Is that all?"

"Not quite." Sylenthros spun around, wearing a scowl on his face. "Remember this, Dane. You can't run from who you are. The past has a way of catching up to us mortals regardless of how fast we try to outrun it. No matter how hard you try to act differently, you are still your father's son and you are still a Trueshot."

It was the first time Dane had ever seen Sylenthros with a serious expression. He was no longer smiling and his face was fixated upon him. He swallowed hard, and though he wanted to back away, his legs refused to move. "You can hate Jonathan Trueshot as much as you want, but he will always be right here." The elf extended a finger and pressed it onto the center of Dane's forehead. "Everything you've known and have been taught has been because of him. Even though Jon is dead, he will continue to be a factor in your life, and you'd do well not to forget that."

Dane fought back the urge to slap Sylenthros' hand away. "Can I go now?" he asked with a huff.

Sylenthros' stern expression melted away and was replaced with yet another smile. "If you'd like."

Dane excused himself and retreated in the direction of the student dormitory. What did the elf know about his struggles with his father? He probably hadn't been with his parents in several hundred years, at least! He didn't understand. Sylenthros was trying to fill his head with all these sympathetic ideas to keep him from hating his precious hero.

As Dane stomped through the garden's threshold, he felt an unnatural breeze that blew past him even though the air was still. He stopped and looked around, trying to find the source of whatever it was that was creating the feeling. That's when he heard Talia's voice coming from somewhere close by.

"That wasn't necessary, you know."

Dane crept along the bushes and peered between their leaves. Talia slowly shimmered into view as she removed an invisibility spell. He could see her standing behind Sylenthros, near the big leafed plant that the elf had touched moments before. "I know you liked this Jonathan but --"

"My, looks like a little bird just dropped in," Sylenthros said loudly over his shoulder, interrupting her mid-sentence. "Good morning, Mistress Frostfire, I see you're still wearing that tacky robe of yours."

"Stuff it, pointy-ears," Talia snapped. The elf merely smiled at her weak retort. "The boy shouldn't be pushed like that, it's his job to figure things out on his own."

"Perhaps," Sylenthros finally met her gaze. "But, sooner is better than later. It's not as if humans have a long life-span like that of a race as glorious as the elves, so it's better he gets things sorted out now rather than when he's on his deathbed in a few years."

Why that arrogant bastard! Dane thought. Fortunately, Talia jumped in for his sake.

"He's got a few decades ahead of him, you dolt!"

"There's not much difference between a few years and a few decades when one lives centuries," Sylenthros pointed out, with a grin on his face.

"Whatever the case may be, he has plenty of time to learn things on his own and to develop his own perceptions of the world around him. And you shouldn't be forcing that on him when he's still young."

"Was that all you came to tell me?" Sylenthros said in a falsetto. Was he mimicking something Talia had said at one point? Dane thought his demeanor was oddly childish for someone so powerful. How did someone like that end up on the Council of Five?

He thought it would be best for him to leave while his professors were still arguing. He didn't want to be caught. The foliage he hid behind offered only a small amount of camouflage as small coins of light dotted the walkway behind him. He pulled back from the bush slowly so as not to rustle it, and tiptoed away.

"Our agents have finished compiling their information about the Tran incident," Talia said.

Dane stopped in his tracks and listened, his curiosity piqued. He didn't realize that the Council was still investigating the incident. It shouldn't have surprised him. The whole affair seemed far too important to them, leading Dane to believe that there was more going on than they let on. Maybe they feared the orcs, but he couldn't imagine that anyone could be more powerful than the sorcerers who inhabited the academy. From what he'd seen, the orcs were primitive at best, with tents that barely passed as shelter and wearing the skin of animals over their bodies. They couldn't possibly hold that much power, at least not compared to Talia or Sylenthros.

"They're a year too late," Sylenthros replied with a sigh. "What did they find out?"

"It's faint, but there's still a trace amount of magical energy in the area," Talia explained. "Just enough for them to sense even after all this time. They mentioned that it felt extra-planar. Whatever the Fergoth were doing, it was in an attempt to pull something into this world."

"Sytarel?" Sylenthros asked seriously.

"More likely an avatar of Sytarel, not the Goddess herself. They were using Tran's children as energy for their ritual," Talia said.

Dane's breath caught in his throat. They only wanted him and the others to open a portal?

Wait, the body has mana in it, Dane recalled from Talia's lecture earlier. *Is it more than what's in the air? Was there not enough mana in the area for them to complete their ritual? That must have been why they needed sacrifices, so they could burn extra mana to make their ritual work.*

"With the added benefit of killing off the next generation of humans," Sylenthros added. "Anything else?"

"Not much. The trail goes cold as it heads into the mountains, so we have no idea where the Fergoth fled. There were also sightings of dire wolves in the area, suggesting that the orcs' ritual has had an effect on the wildlife."

"Pity. Those forests were pristine and untouched by anyone," Sylenthros said, sounding sad. "I'll have to make a trip up there and calm the beasts down. Other than that, there shouldn't be any lasting impacts of the orcs actions. My guess is wherever they are now, they won't be able to make a repeat performance."

"There's still the impact the incident had on Tran and the survivors," Talia pointed out. "Namely Dane."

"My dear Talia, are you developing a soft-spot for the child? I had thought you were a stone-cold ice queen with the way you approach teaching your students," Sylenthros' perpetual grin had returned full force.

Talia opened her mouth to respond, but instead threw her arms up in the air. "Ugh! I don't know why I bother with you. You're an infuriating, egotistical moron!"

"Aw, that's so sweet. I didn't know you felt that way about me."

With a frustrated groan, Talia turned away from Sylenthros. "Just go tend to your stupid forest animals, tree-hugger!" She waved one of her hands in front of her and uttered a cantrip before she disappeared into a portal, leaving the amused elf in the garden.

Having witnessed his professor vanish, Dane decided to make himself scarce before he was caught eavesdropping on their conversation. Assuming the two sorcerers didn't already knew he was there to begin with.

A year later and I still can't rest, Dane thought sadly as he trudged back to his dorm room. *Damn those orcs for what they've done. If I ever see them, I'll make them pay.*

Chapter 19 - Training

28th Day of Manul
125 I.E.

The next day, Dane found himself once again seated in the lecture hall. It was just before the class was about to start, and he couldn't help but notice that there were fewer people in the room than usual. He found that odd, considering the academy punished truancy rather swiftly. Most days saw the room full of students minutes before the professor would come in.

A chair moved to his right, and he saw a boy about his age take the seat. He had a darker skin color, with short black hair and hazel colored eyes. The boy had a slightly round build, one that showed that his increasingly sedentary lifestyle at the academy was starting to take its toll on his body, and likely meant that he spent more time studying than playing in the yard or horsing around with the other students. He was garbed in a plain gray robe similar to the one Dane wore, except the sleeves were long enough that they nearly covered his hands and the bottom hung below his ankles. Perhaps he thought he would grow into it.

Dane glanced around the room before looking at the boy again. There were plenty of open seats, and it bothered him that this person had chosen to sit next to him instead of in a more open area of the class. He wasn't sure where this feeling came from, though. He'd never been one to tell others to go away when approached, but he also never sought the company of other people since he always had so much studying to do.

"Hi Dane," the boy said with a smile. He put his book on the desk, then put his hands on top of it to keep from fidgeting.

"You know my name?" Dane wasn't aware anyone knew him. He never paid much attention to the other students and they didn't bother him either. He liked it that way.

The boy giggled in a way that only a child could. "Of course! I learned it earlier in the semester when you introduced yourself to the class. I kept it in mind after watching your first fight with Heshun months ago. Don't you remember mine?" He tilted his head slightly as he watched Dane attempting to search his memory.

"Um. . . it's. . . Aiden, isn't it?" Dane was never that good at matching names to faces, and he expected to be wrong. Not that being incorrect would've bothered him at all. He didn't know this person, so if he got upset with him over not remembering a name he heard in passing some time ago it was the other boy's problem, not his.

"Yeah, that's right! Aiden Powell, pleased to meet you." Aiden held his hand out, and Dane shook it.

After some hesitancy, he decided to properly introduce himself. "Dane Trueshot."

"Is something wrong?"

Shaking his head, Dane replied, "No, everything is fine. I'm just a bit tired and feeling not all together at the moment, that's all." It wasn't any of Aiden's business to know what was truly bothering him. He decided to quickly start a new topic, in case the other boy had an inquisitive nature that would have him prying into his problems.

"You're part knorian, aren't you?" Dane asked.

"Yup," Aiden replied with a smile. "My mother is human and my father was a full blood knorian. My family comes from Chesterfield, a town a couple provinces to the east."

Dane leaned forward on his desk. "Do you know much about

your father's culture?" He didn't know much about the knorian people's culture, since Lynn had only touched upon it briefly in all his lessons with her. He knew they were a branch of humanity that settled Muriaj generations before the Rogarian Empire ever surfaced, but that was about it.

"Only a little bit," Aiden admitted with a shrug of his thick shoulders. "I'm hoping to learn more after I'm done my instruction in the Academy."

Dane felt a bit jealous of the other boy. Aiden had a rich culture to explore, where as he believed there was nothing left to know about his own people. He didn't have any heritage to look forward to learning about, now that his family was gone.

There's no point in being upset over it, he thought, trying to dismiss the negative feelings before they could set in and ruin the rest of his day.

"Did you notice there's not a lot of people in the room today?" Aiden asked, switching subjects after a brief moment of silence.

"I did. I've been trying to figure out why that is. Even the slackers at least show up on time."

"It's because we're the only one's they let through into magic training," Aiden told him, his face beaming with pride. "The others didn't make it or something. They gotta take remedial all over again."

So that explains why the lecture hall is so empty, Dane thought. He wasn't at all surprised that he was able to make it so far in his studies. He knew he was doing well with the material they were being taught, and was never once sent to the detention hall.

"Are you excited to learn how to do magic? I can't wait. I hope I can help people with what I learn here."

"Yeah, I can't wait to finally learn something of value," Dane replied. Aiden's energy was infectious, and he found himself staring into the other boy's eyes. When he realized what he was doing, he quickly averted his eyes.

Dane knew what was happening. Even someone as young as he knew that he found something attractive about Aiden. Maybe it was his looks, or his attitude, or what he'd seen of his personality. Dane was never one to look at the opposite sex for long. He could appreciate beauty in the way that a painter could appreciate art, but nothing about women excited him the same way that other males did. Having grown up in the woods, away from the influence of the church and society as a whole, he never questioned these feelings, but he knew to keep them hidden from others nonetheless. The way other people talked about him one day finding a suitable wife and raising a family suggested it was abnormal to look at the same sex the way Dane did.

He peeked out of the corner of his eyes and examined Aiden again. His soft, unblemished face practically shone with happiness. Dane wondered how he could be so energetic first thing in the morning. It made him seem that much more adorable, and when Dane realized that, he could feel a surge of adrenaline pump through his veins. He cleared his throat, as it began to feel dry all of a sudden.

"What are you planning on doing once you graduate?" Dane asked, wanting to know more about Aiden and to hear his voice. It was soothing to listen to. Dane had to admit that he could probably listen to the other boy talk for hours and not be bored of him.

Love at first sight, huh? I must be the world's biggest sap, he thought as a smile broke out on his face.

"I wanna be a warmage, to travel with the military so I can help people in need and protect them from monsters. Just like my dad!" Aiden was practically bouncing in his seat from his excitement. Dane couldn't help but chuckle at the boy's exuberance. "What about you?"

"I haven't decided yet," Dane admitted. "I might work with the military, since I don't like the idea of being stuck inside of some dusty library full of moldy old books. I had a teacher that liked that kind of thing once, so I know being a scholar isn't the path I want to take. And I've never been one for research in the first place."

"You should become a warmage with me, since you're in Heshun's class too!" Aiden said.

"Yeah, that's not a bad idea," Dane responded.

Heshun had been teaching them basic combat maneuvers so far, and he was enjoying the swordplay, even if it was just sparring with wooden swords against other students. Training to become a warmage seemed like the perfect fit for him. He looked Aiden in the eyes and smiled.

"I might just do that."

"Then we can train together, and become best friends!"

Dane never had friends at any point in his life, and even though they'd only been speaking for a few minutes, he didn't feel so alone anymore.

"That would be nice," Dane said with a whimsical smile on his face. He found Aiden's attitude infectious and found himself beaming with energy just from being around him.

A door on the left wall near the front of the class creaked open as Talia stepped into the room. Her hair bounced and flowed behind her as she strode towards her desk. A wooden crate floated softly behind her, as if carried by an invisible hand. It lifted itself up and placed itself gently onto the desk, making not a sound as it touched down. She propped her staff up before stepping around to face the class.

"Oh wow, that was neat!" Aiden chirped.

"It's a levitation spell. I read about those in our text."

"I know. I hope we get to learn how to do that one day. I wonder if you can use a spell like that on a person so they can fly?"

Dane chuckled at Aiden's question, and found himself wondering if such a possibility existed. Being able to fly would be awfully amazing, he thought to himself.

After a short pause to let the classroom full of students settle down, Talia cleared her throat and began speaking. "Alright, for those of you who don't already know, you are the top of the class, those deemed worthy enough to command the mighty powers of the arcane. You are but a fraction of the group you were before, but you have all clearly demonstrated a knack for what we have been studying. As a reward for your efforts, we will begin by learning basic fire incantations and some practical applications of fire evocation."

The lecture began with a brief review of the incantation required to evoke a small fireball. Dane had spent some time the previous night memorizing it, word for word, and he made sure that from the moment he woke up until he got to the lecture hall, he could recite it from memory. He was determined to live up to the potential he believed he had. He watched as Talia wrote the incantation on the board at the front of the room using a wand that left a glowing trail of words as she waved it around. It was in the calligraphic script of Arcanus, but when she was finished, she snapped her fingers and it turned into a phonetic alphabet using the Common language, allowing them to read it.

She drew the wand back and underlined the script. After a moment, the magical glowing words seemed to melt downwards and split, showing the translation at the bottom, Oh flickering blaze burn. Fire ball.

"An theros verus. Fiz ban!" Talia read aloud. There were puzzled looks from the students scattered around the room, each of them expecting something to have happened. Talia made an audible sigh and put her palm to her forehead. "How many of you did NOT read the texts assigned to you yesterday?"

No one bothered to answer her.

"You are all the top of the class, and this is what I have to work with? Astonishing. Absolutely astonishing. I expect better from you! You will all be serving the Empire one day." Her voice grew exponentially in volume after a second's pause and she added, "I will NOT tolerate having my reputation as a teacher of the Arts being sullied by your slothful behaviour!"

Even with Dane covering his ears to mitigate the sheer volume of the sorceress' voice, he could still feel a great deal of pain. Whatever magic she was working to make herself so loud worked a little too well, he reckoned.

Talia's voice dropped back to its normal volume. "Do the work I assign or drop out. Anything less than total dedication is a waste of my time."

She took a moment to recompose herself, taking time to glare at the blanched faces of her students and to let her words sink in. Talia could be scary when she wanted to be, and Dane wondered if anyone had seen a softer, more caring side of her like he'd witnessed yesterday in the garden. Despite her strict attitude, Talia had all the qualities necessary to be a kind individual. Maybe she acted strict to keep a distance between herself and her students so they would view her as an authority figure.

"Now, as I was going to say before I was so rudely interrupted by such an appalling display of failure," Talia began, "this incantation must be used to invoke the spell. Keep in mind that these words are merely a focus to help you center your thoughts on your spell-weaving. If you are not focused, or are actively trying to avoid casting the spell even while uttering the incantation, as I just did, it will do nothing. The same goes for any mundane being with no magical ability; they lack the physiological structures in the brain to be able to manipulate mana as we can."

Talia dug into the crate that had floated into the room with her, and produced several small white candles that she set on the desk.

"Now for a demonstration of what I expect from you." She invoked the words of the spell and a fireball shot from the palm of her hand and into a candle's wick, lighting it before the ball of flame dissipated.

"Everyone got that? It's simple." She repeated it twice more, then extinguished the flames. "More experienced sorcerers do not even need the words of power to focus their thoughts on the magic they are trying to work, like so." Talia repeated the process, this time igniting the candles without the utterance of a single word. Her hands moved with a gentle flourish, as though she were conducting a symphony rather than throwing balls of fire around.

"But that will come later, when you've become more skilled. For now, I want each of you who did do their studies to come up here and light one of the candles. Gertrude Crowley, come down here and show your classmates how it's done."

Dane watched as Gertrude tried three times to light the candle before she finally evoked a proper fireball. The next two students to try failed, and the fourth one succeeded on his second try. It wasn't very exciting to watch, but Dane was anxious for his turn nonetheless. He made sure to watch as each of his classmates approached the front to attempt casting the spell and to listen as Talia corrected them on their methods.

"Dane Trueshot, your turn."

"Good luck," Aiden whispered to him as Dane hopped off his chair and proceeded to the front of the room.

"Hold your hand out like this," Talia said as she lifted a hand and held it vertically in front of her with her palm facing the candle. "Then, say the incantation. Focus on the words and imagine the mana around you collecting in the palm of your hand. I trust you know how to do the rest."

"Y-yes ma'am," Dane stuttered.

He was nervous standing in front of a classroom of his peers. It was rare that he had to be in front of everyone but every time he was, it made him sweat and fidget uncontrollably. He tried to ignore the unease spreading through his body, glancing at Aiden for a moment to see the intensely focused expression on his face. He wanted to get it right the first time, to impress the other boy and to prove to himself that he had the potential to be a great sorcerer. Fire was supposed to come easy to him. Wasn't that what Talia had said when presenting him to the Council?

Okay, I just need to focus. . . . Dane began to imagine a warmth traveling through his body up to his right shoulder, then down his arm, like water running along his skin to drip down his fingers. He lifted his hand up as Talia had instructed, and began to say the incantation he'd memorized out of his book.

"*An theros verus. Fiz ban!*" Dane's voice cracked in the middle as he tried to sound forceful. He did his best to ignore the snickering from the other students and to continue focusing on his spell work.

At first, nothing happened, and he began to wonder what he'd done wrong.

Please work! Please don't fail on me!

He was about to begin reciting the incantation a second time when a tiny fireball coalesced in front of his palm and began to spun rapidly. Wasting no time, he mentally ordered it to fly to the candle on desk and light the wick. The ball of fire did exactly as he had commanded, and as it struck the twine, the fireball extinguished itself, leaving only a perfectly lit flame in its place.

"Excellent work, Dane. You're the first one to get it right on the first try. You'll go far here, just as I had expected you would," Talia said, congratulating him. Even though he liked the praise, he wasn't sure if she was saying it because she meant it, or because she was just patronizing him. He could feel the eyes of his classmates on him, probably preparing to lob insults about being a teacher's pet or something else that was equally juvenile.

Despite that, Dane accepted her praise. "Thank you."

"Remember, once you get better, you will no longer need to use the incantation and you can evoke a ball of flame of that size with merely a thought and a bit of concentration." She blew out the candles then gestured for Dane to sit down.

"Alright, Aiden Powell, you're next."

As the two students passed each other down the middle aisle between desks, Aiden clapped Dane on the shoulder. "Great job."

"Thanks." Dane could feel his face flush, leaving him momentarily confused as to why his new friend's words would make him feel uneasy. "Good luck on yours."

"It'll be a cinch," Aiden said with a grin and winked at Dane, causing his face to feel hotter.

As Dane hurried back to his seat and watched his new friend perform the same ritual without any trouble either, he found himself wondering if his life at the R.A.A.S. could get any better.

Chapter 20 - Aiden

23rd Day of Xenar
126 I.E.

Months passed as Aiden and Dane continued to grow closer as friends. They spent their time studying together, working on their magic, and even going out into the town once in awhile. Dane found the change of pace in his usual routine welcoming. He didn't realize how tired he was of his dorm room until he started to leave the academy regularly with Aiden.

The soft trickle of water sounded from behind Dane as he sat next to a fountain. The statuesque image of Archmage Ancherad stood over him with his stone hands raised to the sky, as though praising the Gods. Water arced up over his hands and back into the pool of water below the statue. A golden plaque on the base of the stone read: *Dedicated to Archmage Jean Ancherad for his countless years of service to our glorious Empire.*

Dane and Aiden mutually agreed that the fountain was a great spot to study. They felt at ease in the middle of the serene park. There was little foot traffic moving along the tree-lined pathways. Both boys believed it was good luck for their exams to be studying under the headmaster's watchful eyes, even if it was just a statue.

In Dane's hands was an open tome. His eyes moved back and forth as he read the pages, trying to commit to memory all the things that he needed to know for a performance exam with Sylenthros next week. It was a newer book that was specially made by the collaborative efforts of the professors at the Academy. The pages felt crisp between his fingers as he turned them, suggesting that it had not been long ago since the book had come off the scribe's desk.

"What part are you up to?" Aiden asked.

Dane finished reading to the end of the paragraph and replied, "Um, I'm almost finished reading the theory part." He flipped ahead a few pages to see how much more was left. "I'm about five pages away from the end." Reaching along the top spine of the book, he grabbed the golden tassel that hung there and fit it between the pages, then closed the tome. "Frankly, I'm getting sick of reading about Anarak."

"I suppose, but to be fair," Aiden said, closing his book as well, "Anarak is the Stormbringer, so He's essential to the kind of magic you're trying to cast, isn't he?" He set his text down on the ground next to him, then leaned back using his arms as support. "I envy you, you know that?"

"Really?" Dane asked, surprised. He didn't feel that there was anything worth being jealous about.

"Yeah, I mean, I've seen you a few times in Sylenthros' garden practicing your lightning spells with him," Aiden said. Dane's face flushed when he heard that the other boy had been watching him train. "You have a better grasp of it than me."

Dane could only manage a short response that was choked off by a nervous chuckle. "It's nothing."

"It's true, though!" Aiden insisted. "You pick up new material so fast compared to me."

"I guess," Dane said, trying to dismiss the praise. He liked hearing it, but he wasn't sure how to accept someone's praises without sounding full of himself. He preferred to remain humble if at all possible. "I've only really learned how to conjure lightning. I have no real control of it yet. I've nearly scorched the elf's garden so many times! Besides, you're better at a lot more stuff compared to me. I can't conjure mist or rain like you've managed to do."

"Oh please, as if being able to put a tiny cloud of fog that barely conceals my body amounts to anything," Aiden replied. "Sylenthros could fog up the entire city if he wanted to. I'm certain he has on a few occasions, too. Just because he could."

"But you can at least do it, even if you struggle with it," Dane said. Attempting to conjure a cloud, he struggled to mold the mana into the form that he wanted. Instead of making a fog cloud, he ended up creating too much water and soaked his hand. "I can't even do that."

"It just takes practice. I've been working with Sylenthros for months to be able to do what I can do."

"I suppose." Dane shrugged and didn't let it bother him. He was content with the skills he did have, and even though he was a bit jealous of Aiden, he didn't let that sour his mood.

When he looked back at Aiden, he saw that the boy was still smiling at him. His cheeks looked slightly red compared to what they normally were, but Dane wrote it off as him being hot in the heat and in the heavy gray robes he wore. He wasn't sure what Aiden was trying to get at by being persistent about complimenting him, but it felt good to hear.

"We should probably finish studying so we can get back in time for supper," Dane said. Grabbing his tome, he moved to open it when a hand fell upon his. "What?"

"Hold on, okay?" Aiden asked, and waited until Dane set the book back down.

Aiden twisted around and leaned over to dig into the rucksack that he'd brought with him earlier in the morning. As he fumbled around, trying to get at whatever it was he was looking for, Dane couldn't help but steal a glance at his friend's body. He felt guilty for doing it, but it was a sort of guilty pleasure he enjoyed. Aiden had a soft yet muscled looking body. Over the last few months, he'd grown to fill in his robes properly. He looked powerful, strong as an ox even, and Dane found that kind of power attractive. He closed his eyes and tried to picture what Aiden looked like without clothes on, but then mentally slapped himself for doing that in public. It was bad enough he was fantasizing about his friend, but to do it in public where people might see him? That was even worse.

"You didn't need to close your eyes," Aiden said when the rustling sound stopped. "But I figure that makes this more fun, huh?"

There was a short pause. All Dane could hear was the trickle of water coming from the fountain and the thumping of his heart. Did he get caught? He shifted in his seat to get more comfortable. Dane slowly peeked at his friend, and saw him holding something wrapped in parchment paper with a red ribbon tied around it.

"Happy Birthday, Dane," Aiden said, smiling.

"I don't remember telling you about that. You really didn't have to do anything," Dane said softly. Aiden pushed the gift towards him and set it down on his lap. "It's not like I've gotten you anything before."

"I was born during Aegis," Aiden told him. "You have a couple months to figure that one out." The chuckle and grin that followed told Dane that the boy was mostly kidding.

"Still. . . ." Dane trailed off as he tentatively grabbed the ribbon and paused.

The gift was nicely wrapped, even if the paper was a plain beige color. He didn't want to undo the bow, but there was no way to open his gift without ruining it. Aiden worked hard on the presentation, and he didn't want to pull it apart. The other boy was looking at him expectantly, so Dane pulled on the ribbon. As he did so, the wrapping fell away in a few spots and he could see a green piece of cloth poking out. Curiosity won over him and he began to tear into the paper. After he set the wrapping aside, he examined the gift in his hands.

The green cloth turned out to be a linen tunic. Dane couldn't figure out what plant could have produced such a brilliant green color, but he knew that even a simple dye job could be expensive. When he unfolded the tunic and held it against him, he realized that it was a size or two too big for him.

Aiden seemed to know what he was thinking and said, "I noticed most of your clothes were getting too small for you over the last little while, so I made sure to buy something a bit bigger so you can grow into it. I also knew you liked the color green, and figured you would like this more than a blue one."

Dane tried to smile at his friend's thoughtfulness, but instead he felt sad. He was being given something by someone he cared about, and he realized, it was someone he was beginning to think of as more than just a friend. No one, not even his father, had shown him such kindness in such a simple gift.

"I can't accept this gift," he muttered.

Aiden looked wounded by his words, as if each syllable had been a slap in the face. "Why not?"

"It looks way too expensive. I don't even have any money myself. I couldn't possibly --"

"Return the favor?" Aiden finished, and Dane nodded. "I'm not expecting anything for my birthday. I didn't get you something because I thought you could get me something in return." His face brightened. "I wanted to give you something because you're my friend. Actually, you're the first friend I've made since coming to Rogust."

"Really?" Dane thought that with Aiden's personality, he'd have a huge number of friends. He was always friendly and outgoing, and he liked to do nice things for others.

"Yeah, I'm serious. Besides, in my father's culture it would be considered rude to not accept a gift, so if you don't want to offend me and insult my people, you'd better keep it." Aiden chuckled to himself, unable to maintain a stern expression. "Oh, hang on, I got something else for you." He went back to rummaging through his pack.

"More?" Dane said incredulously.

Though they had been friends for a while, he couldn't understand why his friend would spend so much money on him for something as irrelevant as his birthday. After a moment of searching, Aiden handed him a long leather strap. Dane looked at his second gift, and he realized that it was a belt designed to hold the scabbard of a sword. On the left side was a small hoop he could slip a sword into, and on the right side was a sizable belt pouch that looked large enough to hold his money and a few small rations for longer outings. The flap that sealed the pouch had the initials "D.T." stitched into it in golden thread.

"Wow, Aiden. I can't believe you got these for me." Dane ran his thumb over the leather to feel the smooth texture. It was well-made, on par with the kind of goods he saw from time to time back in Tran. Something like this would not have come cheap, but how expensive it was remained a question that burned in the back of Dane's mind.

"It's no problem. I had some extra gold lying around and --"

"These cost you gold pieces?" Dane swung around, his eyes wide. He'd have to save and scrimp for a whole year back home to have made a single gold coin. "Where did you get that kind of coin? I am not worth that much money."

"I disagree," Aiden said quickly. "I think you were worth every coin I spent on those." He reached out with a thick hand and clapped him on the back. "So are you going to try them on? I know how you like the color green."

"Yeah, I do." Dane looked down at the tunic in his lap. It was a nice shade of emerald green, and he imagined he would look rather good wearing it. He stood up and took off his robes. He could feel the cool spring breeze brush against the bare skin on his torso before he slipped into his new tunic as quickly as he could. Just as he expected, the collar hung fairly low on his chest, and the sleeves went too far down his arms. It felt loose, and every time the wind blew he could feel it crawling into his clothes, making him shiver.

He then picked up his new belt and cinched it tight around his waist. He slid the belt pouch around to his front so he could get to it easily. Turning around to look into the fountain, Dane peered at his reflection in the rolling waters. He had to admit, Aiden had good taste. He was starting to look like a regular swordsman. All he needed now was a blade and some armor to complete the look.

Dane nearly fell into the fountain's waters when Aiden jumped up and draped an arm around his shoulders. "See? I knew you'd like them. You're looking good!"

"Thanks," Dane stuttered, blushing at his compliment. "Where did you get the money for these things?"

"I worked for a bit in a bakery to earn some extra coin. I needed it to pay for postage to keep in contact with my mother, and I just saved whatever I didn't spend. It wasn't anything I didn't use to do at home so it was kind of fun."

"I didn't know you mailed her," Dane said. Aiden had only spoken about his family a few times. He didn't know much beyond the fact that his mother and his twin brother lived on a farm somewhere on the Kelial Plains to the east. It was quite some distance from what Aiden had said, at least a couple weeks even by horse-drawn carriage. Dane figured that if he was mailing her, it would cost a fair chunk of coin to be able to pay a courier to run that far.

Aiden nodded his head, then pulled out a piece of parchment from his pack. "Yup, I got a letter from her the other day, in fact."

When he showed the paper to Dane, he saw the scratchy, almost illegible script written across it. He could pick out a few words here and there, but for the most part it was completely unreadable.

"Did she write it?" Dane asked, trying not to sound offensive.

"Well, no," Aiden admitted and put the letter away. "She can't read or write. My brother, Seth, can at least read even if his writing is horrible. I taught him, ya know? So he reads my letters to her and writes back to me, whenever he feels like helping her out."

"What do you mean by 'feels like helping out'?"

Aiden shook his head. "Mother always said that Seth has too much of my father's blood running through his veins. We're twins, but he's always been more active and a much bigger trouble-maker. He's usually gone from the farm for days at a time without reason, but when he's there, he's always very helpful."

"Did you two fight a lot when you were younger?" Dane asked, and sat back down.

Aiden laughed at him. "All the time. It'd be easier to list off the times where we weren't fighting. It was always such childish stuff too, now that I think about it. Like, one time I found this perfect hiking stick and I'd go walking through the bush with it almost daily. I guess Seth got jealous of me, and he would take it away and hide it whenever he got the chance."

"Of course, I'd always find out it was him, and I'd fight with him to get it back. It was all so stupid. But I guess that's what brothers do, right?"

"I guess so," Dane said, smiling at his friend's story. "What about your mother? What's she like?"

A wistful look spread across Aiden's face and he turned his head slightly to look up at the sky. "She's a wonderful woman. And she's strong, too. Mother has been running the farm since my father was killed in action, and though the family has fallen on hard times, she's always pulled through." He met Dane's eyes and said, "I hope you can meet her one day. She makes the best apple pie I've ever had. Nothing I've eaten here can compare, and even trying to replicate the recipe with a conjuration spell doesn't taste quite right. You and I may be sorcerers, but my mother works some real magic in the kitchen."

Dane began to salivate as he tried to picture what the best apple pie in the world would taste like. He was reminded of the soft, tantalizing scent of cinnamon that he always smelled when he walked into Tran. All at once, he was reminded of how much he wished he could smell such a simple thing again without it being tainted by the stench of the city.

"What's your family like?" Aiden asked.

The happy look on Dane's face faded. "I never knew my own mother. Father never talked about her, and he passed away last year."

A tense moment of silence passed between the two of them. Dane could feel his heartbeat in his chest, and he found the chaotic arrangement of stones in the cobble walkway to be very interesting.

"Gods, I'm so sorry, Dane." Aiden placed a hand on Dane's back, trying his best to comfort his friend. "I didn't know."

"It's alright. Sorry I guess I shouldn't have said it so bluntly. I didn't mean to kill the mood." Dane looked up and smiled. "I'm fine. . . but will you be offended if I don't feel like sharing?"

"Not at all. I didn't mean to step on a sore spot."

"It's okay." He reached down and picked up his book again. "Now, I believe we had a bit more studying to do."

Aiden rubbed his round stomach. "Do you suppose we could wait?"

"Why?" Dane asked, half listening to his friend and half trying to continue reading the page he was on.

"My stomach is growling something fierce," the boy admitted. "Can we get something to eat first and then go back to your room to finish studying?"

Dane stole a glance at the sundial across the path, and noted that it was later in the day than he thought it was. Isabella would be going through the dorms within the next hour to bring the students their suppers.

Marking his page once again, Dane closed his tome and stood up. "Sure, why not?"

Aiden's face lit up as he grinned. "Excellent! I'm starving!"

The pair walked off down the road, heading back in the direction of the Ivory Tower that stood tall above the entire city.

Chapter 21 - Coming of Age

4th Day of Sytarel
126 I.E.

The months crawled by as the Fergoth became more accustomed to their new surroundings. The rough first season they experienced in Zugrul had taught them a lot about how to hunt for their own food and what kinds of plants were edible and could be grown back in the safety of the slums. It had been a long journey, but finally they were able to get by, even if just barely.

It was a hot summer day, and there wasn't a cloud in the sky. The fierce sun beat down on the coast, baking those residents who spent more than a few, fleeting moments outside. The buzz of insects filled the air, as did the exotic calls of the jungle birds that called Rhavik home. Ships came and went often. The port was alive with activity and the shouts of workers filled the slums as their voices echoed off the city walls.

Xellik was sparring with Haij outside their ramshackle home. Their training had become more rigorous and more intense. Sweat dripped in copious amounts off their bodies, and a bucket of water sat nearby, drained of its contents ages ago. No matter how hot it would be, they would not cease in their training.

"Tomorrow's finally your passage into adulthood, isn't it?" Haij asked. He swung at Xellik with his sword, starting above him and coming in low at the orcling's legs, but the younger orc managed to jump back and over the attack with ease.

"It's about time," Xellik said with a grunt of effort as he

retaliated.

"Still bothered that Napir came of age before you?"

"Shut up!" Xellik lunged at Haij with his sword, but the weapon was knocked out of his hands by a swift parry. Wasting no time, he attempted to conjure a replacement sword, but was smacked across the face by the flat of Haij's blade, the tip of which dug in and cut a deep gash across his cheek.

"You know that there's no magic allowed during a spar." The orc pressed the attack and did his best to prevent Xellik from retrieving his sword. "The enemy won't give you time to make a new sword, so you'd best get used to keeping a better grip on your weapon, or learn how to fight without one!"

"Like this?" Xellik stepped forward while learning to the side to avoid Haij's thrust. His fist came up in a swift uppercut that caught the orc in the jaw and left him vulnerable enough to be kicked in the stomach.

The orc hurried to get back on his feet, but he stopped when Xellik's sword was pressed against his neck.

"It's over. I win."

"Never forget that one battle alone is not enough to declare yourself the victor of anything."

"True, but it is enough to declare myself the winner of this battle."

Haij pushed himself up off the ground and sheathed his sword. "Has my father told you how unbecoming that pride is in a leader?"

"More times than I care to count, yes." Xellik frowned at him. "He nags me like he's my father."

"Ever been open to the possibility that he might be?"

"I know enough to say that's a bad assumption to make. None of the shaman that bedded my mother were around to raise me while I was growing up, so as far as I'm concerned, none of those orcs could be my father. Besides, it doesn't matter to me if Bytej and I are of the same blood." Xellik slid his sword back into its scabbard and offered a hand to Haij. "It wouldn't change anything about how things have turned out for us. And besides, a real parent would be around to raise their orcling and teach them how to handle a sword and how to hunt game."

"By that reasoning, that would make me your father," Haij replied with a grin. Blood marred his teeth as it dripped off his lips and into his mouth.

"Shut up," Xellik said, scowling.

"But if that's how you define a father, then Bytej has ensured that you've learned all that, and more, even if he wasn't the one teaching you everything," Haij remarked, standing up and dusting himself off.

"Whatever you say," Xellik said and waved him away dismissively. "Speaking of the old codger, I'm supposed to meet with him to prepare for tomorrow. I've only been out in the jungle a few times, but never alone."

"Then we'll adjourn for the time being and pick up our training when you return."

Haij headed off to spend time with the other hunters in the tribe while Xellik returned to their dwelling to see Bytej. As he'd expected, the shaman was in his garden, tending to the various herbs and plants that he'd been growing since they'd settled down.

To the orc's credit, the plants had flourished well considering the conditions they were growing in. It had taken years, but between having tomes smuggled out of the Great Library in the city proper and his own experimentations, he'd started a tidy business using the herbs and potions he'd been creating. The caste-less were forced to barter and trade amongst themselves using things other than money, and beyond that no one would have anything to do with them except the odd traveler from the minotaur city of Dredal up along the northern coastline.

"I was wondering when you'd show up," Bytej said without looking up from the plants he was tending to.

"I was training with Haij."

Bytej wasted no time in getting to the subject at hand. "Tomorrow you're going to be heading into the jungle on your own. Are you prepared for it?"

"I'm prepared for anything. I can do whatever Napir can do!" Xellik boasted.

"Of course you are. Do you have rations? Water? A bedroll? Flint and tinder to be able to light a cooking fire? A skinning knife?" Bytej asked.

Xellik paused. He hadn't thought to pack any of those things. He'd never been knowledgeable about wilderness survival and most of the necessities that Bytej listed off would've escaped his mind until it became apparent he would need such things.

He was suddenly embarrassed of the brash attitude that had developed due to his high expectations of himself. He'd thought he could waltz into the jungle and hunt down a tiger without any problem. He didn't know where such overconfidence came from, but it troubled him. He pondered how much he relied on his tribe to provide for him, realizing that it was a sign of weakness. As their future leader, he couldn't afford to be that dependant on them, especially now that he was on the doorstep to adulthood.

After taking a moment to think, Xellik begrudgingly admitted, "No, I don't have any of those things."

"That's what I figured. Go inside and prepare your pack then, and fill it with everything you'll need.You'll be setting out just before the dawn."

"That early?" Xellik exclaimed, "But Napir didn't have to leave until mid-afternoon!"

"Orclings leave on the hour of their birth, no earlier and no later. You should know that!"

Xellik cringed at the idea of leaving so early. Though he had magic at his disposal to mitigate the darkness, it still wasn't as good as daylight and he would be left vulnerable to virtually every predator that stalked the jungle.

"After you're prepared, I recommend getting some rest. You won't have much sleep otherwise, and no orcling should have to endure their coming of age without time to regain their strength first."

"Alright, I get it. I'll go get ready," Xellik said before he went off to go pack for his hunt.

That night, Xellik tossed and turned on the floor beneath the warmth of his fur blanket. At first, he reasoned that his insomnia was due to the sonorous snoring coming from the other room after Bytej fell asleep. Their home shook with each breath the elder shaman took. He soon realized that he was unable to sleep because of his fears about tomorrow's hunt. The orc would be in his sixteenth year, and he still allowed fear to control him. He wasn't supposed to be afraid of anything.

No matter how many times he reminded himself of that fact, it did little to quell the storm of doubt that raged through his mind. Nothing he could do helped him to pass out, and before he knew it, the sun began to peek over the horizon just outside his window.

Xellik didn't wait for Bytej or anyone else to wake him and remind him about what he had to do. He dressed himself in a set of leather armor that had been tailored for him earlier that month, and grabbed the pack he had prepared the night before.

Strange, he thought as he hefted the knapsack up off the ground. He could feel and hear something metal rattling around inside. Reaching into his pack, he moved aside several rations and a waterproof box that contained his flint and tinder until he came across a flask. He didn't remember putting it in with the rest of his supplies. Attached to the container was a small note that read: DO NOT READ UNTIL SUNDOWN!

What is Bytej playing at? Xellik thought to rouse the shaman and ask him about the flask, but instead he decided to get moving before he was late. He wanted to be in and out of the jungle as soon as possible.

Xellik left the slums without saying anything to anyone. With a single word, the orcling conjured a small ball of light in the palm of his hand that twirled up into the air and hovered near him, illuminating his surroundings. It would be awhile before the sun's rays would ward off the darkness, and he didn't want to take a chance that he'd be ambushed on his way deeper in.

Though he had only been out hunting with the tribe a few times, Xellik had been paying attention to the trackers and how they did things. His knowledge of animal tracks was crude and mostly self-taught through observation, but he figured he had a good enough handle on how to find something as big as a tiger.

His hunt on that first day turned out to be fruitless. The day passed quicker than Xellik expected. The sun was beginning to set and he realized that it was time to make camp for the night. He struck a small fire and unfurled his bedroll next to it. The sounds of buzzing insects dimmed as daylight faded away. He set a piece of meat over the fire and as it cooked, he dug back into his pack to find his water and skin when his hand brushed against the cool metal of the flask. He pulled it out along with the note, then unfolded the parchment

Xellik,

I'm sure you're curious why I have slipped a metal flask into your pack along with this note. You no doubt have your hands full trying to find and kill a tiger, but there is one more thing you need to do to complete your coming of age ritual.

We elders do not inform young orclings such as yourself about the second yet most crucial portion of the ritual solely out of tradition. Inside the flask, you will find a potion I brewed last night. Drink it when the sun has finally set, and do not panic.

"Thanks for the cryptic little note, old orc," Xellik said aloud to himself. He unscrewed the top of the flask and sniffed. Whatever was inside smelled sickly sweet yet contained a pungent bitterness that made his nose wrinkle. He tipped it back and took a small sip of the potion, finding to his surprise that it tasted much better than it smelled.

Xellik waited until his meat was finished cooking before he washed it down with Bytej's concoction. Nothing happened, though he found it had cleansed his palette a bit. He quickly set up a warding spell to keep watch over him as he slept, then curled up into his bedroll near the fire. Tomorrow, he decided, he'd find a tiger and prove himself to be the rightful chieftain of the Fleshgorger tribe. Only he could fill that position.

"That pride is unbecoming of a true leader."

Xellik sat up with a start. His fire had gone out and was nothing more than a clump of deep red cinders in the center of a ring of rocks.

"Bytej? Are you out there?" Xellik called out.

The gnarled trees around him seemed to warp and bend with the wind, walling him off in the small clearing.

"What's going on?"

An orc's face appeared in the trunk of a tree across from him, the roughly-hewn bark making up the wrinkles in the frown the orc made.

The mouth in the tree moved as the voice spoke again. "What makes you think you're in any position to lead your people? You're still just a baby!" It's voice was gravely and filled with the sound of cracking, splintering wood.

"Who are you to speak to me like that?" Xellik snapped as he sprang to his feet, ready for any tricks the apparition might try. He considered only for a moment the absurdity of talking to a tree, but the more rational part of his mind argued that it could easily be a dream or illusion concocted with magic.

"Why do you think you have the qualities necessary to lead the Fergoth?" the tree-orc asked.

"It is my birthright!"

"Not good enough!" it roared at him. "It takes more than one's ancestry to rule a tribe!"

"Oh? And what would you know of it, tree?"

"Your anger will lead you to ruin, Xellik Fergoth. Just as your mother's refusal to abide by tradition and her pride led her tribe to near total destruction."

The orcling growled through clenched teeth. "Are you saying I am an accident that caused my tribesmen's death?"

"I never said any such thing," the tree-orc replied, though the corners of its lips seemed to curl into a smirk. "Though I suppose if that's what you took from that statement, it is a reflection of your own doubts." The tree-orc stared at him without wavering, its gaze as timeless as the wood it was made out of.

"Shut up! You don't know a thing about me!"

The tree-orc laughed. "I know more about you than you care to admit, child of Sytarel. About your jealousy of your friends. Your envy towards those of your tribe who fawn over Sorda. Your hatred towards Ragash and how he undermines you."

Words failed Xellik as he struggled to reign in his anger. The apparition seemed more than capable of twisting his words around to use as a weapon. The orcling shook the thoughts out of his head and steeled himself. It didn't matter what this thing standing before him was. It was another opponent standing in the way of his destiny.

"I don't care what you are or why you're here," Xellik began as he reached down and fumbled around for his sword, "But I'll make sure you learn to show the High Priest of the Fleshgorgers some respect!" His hand gripped the smooth, leather-bound grip and he grinned as he brought the weapon to bear. However, all Xellik could do was stare dumbfounded as the sword disintegrated in his grip.

"Your weapon is useless here," the tree-orc informed him.

"I don't need a weapon to fell you, tree!" Xellik clapped his hands together, then spread his fingers out as he tried to evoke a simple offensive spell that should've ignited the tree's bark, yet nothing happened beyond a few pops and fizzles.

"The Goddess cannot hear your voice from here, and as such, your magic is also useless. You will not be permitted to leave this place until you have come to terms with your own weaknesses and learn to grow from them."

"My weaknesses? I have no weaknesses!"

"You lack what is necessary to lead the Fergoth."

Xellik held his arms out wide. "Look at me! I have everything I need. I'm strong. I'm powerful. My subordinates fear and respect me!"

"You lack humility and the skills to lead."

"Then tell me what to do!"

"I have already told you what you need. You must learn how to rule fairly and how to get your people to follow you without question."

Xellik plopped down on the ground and rested his chin on his hand. He hadn't expected to spend his coming of age ritual being lectured by anyone, especially not a tree.

Sure, I'm not the smartest orc in the world and I rely on Bytej and the others a lot, but I'm not that stupid. He scratched his head furiously with both hands, wanting to scream something in his frustration but hearing nothing come out of his mouth. Then he paused. *Come to think of it, my so-called people don't even listen to me, and just go about their own business. Do they even view me as their leader?* Xellik looked up at the sky for answers, but found nothing. His gaze dropped to the face of the tree-orc, and the answer was in plain sight. *They don't view me as their leader. They look to Bytej for direction.* His thoughts turned to his conversation with Bytej the day before, and to the biting comments Haij made during their training sessions.

I haven't shown them any real strength nor given them reason to listen to me. It's not about being male or about being a child. It's about being weak.

The tree's frown softened. "Realization is the first step towards redemption, young Xellik Fleshgorger. There may very well be hope for you yet, but only if you commit to the desire to change."

For the first time in the longest time that Xellik could remember, he had no clue what to do and what direction to take. He'd been relying too heavily on Bytej, and now that there was a time where he had to make a decision, he didn't have anyone to advise him or help him through it. Everyone his entire life had been telling him that he needed to grow up and act like the leader he claimed he was, but he never listened and brushed their remarks aside.

Now he was faced with the fear that he may never be able to live up to the potential Bytej had promised he was capable of. And that meant losing any leadership he had over his tribe, as well as any hope of getting out of the slums.

"What do I do?" Xellik pleaded.

"That, young orcling, is for you and you alone to learn. One does not become a wise shaman in a day, nor does one learn the politics of his tribe in a single cycle of the moons," the tree replied.

"If you seek direction, then look no further than your own people. Make peace with an enemy. Listen to their thoughts and desires. Do something to make their lives better."

"That's not helpful." Xellik frowned.

"It was not meant to hold your hand. If you still wish for someone to guide you, then you are not ready to be an adult and you are certainly not in a position to command the Fergoth."

Xellik had to admit that the tree-orc was right. When he was younger he always reminded himself that he didn't need anyone else to be able to lead. So why did he feel and act differently now?

He was disappointed with himself, but stronger than that was his anger, born of the realization that he had become cowed like a simple, mindless peon. He was afraid to face reality and come to terms with the fact he was not ready to lead.

"If there is more for me to learn, then I shall learn it!" Xellik stood up and shouted. "The Fergoth are my people to rule. It is my birthright!"

"Then pay attention to their needs and learn well, young Xellik. Do not forget our talk."

The face in the tree melted away and the jungle around him receded as a deep, unnatural sleep overtook the orcling.

* * * * *

When Xellik woke again, he found himself inside the same reoccurring dream he'd been having since he arrived in Zugrul. The slime-covered stone walls that he had become accustomed to were now clearer than ever before, and he could make out the roughly chiseled texture along their surface. He walked over to them and ran a calloused hand over the cool surface. Strings of the slimy substance stretched between his hand and the walls. He pulled away and wiped the stuff off on his leggings.

Somewhere nearby, he could hear the quiet, slow drip of water. When Xellik looked up, he saw rows upon rows of stalactites hanging from the ceiling. He noticed for the first time that the stone walls only went so high before they melted into the cavern above.

Xellik whirled around to look behind him. The room narrowed until it funneled out into a hallway beyond which he could not see. From the opening he could hear the clip-clop of heavy hooves.

I don't remember hearing that before.

He tried to call out, but no sound escaped his lips. He heard the buzzing voice of the shadow monster echoing off the walls as the hoof steps quickened.

Xellik reached to his side and placed his hand on the grip of his sword, but didn't draw it. He was relieved that it was still there. Whatever he was facing, he'd be ready for it this time.

The beast finally stepped out of the shadows and Xellik recognized it for what it truly was: a minotaur. It's black fur blended easily with the darkness and made his golden eyes stand out, giving him a fierce appearance as he towered over the orcling. Two horns as black as korcyn blood protruded forward, and Xellik could tell that the minotaur took good care of them. They looked capable of goring him easily if he was provoked.

His horns were adorned with a number of feathers from a bird that Xellik couldn't identify, and his robes were made of woven leaves. To both the orcling's surprise and relief, the minotaur seemed to be unarmed.

That doesn't mean he isn't dangerous, he reminded himself. He'd seen enough in his short life to know that an opponent without a weapon could be just as deadly as an opponent with one.

The minotaur's voice still buzzed with energy, but Xellik could not understand what it was trying to say. The beast raised a green-limned hand and tendrils of thorny vines erupted from the ground, entangling his body. The plants dragged Xellik towards the ground and their thorns bit into his skin. The vines began to constrict his body. Xellik gaped in astonishment as the roots squeezed harder until he found it difficult to breath. It was supposed to be a dream, yet he wasn't waking up as the life was squeezed from his body.

Xellik, a soft voice whispered.

The orcling looked up as the voice caught his attention. It seemed to come from nowhere and everywhere at the same time, as if it were both inside his head and echoing throughout the chamber.

The minotaur said something again, and from up above, Xellik could hear the rumbling and cracking of stone as a stalactite was dropped from above. He craned his neck to the side to look up and screamed as it came crashing down on him.

Just before the tip punctured his skull, he woke up to the chatter of the jungle wildlife all around him. The sun's rays beamed through the treetops and he found himself sweating. His head throbbed with a mild headache as well. He rolled over in his bedroll and reached out to retrieve his water skin. However, he stopped moving and inspected his arm once he got a solid look at it.

There were cuts all along his skin.

That was just a dream! That couldn't have been real! What if I'm still asleep? The wounds were sealed, but they were very clearly still fresh. He scratched at one of the scabs with a fingernail and watched as it broke easily, allowing fresh blood to seep from the cut once more. *Bytej's potion couldn't be the reason for this. I'd been having those dreams since we arrived.*

Xellik quickly packed up his small camp and started on the trek through the jungle after feasting on some meat he had left over from the night before. There was nothing else he could do until he could speak to Bytej about the dreams. Perhaps he would know what was going on.

He continued his search for one of the elusive jungle tigers. It was hotter that afternoon than it had been all week, and Xellik felt like he was covered in a thick, sticky sheen of sweat. If there were any tiger around, he reasoned, they would likely smell him coming a league away. He stopped to relief himself and was in the middle of unlatching his belt when he heard something moving around nearby. When he looked up, he saw leaves shaking, but by the time he put his belt back on and ran over to inspect the sound with his sword in hand, there was nothing there.

He bent down to look for tracks, but found there were none. *Odd, the ground is too soft for there not to be any footprints. Must have been some vermin.*

However, later when he stopped to eat some dried meat and refill his water flask at a river, he heard the sound again. This time the ground was clearly disturbed, but the pattern was so indistinguishable that he couldn't tell what had been there.

Is it Korcyn? If those pigs are tracking me, I'm as good as dead. They know this place better than I do.

Xellik turned to look up at the sky, getting his bearings from the position of the sun. If he headed due east, he could find the coast and from there, Zugrul. He didn't want to go back, but he didn't want to fall to a Korcyn ambush, either.

I can't return until I've finished my rite of passage. If I can't find a tiger when Napir found one, I'll be the laughing stock of the tribe. Then no one will accept me as their leader! I can't let that happen. Xellik tightened his belt and kept a hand on the grip of his sword as he continued to move through the jungle and away from Zugrul. *Korcyn be damned, I'll keep going.*

As the day progressed, he heard the sounds in the jungle less and less, but that wasn't what unnerved him the most. It was the fact he was still being stalked by something, yet not seeing anything out there. By mid-day, he felt his luck had begun to turn. He looked through a set of pushes and saw the telltale paw prints of a big cat. He followed them for a time, hacking away at any foliage that obscured his vision. Eventually, he found that the tracks looped back around to the east, back towards Zugruli territory.

Wait a second. . . . Xellik's eyes traced a path along the footprints and saw them take a sharp turn to the south, and then a short distance away they turned to the west. *It's trying to come up behind me!*

The bushes rustled violently behind the orcling and he rolled to the side, nearly being swiped in the back by the tiger's claws. In a flash, he swung out with his sword, drawing blood along the striped beast's left flank. The tiger roared and darted off, disappearing into the foliage. Xellik stood still, holding his sword as he scanned the area around him. He refused to move, afraid that he might not hear the jungle cat before it struck again.

Unfortunately for the orc, the tiger proved more stealthy than he gave it credit for as it pounced at him from the side. Xellik tried to dodge but the tiger was too quick, and it clipped him in the shoulder with an unexpected amount of force, knocking the orc off his feet. Blood spilled from two deep cuts where the tiger's claws had hit him, and he winced in pain when he hit the ground. Before he could blink, the tiger pounced on him and knocked the wind out of his lungs. Its paws kept his arms against the ground and its claws dug into his skin.

I didn't expect it to be this quick!

The tiger's fanged maw moved swiftly towards Xellik's neck, and time seemed to stand still. He could distinctly remember counting each of the tiger's yellowed teeth, and watching the way the beast's spittle seemed to pool in the corners of its mouth before dripping down onto his chest. He couldn't overpower the animal to remove his hand, and he realized he'd be too late. By the time he could bring his sword up to strike, the tiger would've likely taken his throat out.

With no other options available to him, Xellik lunged forward before the tiger could bite him. He craned his neck up and bit the cat on the nose as hard as he could, and felt warm blood squirt into his mouth before the beast rolled off him with a high pitched yelp and a groan.

Free of the tiger's grip, Xellik skittered in the opposite direction and sprang to his feet. He watched for a moment as the cat writhed in pain, but he didn't waste too much time watching. He knew that the creature would soon be back on its feet and he'd lose whatever advantage he'd gained. He gripped his sword tightly and spun it around until he held it upside down. He drove the blade into the beast's head, then leaped backwards as the cat tried to swipe at him before its body's movements were overtaken by its death throes. It collapsed within seconds and Xellik watched as the rise and fall of the tiger's chest slowed, then ceased entirely.

Though he was panting and his arms ached, Xellik felt a sense of elation surging through his body. He'd done it, he'd felled the tiger. After a short break to rest with a small meal and a big gulp of water, he got to work skinning the best on the spot. He realized that this had been the first time he'd ever had to skin an animal before. As he felt the knife slicing through the tiger's flesh as easily as it could slice through a slab of butter, he felt nauseous.

A stench wafted up from the open cut and he turned to the side, throwing up the meal he'd just eaten. When the heaving stopped, he continued his work until the pelt was removed. He was grateful that no one was around to see him get sick like that. Once he was finished, he adorned himself in the pelt and left, leaving the rest of the carcass behind for scavengers to pick clean.

Xellik could hardly remember the trek back to Zugrul, but he did remember the congratulatory praise from his friends as he arrived in the camp while draped in the hide of the tiger. He remembered the reaffirming nod he received from Bytej and how he and Haij had clasped their hands together before the older orc patted him on the back. He remembered having his head shaven, and the mark of the Fergoth tattooed upon his brow.

He was finally a true orc, one that was ready to learn how to lead his tribe.

"So, what are you going to do now?" Bytej asked that evening as he, Xelilk, Napir, and Haij sat around a fire they had started. They drank from mugs filled with orcish moonshine that Bytej drew from a cask sitting next to him.

"Now? Xellik thought for a moment. "I want to lead, but first I need to learn."

"About what?" Napir asked.

"How to be a good leader, so that I can pick us up out of this squalor," he replied with a wave of his hand directed at their surroundings. "We deserve better than these slums. We are the children of Sytarel, and we belong in there!" Xellik pointed at the walled city of Zugrul. "I'll learn how to be a better leader so that one day we will be allowed into that city."

"You've already taken the first step in getting us there," Haij said and raised his mug. "Cheers, to our future leader!"

They clacked their cups together and tipped their drinks back. Xellik paused as he looked to the flickering lights atop the walls. He glared in the city's direction, knowing that somewhere beyond there lay the key to their liberation.

Chapter 22 - Fears

23rd Day of Thessix
126 I.E.

Due to Dane's lack of money since being admitted to the Academy, something that he shared in common with Aiden, they had been put to work by Heshun to pay for their tuition. It started out simple at first with jobs such as cleaning classrooms at the end of the day. Once they had passed basic combat training, the jintaren had upped the ante and tasked the two of them to clear the cellars out on a daily basis, to get rid of any vermin that may be roaming through them. It was a job that Dane thought was more suitable for a cat than a sorcerer, but over time he quickly learned that the magically augmented rodents would've been too much for a simple house cat to handle.

"Magic is volatile and the side-effects are often unpredictable," Heshun had explained to them after their first day in the cellars. "You've just seen first hand what it can do to the pests crawling around our food stores. They're bigger, faster, more aggressive, and breed at an accelerated rate."

"So there's going to be more of them?" Dane asked. "When?"

"Could be as soon as tomorrow. Maybe even tonight, if we're unlucky. Which is why you'll be doing this daily to pay for your tuition."

"And you don't want us to use our magic. That's swell," Aiden said, exasperated.

With time they came to better understand why Heshun forbade

magic and why he forced them to use the spears given to them. Unleashing magic in the storeroom could cause a fire, and if that happened it would undoubtedly destroy the goods stored there.

If the magic seeping down from the Academy above us created these monsters, I hope it's not done anything to the food we eat. Dane tried not to think about it as he patrolled the cellar. He'd asked Sylenthros about it once, and was told that the crates were magically sealed to prevent contamination

Something skittered in front of him, knocking over a small jug. The clatter of clay smashing against stone brought Dane out of his thoughts as his eyes swept around the room to spot a giant rat dashing away from him.

"Get back here!" Dane shouted, stabbing at the rodent with his spear. It was the size of a small dog, with a thick, snake-like tail that dragged along the ground behind it. It squeaked as it dodged and wove around the spear's strikes, trying desperately to get away from him.

A second spear appeared before him and skewered the rat. The rodent squealed and writhed on the tip before finally going limp. "Having trouble, Dane?"

The man looked up and saw his friend standing before him with a self-assured smirk on his face. Aiden had grown into a heavy-set adolescent since hitting his growth spurt sometime in the last couple months. He was unable to shed the soft layer of fat from childhood. He had clean cut hair and sported a thin beard around his mouth. He stood proudly with broad shoulders. His round belly hung firmly instead of sagging like a sack of potatoes, and that only made him look more powerful rather than slothful or lazy.

It struck Dane as odd that even though Aiden had a strict regiment of combat training and exercise, the man never seemed able to shed the extra weight, and it only further perplexed Dane when he had learned that the other man had far greater stamina than himself. He chalked it up to Aiden's knorian heritage.

Either way, he's become quite the attractive man, Dane thought, a smile spreading across his face. *At least I got good taste.*

"Done your side of the cellar already?" Dane asked.

"Yup!" Aiden replied with a grin.

In all the time that Dane had known the boy, nothing had managed to temper the fiery passion for life the other youth had. He was still just as energetic as the day they met. Aiden moved to the side and shook the dead rat off his spear and onto a growing pile of vermin corpses that were stacked away from the stored goods.

"Then you can help me finish my side," Dane said. "You know, the bigger one." Aiden shrugged and tried to suppress a smile.

"I thought you liked them big," he commented, nudging him with his elbow.

Dane smacked his friend in the stomach, and Aiden laughed at him.

"We only have a few more months until our Test. Can you believe it?" Aiden asked as they wove around piles of crates and barrels, searching the rooms for any remaining pests. "It's come so fast."

Dane stabbed another rat and kicked it off to the side. "I don't think I'm ready for the Test, much less our finals with Heshun and Talia. I'm much too nervous, and I can barely focus on my studies as is. They still haven't told us what to expect."

Aiden nodded. "Maybe they want to see how well we can think on our feet?"

"You might be right. That doesn't make it any less nerve wracking."

A spider slipped down between the two boys, and Aiden let out a startled scream. He quickly evoked a fireball and incinerated it as it reached towards him with its prickly appendages and snapping mandibles. A trail of fire climbed up the webbing, but it dissipated before it reached the ceiling.

"Aiden!" Dane cried out. He hoped that no one had sensed the use of magic coming from the cellars.

The other man shrugged his shoulders. "It scared me. I couldn't help it."

Dane shook his head and chuckled. If Heshun found out that they were using magic in the store rooms, he'd chew them out again and punish them. He was frightening enough on a day to day basis, but he could be downright terrifying when he was angry, and it was very easy to set him off when someone directly disobeyed one of his explicit rules.

When both of them were sure they had scoured the place of all vermin, they used a torch to incinerate the piles of bodies they had left behind as they went. The fire could be better controlled since it was not magical in nature and unaffected by the residual arcane energies in the area.

When they finished, both boys slumped back against the cold walls to rest. Dane wiped his sweaty brow with his forearm and closed his eyes, sighing. It seemed like such simple work, but swinging a seven pound spear over and over again was more tiring than it had first appeared. His stress about the upcoming Tests certainly didn't help any, and he was sure he was going to end up in an early grave because of how much he'd been worrying about it. When he opened his eyes, he saw Aiden leaning over him with a concerned expression on his face.

He couldn't help but notice that the man had a pleasant smell about him, even though it was faint beneath a layer of grime, sweat, and vermin blood.

"Do you mind?" Dane asked, raising an eyebrow at him.

Aiden ignored the question. "Are you okay?"

"Yeah, fine. You know I don't have your stamina," Dane reminded him. He couldn't keep up with Aiden, no matter what they were doing.

"Not like this. Are you sure everything is alright?"

"It's just stress, that's all. I'm fine, really," Dane lied. In truth, having the other man so close to him was making him feel awkward, even if his heart fluttered at the prospect of Aiden only being a couple inches away.

Aiden stood close enough that Dane could reach out and touch him with little effort. Heck, he could lean forward and plant a kiss on his lips if he wanted. And he desperately wanted to. Nothing would make him happier than to express his affection to Aiden. Being around him made his heart race and his mind wander. Dane could feel excited as a child stuffed with chocolate as long as Aiden was around. His positive outlook on life was infectious.

"Alright, if you're sure you're okay. . ." Aiden said, sounding disappointed. Was it Dane's imagination, or had he seen a flash of red on his face? It was likely because Aiden was exhausted from their work. Or was it? Dane couldn't decide whether or not he was given an opportunity to explain himself.

Dane watched him for a moment longer, but it seemed as though Aiden was back to his normal self. Dane couldn't risk sharing his secret. It was too dangerous. People like him were detested. They were chased with pitchforks and torches, the snapping jaws of hounds on their heels. The terror of being found out for being a deviant gripped his chest and squeezed, making it difficult to breathe. More than that, he was scared he would lose the most important person in his life.

"I'm going to go get some dinner. I'll meet you back at your room later tonight and we can go over our notes, okay?" Aiden asked, and Dane nodded. "I'll see you then." He stood up and smiled, waving a goodbye before he scampered off to leave the dank cellar.

Dane exhaled and slowly began to laugh to himself. "Gods only know how he keeps going like that," he said before he pushed himself up to his feet using the butt end of the spear. His stomach began to growl like a caged animal.

I could use some food, too, I guess. He thought about perhaps joining Aiden for dinner and meeting up earlier than originally planned, but he had something on his mind that was nagging at him. *I want to tell him, but how? I need to know his answer. I have to know if he shares the same feelings as I do.*

As Dane left the store house, bidding the quartermaster a good day, he stopped outside the doors and sighed as he looked upwards. He could faintly make out some of the stars as the sky darkened, and he remembered how he and Aiden would sometimes walk through the Academy's grounds late at night to talk or get some fresh air after their studies had concluded. Aiden always loved to point out the constellations as he learned them, and looking at them now reminded him of how much he cared for the man.

Dane sighed, and smiled. *I've really fallen hard for him, haven't I? It wouldn't be so bad if I could tell him. Xenar, what should I do?*

As he thought Xenar's name, he instantly thought of Othur. The ursar had always offered him a place to go when he needed a soul to confide in. Dane had thought about telling the monk about his problems and asking for advice, but even though they didn't cling to the close-minded religious zeal of the Church of Laren, he wondered whether Othur would treat him the same way as any human would if he revealed his sexuality to him.

He'd been feeling indecisive about the idea of asking Othur for advice for a long time, and as he headed back to the dorms, he hesitated and looked longingly at the main gate.

Dinner can wait.

* * * * *

"Thanks for seeing me tonight," Dane said, bowing before he took a seat in front of Othur. He sometimes wondered if he bothered the ursar, but he was never turned away. There had been times in the past when Dane was forced to wait a while to speak to him, but those were few and far between. Somehow, Othur was always available when he needed him.

"Of course, Dane. That is what this temple is for," the ursar responded, "Now what is it you wished to talk about?"

Dane thought for a moment how to approach the subject. He wasn't sure what Xen taught about homosexuality, but he felt that he'd be safer in the temple than with the Church of Laren.

Knowing that the next few words out of his mouth would sound stupid, Dane said, "Well, I had a friend approach me the other day, and he admitted to having feelings for me," Dane began to lose eye contact with the ursar as he spoke, "A male friend, that is. And I'm not sure how I should feel. I know how the Church of Laren views homosexuals but I don't know what Xenarian principles think of it."

"We have our thoughts on the matter, but the more important thing is, how do you feel about it?"

Dane wasn't expecting that kind of response. He anticipated shock, or perhaps for Othur to look uncomfortable upon hearing his story. That would have been what most people's reactions would have been if they learned of a sexual deviant in their midst. Dane began to stutter as he answered. "Well, I uh. . . I worry about his safety. What if he says something to the wrong person and gets hurt for it? Is there no sanctuary for him to run to if he gets into trouble?"

"That doesn't answer my question, Dane," Othur said flatly. He stared at the boy, unblinking and without breaking eye contact.

The human sighed. "Yeah, I know." He rubbed his eyes with a thumb and forefinger as he spoke the next words. "I can't lie, it sounds so stupid." Dane met Othur's gaze, staring at the fiercely green eyes. "It's me, I'm the one who has feelings for another man."

"I figured as much. Don't make that face, you'd be amazed how often someone begins a conversation with 'I have a friend that. . .' when they're embarrassed or afraid to say something about themselves." Othur interlaced his fingers and rested them in his lap. "You fear repercussions."

The man's shoulders slumped. "I do. Aiden is my only friend. I don't want to lose him, but I feel like not telling him and secretly eyeing him from a distance is wrong."

"Dane, if you want advice on how to help a friend, I can give it to you. And if you need advice or someone to talk to when you yourself are coping with a problem, I can help you there, too. But I need you to be fully truthful with me when you come to see me, otherwise I may give you misguided wisdom that could very well do more harm than good."

"Yes, of course," Dane said.

Dane began again at the beginning, this time telling him the truth. It was embarrassing to admit some of the things he felt for Aiden, but he realized the importance of getting it all out in the open so that Othur could help him. He talked about the day they had met, and that he knew even before then that he liked men. It was like a lamp being turned on, a single spark that ignited a bright flame of passion in his heart. Dane never realized how much he wanted to be with Aiden, and that it was almost an all-consuming desire as he put off everything to be with him when asked.

"It sounds like you've had a lot on your mind lately," Othur said as he nodded his head sagely. "Were you afraid to talk to me sooner?"

"I was, yes. I've been talking to you and learning from you for a long time, but this was a bit too personal, and it terrified me."

"That is somewhat understandable," Othur said. "Human society is not welcoming to that which is. . . different from the perceived norm."

Dane felt his body stiffen when he heard that word. "Different". That's what he was, and though he knew that he wasn't like others, it still stung to hear it spoken out loud. Dane tried to relax. He knew that Othur was merely stating his observations and wasn't trying to be judgmental.

"I can help assuage your fears a little," Othur said, and waited for Dane to nod before continuing. "We who follow Xen do not see any inherent evil in love, no matter what form it takes. It could be between a man and a woman, two men, or two women. It could even be interracial, like a love between an ursar and a human, for example. As long as it is consensual and both parties care for each other, there is no harm in the way love blossoms."

"That's a relief. I came and talked to the right person then," Dane said with a sigh. It felt like a great burden had been lifted off his chest, as if the weight of a thousand stones had been picked up off his body in a single great tug of a giant's hand.

"As for your fear of rejection, I can't help you much there," Othur admitted, and looked pained. "As much as I wish I could help alleviate the pain you are feeling, and to take the worry away from you, I cannot. Everyone of every race must face rejection of some sort at some point in their lives."

"However, I can tell you're focusing too much on something." Othur leaned forward in his seat. "You seem intensely focused on having control over your life, and sadly, what you seek is to maintain an illusion of control. You can't predict how anyone will react towards you for being who you are, and your idea of maintaining control over your life is to default to not telling anyone to preserve yourself, even if that's not really control and even at the cost of your own emotional well-being."

"How is it not control? I made a decision, didn't I?" Dane asked. He felt offended by the ursar's words.

"Inaction is, in itself, not a choice as we see it. Rather, it is a desire to remove one's control from a situation so that one does not need to make a choice. It gives you the illusion that you have control over your life, when in fact what you are doing is akin to riding the current of a river. You have no ability to change your course, and you cannot go against the current."

Dane admitted that Othur had a point, and it was spelled out fairly clearly. It didn't make it any less insulting in Dane's mind. He suppressed the urge to want to snap at the ursar and took a few deep breaths to calm down. Even so, his agitation hadn't escaped Othur's notice.

"My words seem to have angered you. I apologize," he said solemnly. "But that is often the consequence of looking at the truth. You will feel frustration, because now you have to change something about yourself to cope. Or you can do nothing at all and continue to live the way you have been. Either way, you will feel pain. The only difference is that one path is a long and winding road full of hardship and sadness, while the other is a temporary hurdle you must overcome. Both will come with their own challenges, but learning to do what is best for yourself in the long run is something we all must learn for ourselves. It is difficult, if not impossible, to be taught."

"I understand what you're saying," Dane said quietly when he'd reigned in his emotions. "Is there any advice you can give me for dealing with my feelings for Aiden then? I don't know if, or when, I'll ever be ready to tell him." He broke eye contact and looked away, embarrassed. "I'm not very good with other people, even if I've spent every day with Aiden since we met."

"There's a few things I can tell you," Othur said as he lifted a paw and counted with his fingers. "One, don't put all your hopes and dreams on a single person like you have been doing. Whether they reciprocate your love or not, it's not fair to hinge it all on one person. That's a burden no one should have placed on their shoulders."

"Two, focus less on your desire for control and learn to accept the fact that you cannot control everything in life. And finally, there's only one way for you to know for sure if you'll be rejected: You need to ask this Aiden what he feels for you."

"It sounds hard," Dane said, thinking Othur's words over.

"Nothing worth doing is ever easy. Being happy isn't easy either, but you need to learn how to be happy with yourself and with who you are before you can be ready to love anyone. Do you think you're ready for a relationship with Aiden if he were to return your love?"

"I want to say yes, but I know that I'm not at all ready for it," Dane admitted after a moment of thought. "I know it sounds sappy, but my heart wants him badly, despite me knowing in my mind that I'm not ready."

"The struggle to unify the thoughts of the heart, the mind, and the soul is one we all must deal with, and it is one of the goals of Enlightenment."

"Can I ask you something?" Dane asked and the ursar nodded. "What would you do in my position?"

"I can't answer that," Othur said, shaking his head. "If you're looking for direction, no one can show you the path. You need to look inside yourself and ask yourself those questions that are impossible for others to answer. Only then will you know the correct road to travel."

"But --"

"No buts about it," Othur said forcefully, holding his paw up to stop him from speaking any further. "No one can help you, except for you. I know it's hard and the future doesn't look perfect, but I know that in time, you will overcome your demons and you will be able to be happy. You've made it through worse things than a broken heart, right? Whether you end up being happy with Aiden as your mate, or with another man, or even just being happy with yourself, I cannot say. We are all traveling different roads through life, and none of us knows what's just beyond that next bend called Tomorrow."

Dane nodded. These weren't the answers he was hoping for, but they were something. They were better than nothing, at least. He stood up and bowed. "Thank you for speaking with me tonight." He held his hand out to help the ursar to his feet.

Othur patted Dane on the shoulder when he stood up. "I'll see you again soon, I'm sure. Just come and visit me sometime when you have something good to talk about for a change." He gave the boy a wink before they parted ways.

* * * * *

A few weeks later, Dane found himself in his room studying with Aiden again. The air inside the dorm was comfortably warm, except for the space next to the window which allowed a draft in from the cool autumn night. He sat on his bed beneath the warmth of the lamp, with his book spread out across his lap as he read. Aiden had sprawled out on the floor and propped his head up on his elbows, reading quietly to himself.

Dane's eyes kept drifting off the page and tracing themselves over the curves of Aiden's body, lingering momentarily on the face he'd fallen in love with. A sigh involuntarily escaped his lips and he quickly looked back down at his book before the other man looked up at him.

"Is something wrong?" he asked. "If you're feeling tired, we could take a break."

"I'm fine," Dane lied.

"Are you sure? You've been quiet all night."

"Isn't that what one does when they're reading?" he said with a weak grin.

"You usually like to relax for a few minutes every half hour or so, but you haven't been doing that. It's just been non-stop today." Aiden laid flat on the ground, using his thick arms as pillows.

"Is that bad?"

"No, just unusual."

Dane put a bookmark on the page he was reading, closed the tome, and rubbed his eyes. "Yeah, I could use a short break. Did you want to get a drink at the Purple Nymph?"

"Sure." Aiden closed his book and rose to his feet, cracking his back as he moved.

The pair grabbed their cloaks before heading out. Dane would've preferred to use magic to keep warm, but he'd grown tired of people outside the academy looking at him strangely during the winter months. Mundane humans didn't understand the powers of the arcane, and many thought he was crazy for dressing so lightly.

They left the dorms and made their way across the academy towards the Purple Nymph Tavern that lay just beyond the gates, near the Eastgate Market. It was a quiet bar that saw a fair amount of business, especially from R.A.A.S's older students, and it had a more laid back clientele compared to some of the seedier places closer to the docks. It was frequented by poets and bards and storytellers from afar that enjoyed being an attentive audience to perform for.

There was a bard on the stage as Dane and Aiden strolled out from the cold to take a seat near the hearth. The minstrel quietly strummed on a lute as she tuned it for a performance that was about to start. The two young sorcerers ordered their drinks and received them just as the bard began her song. Dane sipped at the bitter, dark ale he'd been served as the first words began to float from the singer's throat.

Dane didn't pay much heed to the lyrics of the song. Her voice was soft and melodic, and her words switched between Common and Elvish periodically. However, Dane was acutely aware of the speed of the song. It was slower in the beginning, sounding almost sad and forlorn. The tempo had picked up during the chorus, and things felt much better. It was a song that spoke of hope even in the dark, and Dane felt better listening to it. He looked at Aiden, who clapped along with the rest of the crowd when the bard's performance drew to a close. He clutched onto the faint glimmer of hope that one day he'd be able to share a life with Aiden, one where they were more than just friends.

Dane tried to drown out his thoughts with another big gulp of ale that finished off the mug.

"You must've been thirsty eh?" Aiden said with a smile.

"Yeah, something like that."

"What do you say we take the rest of the night off from our studies? We don't have that exam with Professor Frostfire until next week, and I still have a few more days to finish my work with Professor Leafsblade."

"Sure," Dane said as he flagged the waitress over. "Drinking until I can't think anymore seems like a good idea to me."

The two men clinked their mugs together and settled in for a long night of drinking while they waited for the bard to begin her next song.

"So, you haven't told me much about your family," Aiden began after his third drink.

Dane looked up at him slowly, then down at his mug, watching his reflection in the dark liquid. "There isn't much to tell. My mother died in childbirth and I never knew anything about her. My father took care of me and raised me for the first twelve years of my life." He took a sip and set the mug back down. "My father, Jonathan, didn't really treat me as well as I would've liked and we were always fighting. He died saving me from the orcs that attacked Tran."

"I heard about what happened to Tran," Aiden said sadly. "It's unfortunate that happened to you. I'm sorry."

Dane nodded, but remained silent. He missed Tran and wished he could go back to those simple days when he could walk into the town and smell the bakeries and see the smiling faces. Compared to Rogust, it was a peaceful, happy village. He wondered how Ted and Lily were doing. Thoughts of the inn came back to him and he remembered his cat Zoey. He pictured the cat sitting on the table, near the window, looking to the south and waiting for his return.

But would he even return in the cat's lifetime? He dismissed the unsettling thought. As long as Zoey was well-fed, she had many years ahead of her.

"Hey, barkeep!" Aiden shouted across the room, "Another round over here." The boy flashed a few coins and in seconds a waitress was walking over with a pair of mugs.

They spent the rest of the night at the tavern and drank until closing time. When they hobbled back to the academy, they laughed at nothing and bumped into each other like a couple of bumbling fools. Neither one of them cared how they looked. They were having fun, and through the haze of Dane's drunken mind, he was enjoying the close contact with Aiden and was trying hard to get even closer to him without his friend noticing. His body was warm and soft. He liked finding creative ways or excuses to touch him. He draped an arm over his shoulder and gave it a squeeze, leaning on Aiden for support. The man bore his weight without complaint, and continued to laugh along with him.

Before they entered the academy grounds, Dane thought through the drunken haze that he could tell Aiden now. He could share everything, maybe even take a risk and kiss him. If everything went south he could blame it on being overly drunk or that maybe Aiden had dreamed it. He didn't want to do that, though. If he tried anything, he wanted to remember it, and he wanted Aiden to know it without being drunk. Something about the idea seemed impure. He had to be honest while sober.

Aiden bid Dane a good night as the latter stumbled into his room and fell face first in his warm bed, the door slowly shutting itself behind him.

Chapter 23 - Ambitions

17th Day of Athril
127 I.E.

With a groan, Xellik sat up from the cold stone beneath him. He was once again in the spacious, stalactite filled room from his dreams. The vision had become so persistent in recent months that he and Bytej had surmised that the dreams were of something significant, but neither orc could figure out what. There was little they could discern from the images beyond that whatever this place was, it was deep underground.

He felt as though eyes were upon him, watching his every move as he scanned the room. The minotaur was nowhere to be seen, but that made him feel more uneasy about the dream. That minotaur was a powerful spellcaster. He could be hiding in the room he stood in or swoop down from the ceiling with his magic. He could kill Xellik without the orc even being aware of it.

Xellik proceeded down the hallway at a light jog. He'd never had an opportunity to venture out of the room before, as he always woke up when the shadowy minotaur appeared. The orc wanted to get out of the room before it showed up like it had every other time.

I hope I don't run into any trouble here, he thought as he took a right curve down a hallway and down a flight of stairs. *I need to find out what this blasted dream is about before something has the chance to try and kill me. If the minotaur's thorns hurt my real body, I'd hate to think that a weapon could do.*

At the bottom of the stairs, Xellik found himself standing in a narrow hallway constructed out of large bricks. The walls were lined with tree roots that glowed with an eerie light, and when Xellik extended his hand and ran his fingers over their surface, he found them warm to the touch. Never before had the orc seen something like it, and it only further blurred the lines between reality and surrealism for him. Where was this place that he'd been dreaming of for so long?

The hallway stretched further into the darkness. The only sound he could hear was the beating of his own heart and the thumping of his footfalls upon the stones. Everything was still and silent. He glanced over his shoulder as he moved, always feeling eyes upon him. He thought that the minotaur would come from the shadows at any moment. Every time he looked back, he chastised himself for his childish fears. There was never anything behind him, yet he still felt he was being watched. There was magic at play, and Xellik was certain of it. Yet when he tried to discern the truth through his own powers, they failed him as they always did. The Goddess could not hear him in this vision, and thus his gifts were useless.

Without steel in his hands or sorcery at his beck and call, he felt exposed. He wouldn't allow his fears to control him, but he would have felt better about his situation if he had some means of defending himself. He used his fears to spur him forward. There was no use in turning back at this point, and he didn't know how much longer this lucid vision of his would last. He needed information about this tunnel system before he woke up.

Xellik continued to investigate the tunnel. He saw nothing that stood out and screamed important to him. The further down the tunnel he traveled, the damper it began to smell. The walls began to develop a thin layer of green sludge that Xellik found slimey to the touch. The floor was covered in it as well, and he began to walk at a slower pace to avoid slipping.

What is this place?

At the end of the tunnel, there was a doorway leading to a flight of stairs. It spiraled down further into darkness. Not wishing to travel back and risk waking before he learned anything, Xellik plunged ahead. He could hear the faint drip-drop of water coming from somewhere nearby as he moved cautiously down the glowing halls.

At the bottom of the stairs, the room opened up to reveal a small altar in the center of a cavern. A moat boxed off a dais from everything else, and it was connected to several small streams that fed water out of the room. Tree roots crept along the ground, reaching desperately for the moat that had been filled by the dripping stalactites above. A bridge had been constructed at the base of the stairs that allowed someone to get across the moat. Xellik crossed the bridge and began to inspect the altar, keeping himself from touching it for fear of traps.

The altar seemed simple enough. It was a thick table constructed out of marble stone that looked smooth to the touch. It reflected the dim light cast off by the tree roots, making it stand out even more. Xellik spotted a number of etchings running along the top rim of the table, but he didn't recognize the language they were written in. They could have been Draconic for all he knew, but he was certain that it wasn't a minotaur script.

Resting atop the table was a metal stand in the shape of a pair of hands. Cupped within the palms was a green stone that had a flawlessness to it that had Xellik in awe of its craftsmanship. It was cut into a rectangle, with facets angled down and to the sides. The orc could even see his reflection peering back at him. The emerald was made so perfectly that Xellik doubted it was made in this world. It was set within a golden pendant, and its chain hung down over and behind the stand.

After a moment of hesitation, the orc put aside his fears and reached out for the stone. When his skin touched the emerald, a jolt of intense pain shot through his head and he let loose a bellowing scream. He attempted to remove his hand from the stone but found that he couldn't release his grip. He felt like the inside of his head was rupturing and he could feel blood seeping out of his ears and sliding down the sides of his head.

"Xellik. . ." a ghostly voice called out to him. It was a soft voice, almost soothing, and that of a female. He could barely hear it over his own screams. "Xellik. . ."

"W-who's there?" Xellik managed to whimper in response with great effort.

"Come to me. . . Come to Batic. . ."

"Where?" He was in too much pain to remember if he'd ever heard the word Batic before, or where this place could be.

"Come to Batic, in the jungle. . ." the voice responded. "Come to me Xellik. . . Your wishes are within your grasp." It repeated itself several more times, each more quiet than the last, until finally the voice faded away entirely.

Once the voice receded, the pain Xellik was experiencing ceased all at once. He was flung backwards by an explosion of force. When he landed, he sat up with a start back in his own bed as if he'd just been falling a great distance.

His head no longer throbbed with pain, but he could still feel the residual ache from whatever had been hurting him in his dream. His body was covered in a film of sweat and his covers clung to his body. He panted as he tried to get his breathing and pounding heart back to normal.

"What in Galria was that?" he asked himself as he stood up in the darkness of his room.

He didn't think he would be able to get back to sleep anytime soon. He threw on a pair of leggings and ended up wandering around the slums until dawn, when he hoped Bytej would be awake. He needed time to collect his thoughts and relax before he could approach the shaman about what he'd experienced.

When the sun peaked over the horizon, Xellik refused to wait any longer. He quickly returned home and pounded on the flimsy door that made up Bytej's room.

Haij banged on the wall nearby. "KNOCK IT OFF, XELLIK!"

The orc ignored him and continued to slam his fist on the door until Bytej answered it.

"What the hell are you doing, whelp?" Bytej shouted as came out. He was still half-asleep and could barely keep his eyes open.

"Where's Batic?" Xellik said simply.

"What?" the older orc rubbed his eyes with the back of his hand and yawned.

"Where. Is. Batic!?" Xellik demanded impatiently. He ignored the angry grumbling the shaman made as he beckoned him into the room.

Bytej thought for a moment. "Batic is. . . I think that's a temple somewhere in the Emerald Jungle." He strolled over to the bookcase and thumbed through some of the tattered volumes he'd managed to collect of the years. "Let's see. . . Batic. . ." he began muttering to himself as he ran his fingers over the spines of several books. "Ah, here we go."

He grabbed a large brown tome off the shelf and began to flip through the pages to find what he was looking for. "Batic's other name is the Temple of Earth. It's been there longer than the orcs have been on Rhavik."

"What's the significance of it?"

Bytej was silent for a moment as he scanned the pages for answers. "It's a holy shrine dedicated to Gaia, the Foundation of the Earth. A flight of dragons used to watch over the temple but since then some druids have moved into the area to use as a place of worship to their god, based on a report from the Zugruli spymaster." He looked up at Xellik. "Where did you hear the name Batic, exactly?"

Xellik quickly recapped his most recent dream, including the artifact he saw and the voice he heard when he touched it. He could recollect the visions with a degree of accuracy that startled himself, to the point where he could remember exactly how smooth the gem was and how the voice in his mind had sounded.

"That sounds familiar. I think there was an old legend I read about that." Bytej skimmed the book quickly. "I wonder if that relic you saw was the Emerald of Deep Earth."

"Is that important?"

"It's just a legend, a myth. The Zugruli orcs have been trying to confirm whether it's real or not, and because of their tenuous peace treaty with the Woodcaller minotaur, they can't get into the temple to verify what secrets it holds without sparking an all out war with them. The minotaur would likely rally every Korcyn rebel in the jungle and storm the city if that were to happen."

Xellik nodded his head. "But if there is a temple dedicated to the God of the Earth, then that likely means that the gemstone I saw is the Emerald in the legend."

"You can believe that," Bytej shrugged. "It's not uncommon for a treasure found in the open like that to be a fake, though. Maybe your mind was tricking you. Which makes me wonder who called you to it."

"Who else could it have been?" Xellik asked. "It had to be Sytarel."

Bytej laughed at him. "I wouldn't put too much faith in such things." He placed the book back in its spot. "Whenever the Gods try to personally get involved in mortal affairs, other deities intervene to help maintain the world's balance. Even a subtle nudge like that would likely prompt something to happen from an opposing God or Goddess."

"I'm sure it had to have been Sytarel. I can't explain why, but I'm sure of it." Something about the message to travel to Batic seemed significant. He couldn't be quite sure of the how or the why. He wondered if accepting his place as an adult and striving to become a better leader had unlocked something within him to be more receptive to the message.

"If you say so." Bytej rolled his eyes. Xellik was too busy with his own thoughts to notice. "What do you plan on doing with that information then?"

"We're going to Batic. I'll assemble our warriors and we'll storm that temple by ourselves if we have to. I'll take that Emerald and use it's power to overthrow Zugrul."

"Hold on there. If you think we're going to just walk in and do what the Zugruli have failed to do for decades, when they have far more soldiers at their disposal, you're insane. And suppose we did succeed in raiding the temple, we don't have the forces necessary to oppose the Zugrul tribe and its allies."

Xellik paused and thought for a moment. Bytej was right. The Fleshgorgers didn't have much in the way of numbers. "We'd need more warriors, wouldn't we?"

"That, and a lot of luck. Where would you even get more orcs to follow you, anyways?"

"There's hundreds of us in these slums," Xellik said, gesturing out the window. "They'll follow if we promise to overthrow the ruling class and take Zugrul for ourselves. They don't want to be here anymore than we do."

"Now I fully believe you've lost your mind. Even if you were to successfully make it into Batic with a force large enough to combat the minotaur, how do you know whatever relics they have there will be enough to aid you in your grand scheme?"

"I know, because that's my destiny, and it's necessary to fulfill my promise to our tribe. I promised them we would not be in these slums any longer, and I'll do good on that promise. The Emerald is the answer to our problems. It must be."

* * * * *

Later that month, Xellik had arranged to have a meeting for all orcs from every caste-less tribe in the slums. He prepared himself mentally all day for giving a speech in front of hundreds of orcs, with every last one of them judging him based on his every word. The meeting was to take place inside a large building to the north of Zugrul, far beyond the walls and in a place that Xellik hoped no prying eyes would be looking.

Even though the Zugruli orcs seemed content to pretend the slums didn't exist, he didn't want to take the chance that one of them would be listening in on his plans.

The hall began to fill with a large number of orcs. Some took seats on the ground, sitting cross-legged or on their knees. Others leaned up against the walls, trying to keep an even distance from some of those around them. There were orcs from all sorts of shattered tribes, from the young to the old, the strong and the weak, the warriors and the shaman. As the room filled and orcs continued to pile in, Xellik felt a small sense of elation. They were all here to listen to him, to give heed to his words and, by extension, Sytarel's. This was their chance at salvation. They rushed to him like children running into their mother's open arms.

"Orders, sir?" Cinra asked as he approached Xellik from the side.

"You and Urzule are to stand watch outside. I want you to alert me should any Zugruli orcs start looking too hard at this place. We don't want them catching wind of our plans."

"At once, sir." The scout took off without another word.

"Napir, Aiph, I want you flanking me on either side. Look intimidating to keep the crowd in line, but I don't want you to frighten anyone or instigate anything." He looked pointedly at Napir. "Got it?"

"Aye, sir." Napir grinned, then took his position.

"How much longer should we wait?" Aiph asked as he moved to Xellik's left. "This room isn't going to hold too many more people."

"It'll hold all the orcs that are willing to join us. We'll wait for the signal from Haij to let us know when no one else is coming, then we'll have him and Bytej watch the doors for Zugruli orcs." Xellik watched the orcs continue to trickle in.

After a few moments, Haij poked his head in and flashed Xellik a hand signal to let the orc know the streets were clear.

"I thank you all for joining us today," Xellik began, shouting over the still murmuring voices of the crowd. He'd cast a simple spell and conjured a scroll he had written over the course of the past few days. In reality though, the conjuration was a cover, to hide the spell he'd actually intended to cast.

"Sytarel thanks you, as well." Xellik's voice took on a strange, dual-tone quality. He spoke as if both he and a woman talked in unison, and his eyes began to glow with a golden fire. The crowd fell silent in an instant.

Xellik was banking on this simple performance working in his favor. Such thaumaturgy was beyond the scope of arcanists and shaman to work, but for a High Priest, it was as easy to work as breathing. The blood of the First Orcs flowed through his veins, granting him a power and connection with Sytarel that others could not achieve. He lifted his arms up, holding them wide to encompass the room as he drew upon his Pact with his Goddess.

"Though some of your people have fallen out of my favor, and have committed grave acts of sacrilege towards me, know that I come to you now to offer you a chance at redemption. I urge you to listen to this orc's words, for he shall be your salvation. Do not spit in the face of this offer, for this is your one and only opportunity to save yourselves from my wrath. Honor guide your hands, my children."

Xellik lurched forward and shut his eyes as though he were a marionette whose strings were cut. He dropped low, nearly falling to his knees, as if unprepared to make himself stand again by his own will. The orc rose again and gasped for breath, panting for a moment, and took a couple seconds to recompose himself.

The crowd before him was utterly silent, and not a whisper passed between their lips. Xellik struggled to keep from smiling. Though he truly was a High Priest of Sytarel, he couldn't believe how effectively such a simple trick of magic could work on the casteless tribes. His power over them was absolute, and they hung on his every word.

"It is as you heard the Mistress say. I am Her hand, Her Chosen. I am Xellik Fergoth, son of Fellis Fergoth and descendant of one of the First. By my birthright, I am the leader of my tribe, and a conduit through which the Goddess works her magic." There were snickers coming from around the room, but they were quickly stifled. "I don't care what you make of such a statement, but that is who I am. I lead my tribe without question," he said, gesturing with his hands to Aiph, Napir, and to several Fergoth tribe orcs sitting nearby, "and they will follow me to the death."

"What is important for you to take away from this evening, if anything, is what we're planning to do. We have been forced to live in these slums, and who is responsible? The misguided leaders of the Zugruli. They have kept us down here, trapped and hidden beneath the shadows of their glorious city. They stamp us into the ground and label us broken and worthless because of their religious zeal."

"When did being an orc mean throwing one another to the wolves?" He made a sweeping motion with both hands, indicating the entire crowd watching him, "Are we not all of the same blood? Carved from the same mold that was handcrafted by Sytarel Herself? Are we not all Her children, regardless of our genders? Regardless of our social standing?"

There were murmurs and nods around the room, though there still remained several dubious glances on some orc's faces.

"When I first arrived on this accursed continent, I made a promise to myself, and my tribe: I would lead us out of these wretched ruins and put us in our rightful place as full citizens of Zugrul and, by extension, the Orcish Empire. Those orcs behind their walls have no more right to that land than we do, and they are not in a position to judge us unworthy of the protections and rights of a Zugruli citizen."

Xellik pointed up to the ceiling. "But do you know who is in such a position? Sytarel. It is by Her will that we are here, and She is the ultimate judge when it comes to our race. No orc has a right to bar us entry into Zugrul, to beat us unmercifully, or to condemn us and our loved ones to a live of slovenly labor in rat-infested homes." Xellik began to raise his voice, speaking louder above the din of muttering. Many orcs were leaning forward, waiting for the next words to escape his lips.

He had to keep the energy flowing, to make sure that when he finally delivered his ultimatum, they would be hanging on his every word. The trick using Sytarel's voice would only hold them for so long. Soon they would likely remember their distaste for the Goddess, and he would lose control if that happened.

"Are we not better than the korcyn slaves that the Zugruli created with their magics? So why do those pigs get to live in slave quarters that are, for all intents and purposes, better accommodations than our own? Why should the slaves have better homes than us?"

Xellik had never seen the inside of the city, let alone the place where the korcyn were kept, but the crowd of orcs didn't need to know that. He hoped that they would fall for his bluff, or if not, that they wouldn't question it anyways.

"We are orcs!" he shouted, and the crowd roared back in agreement. "We are the children of Sytarel! Not those boars the Zugruli keep!" He brought a hand around and jabbed a finger in the direction of the city. "We belong behind those walls. We deserve the right to worship the Goddess in a proper temple instead of in this pit of mud and rubble! Wouldn't you all agree?"

A resounding cry rose up throughout the room as orcs began to stand and pump their fists in the air, proclaiming their agreement with Xellik's statements. His throat was getting hoarse from having to shout over their collective voices, but it was worth it.

"That's why the Fergoth have made a pledge: We will overthrow the Zugruli orcs, and take our place within the city itself, as citizens and as rulers. And all are welcome to join our cause, reaping the rewards of their efforts and effectively redeeming themselves in the eyes of Sytarel. The Zugruli will know the same despair that we have felt for all these years while we wasted away into nothingness. Who's with me?"

The cheers became louder. Those who had been giving him indifferent looks moments before were now standing and applauding, cheering the orc leader on. Some still hesitated, but they too eventually joined in.

"If you truly wish to join the cause, then cast aside all previous allegiances and join us!" Xellik snapped his fingers and a few of the shaman from the tribe came forward, bearing bowls full of a white liquid inside that rolled and sloshed gently as they walked. "Wear the Fangs of our tribe with pride!"

As the orcs began to line up for the shaman to etch the tattoo on their foreheads, Xellik decided it was time to duck out. His work was done, and he felt the others could take care of the rest. He'd ordered them to make sure to leave the vassal orcs' original tribe tattoos in place, and to put the Fangs on another spot. Xellik wanted to be able to identify at a glance who his home guard was, and who was not from his tribe. He also wanted to ensure that the new orcs recognized that he was willing to let them continue to identify themselves as their former tribes, something he felt would be important or sentimental to them.

Xellik stepped out into the brisk summer air as Napir and Aiph came up from behind him. "That went well, don't you think?"

"I can't believe you had them eating out of the palms of your hands," Aiph said. "You've changed something fierce, Xellik. Perhaps I was wrong to think you'd make a bad leader."

Xellik smirked at his friend. "I'll prove to you and everyone else that I have the traits necessary to rule this new tribe. I'll live up to every one of the promises I made in there."

Footsteps approached from the shadows of an alleyway, crunching softly upon the dirt.

"Any sign of trouble, Cinra?" Napir asked without even looking to see who it was.

"What trouble?" a female voice responded.

The three orcs whirled around to see Sorda standing nearby with a hand on her hip, as if she were resting it upon a scabbard. Her hair had a slick sheen cast along its surface from the moonlight.

"What do you want?" Aiph began, but was silenced as Xellik stepped between them.

"You two go on ahead back to camp. I'd like to speak with Sorda alone."

The orcs didn't hesitate. Neither wanted to deal with the female, nor did they want to disobey Xellik's orders. Once they were out of earshot, and once he was sure Cinra wasn't anywhere nearby, he spoke again.

"I trust you came here for a reason."

"Quite the speech you gave," Sorda said. "Had me believing it for a second, too. It helped that it was devoid of the hate for females you usually display."

"People can change," Xellik replied simply.

A tense moment passed between them, and seconds crawled by as Xellik waited for her to continue. She wasn't saying anything, and he gave a resigned sigh.

"I know things aren't exactly as good as they could be between us, and you know what? I'm sorry about all the problems I've caused for you in the past," Xellik began, "There's no need for there to be any bad blood between us."

Sorda seemed taken aback by his sudden apology. She stared at him with a single brow raised. "What are you getting at, Xellik?"

"I'm saying I don't care about what happened when we were whelps. Let's turn over a new leaf and begin a new journey, to move forward as one tribe, with one unified mind." He held out his hand to clasp her wrist in agreement. "How about it?"

She hesitated, staring at his hand then back up at him. "You confuse me to no end." Her hand shot out and gripped Xellik's wrist as he did the same to hers.

To cement things, Xellik did something he never thought he'd ever do in a million lifetimes. He pulled her close to him and kissed her roughly, his short tusks clicking against her teeth. She resisted at first but relented, and eased into his embrace as his hands cupped the back of her hand. He pulled her closer and pressed their bodies together, and he could feel her warmth against him.

Without another word between them, the two orcs retired to Sorda's quarters back near camp. Before he shut the door behind him, Xellik glanced over his shoulder at the lithe form crouching on a rooftop not far from them. He shot a glare at Cinra and the other orc was gone before could blink.

Chapter 24 - The Temple of Earth

27th Day of Zephyr
127 I.E.

Sorda lightly tapped Xellik on the forehead with her knuckles. "Is something the matter?"

"Hmm?" Xellik turned away from watching the sea to look up at her. He was laying against a set of flat rocks, and was unaware of what she'd just asked him. She repeated herself and he replied, "No, just thinking."

"Thinking or plotting?"

"It's the same thing either way at this point, isn't it?"

"I suppose so," she shrugged. "You've been like that more and more lately."

"Tomorrow is an important day. There's too much at stake if we fail." Xellik stood up and cracked his back. "How are preparations coming along?"

"Our tribe is outfitted and ready to go. Ragash is shoring up the numbers and making sure everyone is equipped. Many of the other tribes are still working on equipping themselves for the journey. Truth be told, only a handful of orcs will be able to accompany us to the temple."

Xellik nodded his head. They'd been preparing for their attack on Zugrul the last few days. Procuring supplies for weapons, armor, and food had been more difficult than he'd first thought it would be, but with the entire slums united under him, they'd managed to pull through. They also knew the rough location of

Batic, as well as its defenses. Now the orcs were almost ready to take Zugrul head on. All they needed was the Emerald.

The next day, the Fergoth rose with the sun and met at the outskirts of the slums. A large number of fresh bloods from other tribes had joined them. Though originally Xellik had wanted to only take the home guard with him, he knew politically and from a tactical standpoint that it'd be better to include members of other tribes in his expedition.

"Are we all clear?" Xellik said to Cinra when the scout rejoined them.

"Believe so. I don't see any Zugruli looking our way just yet, but we shouldn't linger," he replied.

"Good. I want you and Urzule to lead. Find the temple and keep an eye out for any threats from the jungle." He turned to regard the gathered warriors. "I know we are few in number, and that a few of you have your doubts about whether we can accomplish a proper invasion into the Temple of Earth. It's my hope, nay, my belief, that our smaller size will be a boon to us, as we can move through the temple much easier regardless of what awaits us there."

"How do we know we can trust you?" an orc woman from the former Stonecrusher clan said. "How do we know you won't do something like stick us at the front to spare your own tribe from any losses?"

"I'm not asking you to trust me. If you don't believe in us, then you should just stay behind. As for the rest of you," he called out, and looked over the crowd. "If you have the will to march with me, then I will welcome you with open arms and I'll ensure your safety."

"Fine by me," replied a Tigra clan orc. "Let's see what this new leader can do."

Xellik smirked at him. "Let's get moving then. Daylight's

burning."

As they entered the jungle, they brought their weapons to bear. Even a group of their size couldn't move quietly and Xellik didn't want to take the chance that they'd be caught off guard by a korcyn rebel ambush or by whatever else that potentially awaited them among the trees.

"How can you know that the Emerald actually exists?" Bytej asked quietly as he fell in stride with his leader. "For all we know, it could just be a myth. This could be a wild goose chase at best, and a trap by someone trying to lure orcs away from Zugrul at worst."

Xellik's eyes swung to the side to look at him. "It's there, I know for certain. Sytarel showed me the way. That relic is the key to overthrowing the Zugruli."

"You don't think Sytarel would have something to say about slaughtering the strongest clan on Galria?"

"It was Sytarel herself that's been dragging me through my dreams into that temple nearly every night since we arrived. She wants me to follow Her directions. She'll lead us to victory and restore our tribe to its former glory."

"Oh by the Gods. . ." Bytej slapped his forehead. "These delusions of grandeur are getting to be too much to bear, Xellik. Do you sincerely believe that everything will go the way you want it to?"

"Yes, of course. If I wasn't certain, I wouldn't be going through with this entire plan in the first place." Xellik could hear the groan coming from the orc beside him. The shaman wasn't one to buy into dream interpretation, but that's where Xellik believed that he was wrong. The recurring dream was purposeful. The details were always the same, and unlike many other dreams he had experienced in his youth, devoid of oddities like extra fingers or his tusks falling out. He didn't understand why he wouldn't believe him when he said it was significant. Bytej seemed to be looking for any excuse to undermine him. Perhaps he didn't like the idea that Xellik was attempting to take the reins of leadership away from him. Bytej wanted to overthrow the dominant social structure of their race, but he wanted to be the head of that. Xellik frowned thinking about this. He was not going to be the shaman's tool for his own schemes. Even if the journey he took was set forth by Bytej, he stayed on the path by his own will.

"Those visions were more than just dreams," Xellik continued. "It felt real. And the voice. . . it had to have been Sytarel. It was too real to be just a dream. The voice called me to Batic, so I'm going." He shot Bytej a cold look. "With or without you. It's your choice if you want to see this through and finally become the dominant clan in this kingdom."

There was very little talking after that as they continued their trek west through the jungle. They kept a steady march westward, following the directions from Cinra as he read from a map of the area that Bytej had acquired. They stopped only when it became too dark to see without the aid of a torch, and set up camp for the night.

The next several days consisted of heavy marching through the jungle. Things were tense as it was, and the after all the walking the warriors following him were beginning to grow rowdy. They were itching for a fight. Xellik began to worry that tensions might escalate before they found the temple. He didn't think that would happen, at least with the Fergoth orcs. Ragash seemed intent on maintaining order, and Xellik was happy to let him do that. There were rumblings of complaints from the other clans that traveled with them. Those were the one's he worried about. That kind of anxiety was characteristically unorcish. Their race was not one given to worrying. It was a sign of weakness, and being weak went against the Strength that Sytarel embodied.

"Ragash," Xellik whispered, calling the clan's most senior

warrior over to him.

"What do you want?" Ragash grunted as he leaned in to hear what Xellik had to say. He didn't respect the orc. He had attained position as leader because of his blood and because Bytej had told them to treat him as they would have treated Fellis. Xellik had yet to do anything to prove his worth, and being given orders like that made the hair on his neck bristle with rage.

"Keep an eye on the other clans," he said in a low voice. He cast his gaze backwards, ensuring no one was listening to their conversation. "Make sure they don't get out of line. The last thing we need is a revolt right now."

"This is what happens when you rush into things," Ragash said pointedly.

They shouldn't have rushed to get to Batic, but Xellik insisted on getting there as soon as possible. Based on Xellik's descriptions of his visions, he had outfitted everyone with shorter swords than they felt comfortable with. Bows would be utterly ineffective, and crossbows were too hard to come by to get more than a couple. He was not looking forward to close quarters fighting with minotaur in cramped spaces... and possibly long hallways that would give the beastmen room to charge them.

"Your opinions are noted, Ragash, but I know what I'm doing."

"See to it that you don't get us killed," he sneered, showing the pointed tips of his teeth before he stepped back in line.

On the eighth day of marching, Xellik was growing impatient. While he trusted Cinra and Urzule with navigating the jungle and acting as their forward scouts, he was concerned that they hadn't yet spotted so much as a trace of the temple.

"Are we even headed the right way?" Napir asked as he pushed aside some ferns.

"Ask Cinra when he gets back from scouting ahead," Xellik told him simply. "He's never led us astray before."

There was a rustling of bushes nearby. All at once, everyone dropped low and was ready for combat. Xellik stayed still for a moment to listen, but there was no further noise. Slowly, the Fergoth began to move westward again, but a few minutes later they heard the same sound once more.

"Something's out there," Aiph whispered, "And it's definitely not Cinra."

"Bytej?" Xellik said, asking the shaman for his advice. "What do you think?"

"Korcyn rebels, most likely," he replied.

Everyone began to reach for their weapons as a scream erupted from the rear. The shouts were quickly stifled as the bushes rustled violently and someone was dragged away. Seconds later, there was a loud keening noise coming from all directions, drawing ever closer with each passing second.

Xellik conjured a sword for himself and dropped low, preparing for whatever was out there. He was expecting one of the boar-men to come charging out of the bush, but what he saw instead defied all his expectations.

Small, pink-skinned creatures came rushing out of the jungle around them. They wore painted wooden masks over their faces that gave them the appearance of having gigantic heads with fang-filled mouths despite their tiny bodies. They wore woven grass clothes around their waists and long black hair hung around their heads. Through the eye holes of the masks, Xellik could see milky, pupil less eyes staring intently back at him.

"They're phens!" Bytej shouted, "Don't let them swarm you!"

Xellik tried to slice one of the little pygmy people in half but the thing was too quick and too small. Trying to swing at them was like swatting at mosquitoes with a battleaxe. "Stand still, you pests!" He evoked a blast of fire but it missed by a large margin as the creature sprang away, chattering incessantly.

"They're just vermin! Why are they so fast?" Aiph asked, astonished at the sight of so many of the things swarming around. He swung a booted foot and kicked one of the pygmy men, sending the creature flying into a tree trunk. The mad keening sound it made ceased as it struck the wood head first. "Step on them or kick them! Forget your weapons!"

One of the creatures dropped from the canopy above and latched onto a chunk of flesh on Xellik's arm. The creature dug in with its teeth and nails, and Xellik suppressed his scream with a snarl. He tried to shake it off but then the phen merely held tighter. More of the creatures were quick to descend upon him as they tried to drag him down.

With a shout, Xellik unleashed an explosion of arcane energy emanating from his body that threw his attackers away, but not before they shredded skin from parts of his body.

Bytej grabbed a thick piece of wood and ignited the tip of it to turn it into a makeshift torch. He swung it around and the phens backed away, screaming fearfully as the flames licked at their flesh. Several of them ran off to the sides, circling around to attack someone else.

"Warleader!" Cinra called out from somewhere. "I've located the temple!"

"Not a moment too soon," Xellik muttered, then shouted to his warriors, "Disengage and make a run for Batic! Follow Cinra to the gates!" He grabbed a phen's skull and crushed it with his bare hands.

As the orcs began to rush headlong through the jungle, they could hear the mad chattering and tribal screams of the phens behind them, above them, and all around the jungle. It felt like they were all over, swarming like a hive of wasps.

"Why are we running from those things?" Napir huffed as he tried to keep pace with everyone.

"I don't want to waste time with those balls of teeth. We have bigger beasts to take care of."

The trees began to give way until they came into a clearing at the base of a sheer cliff. A huge stone doorway was nestled within the side of a mountain. The archway over the door was ornate and meticulously carved with the love and dedication of a skilled stonemason. On both sides of the gate were weathered, cracked statues in the shape of humanoids armored in full plate, with cloaks over their eyes and swords in their hands. The blades of their weapons were firmly planted in the ground. The statues towered over the orcs, and looked down at them like silent, eternal guardians.

"Make for the doors and seal the temple behind us! Move!" Xellik ordered.

The orcs pushed the gates open with a great deal of effort while Sorda and Aiph covered their rear. The mad keening of the pygmies echoed in the trees and bushes all around them, but fortunately the wide space between the treeline and the temple stole the phens' ability to ambush them. Between the two of them, Sorda and Aiph were able to hold their position while Urzule took potshots with her crossbow from the doorway.

"Everyone's inside!" she called, reloading the weapon. "Get in!"

The two fighters disengaged from their battle and all by dove through the stone doors as the rest of the home guard worked to shut them. One brave little phen tried to get through in time, but its lower half was squished between the stones. Even as it lay dying on the ground, it dragged itself using its hands to get at someone. The creature snapped at people's ankles as it crawled along, until Haij stomped on it with a booted foot.

"Whatever God created these things is a sick bastard," Haij muttered, using a stick he found to scrape the remains off the underside of his boot.

"They shouldn't have been this far east," Bytej muttered, consulting a book he pulled out of his pack. "They're usually on the northwestern part of the jungle."

"Who cares?" Haij asked as he plopped down on the stone floor and leaned against a wall. "I need to catch my breath."

"Agreed," Xellik said, then called to the rest of them. "Take a moment to rest, but stay alert. We don't know what's in here."

Xellik thought back to the stone statues outside, and felt that there was something off about them. He'd heard of a construct called golems, beings made from the earth that were brought to life with the use of magic. He'd seen a few at the Zugrul port that were used to move heavy crates around. There was a small bit of fear building up inside him that made him worry whether the statues at the temple doors were animated in a similar manner. Even if they didn't attack when they entered the temple, maybe they would come to life when he would try to leave with the Emerald.

As the orcs stepped further inside, the room came to life with the glow of luminescent globes that lit up along the walls. Though it had been pitch black a few seconds ago, they could now see clear as day. Xellik wasn't the least bit surprised when he found the walls to be constructed out of the same stonework that he saw in his dream. Further inside he could see that some parts of the walls were covered in the glowing roots that had led him down the tunnel. Several hallways stretched out in numerous directions. Xellik paused to think. He had been given little direction as to where to go to find the Emerald's alter, but logically, he figured that it must be at the heart of the temple. There would be no sense in taking any of the side passages.

Xellik pointed down the central hallway opposite of the gate they just entered. "We'll go down there. Let's move."

They headed deeper in, led by the endless trail of lamps that lit their way. As they traveled, they saw more signs of life beyond the countless spider webs they kept running into. They found empty rooms with tables and chairs that appeared to be eating quarters, and upon closer inspection, the rooms were found to have been used recently. The wet, musty smells of the temple obscured the scents of whoever it was who lived there.

"Who would live in a place like this?" Haij asked out loud. He opened up a cupboard and found nothing but clean dishes. They were large and wooden, and there was not a speck of dust on them.

"The Woodcaller Minotaur. They revere this place," Xellik said, "They'd better not get in our way. Come on. We're not here for sightseeing." He paused for a moment and looked at his fellow orcs. The short rest after the ambush hadn't been enough. Many of his warriors were panting and wiping sweat away from their eyes as they passed around skins of water. "I guess we can stop for a longer break. Take a few minutes to drink and have something to eat. We'll need our strength if those minotaur show up."

His warriors sat down and propped themselves up against the wall. They groaned and sighed as they slumped down. Xellik admitted that he was feeling exhausted as well. He would never admit it to the others, and he turned away to take a long sip from his water skin.

After a few minutes, just as they were about to get up to start moving again, there was a clip-clopping sound echoing off the walls.

"Took them long enough to show up," Xellik sneered. "Everyone get up. We've got company."

A voice called out from around the corner down a side passage. "Hello? Is someone there?"

"A minotaur!" Haij exclaimed, and drew his sword.

The furry bull-man was covered in tribal garments. His chest was bare save for a sash draped over his shoulders. He carried no weapons, and the only thing that looked remotely dangerous about him was the pair of massive horns protruding from the sides of his head and sticking out in front of him. They were well-worn, suggesting they had been used before.

"Intruders! Intruders in the temple!" the minotaur called out, darting back the way he had come. "Quick, get Tsaar!"

Xellik ran forward ahead of his warriors and conjured his sword as he charged, swinging upwards at the minotaur. The attack was dodged easily, and the beastman danced backwards as his hooves clapped rapidly on the stone floor. Xellik was faster, and each successive swing of his sword came that much closer to landing a hit. The minotaur would not be able to move his great bulk that quickly for long.

"Be gone! Your presence taints this holy ground!" the minotaur's hands were limned by a dark green aura as he cast a spell.
Behind Xellik he could hear screams erupting from the end of the hall as the roots that crawled along them sprang to life and impaled his rear guard, pinning their skewered bodies to the wall. Their screams echoed off the walls and were choked off by vines that erupted out their mouths and eyes. He had never before considered the nature as a force to be reckoned with. Seeing it at the beck and call of another amplified its power until even the plants around them became terrifying weapons.

With a scream of rage, Xellik swung and sliced an arm off the minotaur before he could cast another spell. "I'll enjoy using you to feed my troops!"

"Strike me down. You will not get far once the Archdruid gets here!" the minotaur spat on Xellik's face.

"Your Archdruid is no match for the chosen people of Sytarel!" Xellik roared and his hand flashed out to grip the minotaur's head. His opponent gasped before he started to scream as the flesh was melted off his bones. Xellik hurled the limp body to the side and turned to Bytej. "I want the side passages blocked off before their reinforcements arrive! We're going to continue moving forward. Hurry up and work your magics!"

The Fergoth moved down the tunnel that Xellik indicated while Bytej stayed behind. The shaman uttered an incantation and hurled a fiery boulder at the ceiling. The explosion rocked the temple and as he retreated back to meet up with the rest of the orcs, the stonework began to collapse in on itself, sealing off the hallways as well as the path they had come from. There would no longer be any turning back, as if Xellik would ever think of doing such a thing after coming so far.

"There they are!" a minotaur at the end of the hall called out.

The roots and vines came to life again, but Xellik was able to duck and weave around them, narrowly being skewered by the spear-like appendages. A few orcs behind him were not as agile as plants burst from their faces. He sliced the roots away with his sword to get a clear path towards the Woodcaller. In his free hand, he cupped a ball of impenetrable darkness that he'd conjured. He hurled the shadow at his assailants. It struck the nearest minotaur, penetrating the thick hide and chilling him to his core. Xellik then led the charge forward, cutting through the Woodcaller's ranks with his shoulders in tow as they fought their way deeper into the tunnel.

"Where to now?" Haij asked. His sword was coated in blood and bits of flesh and fur. They had come to the end of the hall and they only had two choices: left or right.

"Take the left path. Look," Xellik said, "It has stairs that spiral downward. It must be the way we want to go."

They fought their way down the stairs and just as Xellik suspected, as they reached the bottom of the steps, a long hallway extended into the darkness.

"This is it! We're on the right path!" Xellik yelled, licking his lips. They were so close, and he could not be stopped now. He had been waiting for many years to finally realize his destiny, and now that he was within spitting distance of the power that would help him realize it, he grew ever more anxious. "Keep moving!"

Xellik charged down the tunnel and cut a swath through the minotaur and their defenses with ease. It felt almost too easy. How could they be so much weaker than him? He felt no remorse for the minotaur as they screamed and begged not to be killed. They were weak, and they lacked dignity and honor. They were obstacles in his way, and by that definition, they were the sworn enemies of Sytarel. There would be no mercy for any who showed such pathetic traits. He slew all who tried to oppose him, even those who were no longer able to fight. The Woodcaller had to pay the ultimate price for trying to oppose his will.

There was another flight of stairs at the end of the tunnel. They fought their way to the bottom, and just as in Xellik's vision, he found the altar room exactly as he had seen it, except for one minor difference: there was a group of minotaur standing between him and his goal.

At the front was one that Xellik could only assume was the Archdruid. He clutched a pair of scimitars in his hands, each of them glowing with a soft green aura. He had a set of sleeveless robes on that hung down to his hooves, and feathers hanging from his horns. If Xellik had to guess, this was the minotaur that showed up in his dreams. If that were true, then they faced an obscenely powerful magic user, flanked on either side by his bodyguards.

They must have known what Xellik's true goal was. Why else would orcs invade their temple? Shame for them that their entire structure was crammed to the point of making their superior numbers useless.

"Out of my way!" Xellik snarled. He brought his weapon to bear, and his warriors did the same. The minotaur may have had a number advantage over him, but the Fergoth were better and stronger. Destiny had brought them here and they were not going to be stopped.

"No. This senseless slaughter comes to an end," the Archdruid said. "It is unfortunate that you have come all this way only to find your grave."

Xellik tightened his grip. "I'll cut you down like the rest of your kind. Do you think I came all this way for nothing?"

"You came all this way to meet your demise, child of Sytarel." Tsaar lifted a hand to the ceiling and spoke a single word.

There was a cracking sound echoing from above and a stalactite fell from above. It crushed several of Xellik's warriors and the shrapnel thrown out by the impact wounded others.

"Aiph!" Xellik shouted as he watched his friend's body crumple under the stones like a rag doll. His eyes widened in surprise. He watched the dark blood pool underneath the rubble, and saw how his friend's hand twitched once before going still. He couldn't believe that Aiph was dead. They spent their entire youth together, and survived the trek from Tran together. It was impossible. How could he have died here?

He whirled around to face Tsaar. The minotaur was going to pay for killing one of his kin.

"You bastard!" Ragash shouted as he charged on ahead of the rest of the orcs, his large sword held at the ready. "I'll kill you!"

"Go," Tsaar said, ordering his warriors to engage the orcs. The line of minotaur that stood behind him rushed forward, running over the short bridge or jumping over the reservoir of water that snaked around the room.

"Quick, go help Ragash before he gets himself killed!" Xellik ordered as his troops moved to intercept the minotaur.

Ragash didn't wait for reinforcements as his sword flashed out. The sharpened Rogarian steel, which was almost unheard of anywhere outside of Zugrul, sliced through the minotaur with ease.

Even in his revenge-fueled rage he was capable of striking at the weak points in their armor, hacking through limbs and cutting open their throats as he worked. Ragash was in his element, and as the blood fury ran through his veins, he was subconsciously aware that he would not stop until they were all dead, or until they killed him.

Xellik watched as Ragash was gored in the chest by a minotaur's horns. The warrior lifted his arm as high as he could and drove his sword down into the minotaur's skull. The action had cost him greatly, and a battle-axe cleaved his arm off his shoulders.

He couldn't allow another member of his clan to die. Xellik raised his hands with his palms facing forward. "Sytarel, Your humble servant calls for Your aid! Help me protect Your child!" He could feel magical energies gathering around him. Fireflies of mana circled him madly, creating a ring of sparkling energy that only a trained sorcerer could have seen.

"Stop him! Don't let him get that spell off!" Tsaar shouted. He cast a spell of his own and dropped another stalactite, this time aiming for Xellik. It was knocked aside from an explosion of fire as Bytej stepped in to defend his leader.

Xellik huffed a laugh. "Seriously, did you think that would work twice?" A deep blue aura appeared on the orc's hands and part way up his forearms. It slowly lost its color and turned black, as if shadows had enveloped his hands. "May despair befall my enemies as the encroaching darkness threatens to consume them whole!"

The luminescent globes around the room began to dim and fade away entirely as a wall of shadows seeped in through the cracks in the stone. Tsaar ordered his warriors back, but it was too late. Before they could even react, a gout of shadows exploded outwards and engulfed them. There were a few choked screams, but they were silenced quickly as the heat was stolen from their bodies. It was as though the darkness of space had entered the room and sucked all the warmth from them. When the black fog disappeared, the globes came back on and all that stood between Xellik and his prize were his remaining warriors, a pile of dead minotaur, and a wounded Archdruid kneeling on the ground.

Ragash lay among them, writhing in pain as he clutched at the stump of his severed arm. Bytej ran forward, grabbing medical supplies from his pack as he began to apply bandages to his wounds to keep him from bleeding out.

"Haij, get over here and help me," Bytej called, and began ordering his son around so they could keep Ragash alive.

Xellik stepped over the bridge and walked towards the minotaur. His eyes met those of Ragash's, and through the pain he could sense the orc's hatred. He didn't blame him. His nephew had died for Xellik's sake. He broke the gaze, and stared down at Tsaar.

"What is it that you want with our relic?" Tsaar panted. His speech was slow and slurred, and Xellik was sure that whatever defensive spells he had used to protect himself had barely been enough to keep him alive. "Do you even comprehend the power you seek to control?"

"It's our relic now, and I understand enough to know I want it," Xellik told him. His warriors parted to the side to allow their leader to approach the altar. He stepped past the Archdruid, ignoring him entirely. "It's my destiny to possess this Emerald."

"Stop! You don't know what you're doing!" Tsaar begged.

With one fluid motion, Xellik brought his sword around and pressed the blade to the minotaur's neck, the tip biting into his skin and drawing a thin line of blood. "Silence, cow. The only reason I don't cut you down now is because I want you to see that the sacrifices of your warriors meant nothing. I want you to live with that guilt for the rest of your miserable life. How many of your people were slain today? How many died in vain because you tried to stop our destiny from being fulfilled? You Woodcaller paid the price for your mistakes."

Tsaar didn't respond. He lowered his head carefully to avoid cutting himself on the sword that was at his neck and stared at the floor.

"Good cow." Xellik pulled his weapon away and dismissed it before he finally approached the altar.

"Careful, Xellik. It might be trapped," Bytej warned, but the orc ignored him as he wasted no time in lifting the amulet off the pedestal. As he put the chain around his neck, the room was filled with the breathy voice of a woman.

"You came as expected, young Xellik. And I see you've performed admirably in your duties as Her Chosen Hero," the voice said. Or rather, it echoed in their minds.

Xellik recognized it as the one from his dreams. There were mixed reactions among the Fergoth. Many of them were confused, wondering if every other orc had heard the same thing they did. It didn't take long for them to realize that the voice was in all their heads, and they waited with baited breath to figure out where it had come from.

A tearing sound echoed throughout the room, and a blue-white portal ripped through reality. The shimmering light intensified to such a degree that Xellik had to shield his eyes to continue watching. Violent energies spewed from the portal, threatening to throw him off balance. Whatever was coming through was powerful. Out from the portal stepped a creature that looked vaguely human, yet she had large, leathery bat-like wings protruding from her back. She wore skimpy, revealing leather garments and had a whip strapped to her belt. A thin, spiny tail lashed behind her, and looked like it could cut flesh as easily as a sword.

"A handmaiden of Sytarel?" Bytej gawked in disbelief.

"My name is Nazridia, one of Sytarel's handmaidens," the

creature said, "A succubus, if you would prefer. The Goddess has been very interested in you, Xellik."

Xellik blinked at her. "What's your reason for calling me here?"

"Because you're the one who will restore the orcs to their former glory. That is what you wished for more than anything else, is it not?"

"That's true," he admitted, "That's all I've wanted since the human scum pushed us off our land. We've been shoved to the corner of the world and pushed to the brink of extinction by the self-proclaimed 'races of light', and we've grown complacent. I want nothing more than the power to overthrow those worthless Zugruli and to raise a new Empire from their ashes!"

He cupped the relic in his hand and looked at the faceted edges of the Emerald. "I can feel something very powerful in this gem. This has more magic in it than I imagined. I must test its capabilities. It's the key to capturing Zugrul."

"You need to stop! You don't know what powers you're dealing with!" Tsaar shouted.

"But we do know what we're dealing with, Archdruid," Nazridia told him as she walked in a circle around him as a leisurely pace. The minotaur leaned away from her, repulsed by something he saw in her. "It's the Emerald of the Deep Earth, a relic crafted by Gaia himself and sent to the mortal plane. It's been laying dormant in Batic for millennia, guarded by the Thomadis brood of dragons prior to your people settling here. They were the same dragons that shared their knowledge of Druidism with you, were they not? And they tasked you with looking over this Emerald in exchange?"

"Hmph, fine lot of good they did," Napir said. "They just got their servitors killed. Where's the dragons now?" He stood with his hands on his hips and his chest puffed out proudly.

"Return the Emerald to its pedestal, I beg you!" Tsaar turned to Xellik. "In the wrong hands, that stone has the potential to unravel the very fabric of reality. You can't take it!"

Xellik summoned his weapon once again and cut a large gash across the minotaur's throat. Tsaar clutched at the wound and tried to stop the bleeding, but it only seeped between his fingers and spilled on the ground. He coughed and sputtered as the blood dripped down into his lungs and choked him as he fell forward.

"Come, we have work to do." Xellik walked off and led his warriors out of the room, with Nazridia close behind.

"What do you intend to do now?" the succubus asked him.

Xellik grunted in response. "I intend to use this relic to overthrow the Zugruli High Priestess and take control of the city. Once that's done, we can reclaim finally reclaim Muriaj."

Chapter 25 - Clashing Swords

"Alright, listen up, pups!" Heshun shouted, his voice echoing off the walls of his dojo. "I'll begrudgingly admit that the lot of you are the best of the worst that I've had all year. Many of you can still barely handle a sword, and I doubt any of you are prepared to take a life with the skills I've taught you. But unfortunately, our military is lacking in strength, and so we need to field you cubs as quickly as possible."

Dane swallowed hard, listening to Heshun speak. His shoulders were so tense that they ached, as was often the case when he was in Heshun's training hall. The man had a presence that bade one to stand up straight and pay attention when he was talking. Heshun never needed to say anything. His body language and the way he looked at you was enough to convey that message.

"You'll be reporting to me later today to complete your final combat exam, to prove to me that you're worthy of moving on to take the Test of Magehood." Heshun paced back and forth in front of the gathering of students, his right arm resting on the sheathed sword at his hip. "I will be your opponent for your exam, so that I may witness your skills up close and personally. If you can't show me what you've learned, you will be failed. Understood?"

No one had beaten Heshun. Dane didn't know how the jintaren was planning to evaluate them, but it couldn't have been in their ability to overpower their teacher. He could feel beads of sweat drip down his brow, but he didn't dare move to wipe them off.

"May I ask something sir?" one student asked, standing at the opposite side of the line from Dane. "Are you going to be trying to mortally wound us?"

Heshun stepped over to him in a huff and leaned forward until his face was practically pressing against the boy's forehead. "What kind of stupid question is that? Yes, of course I'm going to be trying to kill you, just like you should be trying to kill me." He stood back up and crossed his arms. "If I could fail you for asking something like that, I would. But unfortunately, I have to settle for something else." He thought for a moment, then said, "You'll be taking your test first, after lunch. Don't be late or it'll be an automatic failure."

The boy tried to come up with a response, but all he could do was stammer endlessly as he failed to conjure the words he wanted to speak. Dane didn't envy him. He pictured that Heshun's punishment for what was in his mind a stupid question would undoubtedly involve more than making the boy take his test first.

"Is there anything else we should know?" Dane asked. When Heshun glared in his direction, he added, "A warrior should go into battle with as much knowledge as he can possibly get beforehand. You taught us that."

"You'll need to apply everything you've learned with me. Magic will be an important component, so don't forget your spells. I don't care where you learned them or how you apply them, as long as they aid you combat," Heshun explained. "No outside equipment allowed. Just bring yourself and I'll provide a weapon for you." He looked across the assembly and waited for someone to say something more. "Any other questions?"

The response he received was nothing but silence.

"Good, that's what I like to hear," he said after waiting for a moment. "I expect all of you to show up on time. I'll be conducting exams through the rest of the day. And don't give me those looks, I've already informed your other professors that you'll be busy with me for the afternoon."

"What's the order then?" Aiden asked.

"That loudmouth over there," Heshun said, indicating the boy at the head of the line, "will be taking the test first, right after lunch. Everyone else will be taking their tests in alphabetical order. I trust you can figure that out amongst yourselves. Class dismissed."

As the students began to file out of the room, Aiden and Dane lingered behind and moved at a slower pace behind the others. There were only twelve students in total who had made it through the final semester, so it wasn't difficult for either of them to figure out when their exams would take place.

Aiden was counting off the names on his fingers, until he got to his. "Sounds like I'm tenth in line. You should be last."

"No, Zuke should be last," Dane corrected him.

"He was kicked out, remember? Over that incident with the conjured knives."

Dane was drawing a blank for a few seconds, staring at his friend before he remembered what had happened. "Oh right. Heshun couldn't sit straight for a week after that." A grin spread across his face. "If Zuke is gone then you're right, I am last."

"Let's go have lunch together and relax until it's time for our exams," Aiden suggested as they walked down the hallway towards the attached dining room next door. "I'll even tell you about my test before you take yours. How's that sound?"

"Sounds like cheating," Dane said with a wry grin. "You know how I feel about that."

"So you're up for it?"

"Of course!"

* * * * *

Later that afternoon, Dane found himself once again outside Heshun's training hall. He rested his hand on the doorknob, but didn't turn it. He knew what to expect going into it, but he was still nervous. He'd only sparred with the jintaren a few times, and each time he'd been thoroughly bested with ease.

Dane had a small idea about what to expect when he walked into Heshun's classroom that day, thanks to Aiden. Though the students had been instructed numerous times not to speak to their peers regarding their exams, Aiden still told Dane everything about his. It was a benefit of being close. Dane realized he wished they could be closer though. He was happy with their friendship, but he wanted more.

I need to focus on the test, he thought. He stayed his hand and was unable to push the door open. His mind lingered on Aiden, picturing his soft smile and warm embrace.

Ever since his talk with Othur, Dane had been weighing his options and deciding whether to tell Aiden or not. He physically wanted to be with the man and a part of him knew that it went deeper than attraction. It was love. Aiden had shown him kindness and compassion when few others had in his life. They were both capable students and dreamed of the same kind of future. If anyone in this world was Dane's ideal partner, it was Aiden.

Yet the problem remained that Aiden wasn't attracted to men, at least as far as Dane knew. He never saw him with anyone else, as they spent everyday together after classes. He couldn't recall ever hearing him talk about women or who he thought was cute. Perhaps he was more focused on his education than on the fairer sex. It was plausible, as Aiden was a top notch student. A part of Dane questioned that and came to the conclusion that they were one and the same, that Aiden was also like him. It was a long shot, but Dane had to know.

Gripping the doorknob tightly until his knuckles turned white, Dane looked up with renewed resolve. First he would deal with the test and best Heshun at whatever game he had planned for him. Then he would tell Aiden. No more second guessing himself. He feared losing his only friend, but he had to know for certain. He needed to reveal his feelings to him before his longing for companionship turned into a deep depression.

I can do this! I know I can!

Dane moved with a confident swagger as he opened the doors and stepped inside. Despite his inability to beat Heshun in one-on-one combat, he was certain he would pass this test with flying colors.

As Dane approached Heshun, he realized how tall he was. It wasn't something he consciously thought about often. Standing before him and preparing to duel him was enough to remind him that the jintaren were huge compared to their rogarian cousins. Heshun's arms were covered in thick, corded muscles that bulged as he moved. Dane pictured that he could lift him over his head with a single hand if he wanted to.

"It's about time you showed up. I thought I'd have to fail you for your tardiness," Heshun said as he stood up from where he was kneeling near the center of the room. He had a sheathed sword laying on the ground in front of him.

"I was preparing myself mentally to face you," Dane admitted. He knew not to hide his fears from Heshun, as the man had a way of sussing them out and using them against him.

"You're fortunate to not be on my bad side. I was growing impatient. Are you prepared?"

"I'm as ready as I can hope to be, Professor."

"Well, come on. Grab your sword and let's get this over with."

Dane moved to the sword racks on the right side of the room.

He grabbed his favourite blade, a rogarian standard issue short sword, and moved to the center of the room to stand before Heshun. His heart was beating fast and he could feel it throbbing at the base of his throat. He craned his neck upwards to look his professor in the eyes.

His hands fell upon the grip of his sword as he shifted his weight to the balls of his feet. He drew the blade, hearing the distinct scrap of metal against metal as it came out of the sheath.

Heshun drew his own sword and threw the scabbard aside, causing it to clatter noisily as it slid along the floor. Dane could feel how sweaty his palms were as he gripped his weapon, lowering himself so he could spring away at a moment's notice.

A tense silence hung in the room as neither combatant was willing to make the first move. Dane was waiting for Heshun to begin, but for all he knew the man was waiting for him to make the first attack. There was no signal to let him know when to begin the test, but he figured the act of drawing his sword signalled that it had begun.

Heshun lunged at Dane, catching him off guard. The boy brought his sword up and deflected the attack. Dane rushed to get some room but Heshun continued to press him. A swing came down low at his feet and Dane jumped back. Heshun continued to follow through and brought his sword back around to strike at his midsection. The blade cut through his tunic, nearly nicking his skin. It was so close that Dane could feel the wind manufactured by the sword's edge.

"I was hoping a couple years of training would have done you some good. But you're just the same scared little victim you were the day I met you," Heshun snarled at him.

Dane reeled as Heshun backhanded him with a fist. He could feel the cartilage in his nose crack. The taste of iron filled his mouth as blood dripped down the back of his throat. His face stung, and he could feel his left eye beginning to swell from the attack. Losing half his vision at the start of the duel did not make him feel confident he could win. He'd have to end things quick. Aiden didn't have any such bruises on his face after his test.

"You've trained in this room almost every single day for the last couple dozen months, and this is the best you can do? It's amazing the orcs didn't kill you on that day."

Dane could feel a twitch under his eye as his instructor tried to dig at his old wounds, but he wouldn't let his words get to him. "Give it up, Heshun. You're not going to get under my skin this time."

"Is that so? Then why is your sword play becoming sloppier?"

The exchange continued for a few moments, with Dane losing ground. Heshun was right, he was still the inexperienced child that he was during his first lesson. The realization stung, and he struggled to reign in his emotions so that it wouldn't affect his performance.

Dane attempted to swing at Heshun, but his sword fell short. He cursed himself for allowing that cheap shot to take his eyesight. It was already starting to affect his depth perception.

He hasn't even started using magic yet, Dane thought. He recalled what Aiden had said earlier. Heshun had acted the same way, trying to rile the student up and force them to defend against a relentless assault to gauge their ability to protect themselves and how well they could handle a more experienced opponent.

"It still bothers you, doesn't it?" Heshun asked. "Thinking that now you have all this power, and it doesn't matter, because you can't do anything to help those people."

"Enough!" Dane roughly shoved Heshun's sword away and snapped his finger. The action was tied to a spell, a mnemonic action that helped him focus his mind in an instant. The room filled with the ear-splitting crack of thunder that left Dane momentarily deaf. A brilliant flash of white appeared as a bolt of lightning streaked down in an instant from the ceiling. The jintaren moved with reflexes that surprised him as he sprang away from the spell. Dane gaped at him. Lightning moved faster than the human body could perceive. How could he have dodged it?

Did he sense my spell before it went off? Dane wondered.

"Don't be so hasty, boy!" Heshun swept his hand in an arc in front of him, smoke billowing out of his palm. A chill fog began to fill the room and within seconds the man had disappeared into the low hanging cloud.

Everything was silent, and Dane felt goosebumps run up his arms. He could hear his breathing and the steady rhythm of his heart as he glanced about. Not even the vague silhouette of his teacher could be seen. Dane spun around, his eyes darting from side to side as he tried to pinpoint where his teacher was.

Had he been more focused on his hearing and less focused on trying to get a visual on Heshun, he would have heart the boot steps approaching from his right. He spotted a glint of metal shining in his peripheral and on instinct, Dane shifted backwards. The blade of Heshun's sword nearly sliced his arm open, and caught his tunic.

The attack was followed by a second, and a third. Dane's first thought was to panic. He couldn't see his instructor well, but Heshun could seem to see him just fine. The rational part of his mind took over, and pointed out one simple fact: Even if he couldn't see him, he knew exactly where the jintaren was.

Dane stepped towards where the attacks were coming from and ducked to the side. The long sword the Heshun was using prevented him from fighting up-close. At such a range, Dane had an easier time utilizing his short sword and smaller size to greater effect. He missed with a few swings as the jintaren proved to be more agile than his bulk would imply, so he followed up but slamming the tip of his elbow into Heshun's stomach.

His instructor staggered, giving Dane space to strike at Heshun with another spell. He snapped a finger to call down a bolt of lightning that struck near Heshun. He thrust with his sword as Hehsun sprang to the side to avoid being struck by the magic. The sword cut into the jintaren's arm and drew a thin line of blood. As he pulled his arm back, a second cut appeared above Heshun's elbow.

The telltale tickle of mana being manipulated pulled at Dane's mind, and he braced himself for whatever spell Heshun was preparing. He attempted to raise an arcane ward, but he was too slow. A blast of cold slammed into him, forcing the air from his lungs. The magical wind carried him several feet before he toppled unceremoniously on the ground, landing on his stomach. The fog began to clear, and Dane gasped in an attempt to breathe.

The sound of rushing footsteps thumping hard on the floor told Dane that Heshun was charging at him. He rolled over onto his back and leveled out his sword to parry several strikes with the flat of his blade, holding the palm of his free hand against it to support it. His foot came around and slammed into Heshun's hand, knocking his sword away. Dane sprang up and unleashed a ball of fire that exploded and prevented the man from retrieving his sword.

Using all the strength he could muster, Dane threw his weight into Heshun's midsection, knocking him to the ground. He planted a foot on the jintaren's chest so that he couldn't stand up, then placed the tip of his sword against the instructor's neck.

"Do you yield, teacher?" Dane asked, grinning at him.

Heshun made a short huffing noise and frowned. In only a few quick seconds, Dane found himself landing harshly on his buttocks with the jintaren towering over him. His sword was now in his teacher's possession.

"Yield, student?" Heshun shot back, smirking with equal satisfaction.

Dane glanced around quickly, trying to find a way out. He couldn't strike at Heshun with any magic, as it would take too much time to perform. The jintaren was much heavier than him, and Dane didn't have the leverage to shove him off or trip him. He had no weapons in his reach, and he didn't know how to conjure any new ones either.

"*An theros, verus! Fi -*" Dane attempted to throw another fireball at Heshun, but the man thrust his foot into his abdomen, interrupting him mid-incantation.

"Fine, I yield," Dane gasped as he slapped the floor with his hand. There was nothing more he could do.

"At least you know when you're beaten, unlike most of your classmates." Heshun stepped back to allow Dane to sit up. "Your form and technique are unrefined, but so is everyone's when they first start fighting with real weapons instead of sticks. With time and experience, you'll hone your skills and become a good warrior in your own right. Until then, you should focus on doing your best to stay alive. Always expect your opponent to fight dirty or to try and catch you off guard. You left yourself vulnerable to a counter attack and tried to pin a physically stronger opponent. That'll cost you on the battlefield."

"Yes, Professor."

"At any rate, I feel you're more than capable of handling things on your own. You have my permission to go ahead with your final Test of Magehood next month."

Dane's face lit up upon hearing this. "Thank you so much, Professor!"

"Now get going. You have a cellar to clear out, and I have a dojo to clean up."

"Yes sir!" Dane didn't care how many cellars he'd have to

inspect, or how many rats or spiders he'd have to kill. He was happy to finally be done with his training. All that remained was his Test of Magehood.

When he left the training hall, Aiden was outside waiting for him. The portly man was sitting up against the wall and studying his spellbook. Dane smiled when he saw that the man had decided to wait for him before they were due to head down into the cellars.

"That looks like it hurt," Aiden said, grimacing when he saw Dane's swollen eye. "How did it go?"

"I passed! I'm not sure how well I did. . ."

"But you passed, that's all that matters," Aiden finished for him, smiling. "Time for work, are you ready?"

"Now more than ever, yes," Dane said. He paused, then said, "But first, I'm going to get my eye looked at."

Chapter 26 - Love Revealed

5th Day of Sethyr
126 I.E.

It took the boys a couple hours to thoroughly cleanse the cellar. It had been rougher work than usual, and despite the cold weather, Dane was covered in a sticky layer of sweat. It wasn't all from labour, though. He spent a great deal of time when he was alone on his half of the cellar thinking about Aiden and what he wanted to tell him. They were both good friends, and Aiden surprised him numerous times with his kindness. He wondered how the man would react when he told him about his attraction to him.

Aiden was understanding, and he was kind. Dane focused more on his thoughts than on the task at hand, playing scenarios over in his head as to how to approach his friend properly. He didn't like the idea of beating around the bush, and prayed silently to Xenar for the strength to be upfront and honest.

With only a month left of training to go, Dane felt he was well equipped to deal with any problems that might arise. Even if it would make him a renegade, if he needed to run away from his problems, he knew he could be long gone before anyone started searching for him in earnest. Dane no longer feared the consequences of rejection.

After their job was done, Aiden followed Dane back to the dorms and was right behind him as he unlocked his door. Dane invited him over to talk, even though there was generally nothing else to do in his room. Aiden wanted to go into the town, but there was seldom anything happening when the nights were longer than the days. This month was the domain of Sethyr, the Shadowalker. The nights dragged on and the world was held in winter's icy grasp. People longed for the sun to return with the spring, and waited impatiently from inside the warmth of their homes.

"Isabella should be by shortly with dinner," Dane said as he moved to his dresser. "Maybe we'll see if she'll bring your meal here instead?"

"I hope so. I'm starving," Aiden said as he rubbed his belly.

"You're always hungry."

"Not always! Just most of the time," he chuckled. "I don't know how you don't get hungry more often. You're always tired and you work just as hard as me."

Dane began to slip out of his sweat-soaked tunic to put on a fresh one. "I just don't vocalize it like you do. Anyway, did you want some fresh clothes so you can get out of those grimy things?" Dane paused. He'd asked the question without even thinking it. If Aiden wanted to change, he'd have to change in his room. Dane could have sworn his heart stopped for a second as the thought crossed his mind.

It would be a guilty little pleasure to see his friend without a shirt for the first time, and Dane hoped that it wouldn't come off as awkward when he decided to tell him everything. He felt his face grow hot and he subconsciously licked his lips in anticipation.

"If you have anything in my size to spare," Aiden replied, already removing his shirt. "I hate having sweaty clothes sticking to me like that."

Even though he had a drawer full of clean clothes and could easily pull out any tunic to give to Aiden, Dane instead found himself fiddling around. He wondered if he should give something he knew would be too small for Aiden just to prolong the experience. That wasn't right, and it wasn't honorable either. He should be open with Aiden, not secretly idolizing him from the sidelines.

"Dane, is everything okay?"

He pulled his arm back out of the drawer in a hurry with a shirt in hand. "Sure, everything's fine!" He tossed the tan linen tunic at his friend's face, obscuring his view.

Dane took the moment to admire the sight before him. Aiden's chest was covered in a splash of thin hair that trailed down onto his round yet firm stomach. Dane never had the opportunity to properly admire another man, and when he released the breath he was holding, a long sigh escaped his lips.

"That's a happy sound," Aiden said softly as he pulled his head through the top of the shirt. "What was that about?"

"N-nothing."

"Oh that wasn't nothing." Aiden said, his tone serious. He got close to Dane and was looking him in the eyes. "What's going on in that head of yours?"

This is it, Dane thought, watching the way his friend moved. He met his gaze, and remembered an old saying that said that the eyes were the window into the soul. If that were the case, Dane believed that he could lose himself in those hazel depths, and be happy.

Sighing and shaking his head, Dane stepped closer. "Aiden. . . I love you." The words exploded from his mouth atop a long exhale. He wrapped his arms around Aiden and kissed him brazenly on the lips. It was brief, lasting only a couple seconds, but to Dane it felt like minutes had passed. He could feel the softness of the other man's lips. It was the most pleasant thing that Dane had experienced in his short life, but it was unfortunately short lived.

Aiden gasped and shoved Dane away, his eyes wide with shock. Pain flared in Dane's abdomen as his stomach began to cartwheel and his heart began to beat faster. Perhaps it wasn't the best way to tell Aiden, but it was the only thing he could think to do. He tentatively licked his lips. He could still taste the other man.

"What was that?" Aiden shouted, wiping his mouth with the back of his hand.

"Aiden, I. . ." Dane said. He felt light-headed, and the muscles in his legs tensed. His body was telling him to run, to get away from this place as quick as possible. His hand inched towards the doorknob as he fought to figure out what to say.

"Stay," Aiden said, his voice strong and commanding. Dane winced at the tone of his words. He had never seen Aiden mad before, but if the man were capable of anger, he assumed that this was it. "What did you say?"

"I said I love you," Dane admitted. "I love you Aiden. I've been attracted to you since the moment we met, and I've loved you for almost as long. I've wanted nothing more in this world than to be able to say that to you. I don't care at this point what you or anyone else thinks of that statement. I've grown tired of being afraid and of being silent. I would be hurt if you hated me, but I wouldn't care if you struck me or grew angry." He stared defiantly at Aiden, trying to find some meaning in the blank expression on his face. Dane decided he would not run anymore.

After that kiss, Dane knew he could die happy. Even if Aiden didn't return his affections, he had felt more alive in that single moment than at any other point in his life. Let the stones come. Let the pitchfork wielding mobs chase him. He would face them all and stand tall like the mountains before a storm.

It was a long, exhausting moment before Aiden reacted to him. He moved closer to Dane, and raised his open hand in a quick motion. Dane maintained eye contact, and did not flinch as the hand flew towards him. He expected to be struck for his words. Instead of feeling a fist colliding with his face, he felt the meaty arms of the other man wrap around his body once more, engulfing him in the warmth he offered. It was a tighter hug than the one

Dane had given him, and now it was his turn to freeze in shock. Maybe Aiden really had struck him and now he was in a coma, experiencing all his little delusions in his head.

Dane could feel the embrace loosen after a moment as Aiden pulled back, but the man didn't let go entirely. His hands remained firmly planted on his shoulders as he moved in to kiss Dane. This time it was longer, more passionate than the first kiss that they had shared. Dane allowed his eyes to drift closed as he melted into the other man's arms.

Aiden released the kiss and leaned towards his ear. "I love you too, Dane." His voice was low, barely a whisper, but his words rang clear as a church bell. Dane thought he might take flight with how elated he felt.

They worked their clothes off and moved towards the bed. There was a knock at the door, but whoever it was went away without trying to enter. It was just as well, since neither man wanted to answer the door naked, sweaty, and disheveled.

"I love you," Dane huffed as he broke off from another kiss. "I'm sorry I never told you sooner."

"I love you too," Aiden replied as he pulled him back down on top of him.

They turned the lamp off and made love to each other that night, cementing their newfound bond, relieving all the pent up desires both men had had for each other since they'd met. The room grew warm with their passion, and the window became opaque with condensation. They didn't care about the noise they made, or even if someone might hear them. The only people who existed in the world in that moment were the two of them.

When Dane woke up the next morning, he stretched out across the bed to relieve the stiffness in his limbs. His arm brushed alongside Aiden's body. He remembered what they'd done the night before and his face flushed.

"You're finally awake," Aiden stated, tracing one of his thick fingers over his lover's cheek. "Did you know you snore?"

"No, I didn't," Dane said and began to chuckle as his memories came flooding back to him. "I can't believe we did all that."

"I didn't hear you complaining at the time." The other man gently rubbed the back of his hand along the stubble on Dane's face, then pulled him closer to let him lay his head down on his chest. "Did you mean what you said last that, that you've loved me since we met?"

"Yes. I didn't really have a word for what I felt back then. We were both young and I was too naive about the world to really understand it. But looking back on it, I know that it was love." Dane had a wistful look on his face as he looked back on the times they had shared together. "What about you?"

"Why do you think I started talking to you on that day so many years ago?" Aiden scratched at the back of his head. "You were cute, yet sort of. . . mysterious. You were smarter than many of our classmates, but you weren't a snob about it, either. I think that's what drew me to you, and just over time as we got to know each other, I was certain that I loved you."

"You never told me."

"Neither did you," Aiden said as he stuck his tongue out at him. "Besides, I was scared of the same things you were. I mean, who would want to be with a fat guy like me?" He looked sadly at his exposed body. Dane hugged the man tightly, pressing his face into the crook of his friend's neck.

"The only one who matters," Dane said before he kissed Aiden. He didn't know why someone as outgoing and friendly as Aiden would want to be with a brooding, meek individual such as himself, but Dane didn't dwell on it for long. They loved each other, and that was the only thing that mattered. He affectionately rubbed Aiden's stomach, brushing the light sprinkling of hair with his fingertips. He turned up and pulled his friend closer, locking lips with him once again.

There was a knock at the door. "Master Trueshot? Breakfast is ready."

"Leave it outside the door, Isabella. I'll come and get it in a moment when I'm decent," he replied. Aiden stifled a laugh.

As they got dressed, he asked, "So, what do you want to do today? Make up for lost time?"

Before Dane could slip into his tunic, Aiden came up behind him and wrapped his arms around his midsection. "Sounds good. But can it wait a bit?" He traced a line of kisses along the back of his neck.

"Why?"

"I'm hungry."

Chapter 27 - Prelude to the Assault

12th Day of Sethyr
127 I.E.

The Fergoth and their allies gathered in a large hut, the same one that Xellik had gathered the casteless previously. A large table was roughly thrown together. Its legs were not even and it wobbled when leaned on. Xellik didn't need anything extravagant. The slums would be their homes no longer. The city of Zugrul would belong to him and his people soon enough.

Pinned atop the table was an unfurled map. A few rocks were used as markers for known guard positions, information that had been collected in the days leading up to this meeting thanks to Urzule and Cinra. The city of Zugrul was larger than Xellik thought as its borders hugged the snaking coastline. The outer walls were built with only a couple meters to spare before reaching the cliffs. Treacherous waters foamed below around spires of earth that jutted up out of the sea. The Teeth of Narmon, they were called, and the coast was littered with similar spires of rock, making travel to and from Zugrul difficult for anyone but capable shipwrights.

Examining the rest of the map, it appeared as if many sections of the city were tightly packed together. Space was at a premium, and if the Zugruli population and their allied clans began to grow, they would need to build more in the coming years. There wasn't much room for expansion with those walls in the way. It was only a matter of time before they forced the slums further out into the jungle to allow for building up the city. The casteless would have no say in the matter as a new wall would likely be erected around the expansion.

The Zugruli won't be happy until they're swept us under the rug as though we're nothing more than dirt, Xellik thought bitterly. He listened idly as Bytej and a Tigra clan orc grilled Garro for information. The slave had been in the city before, and they wanted information. . . information that they were going to get in exchange for the korcyn keeping his hide intact.

When all eyes turned to him, Xellik used a long stick to indicate a pair of dotted lines that extended from the coast into a water reservoir in the city. It marked an underground tunnel that snaked under the walls. It was long ago sealed up, according to Garro, but there was a latch beneath the reservoir that could flush out all the water and allow the orcs to enter the city from below.

"This aqueduct here will be our main point of ingress for assaulting the Zugruli temple," he said, his voice echoing throughout the cavernous room. "From Urzule's scouting, we can sneak up from the port and along the wall to get to it. The grating over the tunnel is rusted and weakened, so we should be able to blast it apart with magic should strength not be enough."

"What of the soldiers above?" asked the Tigra orc. "They will surely sense magic being used."

"The patrols on the ramparts are few and far between, judging by our intel," Xellik said.

"Can it be trusted?" she asked, noting Garro's presence in the room. "The pig has been given too much freedom."

"His information has been . . . valuable in the past and he has yet to steer us wrong," Xellik said. He felt like throwing up at complementing the korcyn. Garro came in handy when it came to understanding how Zugrul worked. He excelled in areas that neither Cinra nor Urzule could hope to do well. It concerned

Xellik that someone who should be a mere slave could be as cunning as he was. His eyes shone with intelligence. Someone had educated Garro, and they had done it well. Xellik wondered what his former masters had been like.

Changing the topic quickly before Garro became the focus of everything, Xellik said, "I'll be leading the Fergoth towards the temple. Half of my warriors will be leading the charge against the main gate with the distraction force. Normally I would appoint Ragash to handle the front lines, but . . ." he trailed off, leaving everyone present to fill in the blanks themselves. No one liked to be reminded of the crippled, useless orc.

Ragash was absent from their meeting, and had been despondent ever since returning to Batic. At first Xellik believed it was his way of grieving for the loss of his nephew, Aiph, but as time went on he began to see that he grieved and felt pity for himself because of the loss of his arm and eye. He behaved like a brooding orcling, not the proud veteran he touted himself to be. He behaved like his mother had taken away his favorite toy.

With the loss of Ragash's ability to fight, and the death of his last living relative, his pride was shattered. It was scattered to winds, never to return. Ragash should have died an honorable death in battle, but he had been denied that. Now he was crippled and useless. Xellik could likely find work for him in training new warriors, but he saw no need to further shame the orc.

Bytej spoke up, turning his attention towards his son. "Haij, you'll be leading the assault team against the front gates. You can handle it in Ragash's stead."

Xellik nodded in agreement. "You were his star pupil. You can do it, right?"

Haij gulped as his adam's apple bobbed. Slowly, he nodded. Showing fear was not an orcish trait, but once in awhile, an individual would let it slip. This was one such moment for Haij.

Xellik saw through his attempts to mask his unease, and he hoped that the other clans didn't. Their allegiances to the casteless were flimsy as it were. Losing confidence in their leaders would do them no good.

The succubus Nazridia took this moment to appear in the room, her form melting away from the shadows. Those who were not present during the raid on Batic stared, dumbstruck by her appearance. They bowed their heads in reverence towards the Goddess' servant, and a hushed silence fell over the room.

"Your plan is all well and good, Chosen, but Sytarel doesn't look kindly on the slaughter of Her own children." Nazridia stood with her arms crossed, barbed tail thrashing in irritation. "Even if you are Her champion, you are not exempt."

"Do those protections extend to the Zugruli tribe?" Xellik asked pointedly. "They are the leaders of the city and the reason why the orcs have grown so passive since the fall of the Empire."

"Of course not," Nazridia replied. "But you'd best not harm the other clans in the city."

"Then we'll have to infiltrate the temple as quickly as possible." Xellik drew his finger along the aqueduct and up to the basin. "We'll come up out of the sewer here after Haij leads the revolt against the gates. If necessary, we'll incapacitate the guards and push for the temple." He looked to Garro. "You said you can get into the city and stir up a rebellion. Your filth better take care of the stables like you said they would."

"Don't underestimate the korcyn," Garro replied, nonplussed by the prospect of more abuse from the orc. "As soon as the attack begins, the slave pen will erupt in revolt. The stables are nearby and will be the first thing they take out."

Sorda stepped in and pushed Garro aside. "Keep it brief, slave. If it's not about the operation, then keep your snout shut."

The korcyn was taken aback by the suddenness of Sorda's

appearance, but relented. He stood up to Xellik as a matter of principle, but he knew orcish society. The females held more power. Even if Xellik ruled, Garro sensed something amiss about Sorda. It seemed more like she ruled, with Xellik wrapped about her thin fingers. Perhaps the korcyn was being paranoid, being too used to traditional power customs in Zugrul. But something about the way Sorda looked at him suggested otherwise.

Xellik watched Garro's reaction, as though the korcyn was confused about where he was. He was busy staring at Sorda, but not in the contemplative, scheming way that he looked down on him and Bytej. Seeing him knocked off his pulpit was pleasing to watch, and when their eyes met, Xellik waved him off.

"Go tell your slave friends to be ready for tomorrow," Xellik said. "We strike at noon."

The rest of the meeting went smoothly until, after a short while, Ragash entered the room with the echoing screech of the door hinges following him. Sunlight poured into the dimly lit hall, and it was quickly cut off as the doors were unceremoniously slammed shut.

Bytej looked at his friend and grimaced at the way he uneasily walked into the room. He tried to hide the pity he felt for the warrior, but it was obvious to all present how he felt about the crippled orc's appearance.

"It's good of you to join us, old friend," Bytej said.

"What have you planned?" Ragash asked brusquely. He wore a leather headband where an extra patch hung over his gouged eye. Even without both eyes, his stare was still menacing.

"The Fergoth will approach from the coast, up an aqueduct and into the city proper," Xellik explained. He then indicated the gate on the map. "Haij will be leading the rest of the tribe into position outside the gates and causing a distraction for us while the korcyn slaves start a revolt from within the city."

Ragash scoffed. "These are all amateur tactics at best. The Zugruli are well armed and outnumber us. Your distractions will not last long enough to get you into the temple."

"Do you have no faith in the warriors you personally trained?" Sorda asked. Next to Haij, she was one of Ragash's most promising students in the art of war.

"I have faith in my warriors. I merely lack faith in this fool," Ragash said, gesturing at Xellik. "You are all being led by a greater fool than Fellis was."

Quiet murmurings around the room began to grow in volume among the other tribes present. Someone was standing up and questioning their leader, and Xellik was beginning to fear that such dissention would fester if Ragash was allowed to continue spouting such nonsense.

"There's no need for such hostilities between us. We are brothers, are we not?" Xellik asked.

Ragash's nostrils flared as he huffed noisily. He kicked aside a metal brazier, sending embers and coals skidding across the ground. "I have no need for your pity! And I don't view you as my leader, either. You didn't earn that position through hard work or dedication. You are barely capable in martial combat. You have earned that position merely because of your ancestry. It's disgusting. I was maimed in the name of your cause, and my nephew died in your stead. His death was futile because you will accomplish nothing!"

"We are working towards ensuring Aiph's death, and the deaths of those who followed us, will not be in vain," Xellik said.

"You waste your time!" Ragash shouted, then winced as his hand flew up to the stump at his shoulder. He dropped to one knee and tried to regain his balance. When he pulled his hand away, his bandages were soaked with fresh blood and it covered his palm.

Bytej rose from his seat. "We need to restitch your wounds and apply new bandages."

Ragash slapped shaman away like a common annoyance. His strike was so strong it knocked Bytej off his feet. "I don't need help from the likes of you!" He stood up and limped away, his head swimming. "Mark my words, you all follow a fool's errand. You will all die following that whelp!"

The door slammed shut, and with it came a wave of uneasy silence. Xellik gritted his teeth, knowing that all eyes in the room were upon him. As if they didn't have enough problems to deal with in the slums, now they had Ragash spreading his blasphemy, tainting the minds of his followers.

It took a great while to get the other orcs back on topic once Ragash was gone. They were more focused on what he said, and were increasingly weary of Xellik himself despite their allegiance to him only moments prior. Was their faith so flimsy that they would falter upon hearing a crippled orc's ravings? Ragash had no say in what the Fergoth planned to do about Zugrul. Not since his dismemberment.

The other orc clans, those that still had unwavering faith in Xellik's goal, insisted that Ragash's dissenting remarks needed to be taken care of. Xellik couldn't abide by that though. Even though Ragash was a powder keg waiting for an excuse to explode, he couldn't kill one of his own clanmates. It was sacrilege. The other clans didn't understand what that meant. Sytarel had been out of their reach for too long, and they could scarcely recall the sound of Her voice over their own defamations of the Goddess.

He remembered the day they arrived on Rhavik, and his first experiences in the slums. The image of the burning effigy of Sytarel filled his mind. Xellik never did figure out who was responsible for it. It was a reminder of how long the casteless had been in Zugrul. It would take years, possibly even decades, to bring them back under Sytarel's watchful eyes.

The new warlord wished that was the only problem he had to deal with. There was still the matter of Garro that needed to be looked into. The korcyn was too brazen, speaking openly and without fear of reproach. Xellik knew that killing him before this attack on Zugrul would deprive them of information he might still be withholding as well as the allegiance of the korcyn slaves. Not that they needed the boarmen to help them accomplish their mission, but their distraction would serve to mitigate losses on Xellik's end.

"Are we alone?" Xellik whispered. He glanced around, trying to see if Garro or someone else might be lurking in the shadows nearby. Lately it had felt like eyes were always on him. More than just Sytarel's eyes, he thought.

"It appears so," Bytej said.

"Have Urzule keep a close eye on Ragash," Xellik said. "He can't be allowed to continue spreading his ideas amongst our people."

"And what should she do if he continues?"

Xellik didn't have any idea. Urzule was a good scout and spy, but even she could do little against Ragash's sheer strength. Without the use of her weapons to harm him, he doubted she could keep him contained.

"Tell her to use her discretion," Xellik replied after a moment of thinking.

"In other words, you have no idea," Bytej said, stroking his chin.

"Shut up. We also need to do something about the korcyn filth."

"You mean Garro?" Bytej asked, and Xellik nodded. The shaman grunted, and said, "You fear him."

"Of course I do. He's too cunning. He needs to be dealt with."

Xellik knew the perfect way to do it, too. After Zugrul was secured, he would have another orc pull Garro aside, away from his korcyn allies, just to lure him into a dark recess behind a house or a shop. Xellik would be there, waiting for him, his blade already summoned. He'd grab him by the mane and slit his throat, and watch as the life faded from his eyes. The body would then be flushed out the aqueduct and set adrift in the sea to be eaten by fish. The korcyn would never know of his demise, and they could play it up as though it were them giving Garro his freedom for his services to the Fergoth.

"No," Bytej said. "That would not be wise." He came to an abrupt stop and waited for Xellik to turn and face him. "The korcyn maybe filthy rejects, but they are still our allies. They are one of the linchpins of our assault. If we don't have that distraction, we will lose many more of our own warriors dealing with Zugruli soldiers."

"I meant after this business is done."

"I still say he should be left alone." Bytej conjured a flame that hovered into his palms, and with a few ministrations of his fingers, shapes began to move and dance within the fire. "Look. If you do anything to Garro, either now or later, it's going to spark a revolt among the slaves again. If that happens during the chaos following our capture of the city, we won't have the power to put an end to it and the Zugruli might bounce back to reclaim everything."

Bytej snuffed the flame out. "What kind of message do you think that will send to the rest of our allies if they learn about Garro's death? That their reward for helping your ambitions is death? If you dispose of people as soon as they have no use to you, you'll eventually run out of allies to call to your aid when you need it."

"They won't care about the korcyn," Xellik said.

"It doesn't matter whether it's korcyn or orc, they will still be wary of you. Perhaps enough to turn traitor and ally with whatever Zugruli sympathizers are left after we're done."

Xellik scoffed derisively. "Damn the politics of these fickle clans." He wiped his sweat slicked brow and flicked his hand clean. "If we leave the korcyn alone, they might revolt anyways if they're feeling particularly vindictive towards us."

"Killing Garro will turn a 'maybe' into a 'definitely'," Bytej warned. "You are new to dealing with the wide-spread consequences of your power, so listen to your elders when they tell you that it's a very bad idea to go offing someone who has been fairly supportive of our efforts."

Xellik threw his hands in the air and paced away in frustration. Didn't Bytej understand the danger of keeping Garro alive? The korcyn always talked about 'the Dawn' this and 'the Dawn' that. Xellik was convinced it was some sort of movement or organization that none of them knew about. It could present a threat to the entire kingdom if left unchecked. If only they hadn't needed the slave in the first place. While he was teaching them all of Zugrul's secrets and how to survive in this inhospitable land, Garro had been milking all the information he needed out of them.

"If we can't kill him, then I want to be rid of him as soon as the city is ours," Xellik said. "As long as he's around us gathering information, he can turn around at any time and use it against us. We need to keep him away from us, even if that means pawning him off on some other orc. Got it?"

"Fine. Now can we get back to camp? We skipped lunch and it's nearly suppertime," Bytej said as he started back.

Xellik nodded and looked up towards the city's walls. He saw a vague figure standing atop the ramparts with the sun at their back. The bat-like wings splayed out at her sides gave Nazridia away. Red, piercing eyes looked back down at him, as though trying to bore into his skull and read his thoughts. She flapped her wings and took off for parts unknown, but something told Xellik that the succubus would always be watching him. He shuddered to think that he might not get a private moment ever again. Perhaps this is what it meant to be a God's chosen one. He stomped off back to his home, to prepare for their coming attack.

Chapter 28 - The Test of Magehood

13th Day of Abyss
127 I.E.

A month passed quicker than Dane had expected, and as spring approached, so too did the Test of Magehood. Adepts all throughout the academy were trying to practice and cram as much knowledge as they could into their minds. It never felt like it was enough. There was always something more to learn and something else to master. Not a moment went by where Dane felt like he was prepared. He tried not to stress about it, but that proved difficult when a single reminder loomed over his head.

This test would determine his entire future.

Aiden placed a hand on Dane's shoulder. "Are you ready?" he asked.

The two men stood before a large wooden door decorated with golden filigree. Beyond this door was where adepts took their Test of Magehood, to claim the title of sorcerer and become a servant of the Empire. No one knew what lay beyond this door. It was said to be different for everyone who stepped inside. No one could be sure though, as graduated mages never spoke of their Tests, even when asked about it. Everyone thought they were bound to some sort of agreement that prevented them from speaking, but the haunted, hesitant way that these graduates responded suggested otherwise. Something about the Test changed people, but Dane couldn't be sure how.

"I believe I am," Dane said. He shook his head. "No, I'm

probably ill prepared for this."

"Hey, don't talk like that." Aiden placed a finger beneath Dane's chin and lifted his head up to look him in the eyes. "We studied hard every day since we got here. You are ready," he assured him as he gave him a hug. "Good luck in there. I'll meet you back at your dorm later tonight after my test, okay?" As he pulled back, he kissed him on the cheek discretely.

"Okay. Thanks," Dane said as he waved goodbye to his friend. He watched Aiden walk down the hall, away from the door and back to the waiting room to begin his own Test.

If Aiden had faith in him, then Dane knew he could do it. Whether he was prepared or not, as long as that man was beside him, he could do it. Taking a deep breath to calm down, Dane steeled himself and approached the door. It creaked open as he approached it, allowing him to enter.

The room that lay before Dane was bare, save for a bright lamp hanging overhead. There was a well-cushioned bed sitting in the center of the room that faced towards the door. The linens were clean; he could tell by the smell as he walked towards it.

This is where I'm taking my test? Dane thought. He looked around, searching for a window or seats, but there was nothing. The walls were bare and painted white. It was drab and lonely. If he were to stay in this room for too long, he would likely go insane from boredom.

Where is the Council supposed to sit? Aren't they supposed to watch over the Test?

Dane was not kept waiting long as the door swung open to admit someone else in. He turned to face the newcomer, expecting either Talia or Sylenthros to explain the nature of this room. Instead he saw a tall, ursine form push his way through the door.

"Othur?" Dane said, surprised to see the black-furred humanoid padding quietly over to him. "What are you doing here?"

"I hear you're taking your final proficiency exam today," Othur said, smiling to him. His arms were behind his back, and Dane noticed that he rarely stood like that. "I believe congratulations are in order for making it this far."

"Thanks but . . . I haven't even started my test yet."

"That's why I'm here," Othur explained. He gestured to the bed. "Please lie down, and all will be made clear in short order."

Still confused, but not one to question the ursar when he said something, Dane moved to the bed and laid down on his back. The lamp was bright and irritated his eyes, so he kept them closed. He began to realize how quiet the room was. The sounds of people moving about in the hallway were blocked out by the door. It was peaceful, and Dane felt his muscles relax after a few seconds. He could feel something cold and hard being pressed against his forehead.

"Now, keep your head still," Othur instructed as he nudged the object little by little until it was stable. "We don't want this falling off."

"What is it?" Dane asked. It felt like a stone of some kind. He peeked one eye open and looked at Othur. "And why are you doing it?"

"This is how the Test will begin," Othur said. "This stone will record your thoughts, your feelings, and your experiences as you go through the procedure. Mistress Frostfire and the others will be reviewing your performance later today."

"And they get you to do it?" Dane knew that the ursar temple had a powerful backer helping fund their organization, but he didn't imagine that it was the R.A.A.S. itself that provided them with money.

"Of course. We work with them to conduct the tests," Othur replied, stepping back. "Your emotional and psychological state is as important as your ability to use magic. This procedure will help the Council better evaluate you."

Dane swallowed audibly, feeling sweat roll down the sides of his head. "So they'll know what I'm thinking?"

"No need to be afraid," Othur chuckled. "They will merely be aware of how you react to your test. Now then, I believe that's enough questions, hmm? Your test will begin now. No need to hold up the rest of your classmates by occupying this room any longer than necessary." He ruffled Dane's hair lightly so as not to disturb the stone resting on his forehead. "Sleep now. When you awake, you will understand everything."

Dane opened his mouth to ask more, but when he did, he yawned. A cool wind caressed his body and it was followed by the rustling of leaves in the trees. All thoughts about the Test, his life at the academy, and even of his partner Aiden began to vanish as he fell into a deep slumber.

* * * * *

The flap of the tent burst open, and Dane looked up from his map of the surrounding plains. He regarded the scout with a curious glance as the man saluted him.

"Lieutenant, we've located the gnoll's den," the scout told him. His face was flushed and his skin covered in a sheen of sweat. He'd been riding hard.

Dane couldn't blame the man for exhausting himself. Seahaven's roads were being plagued by the marauding hyenamen, all but destroying their economy and ability to feed its citizens. The military had been called in when the local militia was unable to do anything about it, and Dane's squadron was the one that had been sent to look into matters.

"Where abouts are they?" Dane asked, beckoning the scout over. The clink of his chain mail sounded as the man half-jogged towards the table.

"Two leagues north-east of Seahaven, near the road . . ." The man looked at the map, taking a moment to make sense of it. His face lit up as he identified a local landmark at a crossroads. ". . . here!"

"Any fortifications?"

"None that I could see, sir. They have four guards posted outside, but there's likely more inside the den. The entrance is small, so I don't believe they have any major fortifications inside."

"Good work." Dane patted the man on the shoulder. "Get yourself some food and rest up. We ride in an hour." He looked over to an armored soldier sitting in a chair next to him. "You got that, Corporal?"

Lowering the book, Aiden looked at him and nodded. Grim determination filled his eyes. This is what he had trained for, what they had both trained for. The people of Seahaven needed their help, and as warmages of the Empire it was their duty to see this mission through.

How long had the two of them been in the same unit? Longer than Dane could recall. They'd been on countless such missions into the hinterlands to reinforce the smaller villages near Rogust. The monsters in the region were growing restless. Something had stirred up the hornet's nest, and now Rogust was swarmed with bandits, beastmen, and all manner of problems.

If only we weren't short handed after the Jintaren Incursion, Dane thought, rolling up the map. *We're spread too thin to contain these problems before they get out of hand.*

Aiden tucked his book away in his pack and stood up. His back gave a few alarming pops as he stretched. "I'll prep the horses. We'll be ready to ride in thirty minutes."

"Don't dally," Dane said as he moved to get his equipment. "It's time we took care of this once and for all."

"Aye, Lieutenant." Aiden left, brushing past Dane with a gentle touch of his arm.

He was too focused on the task at hand as he ran through several strategies in his head. The advantage of being a sorcerer was having numerous tactics available that mundane units never had.

A direct assault would be quick, but we don't know their numbers, Dane thought. He opened up his trunk at the foot of his cot and pulled out his equipment. *We could strike from range, but we wouldn't have any cover. Magic could take out the guards but that might alert the rest of the gnolls in the den.*

Dane slipped a chain mail shirt over his shirt, careful not to get his hair caught in the links. His sword slid into the loop on his belt. The weight of the weapon at his hip was a constant reminder of the power and authority that he wielded, something that he didn't take lightly. At the bottom of the chest were his mithril bracers, the ones his mother had made. He clasped them onto his forearms, and watched as the polished surface shimmered in the lamp light.

Eliminating the guards comes first so we can secure the perimeter. We could sneak up on them at night, but their ability to see in the dark will make that difficult. The gnolls possessed infravision, the ability to see body heat in the dark. They would spot them long before they arrived at the den. *Magic should be able to mask our approach, but only for Aiden and I.*

Opening up his spellbook that he kept in his rucksack, Dane flipped through the pages in a whirl of parchment. He came to a stop at one page and began to trace his fingers under the lines of a spell. Globes of white lights flitted around him as though the stars had come down from the skies to dance around him. His eyes glowed with an unearthly light as he committed the spell to his memory.

Dane snapped the book shut and the lights faded. He was ready.

It didn't take long to arrive at the landmark that the scout had indicated. Off the side and nestled within the split of a fork in the road was a large stone obelisk. Such monuments dotted the landscape and the surface was etched with directions to the nearest towns. One side pointed back towards Seahaven, while others pointed to the borders of neighboring provinces.

"It's off in that direction," the scout said, indicating to the northwest. "There's some rolling hills as you approach the den, but there's little cover we can use."

"We should wait for dark before we strike," suggested a sergeant under Dane's command.

"It won't matter whether we approach the den at night or during the day. They'll spot us a league away if we're unlucky." Dane turned to Aiden. "Corporal, do you have Dashan's Cloaking written into your spellbook?"

Aiden reached into his saddlebag and pulled out his tome, flipping through the pages as he searched for the spell in question. "Yes, I do." The man went about memorizing the spell without waiting for orders.

"The Corporal and I will approach the den under cover of magic," Dane explained to the troops that sat mounted on their horses. "Follow the scout and wait beyond the hill, just out of sight of the den. Once you see our signal, charge for the entrance. Eliminate all who stand in our way. Understood?"
"Yessir!"

"Let's get going, Corporal." Dane snapped the reins on his horse and sped off across the prairies. They were headed towards certain danger, but between his magic and Aiden's, the gnolls would stand no chance against them.

The rolling hills came to a crest before making a sharp descent into a shallow valley. A creek snaked its way through the bullrushes at the bottom. Dane moved his horse precariously over towards the creek, crossed it, then dismounted. They would have to continue on foot from here. The spell wouldn't hide his horse or the noise it made when it moved.

He waited for Aiden to do the same as the boy let his horse rest by the creek. He patted his mount on the side, then jumped off to join Dane. With their equipment in hand, they ascended the hill and dropped to their bellies as they neared the top.

"Do you see anything yet?" Dane asked as he peered over the crest of the hill.

"There," Aiden whispered, pointing to their left. "I see one of the gnolls."

Dane traced a line from his finger over to a steep hill across the prairies. There he could see the small forms of beastmen lazing about in the field. He couldn't quite make them out from this distance though.

Touching his temple with his fore and middle finger, Dane blinked as he channeled mana into his body. His vision zoomed ahead, magnifying the creatures in the distance. They were still half a league away, but he could see them as though he stood next to them. They were armed, with crossbows and swords. Nothing fancy, judging by the tarnished wood and nicked steel. The Empire's seal could be seen on some of their equipment. The scavengers were merely using what they had stolen.

"We need to eliminate the guards first to secure the perimeter," Dane said, dismissing his vision spell. His head swam for a couple seconds, making him nauseous. He kept his eyes closed while talking. "There's four guards according to the scout, so we'll each have to be quick and take out two of them. Use Dashan's Cloaking to conceal yourself and sneak up on them from down wind."

"And run them through, right?" Aiden asked grimly, though he already knew the answer.

Dane nodded. He didn't like the idea anymore than Aiden did, but being a soldier meant having to kill. Even though their enemy wasn't a human, Dane would still have preferred to take them prisoner rather than take their lives.

That is a sign of weakness, he recalled Heshun saying once during one of his lessons. *The enemy will show you no mercy, so don't show them any, either.*

"Let's move out. We don't want to keep the troops waiting." Dane took a deep breath and focused on the spell he had forced into his memory. The words and motions necessary to call upon its power came to him instantly.

"*Tritimo ketimae, Dashan Glokun!*" Dane thrust his hands into the air then pulled them down, as if closing the drapes of a window. He watched as his body faded away like dust in the wind. In seconds, he could no longer see himself. Aiden was gone as well, having used the same spell.

"I'll take the one on the right," Dane said, rising to his full height. "We've got ten minutes before the spell drops off. Let's move."

"Right."

The only indication that Dane had that his partner was still beside him was the sound of his feet tromping on dirt as he jogged. The blades of grass parted to let him through. Dane hoped the gnolls weren't perceptive enough to see that.

He followed the wind, swooping around his target while keeping an eye on him. As long as he stayed down wind, the gnoll wouldn't know where he was. It was just like hunting an animal. A sentient animal that could wield a sword, but an animal nonetheless. The sound of Aiden's footsteps faded into the distance as he advanced on his own mark, leaving Dane alone in the middle of the field. He hoped that his spell was still holding, and looked down at his hands to double check.

I have to stay focused or the spell will drop, Dane thought, creeping ever closer towards the gnoll guardsman. *One thing at a time: Take out the guards, and the rest will be easy.*

Dane stayed downwind from the gnolls. Their canine heritage gave them an edge in sniffing out prey, and he didn't want to give his position away. His eyes glanced from the ground, to the gnoll he crept towards, and back again. If he stepped on anything, the gnoll would hear it.

With only five steps left between him and the beastman, Dane had a startling thought. The way they were going about this wasn't right. The gnolls weren't being given the chance to defend themselves. By Xenar's teaching, even the act of taking the creature's life was akin to murder. Hadn't Othur taught him that once before, warning him that the path he was on would cause him to stain his hands with blood?

The gnoll was repugnant. Its hide was mangy, its fur missing in spots. The exposed skin was red and irritated. Both ears had bite-shaped holes cut out of them. It wore a chain skirt laid over a kilt of some sort, but it was in terrible condition. These creatures were barely getting by as it was. He could see the stringy muscles on the all too thin arms. They didn't attack caravans out of malice. They attacked out of necessity, to get the food they needed and the equipment necessary to pillage in the first place.

But they kill their prey, Dane reminded himself. *They feast on the fallen and leave nothing undefiled. Even if what they do is necessary to survive, they could have stopped stealing and killing any time they wanted, but they didn't.*

Dane shook his head clear. He was given a mission, and there was no use questioning his orders. They were to exterminate the gnolls for the safety of Seahaven, and that's what they were going to do. Religious morality had no place on the battlefield. He uttered a prayer asking Xenar for forgiveness, and began to stalk forward once more. There would be time later to atone for his sins.

Now was not that time, and he quickly dismissed the nagging feeling in the back of his mind telling him to stop.

A good soldier never questioned orders. When told to march, you asked how far. When told to take up your weapons in defense of your countrymen, you asked where your blade shall be pointed. Even though Dane was an officer, he was still only the lowly rank of lieutenant. He wasn't ordered to think, except about how best to utilize his troops.

Blinking once, Dane's furrowed brow disappeared and his eyes held a deadly sheen. He was not Dane, the follower of Xen. He was the soldier, the killer. He was the arm of the Empire, and the Empire said these gnolls were to be put to the chopping block.

He chest felt tight as he tried to hold his breath. Dane exhaled painfully slow through his nose, paused, then breathed in again as he stalked forward. He tightened his grip on his sword. The gnoll was within arms reach, and he could smell the mangy, unclean fur as he drew near. It smelled of bad cabbage and sweat, making Dane's nose wrinkle in disgust. Hadn't these beasts ever heard of hygiene? In a couple seconds, he supposed that it wouldn't matter.

With his sword poised to strike, he took another step. The guard wasn't wearing a helmet, and his thick neck was exposed. It watched the plains with bored, half-lidded eyes. He turned away from Dane and started to walk away.

Now!

Thrusting forward with his sword, Dane's blade burst through the front of the gnoll's throat before its mind could register what was happening. Blood spurted from the wound, running down the blade and eventually onto Dane's hands. It was warm, yet quickly cooling and he shivered. Everything that made the gnoll what it was faded from its eyes, a pale glassy look overtaking it. It paused in its tracks, released a choked gasp, and fell forward.

Across from Dane, he saw a shimmer as a red line of blood

ripped open another gnoll's throat. Aiden had done his part, and now only two guards remained. They would have to be quick if they didn't want the fallen bodies to be seen.

Wiping his sword clean on the gnoll's kilt, Dane moved towards the other guardsman. He didn't have much time. It wouldn't take long for them to pick up the scent of blood, and he could feel his invisibility spell growing weaker. They were almost at the time limit.

Dane was twenty paces from the gnoll when Aiden took down his second target. The last guardsman noticed his companion falling over dead, and opened his mouth. It shouted something in gnollish, and a long howl followed that echoed across the plains.

I was too slow! Dane thought. The gnolls knew they were here.

Dane lifted his free hand, pointing at the gnoll while backing away. He focused his energy into his hand, then snapped his fingers. Thunder boomed overhead as a bolt of lightning streaked down from the heavens. It scorched the gnoll and the ground around where it struck, silencing the beastman as its muscles seized.

Unsure of whether his troops would understand that something was amiss by seeing the lightning bolt, he lifted his hand into the air as a ball of red appeared in his palm. With a command word, the orb shot up into the sky and exploded into a brilliant spray of multi-colored lights.

Within seconds of the flare going into the air, a wave of mounted horsemen came spilling up over the hill with their weapons drawn. They made for the den as gnolls began to come up out of their burrow.

The battle cries of the gnoll raiders echoed over the fields. They were outnumbered two to one by the military, but they didn't back down. As they appeared from the tunnels, Dane and Aiden flanked from the sides, unleashing explosions of fire and lightning to reduce their numbers. It was one of the first times that Dane could recall ever using his magic so destructively. It came to him frighteningly easy, and it scared him to think that he had this much power at his beck and call.

All the better to protect the people, he affirmed grimly as he cut a gnoll down with his sword.

He could hear the whines of his men's horses as they were shot by crossbows. They toppled over, crushing their riders as they skidded along the ground. The soldiers responded in kind with a volley of arrows that thinned the gnolls numbers.

The battle didn't last more than a minute, and time seemed to slow as Dane took in every detail. From the top of the hill, several gnolls spilled out of a hidden hatch with crossbows pointed at him and his men. Dane could feel a bolt whizz by his ear as the gnoll narrowly missed. He conjured another bolt of lightning from the skies, striking two of the archers.

One of his men screamed as an arrow found a home in his head. His half-helm had not been enough to protect him. His body rolled off his horse onto one of his allies, knocking that man over. Dane's men in the rear line retaliated with another volley of arrows, knocking the last of the gnoll marksmen off the hill. Their corpses looked like mangy pincushions, and they whined as they breathed their last breath.

Aiden was locked into a fight with three beastmen on the opposite side of the battlefield. They were pushing him further away from the safety of his allies, and trying desperately to surround him. Between a magical ward maintained with one hand and his sword, he was holding them back. They were pressing in close though, and Dane knew it was just a matter of time before they overwhelmed him.

It was time likes this when Dane wished he still carried a bow with him. His magic would be too destructive, and would likely catch Aiden in the crossfire if he tried to use a spell. His only other option was to clear the forty some feet between him and Aiden to lend him his aid.

Taking off at a sprint, Dane felled any gnolls that got in his way. Whether by sword or spell, they died easily as he sped through them. His body was covered in cuts and bruises as they feebly tried to retaliate, but his attention was on Aiden, not on his attackers. In a few heartbeats he stood behind Aiden's attackers. He drove his sword through a gnoll's back and pulled back out.

"Behind you!" Aiden said as he killed one of his attackers, now able to deal with the two remaining gnolls on his own.

Dane spun on his heels as he pulled his sword back, his arm following the line he traced with his eyes. The gnoll who tried to sneak up behind him was now a headless torso as its scarred head rolled away from the force of Dane's swing.

With their archers gone and many of their kin slain, the few remaining gnolls cried out in their harsh tongue and began to retreat across the fields. They dropped low, running on all fours to hasten their retreat.

"Mow them down!" Dane ordered his men, "Spare none of them. I don't want them coming back."

He looked to Aiden, and the man appeared pale. "Are you alright, Corporal?" he asked.

"Thanks for the save," he replied, breathlessly. "That was almost too close. It was all I could do to stay alive."

"I'm glad I got to you in time," Dane said, squeezing Aiden's shoulder. "Rest a moment. We're not done here yet."

With the battle winding down, Dane took time to assess their losses. Six of his soldiers had been killed during the battle. Several more were lying on the ground, writhing in pain. The medic would have her work cut out for her with patching these wounds. They still weren't done the job though, as the gnolls' underground den still needed to be scoured for prisoners and stolen supplies.

"Tend to the wounded," Dane said, sheathing his sword. "Do what you can to get them back on their feet, and have them rushed to Seahaven's infirmary." He pointed to Aiden, then to several uninjured soldiers and ordered them to follow him. They needed to be sure the gnolls were all gone, and to retrieve any of the stolen goods that they could find. The people of Seahaven would sleep better at night if they did.

Darkness descended down a steep ramp as the burrow went into the ground. Cool air rushed up from below, chilling Dane and causing him to shiver. He indicated two soldiers and ordered them to watch the entrance, and had the other come with him and Aiden.

"This stone looks well hewn," Aiden said, inspecting the walls in the dim flicker of torches. "This tribe must have been here for a long time."

The barrow was hardly occupied. Those that remained in the soldiers' way were the late comers and the cowardly, those that hadn't heeded the calls of their kin. They fell easily to blade and spell, and soon the compound interior was secured. The flickering of torches was the only light found in the depths of the cave.

"Bring the wagons to the den," Dane ordered his men. "We're getting this place cleaned out and returning to Seahaven."

The men couldn't take more than a few steps before the ground began to shake beneath them. An explosion echoed through the caves, knocking loose the ceiling above the soldiers' heads. Dane's ears rang as he was thrown deeper into the cave. The force of the blast quaffed the torches and bathed them in darkness as the tunnel began to cave in around them.

Chapter 29 - Fate

Dane coughed as dust coated his throat. He struggled to get a breath of fresh air. The rumbling around him came to a stop, save for a few loose pebbles that bounced along the debris behind him. He opened his eyes, but it was too dark to see anything.

"Well isn't this just great," Dane said. He jumped at the sound of his own voice as it echoed back at him. How far down did this tunnel go? In the darkness, his mind conjured beastial shapes that rushed towards him with weapons raised. Panic began to overtake him, shutting out the rational part of his mind as he pictured dozens of gnolls advancing on him, spit dripping from their toothy maws.

It would be easy for them to finish him off. They could see in the dark. A single gnoll would be more than enough to finish him off. Then he would become a veritable feast for the dogmen.

Panting to catch his breath, Dane backed up against the wall. He tripped over something and fell backwards. His mind told him that it was the dessicated remains of those who had come before him. He screamed, and then clapped a hand over his mouth as the tunnel filled the sound of his shouts.

No, this isn't happening! My mind is just playing tricks on me! Get a grip, Dane!

Dane curled up, pulling his knees close to him and shirking away from the darkness. He sought the refuge offered by the tunnel wall to reduce the number of places any threats could approach him from. The seconds crawled by and felt instead like hours. There was no way of knowing how long he'd been in the darkness.

He waited, anticipation building until it choked him, rendering him unable to breathe or to even swallow the saliva that built up in his mouth.

Dane wasn't sure how long he was kept waiting for something to happen. He wanted to shout into the darkness, but his fear kept his mouth firmly shut. As time passed, he calmed down, and logic began to return.

Feeling the ground around him, he brushed against whatever he tripped on. It was a loose rock. Exhaling a deep, rattling breath, Dane stood up. He stayed near the wall. It was too soon for him to try testing his luck.

Dane patted himself down to check for injuries. Other than a couple bruises, he seemed fine. He was impressed that he'd managed to survive the cave in without anything more than some dings and scratches. He wondered what could have caused the cave-in. The gnolls must have been ready for an attack to happen long ago, and prepared a trap just in case some humans were foolish enough to wander in, just as he had done.

Boots scuffed on stone to Dane's left. He realized he wasn't alone. He could hear someone else coughing as well.

"*Verus!*" Dane recited, conjuring a ball of fire that hovered over the palm of his hand. The tunnel was illuminated by the dull orange flicker of flames. If something hadn't known he was there, they did now. The flames painted him as an easy target that could be picked off from the shadows. He reached down and grabbed one of the snuffed torches, reigniting it and holding it above his head.

Laying in the dirt next to Dane, he saw Aiden struggling to stand back up. He was covered head to toe in dirt, and he looked like a stone statue coming to life. His face was pale and caked with dust. His eyes were shut tight, and tears worked to cleanse his eyes of the foreign material.

"Are you alright?" Dane asked, bending down to look his partner over. He set the torch down on the ground to free up his hand.

The man nodded, still unable to answer him with words. The cave-in had narrowly missed his legs, though he had an open cut on the back of his calf that was still bleeding, albeit slowly. Dane worried that Aiden wouldn't be able to stand and that his legs might give out. He needed to see a medic as soon as possible, but they were on their own for now and it would be a while before someone could tend to his wounds properly.

Reaching into his belt pouch, Dane produced a roll of gauze and splashed Aiden's wound with some water from his waterskin. The blood was washed away, but the wound continued to bleed. He bent Aiden's leg upwards and worked to quickly tighten the gauze around it. He pulled it tight and told Aiden to keep his leg elevated above his chest until it stopped bleeding.

"Thanks," Aiden said, laying down on his stomach in the dirt. "I hope I can see a medic soon." He looked back at the collapsed tunnel. "Did anyone else get caught in the trap?"

"I hope not. I didn't see how close everyone else was." Dane frowned as he examined the area they had come from. No light found its way between the stones, and the sounds of his soldiers' voices were quiet. The collapse was thick, and it would take his men some time to get them out. He hoped that his troops were preparing to dig their way in.

"I think it would be best if we waited for them," Dane suggested. He retrieved his sword and slid it back into his sheath.

They weren't sure how long they were waiting, but both men could hear the frantic digging through the tunnel next to them. They passed around some trail rations and ate in silence. The light from the torch started to go out which forced Dane to light a second one, and eventually a third. By that time, Aiden's leg had clotted and he was able to stand up, though he had a slight gait that favored his left foot.

Once he felt confident enough to walk, Aiden began to pace around. He was feeling anxious, and Dane felt the same way. He wanted to get out of this cave and get somewhere safe. It was strange for the gnolls to trap them in the cave and not come to finish them off. Perhaps there were none left to harass them. Or maybe the collapse was meant to bury anyone who might try to raid their den.

Whatever the case may have been, they were stuck there. Dane took a closer look at the cave-in. It wouldn't have been hard to blast their way out, but without any means of supporting the roof, they would only make things worse. Teleporting didn't seem to work either. Now that Dane thought about it, he hadn't been able to use portals since he'd begun this mission. He had never heard of portal magic failing after consuming energy. It would have to wait until he was back in the capital to investigate.

The crunch of leather on gravel echoed up from deeper in the tunnel. Whoever was down there started to run as the sound grew closer.

"Aiden, get back in the light!" Dane shouted, drawing his sword.

Aiden was too slow. A curved blade of swirling energy burst through his armor and out his stomach. He gave a choked cry as a spurt of blood flew from his mouth, his eyes wide with surprise. The man hadn't even had a chance to reach for his weapon, much less defend himself. He groped futilely at the spot where he'd been stabbed, and stared down at the blade in disbelief. From behind him, Dane could see their mystery attacker's gleaming fangs that stood out against his sinister silhouette.

"Aiden!" Dane cried. He rushed forward to help him, but it was too late. Aiden's face was already going pale from shock, and no medicine in the world would be able to cure a stomach wound that severe.

The creature laughed, shoving Aiden off his sword and into Dane. He collapsed with his lover on top of him, blood running over his body. Time seemed to slow as the watched the final glimmer of life fade from Aiden's eyes.

"A-Aiden . . ." Dane had trouble speaking. His throat felt parched and it cracked when he opened his mouth. "Stay with me, please!"

"Don't worry, you'll be joining him soon enough, human."

Dane stiffened upon hearing the creature speak. He recognized it, but he couldn't recall from where. It filled him with a primal terror that had him wanting to flee, to escape into a portal and to hide away forever. But his magic wouldn't listen to him! It had failed him when he needed it most, and now Aiden was dead and he was in mortal danger. The darkness grew thicker and the ring off light cast by Dane's torch grew smaller as the shadows swelled.

"Who are you!?" Dane yelled, trying to move out from under Aiden's corpse.

The creature stepped into the torchlight, and Dane gasped when he saw that it was an orc. His eyes ran over its body, and came to rest on the tattoo on its scalp. He knew that mark: the fangs of the Fergoth tribe.

The orc wore a suit of armor decorated with a tiger's pelt. His shaven head gleamed in the light. From his neck dangled a golden chain upon which an emerald of impossible beauty hung. Through the gaps in the orc's armor, Dane could see thick muscles that looked capable of ripping him in half.

The magical scimitar in the orc's hands vanished as if it weren't even there. He reached forward, grabbing Aiden's body and throwing it off to the side. Dane watched in horror as his lover collapsed in an undignified heap. He didn't get to stare long as the orc grabbed him and pulled him into the air with the ease of a parent picking up a baby.

"I've been waiting for this moment for years, Dane Trueshot." The orc punched Dane in the jaw, causing him to see stars. His teeth clacked together painfully, and though it hurt, it helped to wake him up from his stupor.

"*An theros verus! Fiz ban!*" Dane blasted the orc in the chest with a fireball. He fell from the orc's grasp, and the monster stumbled back. The spell scorched his armor, leaving a blackened smear across his breastplate.

"How do you know my name?" Dane asked. He dove away and reached for his sword, taking the grip in his white-knuckled hands. His body was tensed and ready to spring into action. It was time that he finally put the ghosts of his past to rest . . . even if it ended up being the last thing he ever did.

"You should remember that night when we came to Tran . . ." the orc said. "You were the human I pummeled in the holding pens. I'm amazed you're still alive, to be honest."

Dane frowned, thinking back to the night that he had been taken hostage by the orcs. He remembered being singled out. They had exchanged names before getting into a fight.

"Xellik . . ." Dane said, and the orc's smile told him he had guessed right. "Why are you back? The Fergoth were chased out of Rogarian territory!" His voice took on a high pitch, making him sound more afraid than he intended.

"I have unfinished business with Rogust," Xellik replied. He stepped towards Dane. The man hurried back to keep his distance, an act that made Xellik laugh. "Still a terrified little whelp, just like the day we met. You were weak back then, with no magic to call your own. You have just as little power now. What do you hope to be able to accomplish with that pig sticker of yours? With your fledgling magic? Your power pales in comparison to one who has the strength of Sytarel at their beck and call!"

Xellik's hand began to glow as he spoke something in orcish. Ethereal, golden chains burst from the ground with thunderous rattling. Dane slashed at those he could, breaking them in half and causing them to disappear. He didn't see the one coming from behind that lashed at his sword arm, wrapping itself around him. It pulled tight and dragged him back towards the wall.

More chains lunged towards him. Tendrils of energy snaked their way around his body and held him still. Dane managed to keep a grip on his sword, but it did him no good without being able to move his arms. He struggled against the chains, but they held fast. They could contain a minotaur if Xellik wanted them to. What could Dane hope to do with his meager strength?

"You simpering humans worship inferior gods. The Strength and Honor represented by Sytarel is what makes us superior, what draws Her followers together and makes them powerful. Only the strong shall inherit this world." Xellik brandished his scimitar again. The hilt appeared first in his hand as the blade extended outwards. The tunnel was alight with its unnatural glow.

Dane struggled against his bonds again, even knowing that it was futile. But what else was he supposed to do, wait for death to claim him? He wasn't going to sit and wait like a caged animal. He had to do something.

"Where's the honor in killing a restrained opponent?" Dane asked, grunting as he strained more. The shackles rubbed his limbs raw, and blood seeped along his skin.

"Only those who are strong deserve an honorable death," Xellik told him. "One such as yourself deserves a coward's death, and who better than one of Sytarel's followers to send you to the afterlife?"

Dane watched as the orc lifted his scimitar. Only mere seconds stood between him and certain death. What could he do with his body bound as it was? What spells did he know that he could use without moving his hands?

Of course, there is something I can use! Dane thought. It was a simple offensive spell that he always discounted as being too weak, but it was also one that Aiden swore by time and again.

Gathering as much mana as he could in his hands, Dane cried out, "*Effervan tojitiscah!*"

Wriggling the fingers on his unoccupied hand, Dane conjured arrows made entirely of mana. They zipped around unerringly around the cave like flies, then found a home in Xellik's wrist. The orc shouted in pain, letting go of his weapon and reflexively reaching up to cradle the wound. The scimitar vanished as he let go of it, and to Dane's relief, so did the chains as the orc lost his focus on the spell.

No man could stand toe-to-toe with an orc for long and expect to live. Dane knew this, and he understood that he needed to be quick. Xellik wasn't expecting an attack so soon and stared as Dane's blade flashed out, aiming for his unprotected neck. The orc grunted as he leaned away. A thin line of blood appeared on his cheek where the sword cut him.

With a snarl, Xellik wheeled about as his magical weapon materialized in his hands again. Dane raised his own blade to deflect the attack. The ethereal scimitar passed through his steel sword as though it wasn't even there. Dane couldn't pull back fast enough, and he felt the weapon slice into his arm. It cut deep, severing muscle tissue with ease.

Pain flared up from the wound and Dane cried out. In all his time fighting, he'd never felt a pain quite like this. Even sparing with Heshun was less painful. He nearly dropped his weapon, and only the harsh reprimands of his instructor echoing in his memory allowed him to keep a grip on it.

Xellik pressed the attack, and Dane was forced to dodge backwards again and again to get away from him. He felt cold stone against his back, and realized that there was no longer anywhere else to run. The orc grinned with his yellowed teeth as he hefted his scimitar in position to strike.

Dane had to think quickly, knowing that his more destructive and flashier magic would likely bring the entire cave system down on their heads. It would kill the orc, sure, but he'd like to be able to live through this fight. He channeled as much energy as he could muster into his sword, and lightning began to crackle and dance along the blade, as though it were in the hands of the Stormbringer Himself.

This time when Dane attempted to deflect Xellik's attack, his scimitar did not pass through the enchanted weapon. The magic that Dane had ensorceled his sword with made it capable of touching the ethereal weapon. Xellik's swing flew wide to the side, leaving himself open so that Dane could strike.

The man didn't go after the open space in Xellik's armor. Instead he thrust forward, and with the magic reinforcing his steel blade, it punched through the orc's breastplate and drew blood from a wound in his stomach.

Xellik stumbled backwards, placing a hand over the hole in his armor as his life force dripped between his fingers. He looked down and inspected his wet palms, gawking in disbelief.

"Damn you . . . I will bring this entire cave down on us if I have to!" Xellik shouted as fire began to glow in his fists. A fireball exploded from his hands, striking the roof with enough force to make the ground shake.

"You'll kill us both!" Dane shouted. Chunks of rock fell from the walls and ceiling. He jumped away from the new collapse, knocking aside an attack from Xellik as he sought safety on the other side of the wide tunnel.

"Sytarel will never allow one of Her children to fall before the likes of you!" Xellik unleashed another blast above Dane's head.

The man felt a chunk of stone fall onto his collarbone and he heard the crack of bone. He tottered to the side but caught himself by widening his stance. He wasn't going to allow himself to be brought low by such tricks.

As Xellik was readying himself to cast another spell, Dane thrust his free hand outward. His body screamed at him as he moved, but he couldn't stop fighting yet nor succumb to his wounds. Speaking a single word of magic, he loosed an invisible wave of arcane energy. The force impacted the orc in the stomach, aggravating his wound and knocking the air out of his lungs. His hand dropped and the fireball flew straight for Dane. He erected a magical ward, but he reacted too slowly. Some of the heat from the blast managed to get through his defenses and scorch the skin on his arms. His skin blistered and turned a fierce red.

The pain was almost too much for Dane to bear, and darkness began to overtake him. He couldn't let himself give up yet. He had to remain strong so that he could defeat Xellik and put an end to whatever plot he and the gnolls were cooking up. It was hard to maintain his will, to overcome the desire to allow unconsciousness to claim him. His body wanted to give out beneath him and send him toppling to the ground where he would be helpless before the orc.

Xellik was in just as bad a position as he was. He hadn't stood back up from when Dane knocked him over, and the ground was coated with his blood.

Dane shambled towards the orc, sword still in his hand. He noticed that there was a large cut along the top of the orc's skull, and it bled profusely down the side of his face.

"Your kind took everything from me," Dane said as he moved towards Xellik. His words were slurred, and he could taste blood in his mouth. He snorted back snot and spit to clear his throat. "My father . . . my village . . . my lover. My soldiers and the people of

Seahaven suffered because of you . . ."

He stood over Xellik, his sword lifted above his head. The tip was aimed for the orc's skull. Dane had waited many years for an opportunity to strike back at the clan that had ruined his life. He feared the orcs, but simultaneously he wanted to get back at them for everything he'd been through, for all the nightmares he'd endured, and for making him feel helpless every waking moment of his life.

Now he wasn't helpless. Now he had the power to do what needed to be done.

"Good riddance!" Dane stabbed downwards with all his strength.

Xellik roared as he came to life in that instant. His clawed hands gripped Dane's throat and squeezed. The man's chest felt hot as he fought for every breath. He missed his mark and jabbed Xellik in the shoulder instead. The orc had made a grave mistake in leaving his sword arm free though. The blade didn't miss a second time, and as the metal punched through his skull, Xellik's grip on Dane's neck loosened. He let go of his sword and shoved the orc off him. He dragged himself with his good arm, coughing as he struggled to breathe. The crumbling sound of rock gave way as light poured into the tunnel, and Dane looked up towards the relieved faces of his soldiers before their forms grew dark and he passed out.

Chapter 30 - Returning to the Waking World

13th Day of Abyss
127 I.E.

Dane opened his eyes with a start and gasped, as though he'd been holding his breath for an eternity. His heart felt like it might burst from his chest at any moment and a cold sweat covered his body. He tried to move, but his muscles would not respond to him. He felt cuts along his body, though there was nothing there.

"There, all done!" Othur said as he strode into the room and retrieved the stone from Dane's brow. He tucked it away quick as he could. "How are you feeling?"

"Where am I?" Dane asked, his eyes not quite focused enough to see the bare room around him. "What happened to everybody? To Aiden?"

"Slow down. Everything is alright. You're still at the Academy."

Dane struggled to move his hand and reached for his head. It throbbed painfully with the worst migraine he'd ever experienced. "But the gnoll den . . . my men died, and so did Aiden . . ."

"Fortunately, it was all an illusion my friend." Othur produced a cold, wet cloth from somewhere and used it to wipe the sweat from Dane's forehead. "Come now, let's get you back to your room." He offered a paw to help Dane up, but the boy brushed him off.

"No, I need to find Aiden first!" Dane rose in the bed, and felt a wave of nausea over come him as he did. The room spun, and he couldn't hold the rising vomit in. He threw up upon the ground, his stomach churning and his chest heaving. "What's happening to me?"

"The Test takes its toll." Othur gently rubbed Dane's back, trying his best to soothe him as the boy coughed up the contents of his stomach. "Your mind can't make heads nor tails of the experience, and takes it out on your physical body. It leaves you mentally and physically scarred.

Othur sounded sad, almost disappointed. It was little wonder then why the Academy used the ursar's services when conducting their Tests. He would be better able to handle the needs of the students in a time of crisis.

Dane tipped his head between his knees and panted, trying to keep from vomiting again. The smell of his sick didn't help any, and made it all the more difficult, but he was afraid to sit up straight.

"So it wasn't real?" Dane said, hardly believing it. "No one died?"

Othur squeezed his shoulder then. "It wasn't real. It was all in your mind." He knew the boy would listen to him, more so than most, and it would not take long to calm him down. Dane had been through more in his life than most, and he was better suited to dealing with tragic and horrible images. Many students left the Academy with mental scars that lasted years, if not decades. It was all in their best interests, or so the professors said, and Othur normally believed them. But seeing Dane the way he was made him feel uneasy about the procedure now. Hadn't Dane been through enough? Was it necessary to pit him against all the things he feared as well? The boy's mental turmoil made him feel sick, and Othur tried to block out his empathic response before he, too, felt as Dane looked.

"So I'm not alone . . . and the orcs really are gone." Dane heaved a great sigh of relief and laid back down on the bed. "No more people died because of me."

Othur nodded, but he wasn't sure what to say to ease the boy's mind. He had a long road ahead of him as a soldier, and as a person who cared deeply for the lives of those around him. He suffered a great deal from his survivor's guilt. Would he really be ready for the life of a soldier? Could a kind person like Dane take another's life when ordered to do so, when he was still cultivating his belief in Xenar and His teachings?

Ruffling Dane's hair, Othur said, "Rest for a few minutes. I'll get someone to clean this up and then we'll get you back to your room, alright?"

Dane didn't hear him. He was quietly snoring, a line of drool dripping from his mouth and onto the pillow.

* * * * *

Dane woke up later that day in his bed, feeling groggy and sore. His mouth felt full of cotton, and he briefly wondered if he had been drunk the night before. The covers were hot and felt sticky from his sweat in the hot room. He threw them aside and felt a chill pass over him as the cold air touched his skin.

Who removed my clothes? he found himself wondering, and felt embarrassed despite being out cold since the Test.

As Dane sat up, he felt a sharp pain in his head and laid back down. His headache had subsided somewhat since his Test, but it still throbbed painfully when the lamp light flickered in his vision. Dane draped an arm over his eyes and breathed deeply. Dust motes floated in the sunlight and he heard birds from Sylenthros' garden. Were it not for the headache, it would have been one of the more relaxed mornings he'd experienced at the Academy. Dane got up slowly and began dressing himself with a bit of difficulty due to the stiffness of his body.

There came a knock at the door. "Master Trueshot? May I come in?" a timid voice said from the other side.

"Yes, come in Isabella," Dane replied as he pulled on his leggings.

The servant girl stepped into the room and set down a tray of food for Dane. "The Council requests your presence at the Ivory Tower. Please head there after you have eaten."

"Thank you," Dane gave her a weak smile. She bowed and excused herself to go tend to the other students in the dorm.

As he finished his breakfast, Dane tried to recall the Test. It left him with a lingering feeling of dread and of loss, but he couldn't pinpoint why that was. He had vague flashes of images and of words exchanged between himself and others that were there. Othur said they weren't real. Perhaps the conversations he had weren't either, and that's why they were fading from his memory so quickly. They were becoming more incorporeal by the second and he imagined by the end of the day he wouldn't remember what his Test was about either.

Maybe that's why graduates never talked about the Test. They couldn't remember except for whatever scars had been left in their minds. Something about it was unsettling, and Dane didn't want to be alone. He longed to seek out Aiden, but it would have to wait until his meeting with the Council.

Dane headed out of the dormitory and focused his thoughts on the Ivory Tower, imagining the door to the Council's chambers at the top floor. He could picture it vividly in his mind, having seen it many times before. Not wanting to walk up all the steps to get to the Council's chambers, Dane recited the words to a portal spell and faded away as he stepped into the rift. He reappeared before the chamber doors. Teleportation had long ago lost its ability to upset his stomach, and it had become one of his favorite spells to use.

He smoothed out the wrinkles in his clothing and tried to fix his hair. Dane grabbed the large metal ring on the door and banged it against the wood. He was beckoned inside and he headed in to see the Council already seated at their table.

"Good day, Professors," Dane said, and they all returned his greeting.

"I'm glad to see you're awake. How are you feeling?" Ancherad asked.

"I've felt worse than this," the boy replied, shrugging.

"We have many students to review today, and yours will be short, so I'll be brief. We have reviewed the recording of your Test and have come to an agreement about your performance," Ancherad said. He held a piece of parchment in his hand and was looking over it periodically as he spoke. "You are over-confident in your own abilities and rely more on your magic than on your allies. You also display a lack of self-control over your emotions when faced with the things you fear." He eyed Dane, drawing his attention to him. "That's something you will want to hide from your subordinates in the future."

Dane hung his head, touching his chin to his chest. His face felt hot, and he was sure that it had turned red, showing his embarrassment to everyone in the room. Fresh images filled his mind as the Test replayed in his head. He remembered the plan now, though it wasn't in the clearest of details, and the orc. He could remember the yellowed tusks, the sinister laugh, the force of his blows . . . why did it scare him so much?

"However . . ." the Archmage continued, perking Dane up a bit, ". . . regardless of those facts, you still demonstrated superior situational awareness and tactical skill that allowed you to limit the injuries you and your comrades sustained. Your offensive skills could use some polishing, but a strong defense can serve in its place until you become a more seasoned warrior. You utilized your knowledge of the situation and the abilities of your soldiers well when executing your operation."

He went on further to discuss the more detailed aspects of his performance, such as his selection and use of spells, his conservation of mana, and his swordplay. Aside from a harsh comment or two about his selection of spells, and his reckless use of magic as a whole, most of the feedback given to Dane was very positive. However, there was one detail that still bothered him that they had yet to bring up, and he waited for them to finish before he spoke.

"I had a question: You've all told us that the Test was dangerous. I can remember the feeling of being wounded in that place, the bite of the orcs' sword, the impact of the falling rocks . . . Was I in any real danger?" Dane asked. Heshun snorted at his question. Talia merely turned away, preventing him from reading her expression. Ancherad showed no signs of any emotion, as was typical for the headmaster.

Sylenthros, however, let out a boisterous laugh. "Of course it was dangerous. You felt pain and you have been left with mental scars that will likely never fade away. You might not have died, but chances are you could have easily been left a vegetable for the rest of your life, if you were unlucky. But with the magic we're talking about, the odds are a hundred to one, and that's only if you failed."

"So you lied? There was never any harm?"

"Life is not a renewable resource," Sylenthros pointed out. He leaned forward on his elbows and tented his fingers. "Sending adepts to their deaths after years of training? Why, that's about as smart as her fashion sense is good." Sylenthros thumbed in Talia's direction. He smiled at her when she in turn shot him an icy glare. Dane noticed that her fingers twitched and tapped on the table. A layer of rime began collecting around her hands, but it dissipated as quickly as it formed.

"Sylenthros . . ." Ancherad said with an exasperated sigh.

"Right. Well, few people actually die during their Test. Most deaths are a result of a weak-willed individual whose mind can't determine fiction from reality and their brains simply shut down. Like I said, slim odds, but a possibility nonetheless."

"Then why tell us for all these gods-damned years that this Test was dangerous?" Dane snapped. He didn't care if he was in a room containing the four most powerful sorcerers in Rogust. They didn't have any right to do that to him and countless other adepts who had stood before them. "If we knew ahead of time what risks were involved, what the consequences of failure would be, we could have prepared better! How many people failed this year and will be left broken because of it?"

"It's part of the Test," Talia said. She sounded disappointed, but Dane wasn't able to tell if it was because of the years of lying and secrecy, or because of his outburst. "You need to recognize that in the real world, you won't always have time to prepare, and you need to be able to handle what comes your way on the fly. We need to make sure that only those with the strongest resolve, who are willing to lay their lives on the line, are suitable for the role they'll play in serving the Empire. You passed that part with flying colors, as expected."

"A warrior needs to be able to face his fears head on," Heshun added. "Even though you were led to believe that the Test could be deadly, you still faced it without hesitation. Knowing fear and how to handle it is part of the Test. Subjecting you to your greatest fears was also an aspect of what we were evaluating, and you were able to avoid becoming paralyzed by them. Fear of loss, fear of people dying for your sake, fear of the orcs . . . You overcame them all, to a degree."

Dane froze, an icy grip clutching his chest. He could remember his Test more clearly. His men dying to fulfill his orders, their screams etched in his mind. He could see Aiden's shocked face as a blade burst from his chest, blood seeping from his lips. And the orc . . . Dane shook his head, trying to clear it. He needed to leave. He needed to be with Aiden. Othur said he was okay, but he had to be sure.

"So what happens now?" Dane asked, trying to get things to proceed quicker. His thoughts were cycling between his Test and his lover. He didn't care about what the Council still had to say.

"You're to be placed in a unit and given a rank. Professor Halgrind was once part of our military, and since his service he has worked here as a liaison with some of the higher ups in the chain of command." Ancherad gestured to the jintaren. "He's the one responsible for sending off warmages and sorcerers to help defend the realm."

"I've had you placed with Digran's Dreadnaughts, an infantry unit that operates here in the homeland and throughout the Kelial Plains. You're serving under Commander Ghestalt Digran, and have been granted the rank of Ensign. After a year of service, your rank will be boosted to Lieutenant once you have proven yourself a capable leader."

"I'm getting a commission?" Dane asked, hardly believing their words. Ensign was the lowest rank of commissioned officer within the Empire, but it still carried a great deal of weight within the military. He was selected by the Emperor himself to take up this position. He couldn't believe it!

"Yes, and trust me when I say that it doesn't happen very often. Congratulations, Ensign Trueshot," Talia said, smiling. For the first time since meeting her, Dane didn't question the sincerity of her praises. She snapped her fingers and a tabard appeared before Dane, floating just in front of him. It was royal blue with a white trim. A regal 'R' was embroidered on the front. Resting on top of it was a small copper pin in the shape of a sword sheathed behind a shield, a mark that signified his rank. "I told you that you would go far here."

"Of course," Sylenthros said, "It helps that Digran needs a fresh officer to help lead his unit, and you were the most likely candidate we had." The elf shrugged, then added, "I'm sure you'll like your placement."

Dane nodded, then saluted them. "Thank you for your confidence." He bid them farewell, then teleported back to the dorms.

With his new tabard tucked under his arm, Dane went straight for Aiden's room. Marked by a #42, he rapped on the door harder than was probably necessary. He was impatient, and he had to see his partner. He had to be sure he was okay. He was about to knock a second time when Aiden opened the door wearing nothing but a pair of breeches.

"I was getting changed, sorry," Aiden said sheepishly as he stepped aside to allow Dane in. He smiled, and once Dane set his tabard down, he gave the man a hug.

"I'm so glad you're here." Dane gripped the man tightly, pressing him close to his body and feeling his warmth. The Test hadn't been real. Aiden was still by his side. "How did your Test go?"

"It didn't go so good," Aiden said, scratching the back of his head and giving Dane a nervous smile.

"Well, you've got a smile on your face, so you didn't fail, right?" Even if Aiden hadn't been smiling, Dane knew he would've passed with ease. Aiden never failed at anything he set his mind on.

The boy leaned up against the dresser and placed his hands at the edges to support himself, while Dane sat down on his bed. "Yeah, I passed. But I was only ranked as a Corporal, sadly." He chuckled, "Though, I guess I don't really care about my rank all that much. I just want to get out there and start making a difference, you know?"

"Yeah, I do. It's still a better rank than being a private, and a lot better than failing. Congratulations." Dane smiled.

There was a short silence that hung between them as they basked in their victory. Aiden ended up being the one to speak first. "So what unit did you get placed into? They stuck me in the 81st Mobile Infantry Division. Digran's Dreadnaughts."

"Really?" Dane said, not believing his words. Aiden nodded his head. "That's my unit. I was put in as Ensign."

Aiden beamed a smile at him. "I'm glad to hear that. So we really will work together to become great warmages, just like we said we would when we were kids."

"Yeah, we'll be heroes." Dane felt like a kid once more, and he was incredibly happy with how things had turned out. He wondered if it was luck or fate that had put them together in the same unit, or if someone had been looking out for them. It didn't matter which it was. Dane was just happy that he would get to continue working together with Aiden.

"So I guess that means . . ." Aiden paused, a grin spreading across his face.

"What?"

"I have to take orders from you, for once huh?"

Dane smacked him on the shoulder. "Shut up!"

The man laughed at the embarrassed look on Dane's face. "Come on, let's got to the Purple Nymph and celebrate!" Aiden suggested as he pushed himself off of the dresser.

"Sure, I'll drink to that," Dane said with a grin, and followed his friend out of the room. As he closed the door behind him and fell in pace beside his friend, his thoughts turned to Jonathan. What would his father think of him now that he was about to head out into the world all on his own, as an officer in the military no less? He hoped that the man would at least be proud of him.

Epilogue

15th Day of Sethyr
127 I.E.

A thunderous boom shook the Temple of Sytarel within the heart of Zugrul. High Priestess Foa Zugrul, leader of the entire orcish kingdom, turned to her scrying mirror and waved a hand over it. The image of a fully armor-clad orc appeared in the glass. Another boom rattled the frame and it tilted to the side.

"Commander! What's going on?" Foa barked. "What's causing all this infernal shaking?"

"We don't know!" the female responded.

"What do you mean you don't know?"

"It's just as I said, High Priestess, I -" the Commander was cut off as a third, more forceful quake reverberated throughout the city. Her attention turned to something above her, and the Commander's mouth could only hang open as a black shadow descended upon her and the scrying spell was cut off.

"Damn it!" Foa spat, punching the mirror and shattering it into hundreds of pieces. First the korcyn began to revolt within the city, and now the casteless outside were up in arms about something. What were her warriors doing? Could they not contain a simple uprising of riffraff?

She ran through the temple, and bolted down the center aisle past all the pews. Whatever was going on, she needed to get somewhere safe. The golden chandeliers above rattled and shook with every tremor, threatening to snap and descend to the ground.

The reverberations were happening at regular intervals. They couldn't have been explosions. Had the casteless allied with a giant?

As she reached for the great iron wrought doors, their form bulged inwards as a great force slammed into them. Foa fell backwards and scrambled away just as the doors came right off their hinges. Smoke and debris filled the room, clouding the entrance. The twisted metal spiraled across the floor, destroying chairs and ornaments in their wake before coming to a clattering halt along one of the walls.

"What is the meaning of this intrusion!? Who dares defile the sanctity of this temple?" Foa shouted as Xellik and his home guard barged into the temple. "Guards! Guards!"

No one came to answer her pleas as Xellik stepped right up to her and stood face to face with the elderly orc. Foa tried to cast a spell, but Xellik waved his hands dismissively and the mana she had gathered dissipated.

"What is this? You dare to interrupt the spell-work of a High Priestess?" she huffed. She raised a hand to strike him but he slapped her arm away.

Xellik smirked at her and conjured a sword from thin air. Foa's eyes widened as he tightened his grip on the magical weapon and pointed the curved blade in her direction. Only a priestess of Sytarel could conjure such a weapon! How was it that a mere male could achieve such a feat?

"You poor, foolish old crone. You have sat far too comfortably atop your pedestal, and you're unaware of that which goes on around you." He wriggled his fingers and crystalline chains burst from the ground. They lashed out and wrapped themselves around her arms, legs, and throat. Each length of chain tightened and pulled her down to her knees, holding her arms apart so she couldn't work her magic. Xellik stood over her and put the blade of his sword to her neck.

"Sinner! Blasphemer! Sytarel will strike you down for this treachery!" she screamed. "You're dead! Do you hear me? You're all DEAD!"

"Who do you think granted me my power, crone?" Xellik said, and looked up.

A form descended from the ceiling, her shadow blotting out the lighting from the chandeliers. Nazridia's wings fluttered and kicked up a plume of dust as she slowed her fall and landed next to Xellik. She folded her arms and tucked her wings behind her, while her whip-like tail flicked back and forth threateningly. The priestess eyed Nazridia warily, fear playing across her face. Even one such as herself could not deny the existence of the succubus before her.

"Dear, misguided Foa Zugrul . . ." the succubus began as she brought her tail forward and traced the barbed end over Foa's face, leaving a trail of blood as it cut into her skin. ". . . when was the last time you heard the Goddess' voice? When was the last time you carried out Sytarel's will? How long have you led the orcs by your own whims?" She pulled her tail back and then lashed out, cutting a large gash across Foa's cheek. "You are a fool. You have forsaken your Goddess, and in return, She has forsaken you!"

Xellik reached into his armor and tugged on a chain hanging around his neck, pulling out a green amulet. "Do you know what this is, Foa?" he asked as the Emerald slowly spun back and forth. "It's fine if you don't want to answer. This is the Emerald of the Deep Earth, and it houses tremendous amounts of power. It's the relic the Zugruli sought and never managed to claim for themselves. And now, through Sytarel's graces, it belongs to me. I will become the future ruler of the orcish race." He clutched the gem in his fist, and even though his grip was tight, a brilliant green light seeped out between the cracks in his fingers.

The roof rumbled and was torn away by a giant hand. Foa looked up, and saw a gigantic stone golem standing over her, its rocky skin covered in a layer of moss and leaves. Xellik watched as the Batic Golems reached down and pulled Foa upwards, the chains holding her shattering as they grew taut and rigid.

"Traitorous scum! You will all be struck down by Sytarel's wrath!" Foa spat as the giant golem constricted her.

"No, Foa," Nazridia corrected as she leaped up from the ground and fluttered near the orc woman. Foa writhed and screamed within the stone grip of the golem. "The only traitor here is you."

The Batic Golem crushed her body and a choked off scream was followed by the sound of every bone in her body breaking.

Xellik looked up at the golem as it awaited its next order. It had already frightened off every guard in the city, and now it stood silently, watching over the temple that it had just ripped a hole into. "Throw her into the sea. I don't want her corpse defiling any part of my city. Let the fish feed on her."

The golem shifted and cracked as it pulled its arm back before hurling Foa's body towards the port and the sea beyond.

"What now?" Bytej asked, stepping up beside his leader.

Xellik turned and dismissed his sword, then tucked the Emerald back beneath his armor. "Haij, Napir, Sorda and Bytej will come with me. The rest of you, watch the doors and secure the entrance. It's time to officially make this city mine."

Nazridia came down to join Xellik, a smirk plastered on her face. "What is it you plan to do now that Zugrul is in your hands?" she began as the orcs moved through the temple. "Continue the same traditions as your predecessor?"

Xellik scoffed at her. "No. I plan to retake Muriaj, in good time. I'll gather my forces and in a year's time, I shall assault Muriaj, and wipe out the Coalition for everything they've done to Sytarel's children."

The succubus cackled. "It seems my Mistress was wise in choosing you as Her vessel to enact Her will. Very good, Warlord."

She fluttered up towards the hole in the ceiling, then shouted down to him. "I shall see you again very soon."

Just watch, Sytarel. I'll bring the orcs back to their rightful place as rulers of Muriaj!

* * * * *

14th Day of Abyss
127 I.E.

Dane took Talia's hand in his own and gave it a firm shake. "It's been a pleasure learning under you, Professor Frostfire." He couldn't believe that after all this time, all the trials that he'd endured since Tran, that he was finally free to go out into the world. Granted, he was a soldier of the military, but at least he was no longer stuck in the Academy, or an orphanage, or in his father's home. The world was open to him.

"The pleasure was all mine," she said with a smile. "You're one of the better students I've had in years, and you cared a lot about your studies. You worked hard to get to where you are now, and have advanced so quickly. I know you'll be successful out in the real world."

"I appreciate that," Dane said. "I think I'll miss this place, after a time." He looked across the room. The desks were clean and unoccupied. The spot at the back of the room where he and Aiden sat would become some new pupils favorite seat. He almost felt jealous losing his spot. But it wasn't really his anymore, was it?

"Come back and visit sometime," she replied. "Even if it's just to say 'Hello', at least then you won't truly be gone. And remember, if you ever need it, the library is always yours to use."

"I'll make sure to keep that in mind." Dane shook her hand once again, then added, "I should get going. I don't want to keep my new commander waiting."

"Stay safe, Dane Trueshot."

Dane nodded, then left Talia's lecture hall to go catch up with Aiden. Once he was out of the classroom, he teleported away into Sylenthros' garden elsewhere on campus. He spotted Aiden a short distance away, bidding farewell to the elf. Dane stayed back until the two were done talking, as he didn't want to interrupt or listen in on their conversation. Such words were private, to be shared only between the two of them.

"You don't have to stand so far away, Master Trueshot," Sylenthros said, flashing his pearly white teeth. "I'm not going to bite."

Aiden smirked at Dane as he moved over to join them. "I didn't want to butt in," he replied, shrugging.

"We've already said our goodbyes," Aiden told him.

"I feel that I need to thank you Sylenthros. For telling me about my family and for helping to train me," Dane said, shaking the elf's hand. "I doubt I'd be half the sorcerer if I hadn't met you."

"With the way Talia teaches, I'm surprised you're half the sorcerer you are now," Sylenthros replied with a smirk. "Pleasantries aside, aren't you due to meet with your Commanding Officer shortly?"

"Yeah, we're supposed to," Aiden admitted. "I've just been hesitant to leave the Academy. It's been like a second home to me."

"Me too," Dane said. The Academy had been the only home he'd known since he lived with Jonathan. He was feeling uneasy about leaving everything behind to live in a barracks on a military base, even if he was welcomed back on the school's grounds.

"You'll both be fine, I'm sure," the elf reassured them. "That is, as long as your CO doesn't kill you for being late."

"You've got a point there," Aiden said as he moved to stand beside Dane. "We'll clear the city in minutes though, so I'm not worried. Thanks for everything, Professor!"

"Yes, thank you, sir." Dane reached out to grab Aiden's wrist and focused his mind on the Academy gates. A portal opened up and they stepped through it, vanishing with a pop as the rift closed. They tread through the park outside the grounds, and once they were at the edge of Eastgate Market, he turned to look back one final time at the Ivory Tower that stood tall over the entire campus. He hoped that he'd be able to see the Academy from wherever it was that they'd be staying, so he could look at it every morning when he woke up.

"Come on, Dane!" Aiden called out. "We need to get moving."

"Right."

They crossed the city as quickly as they could, following the cobblestone road around the market as they headed south around the Academy. Once Aiden had a clear view of the base, he beckoned Dane over. It was a large building that sat at the top of a sheer cliff, below the Emperor's palace. The barracks was a u-shaped and constructed out of brick, with towers at every corner. There was a smaller building situated in the center for the high ranking officials and consuls to the city. The roof was capped off with blue shingles and the blue-and-white banners spilled out from every available window like water off a cliff. A stone wall surrounded the outside of the building, and more banners hung there as well.

Above them was the Eagle's Watch, a huge cliff where the palace was build into. It hung over the city and looked out over the land. The shadow it cast was ominous, yet reassuring to know that the people who ruled Rogust also looked after its people. Or so Dane hoped.

The two sorcerers made their final jump through a portal, coming out at the bottom of a large flight of stairs that headed up the hill where the base was situated. Dane carried his belongings in a rucksack he'd brought with him from the Academy. He'd polished his bracers and wore them proudly on his forearms. His spell book had been tucked reverently within his rucksack, along with a few other personal belongings that he'd acquired over the years. The belt that Aiden had gotten him for his birthday all those months ago was on his waist, and he waited to be able to fit his own sword into it finally.

"Are you ready?" Aiden asked.

"Yeah, I think so." Dane smiled at his mate. His eyes caught the glint of light off the golden band on the boy's finger, and he became aware of the matching ring on his own hand. His voice dropped to a whisper and he added, "I'm ready for anything as long as you're here."

Aiden returned the smile and they headed up the stairs into the courtyard, ready to begin their tenure as soldiers of the military.

About the Author

Tyler Zilkie lives in Winnipeg, MB. He began penning what would become *Shadows of* War over seven years ago. He graduated with a Bachelor of Education in 2014 and earned the Sheldon Oberman Award for writing excellence from the Manitoba Association of Teachers of English. He hopes to one day be able to share his love of writing and stories with his students.